WICCHE HUNT

The Sea Wicche Chroicles

SEANA KELLY

This is a work of fiction. Names, characters, places, and incidents are either products of the writer's imagination or are used fictitiously and are not to be construed as real. Any resemblance to actual events, locales, organizations, or persons, living or dead, is entirely coincidental.

Wicche Hunt: The Sea Wicche Chronicles

Copyright © 2024 by Seana Kelly

EBOOK ISBN: 9781641972611

KDP POD ISBN: 9798322725978

IS POD ISBN: 97816419728731

ALL RIGHTS RESERVED.

No part of this work may be used, reproduced, or transmitted in any form or by any means, electronic or mechanical, without prior permission in writing from the publisher, except in the case of brief quotations embodied in critical articles or reviews.

NYLA Publishing

121 W. 27th St., Suite 1201, NY 10001, New York.

http://www.nyliterary.com

For Mothers and Daughters

I Fortunately Know a Little Magic

Seagulls dove and wheeled over the roaring ocean. Spray misted the air as I closed my eyes and breathed it in: the salt, the pine, the hot dude next to me.

"Did you remember to send that demon your lemon bar recipe?" Declan, a tall, bearded, broad-shouldered, all-around-jaw-dropping werewolf, jogged beside me down the steps to Lands End in San Francisco, holding my gloved hand.

I'm Arwyn, the sea wicche of Monterey, and I was on a demon fact-finding mission. "Of course I did. I even sent a video of me making them." I didn't want him thinking I'd reneged on a deal. "In fact, I sent a few more recipes to butter him up for tonight."

"Good thinking." Glancing down the stairs, he ushered me off the path, out of the line of tourists.

The sun was setting over the water, waves splashing on the rocks below. We were at the spot where the ocean met the bay. We waited for a large family to pass us on their way up. It wouldn't do to disappear into a magical bookstore and bar right in front of nonmagical folk.

I pulled out my phone and took a panoramic photo. The gloves I wore had connective threads at the fingertips so I could use touch screen devices. You might be wondering, *Arwyn, why not just take off the gloves?* Well, I'll tell you. I'm a wicche, specifically a Cassandra. Our gift is prophesy. I wear gloves because I also have a—I guess we'll call it a gift—for psychometry, meaning I glean information by touching things.

On the one hand, useful. On the other, a nightmare for most normal human interactions, especially dating.

After the family passed us, I put my phone away and Declan grabbed my hand once more. "I'm hanging on to you," he said as the stairs turned. "If her wards try to block me, I'm hoping you can drag me through with you."

"She said she'd tell the wards you were coming." *She* being Sam Quinn, the owner-operator of The Slaughtered Lamb Bookstore and Bar and a newly discovered cousin of mine. Sam was part Quinn wolf, like Declan, and part Corey wicche, like me.

Between one step and the next, the glorious purpling sunset and crashing waves disappeared and we were in a dark stairwell, lit by flickering wall sconces. I experienced a moment of panic and realized Declan must have too because we'd both clutched the other's hand hard.

"I guess it worked." The rumble of Declan's voice in the dim light put me at ease.

Within a few steps, I heard the low murmur of conversation. I pulled up short two steps later, though, when I heard growling.

Grinning, Declan urged me along. "It's a dog."

Light from the bar hit the landing below and there we saw a black wolfhound growling up at us—well, Declan really. Clive, Sam's vampire husband, had mentioned they had a puppy.

"Fergus! Don't growl at customers. That's not polite puppy behavior." At the sound of the woman's voice, the dog sat and stopped growling. Mostly. He raised his lip on the right side of his muzzle—away from the bar—showing us half his teeth.

Ha. I loved the little shit already. When Declan and I reached the landing, we both sat on the stairs and waited to pass inspection. Fergus, which was apparently his name, leaned forward and sniffed at us both. Declan got a wary look and a low growl as the dog positioned himself between us, his back to me, protecting me from the werewolf.

Declan shook his head as I laughed and kissed the top of the pooch's head.

"See?" I murmured, getting up. "He knows you're sketchy." Fergus kept to my side down the remaining steps and into the bar. Holy—I'd seen it in my visions, but those had been pale representations of the real thing.

Waves splashed against the wall of glass, the sky going indigo over the North Bay mountains. The sea level was about five feet above the barroom floor. Kelp bobbed and fish slid through the dark water.

The voices around me were so much white noise. I skirted around tables until I was in front of the window. I knew I was surrounded by wicches. I recognized the buzz of their magic. As I didn't feel hostility from them, though, I sat on the floor, placing my hands on the glass. Almost at once, a tentacle reached up from below and slapped the window, its suckers separated from my hand by a half foot of aquarium-grade glass.

"Hello, you," I whispered. Three more tentacles hit the window as she rose from under the bar. Resting my forehead against the cold, slick surface, I watched the octopus undulating in the waves, one rectangular eye on me. "You I shall name…Violet." The gray tentacles turned a lovely purple. She approved.

Two seals swam in loops, each coming a bit closer with every swoop. "Thank you for the welcome." They surfaced, barking their greetings and making me laugh.

I saw movement out in the depths but couldn't make out what was there. Chairs scraped the floor around me as people moved away. The bar had gone silent. Why—oh, now I saw. My focus had been too narrow.

Violet slipped down below The Slaughtered Lamb again and the seals shot off toward the Golden Gate Bridge.

"What are you doing out there? It's late in the season for you." A gray whale, fifty feet long, swam close to the glass, his huge black eye on me. I felt magic gathering around me, so I held up a hand to the wicches behind me who were readying spells. "Don't."

He moved closer. I returned my hands to the glass and whispered, "Safe travels, my friend." Breaching the surface, he flipped onto his side, swamping the window with a tidal wave of water. Vocalizing, he made a croaking sound that was dangerously close to a laugh. Cheeky bastard.

"As you were," I said, standing up. "He was just passing by and detoured to say hi." I went to Declan, who stared out the window in awe, Fergus held under his arm. "I want glass panels in the new deck so I can see down into the water."

He shook his head, breaking the spell. "You can just look over the edge of the deck. And Cecil and Wilbur might not appreciate you spying on them." The gangly pup, who was all legs and huge paws, wriggled, so Declan put him down.

Hmm. That was a good point. "New thought: glass panels, but I paint the bottom so you see tentacles that are pushing up out of the water to crush the Sea Wicche art gallery."

"I can't believe that just happened." Sam, The Slaughtered Lamb owner and recently discovered Corey cousin, was behind the bar. She had long brown hair braided down her back, leaving her lovely face unframed. She had Corey green eyes and a cleft in her chin that must have come from the Quinn side of her family tree. Shaking her head, she asked, "What can I get you two?"

"Beer. Whatever you have on tap." Declan took the empty stool in front of her. He'd thought he was the last of the storied Quinn line of werewolves. Like me, he'd found out that he, too, had a relative, one who had been hidden most of her life.

Taking the seat beside Declan, I said, "We've worked it out. Declan here is your uncle. And I'm fine with water."

Sam grinned, and it lit up the bar. There was something about her that made you feel safe and welcome. I couldn't explain it. "Was your dad Alexander?" she asked. At Declan's nod, she said, "I'm his son Michael's daughter." Shaking her head, she glanced over at her ridiculously handsome vampire husband, Clive. "This is my Uncle Declan."

He ran a hand down her back. "So I heard." He had a beautiful English accent, chiseled features, thick dark blond hair, and gray eyes that went soft whenever he looked at his wife. I'd seen him in a rage, eyes black, fangs descended, so I knew just how terrifying he could be. Now, though, here with Sam, he was a different man.

"That," he said, gesturing toward the window, "was the most extraordinary thing I've seen in my very long life. Do whales often drop by your gallery in Monterey?"

"Depends," I said, tipping my head back and forth. "If it's their migratory season and I'm out on the deck, I often get a few visitors. Not close like this, though. The water's too shallow for gray whales right next to the gallery. They're maybe fifty yards away. I've taken some great shots of them, though. Once the renovation is complete, I'll have a wall for my photographs."

"Oh," Sam said, like a thought had just occurred to her. Clive smiled and nodded, almost as though he'd heard her thought. "Can you do a portrait of Fergus for us?"

I glanced around the bar, looking for him, and found him once again on the landing, keeping a suspicious eye on all of us. I took out my phone, fiddled with the settings, and slid off the stool to take a few. "I'll see what I can do now. If I don't get anything good, we can schedule a session."

Sam bounced on the balls of her feet. "Perfect." She looked past me into the bookstore. "Fyr?" she called.

Out of the bookstore strode the most Thor-looking mountain of a man I'd ever seen. He had long blond hair, dragon-green eyes—you know what? Just picture Thor and you've got it.

"Can you watch the bar?" Sam asked Thor. "We need to go back and have a chat with our guests."

He nodded, grabbed a bar towel, and folded it into his waistband. It was nothing, the most basic of movements, but most of the people in the bar—including me—couldn't tear our eyes away from him.

Fingers snapped in my face, and I startled, finding Declan staring at me, eyebrows raised. *Oops.* I shrugged. It wasn't my fault the gorgeous man walked in front of me. I'd been minding my own business, framing dog photos. I can't be held accountable for noticing gods walking among us.

I caught up with Sam. The kitchen was remarkable. Her countertops were like my floors, but her concrete was stained the blue-green of shallow water. The dark floor gave just a bit with each step. "Cork?" I asked.

Dave, Sam's half-demon cook, looked over his shoulder and nodded. He wasn't wearing the glamour I'd seen him in, that of a tall, muscular, bald Black man. How freeing The Slaughtered Lamb must be. No humans could get in, so supernaturals could be themselves. In Dave's case, he was still tall, muscular, and bald, but he was now also red-skinned and black-eyed.

"Yeah," he replied. "Cork flooring is easier on the knees and feet." He tilted his head toward the counter to his left. "Wolf, I put a cheesesteak aside for you, if you want it."

"Thanks." Declan grabbed the plate and followed Sam through a dark doorway. I paused, taking off my backpack and pulling out a gift cocooned in Bubble Wrap.

"Thank you for meeting with me again. As a token, I made Maggie a little something for your garden."

Dave wiped his hands on a dish towel and then tossed it onto the nearby island. Leaning against the counter, he studied what was in my hand. "This is for Maggie?"

I nodded.

"Can I open it?"

"Please do." Hopefully, he'd like it too. "It's glass," I warned. I didn't want it broken before it made it to her.

He unwrapped an eight-inch-long glass hedgehog. I'd remembered he'd said his girlfriend wanted a pet hedgehog but couldn't have one, as they'd been living in an apartment. Now that he'd rescued her from a couple of demons, they were looking for a house with a backyard.

"I'd never tried to make a hedgehog before." I thought it had turned out well, though. I'd pulled and snipped the ball of hot amorphous glass, shaping sparkling brown quills, and I'd made the sweet, tapered face a color somewhere between tan and pink. When Dave came close to smiling, I thought my payment had been accepted.

"Go on," he said, waving me toward the door.

Before stepping through, I looked back and saw him gently placing it on his desk. The world went dark again, like when we'd went through the ward on the stairs, and then…oh, it was an apartment. The living room was cozy, saddle brown walls, mahogany wood, and beautiful green leather couch and chairs. They'd moved one of the wooden chairs from the bar in as well.

Declan was sitting on the couch, chatting with Sam and Clive, who were in the matching chairs. Declan patted the cushion beside him. Instead of sitting, though, I went to a painting hanging on their wall.

It was Paris, unmistakably Paris at night, the Eiffel Tower lit up in the distance. This wasn't the painting of a street artist cranking them out for the tourists. This packed an emotional punch. The colors, the brushstrokes, the dreamy quality of the moon glowing behind snow clouds…

"Do you like it?" Clive asked. I hadn't seen or heard him move. If I thought too much about it, he'd scare me, and I didn't want to be scared of him.

"I do." I scanned the corner for a signature and recognized the name. He was a master.

"It's the view from our hotel room balcony," he said. "We went to Paris for our honeymoon."

"Clive hired the artist and then booked him into the suite we'd stayed in so he could get the view exactly right," Sam explained. "I love it so much. Sometimes I just sit here, fall into the painting, and visit Paris in my memories."

Dave walked in a moment later, carrying a plate of lemon

squares, placing them on the coffee table. Clive and I took our seats.

"Well?" I asked the grumpy demon. I hoped he was happy with the recipe results.

"You tell me." He handed me a pair of chopsticks before sitting on the wooden barroom chair.

He'd remembered. Gloves made eating finger foods tricky. I used the chopsticks to pick up a lemon bar and place it on a napkin before using them again to pluck off a piece and pop it into my mouth. *Mmm.* "They're delicious."

He waited, clearly wanting a better critique than that.

"This is a taste thing, okay? I like a little more lemon zest in the shortbread crust and sprinkle a little less sugar on the dough before you bake." I turned the bar over to study the bottom. "I'd go another minute, maybe even two before you combine the crust with the lemon filling."

Nodding, he crossed his powerful arms over his chest. "Okay, good."

Declan put his empty plate down and grabbed a lemon bar. He took a bite, *mmm*ed, and said, "Excellent."

Sam took a bar and curled her legs up under her. "So," she said, glancing between me and Dave, "what questions do you have for our former resident of Hell?"

I took another bite and then put the napkin with the bar on the coffee table. "How do we find and stop a sorcerer?"

Dave blew a gust of air through his nose. "Good luck. We were hunting our own for quite a while. I can tell you that sorcery bleeds over into the mundane world, so sometimes you can track the incidents of bloodshed or death to the sorcerer's doorstep."

"Yeah," I said. "We've been seeing that. The detectives I spoke with said violent crimes have been getting worse and more frequent for a decade or more, but they didn't say anything about a specific area where it was happening."

He nodded. "Which tells us this isn't a new arrangement. See if you can get them to map it for you anyway. You may notice a pattern."

"According to you guys and my mom," I began, "my aunt—the sorcerer causing you all those problems—trained Calliope, my cousin and our latest sorcerer. Mom says Cal began studying with my aunt when she was young, at maybe eight or ten years old, so seventeen-ish years ago."

"And you never saw any black in her aura?" he asked.

When I shook my head, he paused, staring into the middle distance. "So why is there no black and why haven't there been violent crimes near her the last seventeen years? Hmm. Has she changed locations, moved closer to Monterey?"

I shook my head. "She's always lived with her parents."

"Ask your police to check nearby communities. She doesn't practice sorcery in the bedroom of her parents' home. She has to have a workshop someplace where she has privacy and isolation. It wouldn't do to have neighbors hear chanting in the middle of the night. Maybe also check records of properties owned by Coreys. She needs a place to work that isn't too far so she can be there when a family member calls for her."

I reached into my backpack, pulled out a small notebook, like the one Detective Hernández used, and began jotting down what we needed to do.

"I haven't worked with a sorcerer in a while," he continued, "but I did it for a very long time. Most of the wicches I worked with tried to hide the marks of sorcery. I've only known of one, though, who was able to do it."

He scratched his jaw, thinking. "He was a Corey. I'm almost positive. Maybe four or five hundred years ago. Maybe Ireland." He shook his head as though trying to jostle his memories into place.

"I didn't work with him, but I remember hearing mumbles about a spell that could wipe an aura clean. I know who your cousin's demon is now and I don't believe he was the one working with that sorcerer either." He shrugged one large shoulder. "My guess is there is a Corey spell, maybe even a black magic grimoire with many spells, that's passed down from one sorcerer to the next."

As soon as he said the words, I felt the truth of them. "That may be why there are so damned many of them in my family tree."

"Our family tree," Sam said, pointing to herself, Dave, and me.

"Yeah, *our*." I knew that should have made me feel better. I wasn't alone in all this. Unfortunately, hunting down and stopping Calliope felt very much as though it had been laid squarely on my shoulders.

TWO

We're Ready for Your Close-Up, Stheno

"Do you have any suggestions on how Arwyn can protect herself?" Declan asked.

Dave nodded. "There's a spell that might work." He paused, looking at Sam. "She knows a good one too."

At that, Sam popped up and ran into the bedroom, coming back a moment later with a cracked leather grimoire under her arm. She sat and waited for Dave to share his first. I took notes and was able to practice it on him. On the third try, he disappeared. We all looked at one another.

"I didn't just hurt him, did I?" There went my inside source to all things sorcery.

Sam waved her hand, brushing off my concern. "He's fine. He'll make his way back soon enough." She looked toward the kitchen doorway. "Hmm. Be right back."

She returned a moment later with a bottle of orange soda for me. She'd remembered. "I just wanted to check he didn't have the oven or the burners on. Whoever didn't get their dinner is out of luck at this point, but at least there won't be a fire."

She went to her chair, grabbed the grimoire, and opened it to a marked page. "Here. You can take a picture of it. The handwriting is really hard to read, but the spell works well." She placed the book on my lap and I took out my phone, snapping a pic.

"Are there others in the book I should look at?" I asked.

She thought a moment. "You know what? You should just take it and look."

I started to protest, but again, she waved off the concern.

"I'm not that kind of wicche, not a normal one." She shrugged. "I was pretty surprised when that one worked and all these dark shadows rose up from the floor, taking bites out of Dave and then dragging him off this plane, down to Hell." She shivered. "It was horrible."

I took another look at the spell. "You did this to Dave?"

She looked so upset, I wished I could have pulled the words back.

"At the time," Clive began, "Dave was being possessed by your aunt Abigail and her demon. He was choking the life out of Sam with a burning hand. It was either use the spell or die."

"He was gone for days, though," Sam said. "I was so afraid I'd done permanent damage."

"Fuck," Dave said, walking back through the doorway. "Like you could." He patted my shoulder as he passed. "Good job."

"Are you sure?" I asked Sam, holding up the grimoire.

"Absolutely. Stheno and I went through a bunch of grimoires looking for any spells that might help me with Abigail, but we bookmarked ones that just looked good. I couldn't do them," she said, holding out a hand to Fergus, who'd just trotted in. "Owen, the Slaughtered Lamb manager and wicche extraordinaire, said there were some really good spells in there. He took pics and shared them with his family."

She nodded encouragingly. "I hold on to it because I love books, especially grimoires, even though I can't perform the magic. You, though, actually need it to fight off a sorcerer. Take it."

"Thank you very much." I slid the book carefully into my back-pack, considering. "Why do I know the name Stheno?"

Sam and Clive shared a look. "Well," she said, "have you studied Greek mythology?"

I had for a project I'd worked on years ago. "I made a glass sculpture of Medusa's head for a client. It turned out well. I don't understand, though, how—"

"Stheno is Medusa's sister," Sam said. "There are three gorgons: Euryale, Medusa, and Stheno."

I'm not sure what look I had on my face, but Sam looked concerned.

"You know a gorgon?" I shouted.

She nodded warily.

I grabbed Declan's knee. "Oh my—would she be willing to sit for me? In fact, she doesn't even need to do that. I could just take some photos and paint from that." An actual gorgon. She knew an actual gorgon. Who the hell were these people?

"Show her the pictures from your wedding," Dave suggested.

This time, it was Clive who went to the bedroom. He returned with a framed picture of a huge group of people. They were in the bar here, laughing and drinking.

Clive pointed to a gorgeous smiling woman with golden brown skin and waist-length coils of black hair. "That's Stheno. And that's Medusa." He pointed to another woman, her face obscured by a huge glass of red wine. "And Euryale." The third sister looked taller and thinner, more austere than the other two.

"You had all three sisters here for your wedding?" That was insane. Wait. What the hell?! I looked between Sam and Clive. "The queen attended your wedding?"

Sam leaned forward, grinning. "You can see her? These guys can't. See, she's way in the back. She just popped in for a moment. I don't think she wanted our fae guests to start dropping to the ground, kneeling before her."

Declan looked over my shoulder. "Where?"

I pointed at the queen and Declan shrugged. "It looks a little shimmery, but it could just as easily be light reflecting off the flash. I don't see her."

Clive returned the photo to their bedroom.

"I can ask Stheno for you," Sam volunteered. "She'd probably dig it, but I don't know how they are with their images being out there. They know we keep that picture in our room."

Clive took his seat again. "Our friends know we keep their secrets, just as they keep ours. You two are now a part of this, which is why I shared it with you. Sam will ask, and given how Stheno feels about my wife, she'll probably agree."

Elated at the prospect, grimoire safely stowed, we finally took our leave. The drive home was lovely, Declan keeping mostly to the coast route. It took a little longer but was worth it.

"Are you nervous?" I wasn't sure if he wanted to talk about the upcoming Alpha challenge or not. Declan was a Quinn, one of the last of the werewolf origin line. Because of that, even as a child, he'd been challenged often. His parents had been killed when he was small, his human mother's sister taking him in and raising him. They'd both been quite shocked the first time he'd shifted.

After that, they'd moved often, especially when the local pack would get itchy about a dominant—even an adolescent—in their territory. He'd had to fight a lot and hadn't, at that age, learned restraint. Consequently, he'd left a lot of dead wolves in his wake. After his Aunt Sarah was killed, he just moved on when there was trouble. He couldn't take the blood on his paws. That had worked for him until recently, when he'd decided to stay, local Alpha's hissy fit be damned.

"Nervous?" He glanced over at me. "About—oh, that." He shook his head. "Not nervous, no."

"Maybe he'll back down and you won't have to kill him." I was pretty sure I knew what was bothering him.

He held my gloved hand. "That won't happen. Alphas don't turn tail. There's a healthy dose of testosterone and arrogance that goes with being an Alpha. This one in particular has spent his life being the golden boy in town. Ladies love him. Men want to be him. I doubt he can conceive of losing. He'll cheat to assure his win, but he won't back down."

Declan squeezed my hand. "What about you? Nervous about the opening?"

I stared out the truck window at the moonlit waves. "Thankfully, a gallery opening involves far less bloodshed, so there's that."

He laughed.

"I don't know. I've been dreaming of this for so long, I want it perfect. The mural's almost done, but then I need to paint inside and place all the artwork. And put those stupid price tags on them. And, and, and. Usually it's nightmares waking me up in the middle of the night. Lately, it's been stuff I need to get done before the opening."

"You know it doesn't all have to be done before you open, right?" He rubbed his thumb over my glove. "It's not a finish line. When you open the doors, you'll be inviting people into The Sea Wicche to see where you are now. An artist is always changing and growing, though, so every time they come back, there'll be something new."

I let out a breath. That was true. I didn't think I had it in me to be that relaxed about my gallery finally opening, though.

"Shall we discuss the elephant in the truck?" he asked. "Or should I say the grimoire in the backpack?"

"I hate it all. I have so many plans, so much work to do for what I love, but in the background all the time I'm wondering what Calliope is up to. Where are she and her demon? Has someone else been hurt that we don't know about? Why kill Aunt Sylvia?" My voice caught on her name.

Turning away from the window, I watched Declan drive. "I know people always say, *She was the kindest person in the world. She lit up a room*, but in her case, it was true. I'm an asshole. Lots of people hate me, but Sylvia? No. You couldn't."

"A. You're not an asshole. B. Someone could. Her daughter."

"Yeah, you're right. Cal's the asshole." I stared down at his strong, warm hand wrapped around mine. "I can't get it out of my head. When we were in the hospital and Sylvia was in a coma?"

He nodded.

"I was touching Sylvia, listening to the voice in her head." A tear ran down my face. "Sylvia died with her own daughter's voice in her head, telling her how much she hated her." I wiped my face dry with my free hand. "I want to do Calliope harm."

"Understandable."

"The spell Sam showed me in the grimoire was scary. I can't imagine calling up demons to send someone to Hell. For Calliope, though... I'm looking forward to studying it, seeing what else it might have. First, though, I want to do some research. I don't want to take spells from a dark grimoire. My family has too great a proclivity for black magic as it is. I don't need to make it worse by studying some other family's black grimoire."

"Good," Declan said. "Sam is so sweet, it's hard to think of her engaging in black magic, but that spell sounded horrible."

"Dave said it was a good one—effective, that is. And Clive said it was life or death. Sometimes you have to do what you have to do in order to survive for the next fight. And Sam is a survivor."

Declan let out a gust of breath. "Yeah, sometimes you do." And we were back to the Alpha challenge. In order for Declan to survive, Logan had to die.

We were quiet for the rest of the drive, each lost in our own thoughts. When Declan pulled up to The Sea Wicche, there was already a familiar car parked in front.

"Looks like the good detective needs you again," Declan said.

THREE

Admit it. She's a Dick

As I slid out of Declan's tall truck, Detective Hernández slammed her door and came around the front of her car to meet us. She was my age—twenty-eight. We'd gone to school together. We'd known of each other but hadn't been friends. I was the weirdo with long, curly hair that was a mélange of brown, red, and gold. People had been accusing my mom and then me of dyeing my hair ever since I was a toddler.

Sofia Hernández, though, had been cool and liked by just about everyone. She was athletic, studious, and seemed genuinely kind. As I'd been on the outskirts of high school society, though, what did I know? The student who wears gloves all the time and occasionally drops to the ground in a seizure-like vision isn't on everyone's invite list.

She checked her watch. "Thank goodness. I was falling asleep."

"You should have called. I could have given you our ETA," I said, coiling up my hair and stuffing it down the back of my top. The wind was coming in strong off the ocean.

"I did. It went to voicemail. I was giving it another thirty minutes and then heading home." Hernández ran a hand over her dark brown hair, checking the thick bun at the base of her skull, and nodded hello to Declan. She had big brown eyes framed by dark lashes and a cupid's bow mouth, one she held in a firm line.

I pulled my phone out of my pocket and checked. Yup. Two missed calls. "Sorry. We were driving back from San Francisco on the coast route. There are spots without cell service."

"It's fine," she said. "Kind of relaxing. Just sitting in the dark, listening to a podcast. Anyway, I wanted you to know a woman washed ashore today. She's been identified as Pearl Corey."

"Oh." I went to sit on the steps of the gallery. "I knew it was coming. I saw her death. Still, it hits hard when my visions become reality. We weren't close or anything, but she was a sweet little cousin I watched grow up at family functions." I looked up at the detective as Declan sat beside me, wrapping an arm around me. "You've told her mom?"

Hernández nodded.

"I'll tell mine. We'll go visit Aunt Hester." I thought about it a moment. "You didn't sit outside my gallery waiting to tell me this."

The detective shook her head. "I'm sorry for your loss, but I also want your help. She's been in the water too long. They can't get any evidence off her body at this point." A strand of long hair came loose from her tight bun, and she tucked it behind her ear.

"Come on. Tell me you're not asking me to read my poor dead cousin?"

Hernández didn't flinch. "I'm asking you to read your cousin. I want her killer caught before he does this again. And I waited here because I have a friend who's a coroner. She's on the night-shift. Hopefully she won't be weird about me bringing a consultant. The body's been processed. It's about to be turned over to her mother. We only have tonight to do this. If you agree, that is."

"She hasn't eaten," Declan interjected. "Maybe we should—"

I patted his knee. "It's better if I don't. Less to come back up if the vision is bad."

He pulled me closer. "Right."

"It's about a thirty-minute drive from here. I can take you and bring you back—if you agree," she said.

I looked up at Declan and patted my backpack. I appreciated that he cared and wanted to protect me. It was an unusual experience in my life, but I had to go.

He nodded. "I'll drive." He took my gloved hand and pulled me up.

We let Hernández lead the way. Traffic was already light downtown and became nonexistent once we headed away from the city center. She eventually pulled over in front of a squat, nondescript white building with lettering that read *Monterey County Coroner*.

When the detective got out, she pocketed her phone and pointed to the front door. "Dr. Landscombe will let us in. I called and explained the situation on the way over. I had to do some arm twisting."

Declan and I followed her up the cement walkway. I didn't want to be here. Places like this were crawling with horrible memories, just waiting for me to accidentally brush a wrist or ankle against a doorknob or chair leg, waiting for me to relive someone's greatest trauma.

A pale woman with pinched features, wearing a white coat, walked down the hall toward the glass front doors. She looked up at six-foot-six, bearded Declan and hesitated. Hernández waved and the woman started moving again, pushing open the door.

"Sorry," the doctor said. "I was expecting two women." She gave Hernández a look and said, "Come on, then," leading us down a dingy white corridor. One of the fluorescent panels overhead flickered. This was the beginning of a horror movie.

I found Declan's hand and held on tight, wishing like hell I was in my studio in my comfy chair, a hot cup of tea warming my hands…

"—middle of the room. I'll be over here. I won't leave her unattended." The doctor wasn't happy about any of this. She wanted to help her friend, wanted the killer caught, but it was obvious this was really unorthodox and made her uncomfortable.

"Understood," the detective replied. "I appreciate you doing this."

The coroner nodded and moved to a desk to work.

I handed Declan my backpack and moved to the center of the room, to the metal gurney holding a body covered by a sheet. The tips of two fingers stuck out from under the sheet. Blowing out a breath, I started to tug at a glove and then Declan was there, placing a chair beside me.

"Good thinking." I sat, pulled off the glove. When I did a reading, I centered my thoughts and thought of a question. Otherwise, I could end up seeing her Christmas pageant when she was seven. I needed to know about Pearl's murder, so I thought of that and then touched a finger to her pinky.

Ankles are yanked up and she slides under the water. He holds her legs as she struggles, unable to right herself and breathe. Craig stares down at her, impatient, a look of annoyance on his face. She grasps the edge of the tub, trying to pull herself up. Shaking his head, he snatches one of the crutches she left leaning against the wall and flips it over, jabbing it into the tub. The curve of the shoulder support pins her neck to the floor of the tub, crushing her larynx. Head throbbing, lungs ready to burst, she pushes at the crutch, but he's too strong. Her vision constricts and finally he smiles down at her. Choking, inhaling water, her thrashing is no match for the one who said he'd love her in sickness and in health.

Curled in on myself, head throbbing, gasping for breath, I felt the hard linoleum floor under my shoulder, my hip. Declan was hunched over me, trying to figure out how to help. I moved to my knees, ungloved hand fisted against my chest as I desperately sucked in as much air as I could. Hernández crouched beside me, asking how she could help.

Lifting my head, I stared through my curls at the doctor, who watched from behind her desk. Hanging onto Declan's arm, I pulled myself up, still staring at the cow as her chair shot out from under her, dumping her on the floor. Hernández stood to help her friend, took a step in her direction, and then looked back at me, brow furrowed.

"That's not Pearl," I said, voice hoarse, having just been strangled and drowned in that vision. "This is the body of a woman drowned in the tub by her husband Craig." I forced myself to slow my breathing.

Declan grabbed my sleeve when I almost touched him with my ungloved hand. He pulled the glove from my pocket and handed it to me.

"Did you do that?" The detective asked her friend, looking well and truly pissed off.

"I told you before," Dr. Landscombe said, "there's no such thing as psychic ability. I don't want your reputation in the department ruined by a con woman."

Glancing up, I saw Declan's eyes had gone wolf gold. I shook his sleeve until he looked down at me. My back to the other women, I mouthed, *your eyes.*

He shouldered my backpack, wrapping an arm around me. "I'll take you home."

"No. Wait," Hernández said. "I'm sorry. I didn't know she was going to do that. Please. I really do need your help with your cousin's case."

The coroner climbed to her feet. "The victim is her cousin?"

"Yes," Hernández said. "This is Arwyn Corey,"

Declan and I still had our backs to the women, but I could see his eye color was darkening to his natural brown.

The detective moved so she could see me. "I really am sorry. Please don't go yet."

I thought about Pearl and Aunt Hester. Sighing, I nodded and then turned to Landscombe. "Don't fuck with me again." I stared her down until she finally nodded.

"But you're wrong," she gloated. "That one was an accidental drowning in the tub. She fell asleep."

"No. She didn't," I said to Hernández. "She was taking a bath, eyes closed, and her husband grabbed her by her ankles, yanking her up so her head went under the water. She struggled, trying to get out." I glanced at Landscombe. "If you check her throat, you'll see bruising that has nothing to do with drowning. He used the curved, under-arm cushion of her crutch—she'd twisted her ankle badly on a hike—to pin her neck to the bottom of the tub and then watched her die. She won't have too much water in her lungs because he was crushing her trachea as he killed her."

Hernández looked at Landscombe, waiting for confirmation.

The doctor shrugged one shoulder. "I didn't do that autopsy. I don't like this, Sofia. I don't believe any of it. I checked the computer as that one was doing her routine to see who was on the gurney. It was ruled an accidental death."

Hernández took out a small notebook from her jacket pocket. "What's her name?"

"Trisha Hall," Landscombe and I said at the same time.

The detective turned back to me. "Her husband killed her?"

"Yeah," I said. "Craig. There was no emotion. He just wanted it done. Check the prints on the crutches. His'll be in a weird place, gripping the bottom of the crutch. There'll probably be bruising around her ankles that, again, have nothing to do with falling asleep and sliding into a bath."

After a charged moment, the doctor said, "It's true." Her voice was low and shocked as she stared at her computer screen. "Her hyoid was fractured." She touched the fingertips of one hand to her forehead. "How could he have missed that?"

The coroner stood, staring down at the linoleum, shaking her head. "And how could you have known?" she said, mostly talking to herself.

"I'm not here to perform party tricks," I said, voice still raspy. "Get Pearl."

Landscombe didn't like being wrong, didn't enjoy being ordered around, and clearly resented me. Whatever. She stalked across the room, moved Trisha's gurney, checked the tag number on another, and wheeled over Pearl.

Was it wrong that I wanted to punch the doctor in the back of the head? Because I really wanted to.

I sat again and took off my glove. This time, I let my finger hover right above the bloated, discolored skin of an elbow barely sticking out from under the sheet. The body had been washed, but she still smelled of the sea. This was Pearl. Blowing out a breath, I touched her skin.

A quiet coffee shop. Pearl, her hair still long and black, sits alone drinking cocoa, her textbook open, her muffin forgotten. She stops to type into her laptop and then resumes reading.

A handsome young man with chiseled features, dark hair, blue eyes, lightly tanned skin leans on the empty chair across the table and asks if he can take it.

She nods, confused, her face flushing, her Corey green eyes guarded. There are lots of empty tables. Why ask for hers?

He lifts the chair and turns, but then seems to change his mind and turns back, replacing the chair and sitting. Looking at her textbook, he asks if she's studying for the Anthropology midterm as well. She nods, unused to the attention.

Smiling, he leans in and asks if she has Professor Putnum. She shakes her head. He then launches into a tale about the professor, the assistant, and a couple of particularly ridiculous students.

Pearl laughs in sputters and starts. It's like a rollercoaster. She doesn't have time to catch her breath, to get used to the uninterrupted attention of a charming, handsome man. It's all going too fast, and while it's fun, she feels out of control.

No studying is done. He sees a friend and has to run but not before asking her to dinner. She nods, the rollercoaster careening around a curve. They were supposed to meet in the quad, but when she answers a knock on her dorm room door, there he is, throwing her off yet again. She planned to calm herself on the walk, maybe call home to talk with her mother about the garden, but he's already here.

They take the stairs down, avoiding the elevators, and leave without anyone noticing. Pearl is used to not being noticed but is surprised that no one calls out to him. She assumes they'll eat on campus, but instead he walks her to his very expensive sports car. None of this is real. How is she the one with the hot guy in the fancy car?

He takes her to a little bistro. She feels out of place. She and her mother aren't poor, but since the divorce, it's been tighter. Dad, like others in his family, has money, but she and mom have been on their own a long time. She brings forty dollars on the date, thinking that would be enough if they split the bill. With the prices on this menu, she'll need to use her emergency card and then explain to her mother what happened. Mom won't be mad, but it makes Pearl uncomfortable.

Still charming, he holds up most of the conversation with stories about trips he's taken. The rollercoaster jolts forward up a long incline before teetering on the precipice and then racing down, her stomach dropping out from under her. When he kisses her at the end of the night, it feels like an out-of-body experience, like she's looking down from above, thinking her shoes are stupid and wondering why he would choose her.

He touches her hair, telling her how beautiful it is, and then mentioning that she might look even better as a blonde. Yeah, he says nodding. Short blonde hair.

And that's how it goes for two weeks, him showing up when she isn't expecting him, and him sweeping her off her feet while oh-so-subtly suggesting how she could improve. She uses a chunk of her savings to go to the salon he recommends to have her hair cut and colored. She hates it, hates being so visible as the rollercoaster drops again.

He's so pleased when he sees that she's changed for him, he takes her to a fancy dinner at a restaurant on the water. She orders scallops because they're small and he makes her stomach wobble. He orders wine. She doesn't like it, but she keeps sipping, as it gives her nervous hands something to do and allows her to hide, however briefly, behind the glass.

After dinner, they walk on the beach, each holding onto their shoes in one hand and each other with the other. They walk for quite a while. Pearl's teeth are chattering. Instead of turning around, though, he laughs and points up ahead to a place he wants to show her. The cliffs are high beside them, and she sees no one else on the beach, it being such a cold, windy night.

Pearl stops. The tide is coming in and icy seawater is washing over her already frozen feet. He laughs again, tugging her along. It's not much farther. They round a huge boulder and are out of view of most every-

thing. Pearl is wondering if he's going to kiss her again. He hasn't since that first night.

When he moves in close, she is caught between excitement and terror, the rollercoaster going up again. His fingertips brush the long column of her neck. Leaning in, he bypasses her lips and instead whispers, "I've wanted to do this for a long time."

She smiles, but then his fingers tighten on her neck. She can't believe it. Doesn't fight. She stares into his dead eyes, uncomprehending. When he smirks, kicking her feet out from under her, she panics, clawing at his hands, even as black spots blur her vision.

She barely registers the cold when he drags her to the water, shoving her head under as he squeezes the life out of her. The out-of-control rollercoaster slams into a turn and goes flying off into the dark. The last thing she sees is his triumphant smile as he scrubs at his face, washing it away until there are only dead eyes staring into her lifeless ones.

FOUR

Why Is She Still Here?

Two strangled victims in a row made me hate Landscombe even more. The ocean, though, gave me a thought. I needed to start carrying a jar of seawater in my backpack. The ocean always healed me—thanks, Dad—so maybe it would help after readings.

My throat was killing me, my head pounding, but the rest of me felt fine. When I opened my eyes, I realized I was sitting on Declan's lap. He was on the chair, a strong arm around my waist to keep me from tumbling to the floor again. That was nice.

Hernández crouched beside me again. "Your neck," she whispered, her expression pained.

"It'll fade," I croaked. Damn, that hurt! "Water?"

The doctor was already there, with a paper cup of water. I wanted to smack it out of her hand, but I wanted the drink more. I slipped on my glove and took the cup, taking a tiny sip. It felt like knives going down, but then the pain began to lessen. The doctor made to poke at my neck, causing me to jerk and spill some water on Declan's leg. I swear, I couldn't remember wanting to hex someone more in my life! Well, maybe my cousin Colin. He was the worst.

"Could you all excuse me for a moment?" I whispered.

"What?" Landscombe said. "Of course not. I'm not leaving you alone with evidence."

I stood. "She's my cousin Pearl, not evidence." Turning to Hernández, I said, "Can you all just move back, away from me? I need to do something."

Declan moved between me and the other women. "I think I know what this is. She won't touch the body. Let's give her some space now." His deep, solemn voice finally got them moving to the other side of the room.

I took off my gloves and prayed to the goddess to give my voice the strength it needed to send Pearl on to the other side. I closed my eyes and lifted my hands and face to the heavens, singing the song of death for Pearl, sending her on with our love. I was announcing her arrival, telling the souls there that they were receiving a gift of kindness and light, one we hadn't been ready to part with.

Tears streamed down my face, but the goddess had given my voice the strength to complete the ritual. When my last note echoed in the sterile room, I bowed, fingers to my forehead, thanking the goddess and saying goodbye to Pearl.

I stood, wiped my face, and pulled on my gloves, grabbing my backpack and water cup. It was time to go. I went to the door and waited for Declan to open it for me, as my hands were full. I strode down the hall to the front door.

"Arwyn, wait. What did you see?" The detective and the doctor followed us.

"Give me a minute. I want out of here," I whispered, knowing Declan would hear me. Ritual over, the pain and hoarse voice had returned.

He did and passed it on.

Once outside, I went to his truck. "Heat?"

He opened the passenger side door, picked me up, and placed me on the seat. I took another sip, felt it go down easier, and placed the cup in a holder. Declan slid behind the wheel and started the engine, cranking up the heat for me. I unzipped my backpack and pulled out a sketchbook and charcoals.

I slammed the door closed, rolled down the window, and started to sketch the man who'd killed my cousin. Hernández leaned against the truck door, watching me work. When I was done, I took a bigger gulp and felt the pain fading.

Handing the detective the sketch, I said, "That's not him, though."

Landscombe looked over Hernández' shoulder.

"What do you mean?" Hernández was studying the image.

"That was the face he showed her, but it's off. I think the shape of his face is right. The dead eyes are right, but the last thing she saw was him scrubbing his wet hands over his face, cleaning something off. It could have just been makeup. I think, though, it's both skin tone and a fake nose or chin. I think that was why he only kissed her once. That, and it didn't feel like sex drove him.

"It was her first kiss," I continued, throat sore but getting better. "She was too discombobulated to notice anything, but I think the kiss messed up the putty or makeup or something. Maybe he has theater experience. Maybe not. He's a sociopath, I can tell you that, so taking drama lessons fits. He needed someone to teach him how to react like a normal human being."

"Can you start at the beginning?" Hernández asked.

"Sure." I told her all about the short, tragic courtship of Pearl Corey. "She thought he was a student, but I'm not so sure."

"Why?" the detective asked.

"Hard to explain." I thought a moment. "It all seemed contrived, right from the beginning. A quiet girl, hiding behind a curtain of hair, and that's the one he approaches. There were lots of empty tables, but he asks to take her chair? Nah. He wanted to know if someone was coming, someone who might see him and mess up his plans.

"And then he checks which professor she has before talking about a different one. No one recognizes him, even when walking in the dorm or around campus. She sees him as confident and outgoing, but no one even waves at the rich, good-looking, charming guy? I don't buy it. He didn't belong there. He was isolating and manipulating her.

"I mean, is short blonde hair even important to him," I continued, "or does he just get off on making her do something she absolutely doesn't want to do?" I shrugged. "No idea. He paid cash for their meals, so she never saw a card."

"Name?" Hernández asked.

I shook my head. "He introduced himself as David, but I don't think that's it. He's tall. She had to look up to him. Not Declan tall, and Pearl is petite, but probably six feet. Dark hair, blue eyes. He's white, lightly tanned, but that might be makeup. He doesn't feel like an outdoorsy guy, so he's probably much paler than he appeared." I shrugged. "All of that is feel on my part, though. All I know for sure is what I saw."

The doctor scoffed at that.

Tossing the sketch pad into Declan's lap, I stepped out of the truck, forcing Hernández to step back. "That's it. I'm sick of your shit, sister." I held up my fists. Spelling her would have been easier, but I was itching to whoop her the old-fashioned way.

Hernández immediately stepped between us. "Okay. That's enough." She turned to her friend. "You should go in."

The doc was super snooty but left right quick, which, honestly, was all I wanted.

"That one," I said, pointing over the detective's shoulder, "is not your friend. She's an asshole."

"Too bad," Declan rumbled. "I'd have enjoyed watching you lay her out."

"Me too," I groused.

"Hop in," he said. "Let's get you home and fed."

"Thank you," the detective said. "I'm sorry about—well—all that."

"Not your fault," I said, pulling myself back into the cab.

Before Declan could pull away, though, another familiar vehicle parked right in front of us. Detective Osso stepped out of his SUV.

He nodded to Declan and then came to my open window. Osso was a bear shifter. He was almost as tall as Declan but even broader across the shoulders. He was a dark-skinned Black man who wore a perpetual look of annoyance.

"Ms. Corey, as long as you're here, I could use your help."

"No, no, no," I muttered, rolling up the window.

He laid his hand on the top edge of the glass and stopped it. Stupid strong shifter.

"Ms. Corey," he said disapprovingly.

Hernández patted his arm. They often worked together and though she was fully human, she knew that the rest of us weren't. She gestured to the coroner's office. "Joyce switched corpses on Arwyn, so she had to do two readings on women who'd been strangled. Her voice is just now starting to sound like itself. She's already been through a lot tonight."

"Landscombe's on duty? Damn." Patting the glass, he said, "I'm sorry she did that to you. If you're not up to it, that's okay." He paused. "There's just something about this lady. It makes no sense. And she's got this big grieving family, calling me every half hour for an update. I've got nothing for them, so I notified the coroner's office I was coming in to see her. I need to tell her family something. They're heartbroken."

I sighed and Declan patted my knee. He knew I was going to go back in. *Damn it.* I grabbed the backpack and opened the door.

"You should be ashamed," Hernández murmured.

Osso shrugged. "It got her out of the truck."

I trudged past the detectives. "You two both suck."

Osso moved ahead, tried the locked door, and then knocked, his wedding ring pinging loudly off the glass.

Landscombe stuck her head out the door and looked down the hall.

"I can't believe you knocked her chair out from under her," Hernández whispered to me.

"I'd have paid to see that," Osso rumbled.

"Can you check to make sure it's the right body?" I asked him.

"I don't trust her as far as I can throw her. She's a snotty bitch who has a lazy doctor working under her. I called it out and now her ego demands that she bring me low. I'll do this for you, but you have to keep her away from me."

"Done," Osso said. "It helps that she's afraid of me."

The doc looked pissed, but she pushed open the door. "Yes?"

"I need to see my victim and any report that may have been generated," Osso said, voice deep and commanding.

"Reports are available in the secured database. I believe you know that, Detective." She wasn't giving any ground.

"I do," he said. "As of ten minutes ago, it hadn't been uploaded, though, so I'd like to see my victim again and see if there are any preliminary findings."

She didn't let him in, though. She stared around him at me. "Why is she back? I don't want her in my morgue."

Osso nodded gravely. "I can understand that. No one enjoys their errors being brought to light." Before she could respond, he went on, "Regardless, Ms. Corey is consulting on this case. Now," he said, stepping forward and forcing her back, "we won't trouble you any. We just need to see Magdalena Lopez's body."

Landscombe was clearly torn and pissed off. Osso had a right to see the victim. She didn't want me in her facility, but the way Osso conducted his investigation was not hers to oversee. After a moment, she stepped aside, telling him the victim was in the exam room, second door on the left.

Osso, Declan, and I went ahead, but the doctor held Hernández back for a hissed conversation. I didn't have Declan or Osso's superior hearing, but I got enough to know a friendship was going down the drain right now. I would have felt guilty about that, but since Osso hated her too, it took some of the weight off me.

Detective Osso opened the door and the overhead fluorescent lights flickered to life. No gurneys in this room. Just a wall of metal drawers holding dead bodies. Osso walked over and checked the information on each door, looking for the identifiers for his victim.

Halfway down the row, he grabbed the handle and pulled the

drawer out. The overwhelming medicinal scent of the facility couldn't mask the stench of death. And again, it was probably much worse for the other two, as they both had a shifter's excellent sense of smell.

Osso lifted the sheet to see her face and then replaced it, nodding to me. I glanced around for a chair and then saw Declan carrying one toward me. He sat down and waited.

"You're right," I said, sitting on his knee. "It was nice not coming to on the floor last time."

"I really hate seeing you hurting and then crumpling on the ground," he grumbled. "We need to figure out ways to make this easier on you."

My back went up a little, as I wasn't his problem to fix, but then I relaxed back into him. I'd been dealing with this on my own for a very long time. Everyone just took it as normal that I dropped to the ground, often hitting my head. No one, Mother included, ever said, *We need a new plan. Arwyn shouldn't be getting hurt like this.* Having someone care about me and not just what I could do was strange. Not unheard of—Aunt Sylvia loved me for me—but it was unusual. I was, consequently, having a hard time adjusting to and trusting Declan's desire to help.

I took a deep breath and let it out slowly. Grabbing my glove, I looked over my shoulder. "If the smell is getting to me, it must be horrible for you guys."

Both men nodded, their faces strained. Osso moved the sheet so part of her foot was accessible. Touching dead bodies was officially my least favorite thing to do. Nevertheless, I blew out a breath, pulled my glove off, and thought, *Show me what I need to know to find your killer.* I didn't like seeing the parts of people's lives that shouldn't have been open to me. With that thought in mind, I touched a finger to the side of her foot.

FIVE

Entomophobia (a fear of insects. Don't say I never taught you anything)

Early morning. Her car is the first in the parking lot. She enjoys having the school mostly to herself. Archie, the head custodian, is here. He's the one who unlocks the doors and turns off the alarms, but she rarely sees him. He's off doing his own beginning-of-day rituals.

A petite Latina in her late fifties—who doesn't look a day over thirty-two—she wears a dress with sensible heels and a warm cardigan sweater. Her classroom temperature can swing twenty degrees during the school day. Old building, temperamental HVAC unit. Her shoulder-length hair is kept tidy in a bun.

She walks down the dark, quiet halls, thinking about what she needs to get done before the few summer session students begin arriving. She has some copies to make, far fewer than during the regular school year. She's been teaching long enough to remember what it was like before every student pulled out their laptops when they sat down. She's transitioned most of her curriculum to a digital format, but she still has some sheets she likes them to keep in their binders for quick reference when doing their homework. New unit, new sheet. She'll get that done first.

Even though most of what she teaches is on the projector, she still prefers posting key pieces of information, including due dates, on the white board. That needs to be updated too. Then she'll start slogging through the grading, by far the worst part of teaching as far as she's concerned.

Flicking on her classroom lights, she sees hundreds of dark forms scurry under desks and into dark corners. Fear overwhelms her. She'd scream if she could move. When a cockroach darts directly at her, she shakes off the paralysis and runs back down the hall, calling for Archie. The image goes dark and then…

Same day, same outfit. She's walking to her car, feeling around in her bag for her keys. She finds them, presses the button on her key fob, reaches for the door, and then snatches her hand back like she's touched an open flame. The paralysis again. Her door handle is covered in webbing and fly carcasses; a huge spider stands on the dead flies, watching her.

Heart racing, throat closing, she can't scream. A colleague calls good-bye, breaking the stasis. She shouts and the other teacher turns, hurrying over. The image goes dark and then…

Another early morning at school, the halls are darker than usual as a freak summer storm rages outside, causing washouts. The parking lot is still mostly empty. She and her family live close to the academy and so she rarely needs to concern herself with traffic and weather issues.

Yesterday was horrible. The headmaster brought in an exterminator while she met with her classes in the library. It's fine now, she keeps telling herself. Fine. She turns down her hall and wonders why Archie hasn't turned on the overhead lights yet. Yes, it's early, but it's also so dark. She's a grown woman, a grandmother for goodness' sake, and yet she's now afraid of the dark. It's embarrassing.

She's close to her door when she hears footsteps echo in the empty hall.
"Archie?"
The footsteps slow to a stop.
She can't see anyone. "Archie?" she calls louder.
Nothing. "Hello?"
A high-pitched falsetto mocks, "Hello?"
Spooked, she walks faster and so do the steps behind her. When she hears them running, pounding down the dark hall, she sprints. Her hand trembles as she tries to get the key in the lock. Footsteps race closer. She gets the key in, unlocks the door, dives in her classroom, and then slams

the door shut, snapping the lock back in place a moment before fists hammer it. She steps back. Waiting.

The false voice whispers her name over and over. Frozen, she cries silently. The overhead lights in the hall turn on, light appearing under the door. The shadow appears to rock back and forth before it disappears, the footsteps moving away. The image goes dark and then...

After work, still shaken by the strange things happening on campus, she's at a country club, working at a table near the entrance, checking in guests. The school does this every year. It's a fundraiser with a silent auction. Dinner is a thousand dollars per plate. There is a dance floor and a jazz trio. They used to have students serve as waiters, which everyone enjoyed. Parents loved having their children wait on them. Students loved the big tips that ostensibly went to their clubs on campus, though she knew most stayed in the students' pockets at the end of the evening. The only ones who didn't like this practice were the police, who had issues with under-age kids serving alcohol.

She checks her watch. The headmaster doesn't allow the faculty to leave until after eleven. Most of the parents are lovely people. Some of them, though... A man, the father of one of her Government students, is trying to sneak in an extra guest. He contends there are empty chairs. No need for them to go to waste. And he promises he and his guest will bid on at least three high-ticket items.

It's exhausting, she thinks. They all know this is his mistress. Just buy her a ticket instead of all this dickering back and forth. She holds her ground. The event is sold out. She couldn't possibly give away a seat that's reserved and paid for. He stomps off in search of the headmaster, who will undoubtedly fold.

Dinner is complete. The dancing is in full swing. The table no longer needs two people, so she and her partner take turns getting some time away. They've shared this duty for years and have their rhythm down. Sitting for so long is difficult for Magdalena, so she always takes the first break. She usually walks around the pond a few times to work out the stiffness, hits the rest room, and then is back in time for her partner's break.

It feels good to walk away from the noise and forced cheer. She's looking forward to sleeping in tomorrow. She smiles, imagining a do-nothing weekend. It won't happen. She'll end up grading, but it's nice to imagine, especially as she's nearing the end of such a miserable couple of days.

The far side of the pond—no doubt a visual clue for golfers—grows a lovely patch of black sage. She enjoys rounding the pond and getting hit with the minty smell this type of sage produces.

She's learned over the years which areas are often too wet to walk through. She's ruined more than one pair of dress shoes accidentally sinking into a spot of mud. This year she's wearing nice but sturdy shoes, ones that can take a good cleaning if she misjudges the ground in the dark. The parents, after all, don't expect, don't even want, the teachers to be dressed up as they are. They might respect the teachers—might— but they're still viewed in the servant category. She learned that the hard way years ago.

As she's passing behind the tall sage, she hears that high falsetto voice that had chased her in the hall. It whispers her name. Panicked, frozen, out of sight of the marquee, her feet sink into sopping grass. She's covered in goose bumps and her breathing becomes shallow, unsure if the voice is in front of her or behind. She hears footsteps squelching in the wet grass and then that horrible high voice telling her to run.

Breaking through the fear, she surges forward, but one of her shoes is stuck. She pulls her foot out, is scrambling across a wet slope with one shoe, when she hears breathing right behind her. Terrified, she opens her mouth to scream but feels horrible pain in the back of her head. The vision goes dark and stays that way.

My eyes fluttered open, my head in horrible pain. I slumped to the side, but Declan kept one arm around my waist and the other over my shoulder to keep me mostly upright. He'd been careful to make sure he wasn't touching my skin. How had I been so lucky to find someone willing to do whatever it took to ease my pain?

I patted the arm across my chest with my gloved hand. He immediately moved it but kept the one around my waist until I was steady enough to stand. I put my glove back on and leaned against his shoulder.

"Are you ready, Ms. Corey?" Detective Osso rolled the drawer back in and then took out his little notebook and pen.

"Yeah. She was killed by a hit to the back of her head. Which is why mine is killing me."

"My wife always makes sure I have aspirin in the car. Would you like me to get you some tablets?" he asked.

I shook my head and then regretted it. "It'll fade, usually before the pills kick in. Even so, I have a bottle in my backpack too. I'll be okay."

Osso nodded. "Can you tell us what you saw?"

Running it all through for them, I realized I'd been wrong. "When you asked me to come in and read your victim, I had an immediate jolt that the cases were connected, that this woman's death was tied to Pearl's. I agreed in spite of your ridiculous guilting skills—that shit stopped working on me when I was like five." I rolled my eyes and regretted it at once. Not the childishness, but the additional pain it triggered.

"I thought knowing who killed Magdalena would help us identify Pearl's killer, but I was wrong. These are two different killers. This guy wanted to menace her, to make her jump at shadows and change her routines. The thing is, though, he had to—"

"Know her routines in the first place." Osso finished my sentence.

"Exactly." I wrapped one of my hands around Declan's wrist and felt him relax behind me. "How would he know? She used to arrive long before students started showing up for the day, before the rest of the faculty. He knew her car, but then he also knew her habit of walking around the pond at this once-a-year fundraiser."

I started to shake my head again and then remembered. "He didn't just want to kill her. He wanted to terrorize her first."

"The cockroaches," Declan said. "He got in before she got to work to release the cockroaches. Are there records somewhere of people buying those things?"

Hernández shook her head. "Pet stores sell them for feeding to reptiles."

I felt Declan's *hmm* reverberate through my back. It made me feel unreasonably warm and comforted.

"They could have been put in her room the night before," Osso said.

"After the night custodian but before the alarms and locks," I added.

Hernández and Osso nodded, thinking.

"What do you know about Archie or the night custodians? The killer could be someone always in the background, someone people stop noticing." It didn't feel like that, but it was a possibility. "Honestly, I felt anger, vengeance, a need to scare her as he'd been scared. Maybe see if she'd ever reported someone. Teachers are mandatory reporters. Maybe she'd called CPS on someone's parents. Or on another teacher."

Osso nodded, still lost in thought. "We know how to investigate, Ms. Corey."

I felt Declan tense.

"Then what am I doing here?" It was always the same. Desperate for my help when they needed it and then, *Shut up and go away, freak girl.*

Hernández smacked Osso's arm. His usual annoyed look darkened. I could see him replaying the conversation in his head. His gaze snapped to me.

"Sorry. You're right. You've given us avenues to pursue and that's what I'll tell her family. Thank you for your assistance."

"Uh huh." I stood. Declan kept his hands on my hips until I seemed steady. I asked Hernández, "You said you notified Pearl's mom, right?"

The detective nodded. "I went out to tell her this afternoon. I was able to get her to call someone to sit with her." She checked her notes. "An Elizabeth."

I nodded, relieved. "My aunt Elizabeth is a very kind woman. She'll be a comfort."

"Let's go get you something to eat," Declan said, shouldering my backpack.

"Yeah, let's go," I said.

SIX

Grieving the Dead

Once we were back in his truck, he pulled a pair of brand new gloves from his glove box, put them on, and then reached for the back of my head. "There's a small knot. You still have some water in the cup. You should take a couple of those pain relievers in your backpack."

He was right. The pain hadn't faded yet, so I might as well. After I did, I pulled out my phone. "Sorry. This will take a minute."

"No problem. They've boxed us in anyway."

Smiling, I tapped the screen. "Couldn't you just pick up the truck and place it in the road?"

"I could," he said as the phone began to ring, "but I don't have time for secret government agencies snatching me up to experiment on, trying to figure out why I'm so strong. And hot."

"Yes, dear." Mom had picked up.

"Hey. I'm sorry if I woke you. I don't know if you've heard yet, but Pearl was found today. She's been positively identified."

"We know. Your gran and I are with Hester now. Elizabeth was here earlier. John and Selena will be here in the morning. Roger's on a plane. He and Hester may no longer be married but they both loved Pearl very much."

"Can you take me over tomorrow after the Council meeting?"

"Of course. Would you like me to come get you now?" Mom asked.

"No. Detective Hernández told me about Pearl and asked me to come to the morgue to read her, to try to figure out who killed her. I ended up having to read three murder victims, so my head is a mess right now. I'd rather visit tomorrow."

My mom was moving. The low murmur of voices in the background disappeared. "And what did you see?" she demanded.

Declan reached over and rubbed my thigh, listening to both sides of the conversation whether he wanted to or not.

"I just shared that with the detective, Mom. You can't say anything to the people there. It might mess up the investigation."

"I know how to keep secrets, Arwyn. I'm asking you what you saw." Sybil was tough as nails and didn't have much patience for anyone who wasn't.

As she was my mother, head of the Corey coven, and kept way too many secrets, I explained what I had seen, though in less detail than I'd given the cops.

"So she was singled out? Targeted?" Mom's heels clicked in the background. She was pacing in an echo-y room, probably the kitchen.

"That's the way I read it," I said.

"Tomorrow, when the Council convenes, we'll see if the three of us can see anything more." She let out a gust of breath. "I want this bastard found and thrown into a cell for the rest of his natural life," she hissed, trying to be quiet.

"Me too."

"I know you do. All right. I'll tell Hester you'll be here tomorrow. Now go home and rest."

Aww, she did care about me.

"We need you at your best tomorrow for the Council meeting."

Of course.

"Here they come," Declan said.

Osso jogged to his SUV, started it up, and spun it around, heading in the opposite direction.

The tap at the window made me jump. Hernández waited on the other side. I rolled it down.

"I'm sorry about that in there. We both really appreciate your assistance, but I can't help feeling horribly guilty that every time you help us, it causes you pain." She glanced around, uncomfortable.

"I appreciate that," I said. "How about as a thank you, you arrest the asshole who killed Pearl?"

She thumped the side of the truck twice. "I'm on it."

As she walked to her car, I rolled up the window. My phone buzzed in my pocket and Declan started driving.

The readout on the phone said, *Sam*. Why in the world would she be calling me in the middle of the night?

"Hello?"

"Hi. Sorry. I hope you weren't asleep," she said.

"No. I'm still up."

"Good. That's what she said. I had a visitor tonight. Well, she said she's been hanging around since earlier when you visited. She was with you but then—"

"Darling, just start at the beginning," a male voice said in the background.

"Right," she started again. "I have Pearl with me right now. She's afraid to move on, so she's been spending time with all of you. She said she loves your mural. What?" Pause. "Right, okay. She thanks you for singing the song of the dead for her. She felt the push to move on but isn't ready yet."

Declan had pulled over when he heard Sam say Pearl was with her. I couldn't see past the tears in my eyes. Sam Quinn, my newly found cousin, was a necromancer. She could see and speak with the dead.

I cleared my throat. "Tell her we love her and miss her so much."

"She says she loves you all too. She knows she's not supposed to hang around, but she doesn't want to leave everyone," Sam said.

"Remind her Aunt Sylvia is waiting for her with your mom, Bridget. She has two incredibly kind aunts waiting at the head of the line to welcome her and guide her through the next life."

"She's crying but says she knows. She needs me to tell you that she remembers what kind of car he drove. It was a black BMW convertible with brown leather seats," Sam relayed.

"Thank her, please. I'll tell the detective."

"What?" Sam's voice was less clear. "Huh. Interesting. Pearl says he kind of stuttered his name when he introduced himself. She says he said, *D-David*. Like maybe he was making it up on the spot." Sam paused again. "Oh. She said there was a leather portfolio—black—on the passenger side seat that he tossed into the back seat when he drove them to dinner. She says she's positive there was an engraved D on the portfolio."

"I'll let the detective know." I thought about her last moments, the horror that this charming young man had only pretended to find her interesting so he could get close enough to kill her. And poor Pearl, like her mother, had only weak magic at best to protect herself. "Please tell her the whole family is grieving her loss. Tell her I saw what happened. I was with her at the end. She didn't die alone."

"Oh, here. Wait." Sam's voice was distant again. "It's okay. Let's try. Sometimes this works. Come here. You need a hug." Rustling sounds. "There. That worked. You go ahead and cry. If anyone deserves a big cry, it's you." Silence. "I get it, but trusting people, wanting to see the good in them, that doesn't make you stupid." Pause. "Nuh uh. Trust me; I know from stupid, and you're not." She chuckled softly. "See, that's better now.

"Look, here's Fergus." Pause. "He *is* a handsome boy; you're right. Ha, did you see that? He tried to put his paw on your knee. He does that when he thinks someone needs comforting. I've always wondered if pets could see people on the other side. Maybe they can."

There was a soft jingling sound, probably her dog's collar.

"Are you ready to move on? I can help you do that," Sam said. "Oh, no. It's okay. You don't have to yet. Not if you're not ready. If you stick around, though, you have to promise to not visit me in the bathroom. That's creepy." Pause. "Oh, and definitely not when, you know, Clive and I—"

A male voice broke in. "She is trying to tell you not to watch us have sex, Pearl. And I'd like to second that request."

"Ah, there you go," Sam said. "Your eyes sparkle when you laugh."

"Darling, I believe your cousin is still on the line," Clive said.

"Oh!" Rustling. "Sorry about that. Anything else you want to tell Arwyn before we let her sleep?" Long pause. "She wants to thank you again for the song to the goddess. She felt better and stronger after you did it. She wants to thank you for enduring the pain to tell the police what happened. Hmm?" Pause. "Oh, okay. She wants you to call me tomorrow when you visit her mother. She has a message she'd like me to give her. Is that all right?"

"Of course," I said. "I'll call you tomorrow."

"Good. Well, we both wish you a good night."

"And you." I disconnected and just sat there, staring out the truck windshield.

Declan reached for my hand and squeezed. "She's not alone. Sam is comforting her on this side and your aunts are waiting on the other."

"Yeah."

He started the engine again. "I know an all-night fast-food joint on the way back to your gallery. We'll get food and then you can sleep, okay?"

I nodded. I wasn't hungry, but he was right. I needed to eat something. Please, Goddess, no dreams tonight.

I ate half a burger and a few fries on the way home. Having a werewolf around was handy. No wasted food. When he pulled up to the gallery, I touched his wrist.

"I don't want any more nightmares. Can you help me sleep?"

He put his big warm hand over mine. "Of course."

We walked around the back and used the studio door, but not before I leaned over the rail to wish everyone a happy morning. It wasn't light yet, but it would be soon.

"Couch or bed?" I asked.

He scratched his beard. "I think I might just be too tired to let you sleeping next to me in a bed keep me awake." Following me up the steps, he mumbled, "Or maybe not."

I stopped and turned. He'd been eye level with my butt. "Couch?"

Nodding, he turned and trudged back down the stairs, kicking off his work boots. He slouched down on the couch, his legs straight out and crossed at the ankles, his head resting on the back cushion.

"I'm going to change into sweats and be right down."

He nodded again.

I put on my super soft loungewear, brushed my teeth, tied up my hair, and then grabbed two blankets. Before I went down, I remembered to text Hernández.

> Me: Long story. Too tired to get into right now. Pearl's spirit told my cousin who's a necromancer that she remembers that her killer drove a black BMW convertible and though she's not sure if his name is really David, he did have a leather portfolio in the car that had a D on it. Okay, good night.

> Hernández: Wow. Okay. Wow.

When I went downstairs, I found Declan breathing slowly and deeply. As gently as I could, I covered him with one blanket and then tried to lie down next to him, my head on a pillow up against his hip. Once I finally got arranged, my legs tucked up—I needed a bigger couch—a blanket around me, I let out a long breath. I hadn't woken him.

He pulled an arm from under his blanket and rested it on my shoulder. "That was cute," he rumbled. "Wolves don't fall asleep when someone's moving around in the den. Thank you for the blanket, though." He rubbed my arm. "Let's both sleep now."

And I did. Finally.

SEVEN

Otis Joins the Ranks

*G*rowling. *Wolves with their teeth bared snarl and snap, tearing into one another with sharp, deadly claws. Howls. A ring of savage, slathering animals tethered by string as Declan stands in the middle, shoulders straight, accepting what's to come.*

A woman stands in a weak circle of light, darkness encroaching. A man climbs steps toward her, a long needle held at his side. She knows who he is, knows what he plans. She tries to push him away, but he stabs her in the neck, injecting her with poison.

Sylvia struggles in the hospital bed, trapped in a coma of the demon's making. He's crushing her, sitting on her chest. Calliope whispers foul curses in her mother's ear, sharing a look of triumph with her demon.

He waits in the woods, hidden, watching the young boy play with Iron Man and Spider-Man. The boy runs in a loop, both action figures tight in his grip as they fly through the air. He smiles, thinking about his experiments and what a sharp knife can do to skin.

The woman is paralyzed with fear; the dinner party and her work partner are too far away. A high-pitched voice calls her name again. Why is this happening? What has she ever done? She tries to run in the mud but slips. She hears a sharp intake of breath and then nothing more.

Whispers. A long, dark corridor. Thick carpet. Carved wooden walls and doors. A light is barely visible beneath the last door. The whispers make her skin crawl. She moves closer, trying to make out the words, but hears the crack of a hand against flesh, a gasp of pain.

Pearl sits in a coffee shop, typing on her laptop, a textbook open on the table beside her. Long, dark hair curtains her from view, so he moves his seat. He watches her around a man's shoulder. She hides in the far corner. Bitten fingernails with chipped polish. She jumps when a barista drops a bottle. She's barely changed. Still the same scared little mouse.

He can't wait to see her eyes widen in disbelief and terror. God, he loves the fear. It's powerful. Intoxicating. Addictive. He'll make the little mouse squeal. Soon.

I startled awake, early morning light streaming through the windows. Alone, I checked my phone. Three and a half hours. *Damn.* Normally, sleeping next to Declan gave me six to seven hours of solid, dreamless sleep. Perhaps last night was too much. My mind hadn't been able to settle down, especially after watching my cousin be murdered. Most of the images in this last nightmare had been familiar horrors that had woken me many times before. What I hadn't recognized was the one lingering in my head: a long, dark corridor filled with doors. What the hell did that mean?

I sensed a shadow pass over the skylight. Looking up, I expected a dark raincloud. What I found instead were two eyes staring back. I jumped out of my skin. We had a sorcerer and her demon to contend with, after all. Thankfully, what I was looking at wasn't evil. It was the baby raccoon who'd taken to hanging out with me at dawn and dusk while I painted.

I'd named him Otis and he was, no doubt, wondering when I was coming out to play. "Give me a minute," I called and then ran up the stairs to put on work clothes.

It took a while to get set up, tarping the area under where I'd be working today, filling a large basket on a rope with paints, brushes, trays for mixing the paints. My mural went over the newly renovated side wall of my gallery. I made the boards look grayed from the ocean spray, rotted through in places. A long, purple-blue tentacle appeared to break through the decrepit old building. There would be another one bursting through the roof, but that'd be a physical tentacle, like the ones I had coming up from the water, curling around the deck, seeming to be pulling my gallery down into the ocean.

There'd been an article in the online version of the local paper, saying I'd given more than a few fishermen a shock the first morning they'd gone up. Apparently, there were many messages being passed on their radios that morning, as they were all telling each other about the sea monster finally tearing down that old cannery. A few of the boats ignored their normal timetable and swung by for a closer look. Lots of flashes were going off as I sat in my dark studio, drinking tea and smiling.

I'd done it on purpose, putting them all up late at night so the fishermen would be the first to see them. Declan and me, that is. It had been a two-person-with-super-strength job. I wasn't anywhere near as strong as a werewolf, but my father's fae blood made me much stronger than a human.

After the article, I started noticing more cars driving by, watching me work on the mural. A few would honk and wave, but most just slowed down and took pictures. My gallery could use the hype. I was a little off the beaten path and needed buzz.

Once everything was set, I climbed up with a thermos of tea, pulled the rope, hauling up all my gear, and got to work. Almost immediately, Otis climbed off the roof and onto the scaffolding, sniffing around for food, but mostly just watching.

I pulled a muffin out of my overalls pocket, unwrapped the paper towel surrounding it, and then rolled it to him. He jumped out of the way, looking betrayed by my hostility, and then sniffed the air, waddling happily back to claim his breakfast. He picked it up with both paws, plopped his butt down, and ate while I worked. It was nice having company.

My phone buzzed. I pulled it from my bib pocket, saw it was Declan, and tapped speakerphone. "Hi."

"Hey," he said. "I thought you'd sleep later."

"How do you know you didn't just wake me up?"

"Turn around."

I did and saw him over at his property. He'd purchased the land across the road and down maybe an eighth of a mile. It was closer to Cannery Row and had been a combination retail space and amusement area for tourists. Outwardly, it appeared to be a large barn. When you went in, there was a full-sized carousel in the middle with small retail stalls selling souvenirs and taffy, fudge, hairbands, whatnot, all around it. I remembered going there as a child. My mother hated the place. Most of the adults did, as the interchangeable teenagers working the carousel barely glanced to see if the children were secure before starting the ride.

My cousin Colin was screwing around and got knocked off when it shuddered and jumped before taking off faster than usual. And I just realized the teenager at the controls probably did it on purpose, as Colin had been harassing him earlier. Good for him. Colin has always been a dick.

Apparently, years later, a child was seriously hurt riding it. It wasn't human error, then. The owners hadn't been putting money or expertise into the upkeep of the old machinery. A tourist with deep pockets sued and the business went under. Honestly, though, it had been struggling for years.

It was a prime location, but the building would cost more to renovate to get it up to code than it was worth, so it had sat until a woodworking werewolf decided to snap it up and make it a workshop instead of a tourist trap.

One of the carousel animals was an octopus. It was the one I always rode when I was little. If he decided to junk the old, probably rotting, animals, I'd asked if he would give me the octopus. I'd take care of her.

Declan was a gifted woodworker, but because he'd moved around so much, he couldn't take what he built with him. He mostly built to order and moved on. If he'd built pieces that hadn't already been sold, he'd leave them in consignment shops and collect the money when they did. Now, as he'd decided to stay in Monterey, he was renovating the building and creating the workshop he'd always wanted.

He waved and I waved back.

"I was thinking about the sleeping thing as I painted and chatted with Otis," I said.

"Who's Otis?"

I snapped a pic of him eating the last of his muffin and sent it to Declan. "He's my dusk and dawn painting buddy. He scared the crap out of me this morning when I looked up at the skylight and saw him staring back at me. I was late, so he was checking up on me."

Declan laughed. "It's good to have company. Anyway, you were thinking?"

"When we've done this before, I was leaning on you or the top of my head was touching your pant leg. Last night, I was trying so hard not to wake you, I didn't adjust the pillow against your leg. Because of that, my head wasn't touching your thigh. It's a working theory."

"We'll have to test it out," he said.

"I'm twenty-eight years exhausted, so I'll take you up on that offer. Also, if you get hungry, I have muffins in the studio. Courtesy of the nightmare night before last, your choices are blueberry-raspberry or strawberry cheesecake."

"Mmm. I'll definitely be over soon. By the way, I called to say the mural is amazing. I know you're not done yet, but it absolutely looks real. I've had a few cars pull into my drive to turn around and then park by the side of the road, watching you."

"Oh, that's...not at all threatening."

He laughed again. "I had my eye on them."

"Okay, good. Well, this wall isn't going to paint itself." Especially now that Otis was playing with my brushes.

"Try to take a nap later."

"No can do. I have a Corey Council meeting today. Oh, speaking of which, can you give me a ride to my mom's or should I order up a car?"

"What time?"

"Elevenish."

He paused a moment. "I can make that work. I'll pick you up and grab muffins then."

"Sounds good. Happy building!"

"Thanks. And happy painting to you."

I disconnected and put the finishing touches on the tentacle. It was almost photorealistic in its detail. Even this close, I was proud of what I'd created. The flesh was a lightly mottled gray that turned more blue and purple in different spots. I'd used an iridescent paint to highlight the suckers and then a high gloss clear coat just on the tentacle to give it a wet look.

I was letting the clear coat dry while I continued to make my gallery look as though it was one strong gust away from collapsing into the sea. I'd finished the section I was working on and was about to climb up to the top of the scaffolding when a text pinged on my phone. I checked my pocket. It was a text from Declan.

Declan: Check the time.

I did. *Shit.*

Me: Thanks

I collected my stuff, filled the basket, lowering it to the ground, and then turned to say goodbye to Otis. He was gone. Darn. I'd missed him leaving. Oh, well. After hauling in the basket, I ran upstairs to shower. Mother would be most displeased if I arrived in my paint-spattered overalls.

Hair care was always the biggest time suck for me. I could shower quickly, but once shampooing and conditioning came into the mix, forget about it. Wet, my hair hung down past my butt. I'd tried cutting it a few times over the years. It always grew back to the exact same length by the following day. Clearly, it was a fae thing and I just needed to deal with it.

Far more time-consuming than washing was drying. Couldn't I just spell it dry? Sure, but that filled it with static and made it stick up crazy. So, lots of leave-in conditioners and emollients later, I was gently drying with a hair diffuser. Okay, fine. I was vain about my hair. It was a pain, but it was also soft and beautiful because I took good care of it.

My mom would have preferred I wore a dress, like that was ever going to happen. Clean black jeans with no paint spatters, loafers instead of sneakers, and a lightweight lavender sweater was the best she was going to get. I pocketed my phone and a slim billfold. I'd grab my backpack on the way out. First, though, I needed to try something.

When I went downstairs, I saw my driver lounging on the deck. I unlocked the door and opened it.

"Sorry. Running late. Come on in and eat. I need to do one thing and then we can go." I went to my pantry and looked for an empty jar. Ha! I knew this would come in handy someday. When I turned to go outside, I found Declan leaning against the doorframe, watching me.

"You're looking beautiful, Ursula."

Not gonna lie, the voice, the look in his eye, all of it was doing things to me. "Does that mean you're not angry I'm ten minutes late?"

He shook his head. "Not even a little bit."

I patted his chest as I walked by. "Sucker. Oh, and the muffins are on the counter."

I went out to the deck and hung over the railing. "Hello, Cecil!" A tentacle slapped the surface of the water. "Hello, Charlie. Hello Herbert." My starfish friends were looking bright and handsome on the posts holding up the deck. I searched the waves for the gray seal head of Wilbur, a selkie. We played catch most every day. I scanned the deck for his tennis ball but didn't find it. He must not have returned my last throw yet.

I unscrewed the conical hat on the plastic bear and balanced it on the railing beside me. Holding my hand over the water, I began to pull. Water rose like a slow, measured fountain. I could make seawater shoot wherever I wanted. It had been one of my key defenses against my shitty cousins. The slow control was far more difficult, but I'd been practicing.

When it had finally risen to the height of the railing, I flipped over the see-through honey bear and scooped up the seawater, filling the little container. After screwing the top back on, I turned to find Declan sitting on a bench, finishing a muffin and watching me again.

"What are you up to?" he asked.

"I had a thought last night. The ocean always makes me feel better, heals me. So I thought I should start carrying it around with me to see if it works in small doses."

He nodded. "Great idea. It helped when I brought river water to you when we were in that little girl's house."

"Ana," I said.

"I know," he responded, standing up. "Thinking too much about her or Christopher is hard. I only know a small portion of what's in your head, and it bothers the hell out of me. I don't know how you do it."

"Practice. And art. And my ocean friends here. Otis, who's turned out to be a good painting buddy. Baking." I shrugged. "Finding beauty to counter the horrific, I guess."

"I like that." He checked his watch. "We should probably get moving before—"

My phone buzzed.

"—that," he finished.

EIGHT

The Corey Council Convenes

"Should I walk you in?" Declan asked.

"Why in the world would you do that?" I grabbed my backpack and stared at him.

He ran his hand through his hair. "I don't know, do I? It's your mother and grandmother. I'm just trying to be polite here."

I looked up at Mother's pale yellow Queen Anne house. It was three stories with a turret. Growing up, the turret room was mine. Hardwood floors and floral rugs throughout, each room filled with perfectly maintained antiques, it had a distinctly feminine feel. The idea of this big lumberjack standing in the foyer cracked me up.

"Hmm, as someone who cares for you, I'd advise you to save yourself and never look back. As someone who also loves to watch my mother squirm in discomfort, I say come have lunch with us."

He looked up at the big house. "How about if I split the difference and walk you to the door, say hello, and then burn rubber out of here?"

Grinning, I said, "Okay, but if you could stamp your boots a little and leave dirt or sawdust on her perfectly polished floors, I'll make you cinnamon rolls."

"Deal." He got out and came to my side, closing the door after I slid out.

As we walked up the steps between the flowering hedgerow, the front door opened. My mother, in a trim navy blue dress, stepped out onto the porch.

"Ooh," I whispered, "blocked at the door."

"I still want cinnamon rolls," he whispered back.

"Darling, you're late. Lunch is going cold." My mother was a beautiful, if stony, woman. She wore her shoulder-length black hair in a perpetual chignon. I happened to know that when she smiled, it felt like everything in the world would be okay. Unfortunately, I couldn't remember her wholeheartedly smiling since I was little.

She carried the weight of the Corey coven on her shoulders, and it showed in her stiff posture. Green eyes, heart-shaped face, bow lips, it didn't matter. She and Aunt Sylvia could have been twins, but Syl didn't carry the responsibility. She was lighter and freer and cover-model beautiful. The pressure and duty had hardened my mother's features; her immense magical power made her a formidable opponent who most in their right minds avoided.

I loved that Declan pretended like he didn't see the disapproval and didn't feel the hostility. He was just her daughter's—what?— suitor, I supposed, and he was treating Mom like any potential mate's mother. I could tell it drove her nuts, which tickled me no end.

"Sorry, Mom. I was working and then"—I pulled at one of my curls—"you know how long it takes to deal with this."

"Go in. Your grandmother is waiting for you." She finally turned her attention to Declan. "And Mr. Quinn, it was good of you to chauffeur Arwyn to us."

"That was no problem, ma'am. This is a beautiful house you have." He stomped a boot on her porch. "Nice and solid."

"Is that Arwyn's young man I hear?" Gran's voice floated out the door. Dressed in a trim black dress, her silver hair knotted in a bun at the base of her skull, she came to the door and tapped her daughter's shoulder. They looked like an age progression image of the same person. "My goodness, where are your manners, Sybil? Declan, would you like to join us for lunch?"

Mom was used to being the biggest and the baddest, and then Gran came along to put her in her place.

"No, thank you, ma'am. I appreciate the offer, but I have to get back to work. I have some men waiting for me."

"Gran, did we tell you Declan bought the property across the road from The Sea Wicche?" I asked. "He's a very talented wood-worker and he's opening his own workshop with a retail area."

"Is that so?" she asked with a gleam in her eye. "Did you hear that, Sybil? This nice young man is staying. Now that we're neighbors, perhaps you could walk me back to my chair. The years are starting to take a toll."

"Of course." He stepped around Mom and took Gran's arm, walking her back in.

Mom rolled her eyes and crossed her arms. "As if she couldn't run a 5K if she wanted," she said under her breath.

Hiding a grin, I sidestepped my mother as well and followed Gran and Declan through the house. He was just pushing in her chair at the dining table when I entered. Gran gave me a wink and Declan was clearly trying not to laugh.

Rubbing my shoulder, he said, "Call me if you need a pickup." Seeing my mother in the doorway, he added, "It's always nice to see you, Ms. Corey. I hope you ladies have a nice lunch." His footsteps sounded heavier as he left, and I knew he was angling for banana bread to go along with the cinnamon rolls.

"Such a nice young man," Gran said, causing Mom to shake her head as she went to the kitchen.

I spied Declan through the large front window, opening his truck door. He stopped and gave me a big grin before sliding in and driving off. Yep. He'd heard Gran.

"Let me help you, Mom." I went into the kitchen as she was coming out with a tray of English tea sandwiches. Really, Mom? *Lunch is going cold.* Yeah, that happens when you're serving cold sandwiches.

"I'll get the iced tea." I picked up the tray with a pitcher of tea and three cut crystal glasses.

Gran had already taken two of the smoked salmon sandwiches.

There was a bakery across the street from Mom's tea shop. When she had people over, she usually stopped in there to pick up an assortment of these tiny, delicious sandwiches. I chose the chicken and cranberry. Mom preferred the cucumber-dill and the shrimp salad.

I poured everyone iced tea and then sat to eat.

"How's the gallery coming?" Gran asked. "It won't be long now."

I swallowed and then took a sip. "I'm almost done with the mural. Maybe another day or so. At that point, I begin painting the interior."

"Why not have Phil's men do the painting?" Mom asked.

"Because I'm not just painting the walls white. I want it to look like we're under water."

"How can you possibly have time for all that before your opening?" Mom asked, taking a bite and touching the napkin to her lips.

"Yes. That is the issue and why I get cranky when asked to do other things."

"You agreed to join this Council and—"

I cut her off before she really got started. "I know, Mom. You might notice I'm sitting here. It doesn't mean I'm not stressed about getting everything done in time."

Gran reached over and patted my arm. "I know you're busy, but what we do provides protection, direction, even hope for our people." Gran, like Mom, had no patience for gripes about Council responsibilities. I got it. They'd been shouldering it without a third for far too long, but there was little to no care for how hard this was, mentally and physically, on me. Whatever. The sandwiches were good.

When we finished, we moved out to Mom's backyard. It was a showplace. Aunt Hester, Pearl's mom, might not have had a lot of magical ability, but she had ten green thumbs, which is its own magic. There was a screen of tall trees around the perimeter of the garden, with flowering bushes, decorative grasses, beds of blossoms, and vines dripping from the pergola.

My old bedroom had a window to the garden. I'd spent much of my growing up years—if I wasn't across the street in the ocean —sitting in my window seat with a sketchbook in my hand.

The yard had also been spelled. Neighbors could neither see nor hear us. The last time we'd joined hands in a ritual like this, I'd had a vision of issues to be aware of and try to prevent. Mom and Gran had experienced my vision too but from a different angle. We didn't see exactly the same things, which was incredibly odd.

The three of us met in the middle of the garden. I took off my gloves, lifted my arms to the heavens, allowing all my mental blocks to slip away. Voices, emotions, visions swirled around me, but I cloaked myself in the white light of the Goddess. I wasn't sure how I knew what to say, but when Mom and Gran began to speak, my voice twined with theirs.

"We, the Corey three, maiden, mother, and crone, call upon the Goddess for her wisdom and protection. We entreat thee to look favorably upon us and share your insight. We seek only to care for our people. There is darkness in this family. We ask, our most beloved Goddess, that you share with us how we might pluck the evil from the heart of our family. For your guidance, we thank you. Blessed be."

We joined hands and I was slammed with more visions than I could process all at once. My knees buckled.

A darkness hovers over Gran's house, pacing back and forth across her patio, leering in her windows. It tries to seep under Mom's doors. It scratches at the gallery walls. It looms over us every day, waiting for a weakening of our defenses. And under it all is the chanting of Calliope and her demon. It's an auditory arrhythmia. If we listen too long, let it bleed into our souls, our hearts will mimic the rhythm and we, as a family, will seize.

Tourists bump into each other as they ignore the sidewalk, their atten-

tion fixed on the contents of shop windows. A man in a dark coat arrows through the throng, fingers gripped around something in his pocket. He pushes open a door and a bell tinkles. Serena stands behind the counter. She nods to the man, asking if he needs help. Ignoring her, he moves to the back of the shop, knocking over a display of packaged loose-leaf tea.

Annoyed, she goes around the counter to pick up the bags. The man unstoppers the vial in his pocket, quietly takes the lid off one of the glass jars Serena keeps behind the counter, and sprinkles the contents of the vial all over the tea leaves. He's out the door before Serena is done cleaning up his mess. Three customers later, she pulls doctored leaves from the jar, brews them, and hands her customer death in a go-cup.

Uncle John in sitting in his den, a laptop open. Hand over his mouth, he stares in disbelief. Head shaking, he closes his eyes, moving his hand from his mouth to his forehead. "Why? Why would she do this?"

A man stands at the top of a staircase in the foyer of some grand old mansion, dark wood, darker rugs, antiques, low lights. His head is turned, arguing with someone, their voices kept low. Shaking his head, he starts down the stairs and then he's flying. His body crumples at the bottom, his neck at an unnatural angle.

Aunt Hester sits in the dark, staring into the middle distance, unable to move on, unable to live without her Pearl. The phone rings, but she ignores it. The doorbell chimes, but she's beyond noticing. A light layer of dust has settled on her as she waits for death to return. This time for herself.

A great fire consumes a building. The inferno is more flame than structure. A moment later, the edifice gives up the struggle and collapses, shooting sparks swirling into the sky. Under the roar of the fire is a growl and tires kicking up rocks.

An older man approaches a cliff, unsure of why he's there. He feels an obligation but fears he's misjudged the situation, the person. Uneasy, wishing he was home with his feet up watching the game, he greets the one waiting for him. The other points toward the cliff. The man turns his head and then it all goes black as a heavy object connects with the back of his head. He's dragged through brush and then rolled off the edge, falling to the jagged rocks and ocean waves far below.

The glass of a greenhouse glows in the twilight, reflecting the pinks and purples of the sky. A dark figure moves like a ghost across the yard. The door isn't locked. Why should it be? It resides in a spelled garden. The figure goes in, pulls a spray can of industrial lubricant from their pocket, and sprays. They crank the huge silent wheel, opening the windows on the far side of the greenhouse, the ones impossible to see from the house. The figure goes to the heater controls and pushes the power button, turning it off. The figure slips away, content in the knowledge that hundreds of delicate, precious plants will soon die.

A man rides his bike along a narrow road. He knows it like the back of his hand. He's been riding this route for probably forty years. Most of his early morning ride is along empty roads with dense trees canopying the path. Halfway through, he hits the coastline and watches the waves capsize over huge rocks. Sea spray hits his face and for one brief moment, he closes his eyes, relishing the feel. He doesn't see the car, doesn't even hear it because of the podcast in his ears. A silver truck races up behind him and slams into him, sending him sailing onto the bone-crushing roc—

I opened my eyes, head pounding, body feeling too battered to move. I wasn't sure what happened. My fingers tingled. Did Mom and Gran rip their hands away mid-vision?

Mother ran to the house, a barely audible *No, no, no, no* on her lips.

I stayed where I was, wishing for a morphine drip. "What happened?"

Gran stood quietly, hands clasped, lips moving.

"He's alive!" Mom called from the back door.

Gran lost all tension in her body and hit the ground beside me. I forced myself into a sitting position to check on her and then saw she had tears running down her face.

"What?" I asked again.

Mom walked down the steps and helped Gran up. "That was your Uncle Andrew on the bike. When I told him what we saw, he agreed to change his route and to keep changing it until Calliope is caught."

Gran kept murmuring *thank you* over and over as Mom helped her up the stairs and back into the house. I followed, but more slowly.

NINE

The Line Forms to the Left

How had I not known it was Uncle Andrew? I'd even seen his face, seen him close his eyes. How had I not recognized him? Shaking my head, I followed their voices to the sitting room, opposite the dining room. It was a light and airy room, high windows, off-white walls, with a floral sofa and matching chairs.

Gran and Mom looked shaken, their expressions drawn. Voices hushed, they assured each other that they hadn't lost another child, another sibling.

"I'll make tea," I said and headed back to the kitchen. As I brewed a calming blend, I pulled out the cart and cups while wondering what else I'd missed. This had always been my problem, hadn't it? I was shit when it came to visions related to Coreys. I couldn't see myself in visions at all, and I'd missed Abigail and Calliope.

If I'd agreed to join the Corey Council when they'd first asked me at thirteen, maybe Sylvia... How many people had suffered, lost their lives, because I didn't want it, was afraid of it? No wonder Mom had been pissed off at me most of my life.

Without their perspective, the bicyclist would have been just a guy in one of the thousands of visions swirling in my head. They recognized him and called to prevent his death. I would have started baking and ignorantly let him die.

When I eventually composed myself and rolled in the tea cart, Mom and Gran were looking more themselves. I poured, passed the cups and saucers, and then sat in the far chair, feeling as low as I could remember in quite some time.

"Your Gran and I were discussing the vision." Mom took a sip and sat back in her chair. "That was Elizabeth's greenhouse. I called, telling her to check her wards and to put a lock on it. She was very grateful for the warning and will be securing it today."

"Good," I said, pretending I wasn't drowning in a very dark place right now.

"Serena's shop," Mom said. "Did you see which jar the poison went in?"

"It was on the far right, looking at the counter. I think it was a lavender and lemon blend. I'm not positive, though," I said. "The thing about visions is that sometimes they're more symbolic. It might be a Darjeeling or a berry hibiscus, but I saw lavender lemon because that was what I wanted to drink in that moment. It might not even be tea. I think we tell her what we saw, but also alert her to someone coming in and causing a distraction in order to poison her products."

Mom and Gran nodded slowly, taking that in. Mom got Serena on the phone and told her exactly that and to rebuild her wards. Calliope had worked with her on the original warding of the shop, meaning Calliope could take them down anytime she wanted. I stayed out of it. Serena hadn't been my biggest fan before her mother had died and I'd identified her sister as the sorcerer who'd done it. Now? Well, there was a lot of understandable hostility aimed at me.

Once Mom was off the phone, she looked between the two of us. "What was that about John? What was upsetting him on the computer?"

I shook my head. I hadn't seen the screen either.

Gran said, "It was a banking website."

Mom swiped through the phone and called John, Serena and Calliope's dad. As Mom explained the vision, he logged into his accounts, checked balances, and then reset his passwords. He said he'd be contacting the bank to add more security. It was the best we could do at the moment.

"So, she needs money," Gran said. "We'll need to send a message to everyone to change passwords and update security. If she can't steal her parents' money, she'll try to steal someone else's."

"They should probably strengthen all their wards," I said. "Who knows how long she's been planning, stockpiling information, unwinding wards."

"Yes," Mom agreed. "I'll send out the message today." She picked up her phone again and texted.

"Wait until we've finished our meeting," Gran said.

"No. I'm sending Andrew over to sit with Hester. I'll be taking Arwyn this afternoon, but I want someone with her now."

Gran and I nodded our agreement.

"Did either of you recognize the man who was pushed down the stairs?" I asked.

They looked at each other and then shook their heads.

"The house didn't look familiar either," Gran said.

"No," Mom agreed.

"Maybe the one doing the pushing?" Gran asked.

"I couldn't see him," I said. "I don't think he's family, but it feels like he's connected to a Corey. No idea how, though."

"And that other one being shoved off a cliff," Gran said. "I've never seen him before either."

Mom took a sip and shook her head. "Nor have I."

Shrugging, I said, "Me neither. And this is the problem with visions. Sometimes I have no idea what they mean until after the thing happens." I rubbed my forehead. "It's so frustrating."

"Well," Mom began, "we'll think about it and maybe one of us will have an epiphany."

"The fire scares me," Gran said. "I didn't see enough to identify the house. They already tried to burn down your gallery. Are they coming back to do it again? Is it one of our houses? Is the fire connected to that dark presence we saw trying to break into our homes?"

I closed my eyes, calling up the image. "I don't think it's me. The shape of the building isn't right. The gallery is much longer than what we saw. I feel like I should know it, but I can't place it."

Mom stood. "We'll think about that too." She checked her watch. "The family knows we're meeting. If anyone would like to petition our help, they're to arrive in about fifteen minutes. I suggest we use the restroom or whatever we need to do to freshen up. I have no idea how many might come, but we'll need to be ready and welcoming. We haven't had a meeting like this in a very long time, so many people need our help."

Yeah, I felt that punch. Mom was always good at hitting her targets.

She flicked her fingers and chairs that had been along the wall were now fanned out in front of the window. "We'll let people congregate in the parlor while we see petitioners one by one in here." She started to leave and then paused. "Darling, can you freshen our tea? I believe we'll be seeing a great many people."

I did and then I used the time to send a quick text to Declan.

> Me: I had a vision about a building burning. It's not my gallery again. I think, though, it might be your barn. It was hard to identify the shape, but I heard a growl, and the pack is causing trouble. Do you have sprinklers installed yet?

> Declan: No, not yet. I'll get the cameras mounted today and the motion sensors. Thank you.

Even if I was wrong, he was doing things to keep himself safer, which was good. As Mom and Gran were still in the kitchen, I pulled the borrowed grimoire from my backpack and started leafing through it. I read over the marked spell Dave had recommended. It was simple enough and I'd never had trouble memorizing spells. I didn't think I'd ever use it, though. It felt evil.

There were a lot of spells I knew, some familiar with alterations. Most grimoires were specific to a family, the spells recorded the way that family performed the spell. I loved studying other grimoires because it highlighted how varied our magic was, how personal. There wasn't one specific way to access and use magic.

Near the end, I found a spell for finding something important. Mom, Gran, and I had already performed countless spells, trying to find where Calliope had hidden herself. This one was new, though.

"What's that you have?" Gran asked.

"Sam loaned me a grimoire that has a very creepy spell for sending someone to Hell. She wanted me to see it, since we're dealing with sorcery."

Brow furrowed, Gran leaned on the back of my chair. "Let me see it."

I flipped back and showed her. Her gaze slid across the page. Patting my shoulder, she said, "It's dark but not black magic. If it keeps you safe, use it."

She sat on the couch and I put the grimoire away. I heard voices in the entry. There was no time to try the finding spell now, but I'd try later when I had the time and quiet to practice.

More voices were added to the ones I'd heard. Too many people were coming today, some of whom I didn't know, or at least remember. Mom and Gran knew them all, though. They greeted everyone by name, asked after the particulars in their lives, and then gave them the chance to request our aid. Mom and Gran were benevolent queens. I was the idiot to the side, taking notes. The petitioners glanced at me warily while explaining their marriage difficulties, their business troubles, their errant children and infuriating neighbors to Mom and Gran.

I wrote it all down, adding a score to their request, with a bulleted list explaining why I'd given them that score.

I scored the one who wanted us to help his failing online

investment banking business a one. He was gambling away his profits and trying to hide that from his long-suffering wife, who was sitting beside him. She was the Corey. He'd married into the family because he'd seen dollar signs. He possessed weak magic, relying on his wife to do the heavy lifting, so to speak.

How did I know all of this when I hadn't touched him? I hadn't put my shields back up after the vision. I could have, but I was feeling pretty shitty about myself and so left myself wide open to it all, taking the emotional battery. I think Mom, Gran, and I were still connected, which heightened my abilities as well.

My head was killing me and I was trying to will my stomach not to rebel, but I did my job, listening, taking notes, and adding insights.

When a woman embarrassedly asked for our help with her marriage, I wanted to pull her aside and tell her he'd been cheating since the beginning. He was trash and she needed to leave him, to lock him out of her accounts and leave him. Thankfully, I didn't have to. Apparently, Gran and Mom knew about the cheating as well.

Mom advised her to divorce him, to show some self-respect and kick him out. It was harsh, but it felt like she'd needed the kick to the teeth to get her moving. California was a no-fault, community property state, Mom told her, so there may not be much she could do about the money, but that house was paid for with her Corey inheritance and the children shouldn't suffer by losing their home because he was a cruel bastard. Gran even offered to visit to make sure he and his belongings were out by the end of the day. When the woman got shakily to her feet, she stood a little taller, resolved. She'd had enough.

By the time we'd seen everyone, Mom had a series of people scheduled to sit with Hester, and I too had had enough. What I wanted to do was crawl into my bed, close the shutters, turn off the lights, and try to sleep away the pounding headache and nausea. Instead, what I would do was visit Hester and pass on her message from Pearl.

Wait. "That was the connection," I blurted, confusing Gran and Mom, who were picking up their teacups and placing them on the cart.

"What connection?" Mom asked.

"The man thrown down the staircase. It felt familiar but not. I think it's connected to Pearl's killer."

Gran sank back down onto the couch while Mom just stared, waiting.

"I need to talk with Detective Hernández. I think it's the same killer."

"What about that poor man who was pushed off the cliff?" Gran asked.

I thought about it, staring out the front window at the ocean. "It's not the same energy, but it does feel connected. I don't know. My head is killing me. I'll try later after the pounding has stopped. I'll call the detective, though, on the way to Aunt Hester's to give her a heads-up."

"Okay. Mother, I'll get your bag. Are you ready?"

Gran nodded but didn't move. I understood. It had been an exhausting day and it wasn't over yet.

After I returned the tea cart to the kitchen, I grabbed my backpack and waited on the front porch, sitting on the stairs. Mom wanted to send an email to the family, warning them to strengthen their wards and change their passwords. I, however, needed ocean winds to blow the pain away. Oh! The honey bear seawater. I'd forgotten.

Digging into my backpack, I pulled it out, squeezed some onto both gloves, and then placed one hand on my forehead and one on the back of my skull. It was almost immediate, the lessening of the pain. *Thanks, Dad.* And, yes, I had fresh gloves to put on.

"Why on earth are you carrying around a honey bottle?" Mom's voice startled me out of my stupor. She and Gran were standing behind me, wearing expressions somewhere between confusion and concern.

"Oh," I said, twisting the top closed and returning it to my backpack. "It's just an empty container that's light and handy. The important part is the ocean water inside. My head was killing me, and I felt like I was going to hurl—"

"Arwyn, really," Mom corrected.

"I thought I might be sick."

"Did it help?" Gran asked.

Nodding, I stood and shouldered the backpack. "Yeah. It did. It's not completely gone but I'm feeling much stronger than I was a few minutes ago."

"Good," Mom said. "Mother, I made sure Lucy has your number in case she has any trouble kicking that piece of garbage she married out. I don't think she will, though. She sounded determined."

"That's too bad," Gran said as we walked single file to Mom's car. "I was looking forward to putting the fear of me into him."

I opened the passenger door for Gran and then got into the back of Mom's very safe and very expensive sedan. While they discussed some of the petitioners, I called Detective Hernández and told her about the two murders.

TEN

I'm Not Crying. You're Crying. Shut Up

After we dropped off Gran, Mom and I went to Aunt Hester's home and found Uncle Andrew's car parked at the curb.

"Good. He didn't leave before we got here," Mom said.

Mom had just stepped onto the porch when Andrew opened the front door. He came out to kiss Mom's cheek and then nodded at me.

"Arwyn. Thank you." Returning his attention to my mom, he asked, "Do we know when Roger will be here?"

Mom checked her watch. "I thought he'd be here by now." She pulled her brother away from the open door and whispered, "Check the airlines and make sure there hasn't been an accident, or a hijacking, between here and Seattle."

Pulling out his phone, he sat on the porch swing while Mom and I went in to see Aunt Hester.

We found her sitting in near darkness, her chair under a reading lamp that hadn't been turned on. Curtains drawn, the only light in the living room came from the open bathroom door down the hall. She had a wadded-up tissue in one hand and stared down, dry-eyed, at Pearl's high school graduation photo in her other hand. The poor woman had cried every tear in her body. Desiccated, she was moments from blowing away.

"Let me get you some tea, dear," Mom said, walking to the kitchen.

I went to Hester and crouched down, pulling the photo and tissue from her grip. Her ex-husband was the Corey. Hester was a Goode, an old and well-respected wicche family. Pearl had inherited her father's dark hair and green eyes, but Hester was an assortment of pale colors. Light hair, light skin, light eyes, in faded pajama bottoms and a light gray hoodie. She bordered on transparency.

"Let's go out back." Standing, I pulled her up with me. When she tried to protest, to drop back down to the chair, I kept her upright. Fae strength meant she wasn't hitting the ground on my watch.

Keeping an arm firmly around her, I walked her to the door in the dining room that led to the back garden. When I opened it, she squinted at the still-bright early evening sky. Lifting an arm, she shaded her eyes. I considered just letting her sit on her porch but decided against it. She was too far from thriving, vibrant things.

I walked her to a garden bench under a huge crepe myrtle tree that was exploding with bright pink blossoms. Sitting beside her, I pulled out my phone.

"Aunt Hester, did anyone tell you we found Bridget's daughter?"

She didn't respond.

Resting the phone on the bench beside me, I pulled one of her hands between my two gloved ones. "Well, we did." I squeezed. "Do you know how I'm a Cassandra wicche?"

She nodded. Barely.

"It turns out Bridget's girl Sam is a necromancer."

Her brow furrowed as she took that in, still clearly not understanding why I was telling her this.

"Auntie Hester, are you listening?"

She looked up at me, eyes dull.

"I got a call from Sam last night. She had Pearl's spirit with her, and she wanted me to come here so Pearl could pass on a message to you. Okay?"

It was extraordinary, the way life and understanding and hope flooded back into Hester's gaze, and then she was the one gripping *my* hand.

"She asked me to come see you. I'm going to call Sam now and she can pass on Pearl's message, okay?"

Hester nodded, her eyes glowing.

I extricated one hand, swiped through my contacts, hit *Sam* and then the speakerphone.

It rang a few times and then, "Hey, Arwyn. Give me a minute. Owen?" she called. "Can you cover for me? I need to go in back for a bit." The sound changed, the background noise getting quieter.

We heard a growled, "Get out." Hester and I both jumped and then I shook my head grinning.

"That's Dave, her cook," I explained. "He's just grumpy."

"That he is," Sam said. "By the way, thanks for all the recipes you sent him. Those meringue cookies? Ridiculous." She was quiet for a moment. "Pearl? I'll ask. She wants to know if you have her mother with you?"

Like a miracle, tears began flowing from Hester's dry eyes.

"She's here. You're on speakerphone," I said.

Mom came out the back door and then stood still, not wanting to disturb what was happening.

"Okay," Sam said. "Everything I say now is Pearl. When I'm speaking as myself, I'll let you know. Go ahead. Your mom's listening… I love you, Mom. I'm so sorry. I was stupid to trust—"

"No," Hester said, grabbing the phone from my lap. "You've never been stupid. You're my brilliant, beautiful girl, the light of my life." She scrubbed at her streaming tears. "I'd give anything to change places with you. To take your pain. You're the one who should still be here."

"I need you to promise me something," Pearl said.

"Anything."

"I need you to take care of yourself, okay? I need you to live and be happy without me."

Hester shook her head, trying to hold back a sob. Finally, she choked out, "I can't."

"Maybe not now, but with time. You don't need to worry about me. I'm okay. There's no more pain or fear. I just worry about you now."

Hester took a minute, breathing slowly. When she finally spoke, her voice was steadier. "You don't have to worry about me. I'll be okay."

"Liar."

"Someday," Hester said.

"So, I was thinking," Pearl began, causing Hester to release a breath on an almost-laugh.

"Have you, now?" It felt like a familiar pattern between the two.

"Yes, and I've had a scathingly brilliant idea."

"Let's hear it," Hester said, smiling and weeping.

"That poor guy next door needs your help, and you need something to do. Plus, his daughter really needs a fairy garden."

Hester glanced over at a tall fence between her property and the one next door. "I don't know…"

"You don't have to. I know. They're a nice little family of two, just like us, and they could use your friendship and expertise. Besides, you need a project. Our garden is perfect. Theirs is sad. You could make sure the garden is safe for her and her dog to explore and play in."

Hester wiped at her face again. "Why does it matter?"

She was quiet for a while. "I don't know. I guess I just see things clearer on this side. I worried about so many things, avoided things that could have made me happy. I just want better for you. I want everything for you, Mom."

My heart hurt listening to them. Like my own mother and me, they were on their own, my Uncle Roger having left when Pearl was small. We had such a different relationship than these two, though. I looked up, wondering if Mom was as affected as I was and found the porch empty. She'd gone back inside.

"Promise me you'll try, okay? One of us needs to live a full, happy life, and that creep made sure it wasn't me."

"I'll try," Hester forced out.

"Please do. I love you, Mom."

"And I love you, my little one. So very much."

"And, Arwyn?"

"Yes," I said.

"Can you tell the detectives I remember the name of the restaurant we went to. It was the High Tide."

"I'll tell them," I promised.

After a long pause, we heard, "It's Sam again. I'm very sorry for your loss, ma'am."

Hester nodded, a fingertip tracing the edge of my phone case. She didn't want to let go.

"Thank you, Sam. I'm sure we'll talk again soon." I reached over to hit the end button and then waited, wanting Hester to do it.

She didn't. Sam disconnected and then Hester reluctantly handed me my phone back.

"She said she didn't hurt anymore," Hester said. "I can't stop thinking about her final moments, the pain and fear, and I wasn't there to stop it, to save my baby."

"Which is why," I said, wrapping my arm around her, "she stuck around to make sure you knew she was okay. You don't have to keep torturing yourself with that moment. She's moved past it and wants you to as well."

Hester nodded but didn't seem convinced.

"And remember," I went on, "Aunt Sylvia and Aunt Bridget are first in line, waiting to greet her and show her the ropes."

Hester leaned into me and the floodgates opened. I was just about to text my mom and ask for tissues when she came out the back door with a box of them and a steaming cup of tea. She placed the box in Hester's lap and the cup in mine, so I could balance it for her.

Patting Hester's shoulder, Mom said, "Roger's plane has landed. He's going to our mother's, but he'll come see you tomorrow so you can discuss arrangements." Expression strained, she turned and went back in, all without ever looking at me. I murmured soothing nothings while staring at the closed back door.

Eventually, I got Hester to drink some tepid tea and talked her into taking a shower. She needed to wash off the horrible combination of anguish and ennui.

While she got cleaned up and changed, I looked for Uncle Andrew and my mother, not finding them where I'd assumed they'd be—in the living room. I peered out the front window and saw both cars were gone. Shaking my head and blowing out a breath, I checked my phone. Sure enough, there was a text from Mom saying she had to go to Gran's to see Uncle Roger and I should call a cab or that wolf for a ride home.

Aunt Hester lived too far away for what I felt like doing: angry stomping home. I checked Hester's freezer. As I suspected, there were lots of sorrow casseroles, none of which looked great. When I heard Hester's slippers shuffling down the hall, I closed the freezer door and met her in the living room.

"You need food," I said. "Me too, come to that. I can heat up one of the dishes in your freezer or I can order something better to be delivered."

"I'm not hungry, sweetheart. You don't need to stay with me." She glanced around the room. "Is your mom waiting for you in the car?" She curled up in the same chair I'd found her in when we'd arrived.

I sat on the arm of the couch. "No. Mom had to leave."

Hester smiled softly. "Pearl always sat like that." Her brow furrowed. "But I thought you didn't drive. How will you get home?" She glanced around again. "I can take you." She stood and went to her purse in the entryway.

I considered telling her I could call for a ride, but she was more animated, showed more purpose, than I'd seen since I'd arrived.

"That'd be great," I said. "How about if we stop for food on the way and you can eat with me at the gallery."

I felt a *No* coming, so I added, "I'd really love for you to see it, if you're interested."

She looked down at herself. "I guess I should get changed."

"Nah. Maybe just your shoes so you can drive safely. The rest of it, you don't need to worry about." She was wearing a clean pair of faded pajamas with an oversized hoodie and house scuffs.

While she went to her room to put on real shoes, I checked the locks and grabbed her handbag. She found me by the hall door to the garage. Taking her bag from me, she opened the door and waited for me to go first.

"I know a great burger place on the way home. I can run in and get us dinner."

Shaking her head, she opened the drivers' side door. "I don't need—"

I cleared my throat, and she looked over the top of her car at me. I stared back, eyebrows raised, waiting for her to remember her promise to Pearl.

Finally, she nodded and got in. "I could eat."

ELEVEN

Family. Amirite?

Hester didn't eat much, but it was something, and that made me feel better. Her gaze had been darting all around the studio while we had dinner. When it was clear she'd had her fill, I cleaned up and gave her a proper tour, including the gallery.

The building was an old cannery that had been in the family for a while. I had purchased it from Gran and began the arduous task of converting it into an art gallery with a studio. The majority of the building was the gallery-retail space. The grand opening for that was less than two weeks away.

The studio was also my apartment. I had a large work area with a small living room comprised of a couch, a coffee table, a reading chair, and an end table. The back half of the studio was a kitchenette with a restaurant-grade oven for all the baking I did. A small restroom was in the back corner. Upstairs, in the loft, was my bedroom and a full bath. And then on the other side of the studio, opposite the gallery, was the fire room where I did pottery and glass blowing.

The construction was finally done. I just needed to paint the walls in the gallery and start moving in my art. Hester loved the idea of a tea shop in the gallery, and I eventually got her to agree to stop by regularly for a muffin and a cup of tea.

I could have been wrong, but it felt like getting her out of her house—away from the grief that had saturated the furniture and sunk into the floorboards—was helping to lift her mood. Sorrow was coming second to wonder at the moment, so I pressed my advantage and took her out on the deck.

It being summer, the sunset was just now winding down, the sky pink and purple rather than gold and red. I waved her over to the railing and introduced her to Charlie and Herbert.

"Cecil," I called and a tentacle broke the surface. "This is my Aunt Hester. Can you say hello?" Three tentacles swirled at the surface and then went back under.

Hester gasped and leaned farther out. A tennis ball rolled across the deck and came to a stop directly beside my shoe. Dang. That was impressive.

"Wait right here." I ran in the studio door and grabbed the long orange plastic pole with the ball cup on the end. The gizmo was made for throwing a ball to a dog, but it worked great for playing fetch with a seal. Declan had found it for me, and I'd been using it ever since. I picked up the wet tennis ball with the scooper and then went back to the railing.

Pointing out with my free hand, I told my aunt to watch the water. I flung the ball, the plastic arm helping it go much farther than I could have managed on my own. Hester looked confused for a moment and then delighted as she watched Wilbur streak through the water after the ball.

"Was that a seal?" The sight shocked a laugh out of her, her cheeks finally losing their gray pallor.

"That was Wilbur. We've had a daily game of fetch going since I moved back to Monterey."

Shaking her head, she looked down where Cecil had broken the surface and then up at the thirty-foot tentacles that appeared to be pulling my gallery into the ocean. "How?" was all she got out.

"Has no one explained my parentage to you over the years?" I asked, twisting my hair and stuffing it down the back of my shirt, out of the wind.

At the embarrassed shake of her head, I patted her shoulder and waved her back in. "It's okay. No need to feel uncomfortable. Coreys have been looking at me sideways my whole life." I pointed to the couch, and she sat.

"They don't look at or talk to me at all," she said.

"Yeah. Some of us can be real assholes. On behalf of the Coreys," I said, "please allow me to apologize." Opening the freezer, I rattled off all the baked goods I was stockpiling for the gallery opening. One little spell and they'd be thawed and tasting like they were fresh from the oven.

"You're a baker too?"

"I'm a real Renaissance woman." At her confused look, I said, "As you know, I'm a Cassandra wicche. I've had horrible nightmares and visions my whole life. When they wake me up in the middle of the night—and they do every night—I bake. I talk with my friends in the ocean. I draw, paint, blow glass. I do whatever I can to plaster over the dark and traumatic with light and beauty."

I held up my gloved hands. "I'm not a germaphobe. Psychometry. I can read thoughts, see memories, have visions, whatever, when I touch people or things. I'm a clairvoyant and a precog. Also, while I'm a Corey wicche on my mom's side, my dad is water fae. I have no idea what kind—I've never met him—but he's responsible for my affinity for water. And probably for upping my psychic abilities.

"Cassandra wicches usually only pop up in our family every couple hundred years. I got a lot of shit, particularly from my cousins, when I was little. Unknown parentage, long crazy hair that takes on blue, green, and purple hues when I've been in the ocean, knowing what they're thinking, what they've done, being my mother's daughter, all of it made me incredibly unpopular. I'm told I asked for my first set of gloves when I was about three, after I'd told a room full of family members about Aunt Bridget and Uncle Michael's imminent deaths."

"Oh no," Hester breathed.

"Yeah. I was the family's own little harbinger of death. Made me quite the popular party guest." I shrugged a shoulder. "What are ya gonna do? Anyway, about these baked goods," I said, opening the freezer door again. "Which sounds good to you?"

I felt a *No, thank you* coming, so I pulled out a container of lemon bars. "These are my favorites. Can I talk you into one?"

With a little shrug, she said, "I *do* love lemon."

"Right?" With that hurdle cleared, I opened the refrigerator. "I have milk, beer, orange and grape sodas." I leaned on the door. "I can also make some hot chocolate, coffee, or tea."

"I don't want to be a bother," she said, clearly uncomfortable with someone trying to look after her.

"It's not even a little bit of a bother. What sounds good?" I felt what she wanted to choose, so added, "Let me make you my hot chocolate. I think you'll like it." I pulled thin rubber gloves on over my regular ones—no one wants fibers falling into their food—and then got chocolate from my pantry. I grabbed a double boiler and got to work melting dark and milk chocolate. I ran a cinnamon stick over a microplane, added vanilla, sugar, a pinch of salt, and then a hint of chili to give it a kick. Once it was melted and smoothly mixed, I added the whole milk.

"Are you a whipped cream or marshmallow person?" I asked, pouring the hot chocolate into two mugs. I could feel her hesitating. "Just say it."

"Marshmallow."

"A woman after my own heart." I went back to the freezer for a couple of homemade marshmallow squares, did the thawing spell, and dropped them in our mugs. I brought over a plate of bars and some napkins first and then our mugs before peeling off the second set of gloves.

Hester took a sip and then paused, her eyes fluttering closed. "Oh my goodness," she murmured before taking another sip. Her reaction made me feel bright and bubbly inside.

Mmm, the hot chocolate was good. Maybe a pinch more cinnamon next time. I took my chopsticks out of my pocket.

Moved a lemon square to a napkin and then plucked off a piece and ate it.

Hester was watching me, but not in a wary way, which was nice. "You're quite good with those."

I held up the chopsticks. "Finger foods are hard, so utensils are my friends. If I'd brought over plates, I'd be using a fork. Since I brought napkins, I'm using chopsticks. When I cook or eat something tricky, like the burgers we had for dinner, I wear the latex gloves. They get hot, though, so I try to work around them when I can. I'd prefer not to live my life encased in rubber."

She took a bite of her lemon bar. "Oh, my—how? These are incredible."

Smiling, I nodded my thanks. "Like anything, I got good with practice. Mom says she started to hear me puttering around in the kitchen in the middle of the night when I was around six. I think I colored in my room before that. You do anything every day for twenty-two years, you're going to get good at it."

"What I don't understand," she said, "is I married into this family about that long ago and I didn't know any of this about you. I knew you were Sybil's daughter, a gorgeous child with a fairytale-like mane of hair that should be hanging out a tower window—"

I laughed.

"—who kept to herself, had eyes a brighter green that the rest of the Coreys, and was the only one who would check on my girl at family get-togethers."

I took a sip, trying to figure out how to explain my family. "Coreys, like Goodes, are an ancient wicche family."

"A very powerful one," Hester added.

"Yes. And because of that, there's a certain arrogance. Unlike your family, there is a darkness in mine. Yes, we're very powerful, but we also have quite the reputation for sorcery."

"That was the main reason my parents didn't want me to marry Roger," she said.

"That and he's kind of a dick," I said, making her smile.

Nodding, she took another bite of lemon bar. "I was young," she said, which honestly is explanation enough.

"Now, what you also have to remember is that although most of my cousins made my life a misery and many of the aunts and uncles either turned a blind eye to what was happening or joined in on the shit-talking their kids were doing, I was still my mother's daughter and a Corey. Half a Corey is still more Corey than a Goode who happened to marry a Corey."

I rolled my eyes. "Most of them suck, with a few notable exceptions. Aunts Sylvia and Bridget were wonderfully kind women. Amongst the living, Aunt Elizabeth and Uncle Robert? Salt of the earth. Uncle John?" I shook my head, suddenly emotional. "He and Sylvia were like parents to me. They loved me not for what I could do or how powerful I was, just for me."

Hester patted my knee in comfort. "I was so sorry to hear about Sylvia's passing. She was my favorite and the only one who treated me like family."

I nodded, wiping away the sudden tears. "She didn't pass gently into that good night either. Her daughter Calliope is a sorcerer and she and her demon killed Sylvia."

Hester put down her cup. "What? No one told me that."

"We're all about secrets in this family." I put down the rest of the lemon bar. "I'm sure it's been difficult to feel shunned, but as someone who exiled herself, it's probably been better for you both."

Hester picked up her mug and took another sip. "Maybe so," she said, stifling a yawn.

"I have an idea." I flicked my fingers, locking the windows and doors and closing the shutters. I hadn't forgotten that vision during the Council meeting of a demon lurking around my gallery. Fricking Calliope. "How about if you stay here tonight. Maybe being in a different environment will help you sleep."

"Oh, no. I've taken up enough of your time."

When she started to get up, I motioned her back down. "I wouldn't offer if I didn't mean it. I usually end up sleeping on this couch, anyway. The bed in the loft is ridiculously comfortable. And in the morning, you can have a muffin and tea before you head back."

She glanced up the stairs to my loft. "You're sure?"

"I absolutely am. Someone should sleep in that bed, as I never seem to." I pointed up again. "There's a bathroom up there and extra blankets if you get cold."

Looking completely wrung out, she stood and took her empty cup and napkin to the kitchen before trudging up the stairs.

I saw movement in the skylight and had a mini heart attack. Three sets of eyes stared back at me. Otis had brought friends. Pointing to the back porch, I flicked my fingers, making the glass opaque. Hester needed sleep, not furry voyeurs.

Grabbing three muffins, I quietly went out onto the deck. The empty deck. "Otis," I whisper-called. Three little raccoon heads popped out from the roofline. I held up the muffins and heard claws scrabbling on the roof.

Sitting on a bench, I considered how they might get down and decided the scaffolding was probably the safest route. I turned that way, to watch them come around the corner. After what felt like too long, something touched my leg. Otis and his siblings sat in a semicircle around me.

"How'd you do that?" The roof of the cannery was about forty feet high. If they didn't use the scaffolding, how had they done it? Tricky little scamps.

I placed a muffin in front of each raccoon and then sat back, assuming they'd grab them and scamper off. Nope. Each one picked up the muffin and then plopped their butt down and began to eat.

Letting out a breath, I watched my new friends and eventually shook off the day. I had a lot to do tomorrow, so I waved goodbye and went in to sleep. Unfortunately, the day wasn't done with me yet.

TWELVE

Why Do Epiphanies Always Happen in the Middle of the Night?

I ndistinct whispering. A busy hallway. Dark, carved wood, expensive, sound-muting carpet. Children and teens in navy blazers, backpacks on their shoulders, two lanes of traffic, shoulders bumping in the middle. Insults are muttered out of earshot of the teachers who stand expressionless at their classroom doors. That one checks his watch. This one smiles sharply, her eyes distant.

One boy nudges his friend before shooting his foot into the oncoming stream of students, tripping a girl. She cries out, pitching forward, falling on the students in front of her. Now one side of the hall is a jumble of bent legs and arms, spilled backpacks. Others halt as though at a precipice while the students passing on the other half of the hall continue on, heads twisted to gaze back on the carnage.

The boys smile secretly, the tripper feeling overwhelmingly pleased. He did that. The girl had shown him up in English class, knowing an answer he hadn't. As if anyone cares about poetry. She isn't feeling too good now, is she? He entertains himself, playing the moment over and over again.

The friend finally lets out a giggle and then nods toward a boy they're about to pass. The tripper shakes his head. It's too soon, and he knows it. The teachers will be alert, the other students too.

A long, dark corridor. Where have the students gone? Same dark wood *and expensive rug, but this hall isn't filled with teenagers bustling to class. Whispering. Soft voices conspiring behind one of the many closed doors along this dimly lit corridor. Plans are being made. For next time.*

The image jumps.

Delicate hands work the mortar and pestle. Murky light sways, always in motion. Torchlight. Her hand twists, a ring glinting on her finger. A familiar peridot ring. Calliope. Chanting fills the dark stone room, two voices twined. Blood drips on the open page of a grimoire.

The image jumps.

Someone is looking through a narrow slit in the shutters, into the studio where she sees herself sleeping on the couch. A finger with a long, sharp claw taps on the glass. She sleeps through it, but someone else has woken. Someone else is walking quietly down the loft stairs, head swiveling, trying to find the source of the tapping. She pauses at the sleeping figure, pulling up the blanket to cover her shoulder.

The taloned finger taps once more and then drags the claw down the glass. The woman turns to the door, thinking about seals and tennis balls, not the darkness that beckons. She reaches for the door—

"Arwyn? Honey, are you okay?"

I startle awake, my gaze flying to the back door. "Did you hear tapping on the glass? Is that what woke you?"

"No." Hester follows my lead and glances toward the door before focusing on me again. "I heard you whimpering in your sleep. You'd said you have nightmares every night, so I came down to check on you. That's all."

That's all, she said, as though it was nothing. I couldn't remember the last time my own mother comforted me when I cried in the night. And then I did. I remembered exactly the last time and felt sick with it. I'd been six or seven years old, sleeping in the room next to hers. I'd woken from a horrible dream, one that hadn't just scared me but had me crying inconsolably.

My mother was there, asking me what I'd seen. I'd told her Auntie Sylvia had a shadow following her around, one that sat on her chest, took her breath, and killed her. Mom stood abruptly and left the room. She never came back and shortly after that, I moved to the turret bedroom that I'd been asking for. Mom had been saying I was too young to sleep so far away from her. After that nightmare, I couldn't be far enough away.

"You're wearing gloves," I said, staring at Hester's hands.

"Oh." She looked down at her hands. "I wasn't sure if I was allowed to wake you or not, but you sounded so scared, I grabbed that pair that was sitting on your worktable so I could touch you and not make it worse."

She held up a gloved hand. "Are these special? Should I not have touched them?"

I let out a gust of breath. "No. It's fine. I have gloves stashed everywhere around here." Reaching out, I squeezed her hand. "I'm not used to people checking up on me."

She brushed curls out of my face. My heart clutched and I had trouble breathing. Why did epiphanies always come in the middle of the night? I loved my mom but had bitchily been snarking about her for as long as I could remember. In my defense, she could be a real piece of work. But she hadn't always been. She'd been sweet and loving when I was small, and then it had disappeared one night with a vision about her sister.

I'd gone from her baby girl to be cuddled and indulged to the problem child who needed to be endured while being pushed away. I hadn't understood why, to my mind, she'd stopped loving me, but I knew it had to do with the nightmares, the visions. I knew the problem was me but didn't know how to fix it, so I'd withdrawn, not wanting the darkness in me to hurt anyone else.

And now here was Hester, treating me like a child deserving comfort and willing to give it. When my eyes filled with tears, I went to the kitchen. "I could brew some soothing tea, so you can go back to sleep."

"I'm fine. You should try to get more sleep, though."

I blinked my eyes dry and then turned back to her. "No. I'm done for the night. This is when I'd usually bake, but I have an image in my head that I need to get out, so I'll paint. You should go back up to bed, though. Hopefully you can get a few more hours. Thankfully for you, painting is quieter than baking." I smiled, trying to project mental stability, but Hester wasn't buying it.

"Can I hug you?" she asked, opening her arms.

I almost waved her off, saying I was fine, but stopped myself. I walked into her arms and was hugged in a way I could barely even remember. If she felt the tears soaking through the fabric on her shoulder, she didn't say anything. Eventually, I got myself under control and went back to the kitchen to brew us a pot of tea.

"Would it be all right if I watched you paint?"

I nodded, handing her a fragrant cup. "It'll be boring, but you're welcome to stick around."

I was afraid her presence would make me self-conscious and effect the painting, but once I started mixing paints and staring at the canvas, I forgot she was there. My head was in the darkened corridor. I was seeing every detail, intent on recreating the vision.

When I finished, I saw the early morning light leaking through the shutters. Flicking my fingers, I turned off the overhead bulbs and opened the shutters. I'd wash my brushes in a minute. Right now, I needed to let the cold wind skating over the ocean blow the dark images from my head.

I went out on the deck and hung over the railing. "Good morning, Charlie. Morning, Herbert. Greetings and salutations, Cecil!" A tentacle splashed the surface of the water. I glanced around the deck but didn't see the tennis ball. "Good morning, Wilbur, wherever you are."

A moment later, the tennis ball arced over the railing and bounced across the deck. I ducked into the studio to get the plastic throwing doohickey and found Hester standing in front of the painting, studying it.

"Oh—I'm sorry. I completely forgot you were here." I shook my head. "Too used to being alone. I didn't mean to wake you."

She turned and smiled. "You didn't. I was watching you paint. I did drift in and out a little, but the last hour or so, I've been wide awake and watching. You're extraordinary," she said.

The wonder in her voice made me well up again. What the hell was wrong with me? "Let me at least get you a muffin." I hurried past, hoping she hadn't noticed.

"I mean, I watched you," she said again. "The canvas was blank, white, and then you knew exactly what to do, which colors to use, how to apply the brush, how to layer the colors and the strokes until where there was nothing, there's now a creepy corridor."

"Does it feel creepy to you?" I walked back, studying my own work.

"Absolutely. Evil things are happening behind those doors."

Nodding, I said, "I believe you're right about that. I just don't know what those things are yet."

Hester pointed to a painting in the corner. I followed the gesture and recoiled. *Shit.*

"I don't like that one." She patted my shoulder. "No offense intended. You know what I mean, don't you? I keep telling myself not to look at it and then my focus would drift from the corridor to the water. And every time I looked at it, the pinch to my heart became a jab, and then a slice." She paused, staring. "It's what my Pearl saw as she was dying, isn't it?"

I couldn't lie to her, as much as I wished I could. She already knew. I nodded and then she did too.

"I thought so." She looked between me and the painting. "Should I take it? Should I ask for my girl's final minutes?"

I shook my head. "No. This was me working out what I'd seen in a vision. Just like you saw me do with the corridor. Painting what I see can help me process it. Sometimes details I don't even remember come out in the painting. These are like—I don't know —journal entries. They're my dreams. I don't sell them."

I turned Pearl's death to the wall. "She wouldn't want you to see it, let alone have it. You heard her. She wants you to teach your neighbor how to garden." I took her gloved hand in my own. "She wants you to live, not follow her into death."

She nodded, but her heart wasn't in it.

"She'd probably also like it if you helped out your niece."

Hester's focus shifted from the back of the painting to me.

"I could use help in the gallery, a salesperson who knows how to properly brew tea."

Her lips tipped up. "Well, I do know how to do that."

I shrugged. "It might be nice to get out of the house and do something completely different for a few hours a day."

"It might be. I'm going to get out of your hair now. I know you have a mural to finish." She squeezed my hand. "I think Pearl wanted to make sure I was here last night because she was afraid of my being home alone. Thank you for helping my girl take care of me."

"You're always welcome here. I want you to remember that. I'm not used to having someone take care of me after a nightmare, so thank *you*."

She collected her bag and took the muffin I handed her, nodding her thanks. "I'll be back," she finally said as she walked out the back door. She leaned over the railing, said something, and then shook her head on a smile as she left. Hopefully, Cecil had said goodbye.

THIRTEEN

What's in the Box?!

I jogged up the stairs and changed into my work clothes, a purple long-sleeve thermal top, overalls, and paint-splattered sneakers. I had nothing on my calendar other than gallery work. When I came down, I remembered the brushes I'd left sitting out beside the corridor painting. After cleaning and treating them, I grabbed multiple muffins in case I got visitors while I was on the scaffolding.

Attaching my supply basket to the rope, I heaved until the basket was swinging near the top. Sea spray made the bars slippery, but I was agile and the last of the painting went fast. This side of the gallery looked derelict. The two-dimensional tentacle glistened in the sun. Now I had to attach one of my three-dimensional, thirty-foot ones.

It was awkward and tricky, pretending the tentacle was too heavy for me. I used the rope and pulley again to bring it to the top of the scaffold. I'd already painted the hole the tentacle was busting through. Now I needed to fasten it to the building in a way that was safe, secure, and realistic-looking.

Magic works great for these types of situations. Unfortunately, I was out in the open and lots of cars were driving by, gawking at the mural. I couldn't do magic in full view of human eyes.

My phone rang. Declan. I swiped and hit speakerphone. "Hey."

"It looks like you could use some help." His deep rumbly voice made my stomach wobble.

I put down the tentacle and then turned, looking down the road at the barn, where I knew he was. "If I didn't have to pretend to be human strong and coordinated, I'd be done by now."

"Ah. In that case, how about if I run over and pretend to be your very strong and manly boyfriend who helps you do the thing you could easily do on your own?"

I sighed. "Yeah. That'd be good. I need to get started inside. I don't want to waste time, pretending this is more difficult than it is."

"On my way."

A moment later, I saw Declan run across the busy road, in between cars traveling at high speeds in opposite directions. My heart stopped before I remembered he had a wolf's speed and strength. If a car hit him, he'd be more likely to leave a dent than go flying.

He jogged on the shoulder of the road and was climbing the scaffold in no time flat.

I pocketed the phone I'd forgotten about while watching him. "It's not fair that just because you're a dude, you can do super-human shit, and they won't bat an eye. If I try it, they have their phones out recording me. It's bullshit is what it is."

"Blame the patriarchy," he said, picking up the tentacle.

With the two of us working together, we had the tentacle attached in no time.

"Et, voilà!" I said. "Now I need to move this all inside."

"You use a little magic. I'll use a little more than human strength, and we'll get this down in no time," he said, beginning the process of taking down the scaffolding.

It took longer than no time, but once we were done, we both just stared at the mural.

"Damn, Ursula, how do you do what you do? This is unbelievable. I'm standing fifteen feet from the wall and it looks real. A sea monster is tearing apart your gallery."

Thankfully, the second part of the task was far easier. Once we moved the aluminum bars and plywood planks around the corner of the gallery, we didn't need to pretend we were straining under the weight.

I put down tarps, not wanting the floors scratched, and then he stayed to help me erect the scaffold again so I could paint the interior. Magic played a part, and it went quickly.

Declan checked the time on his phone. "I'm starving. Let's go get something to eat. You're buying."

Laughing, I went through the adjoining door into my studio. "Fair. And I'm starving too. Where do you want to go?"

He followed me, scratching his beard and thinking. "What are your thoughts on Mexican?"

"First," I began, shouldering my backpack, "I'm enthusiastically in favor of Mexican food. Second, I have a conditioner that'll help with the itchy beard."

He dropped his hand. "Sorry. I get sawdust in it. I always take a shower when I'm done working. Until then, though, scratch." He paused at my back door. "I can go clean up in your bathroom."

Waving him forward, I said, "Are you kidding? Have you seen me? I'm wearing overalls and covered in paint. Come on. Let's eat."

"Oh. My truck's back at the workshop. Give me a minute and I'll be back to pick you up." He was gone before I could protest.

Honestly, though, he was right. I shouldn't be running across busy roads. I could have a vision at the wrong time and drop right in front of a speeding car. It was why I'd never learned to drive. Too much potential for death.

I took a wide loop around the side of the gallery, checking again that the mural looked the way I wanted it to. Declan's truck pulled up to the curb and I noticed two other cars, parked and taking pics of the gallery.

A middle-aged man in one of the cars rolled down his window.

Brown hair slicked back to showcase a sweaty brow and narrow eyes. He rubbed his lips with his index finger and then said, "Excuse me, miss. Are you the artist?"

I nodded.

"Incredible," he murmured, looking over my shoulder at the mural.

"I'm glad you like it," I said, reaching for Declan's door handle and instead finding Declan's hand.

He opened the door for me but had his eyes on the man. Once I was in, he shut the door, circled around, and slid in. "There's something off about that guy. You have alarms and wards, right?"

"I do," I said, adding another protective spell to my home.

He started the engine, waited for a break in cars, and then reversed and swung around, driving back toward the center of town. "You should hire a guard too. Your artwork is worth a lot of money, so it makes sense, but if that guy's any indication, you need a bodyguard."

"He just liked the wall. Maybe he has a thing for octopuses. There are lots of completely harmless sweaty, obsessed people in the world."

"His scent was off. He had the sour tang of the long unwashed and desperate. His car and clothes were nice. The stench emanating from his body was not." He turned up a hill, away from the water. "He smells sick. Maybe physically, but it feels mentally."

"Okay," I said, having felt a darkness around the man as well. The thing was, most people weren't bright, shiny, and smelling of soap. We all had personal baggage we dragged around while trying to present a stable and contented version of ourselves to the world. He might have been struggling with a new diagnosis or spiraling after losing a job or partner. It hadn't felt like he was an imminent danger, but Declan was right. My artwork was worth a great deal. I needed a security guard to make sure my smaller pieces didn't walk out the door while I spoke with other patrons.

He pulled into the parking lot of a small Mexican restaurant off the beaten path.

"Hey. I thought you were new around here. How did you find Mariana's?" I slipped out and slammed the truck door.

He met me at the front of his truck and took my hand. "Juan recommended this place when I was working with Phil's crew on your deck." He pulled open the door to a busy restaurant.

"Juan didn't steer you wrong. This is one of my favorites."

The hostess, a young Latina with beautiful brown eyes, had her hair pulled back in a messy bun. I understood the challenge of tying up thick hair. Wearing black pants and a white blouse, she held up a finger, asking us to wait a moment while she spoke with another customer.

Checking the lock screen on his phone and then looking around Mariana's, Declan said, "I think we picked the wrong time to come."

"Eh. It's worth it." I pointed to his truck. "I've got protein bars in my backpack if you need something now."

The hostess waved us forward. "Arwyn, right?"

I'm sure the confusion was clear on my face. "I'm sorry…"

She waved away my embarrassment. "We went to the same high school. I was a few years behind you. I remember your hair, though."

I nodded and smiled. "Yeah, I was told people often just referred to me as *The Hair*."

Her brow furrowed. "Really?" She shook her head and lowered her voice. "There are creeps everywhere and at some point, they attend high school."

Laughing, I said, "True. And middle school."

She rolled her eyes. "Middle school was the worst."

A group walked in the front door.

The hostess said, "I have your name on the list, but it'll probably be twenty to thirty minutes. Is that okay?"

I nodded but Declan didn't look happy.

"What's your name?" I asked.

"Beatrice," she said.

"Good meeting you, Beatrice. We'll wait outside."

She nodded. "I'll come get you when we have a table ready."

The benches outside the door were taken. As Declan had nabbed a parking spot one car down, we opted to sit in his truck, windows rolled down. I pulled a chocolate peanut butter protein bar out and handed it over.

Sighing, he took it. "I hate these things."

"Everybody hates them, but sometimes you've got to eat."

Nodding, he bit into it and paused, a disgusted look on his face. Then he stuffed the whole thing in and ate it quickly. Grabbing his water bottle, he washed the taste out of his mouth and then looked at me accusingly. "Why don't you carry around muffins or cookies? You bake constantly. Where does it all go?"

"Well, I have some raccoon siblings that have recently been added to the payroll."

Eyebrows raised, he waited.

"At first, it was just Otis. He liked watching me paint the mural while he played with my brushes. He sniffed the muffin I had in my basket, so I gave it to him."

"That was your first mistake."

I shrugged. "I don't mind classing up his usual meals. Anyway, the next day there were two more little raccoon babies with him, staring down at me from the skylight."

Declan grinned and shook his head. "You're going to have his entire family sitting on your doorstep."

I thought about it. "There are worse things."

"Okay. Besides the raccoons, where does it go?" He glanced over when Beatrice stepped out, but she waved to the couple sitting on the bench.

"There's also a new werewolf in the neighborhood who eats a lot."

Patting his flat stomach, he said, "True." His attention, though, was on all the people waiting for a table.

"We can go somewhere else," I suggested.

"Hmm?" He turned to me. "No. It's not that. I'm smelling something strange. They probably have the back door of the kitchen open. That smell is great. There's another one underneath it. It's like decomposition but not quite." He glanced up at the trees around us. "There could be a dead squirrel in that tree, but I don't think that's it."

I scanned the people too. "Zombies?"

"Bite your tongue," he said, stepping out of the truck.

"That's a zombie's job." Looking over my shoulder, I watched Declan search the bed of his truck and then open the top of his tool chest before rearing back.

He slammed it shut and then got back in, starting the engine and pulling out of the space. "Sorry. We'll need to do this another time. I'll drop you off, and then I have to take care of a few things."

FOURTEEN

Stupid Wolf

"Oh, so we're lying now? Is that what we're doing?" Declan glanced over and then looked back at the road. "What?"

"Pull this damn truck over and tell me what's in the toolbox." I turned sideways and gave him a hard stare. Lying was not okay, even if he was trying to rationalize it as protection. "Are you under the impression I can't take care of myself? That I am not literally made of magic?"

Blowing out a breath, he said, "Let me get us back to my workshop. I'll pull behind the barn so we don't have an audience."

"What's in the box," I repeated.

"A dead animal." He glanced at me again. "It looked like an opossum and an octopus."

I froze. "Pull over."

"We'll be at the workshop in three minutes." He rubbed my knee.

"I swear, Declan, if someone killed Cecil—"

"You saw Cecil this morning, right? It can't be him." He gripped the steering wheel tightly. "The truck is shimmying. I'd appreciate it if you didn't blow up my truck."

Staring out the side window, I bided my time. "What the hell is the matter with this pack? It has to be them, right? Daniel and Kenji said members of the pack forced you off the road." I studied him a moment. "They're your second and third in the pack, right?"

He shook his head. "It's not my pack. None of us have standing in the Big Sur Pack now that Kenji and Daniel broke ties."

"Don't be coy. You'll take over as Alpha. Do you trust them? Are they your guys?" We were only a few blocks from the workshop and I was trying not to jump out of my skin. Or accidentally blow up his truck.

"We'll see." At my sound of annoyance, he added, "Okay, yes. But I'm not Alpha. Anything can happen."

Now *that* distracted me from the octopus. "What do you mean, *anything can happen*? You said you could take Logan, no problem."

He shrugged one beefy shoulder as he pulled onto his property. "They're not known for playing by the rules. If he pulls a gun on me, I'll be dead and he'll remain Alpha." He pulled around the barn and parked.

I punched him in the arm. Hard. "What the hell? If you know he's going to cheat, you don't just go and take a bullet to the head. Since when are you Dudley Do-Right?"

"I have no idea who that is, but I can't remake the pack if I'm as corrupt as their current Alpha. Now, are we checking the toolbox or not?"

"Stupid wolf," I grumbled as I hopped out of the truck. "Go ahead. Get yourself killed. Big dummy."

He put down the gate of the truck bed, waited for me to stomp over, and then picked me up at the waist and put me in. Climbing in a moment later, he wrapped his arms around me.

"I'm very hard to kill. Many have tried and failed."

"I don't care," I mumbled into his chest, punching him in the side. Sort of. My heart wasn't in it.

"I can see that."

I tipped my head back and glared. "I'm going with you. And then if they try anything, I can curse them."

He was already shaking his head. "No. I don't want you there."

My glare turned a hair more homicidal.

"I don't want you to see what I have to do." His hands ran up and down my back.

"Do you have any idea about the sheer tonnage of fucked-up stuff I have in my head? I've been seeing horrible things for as long as I can remember."

"Right. I don't want to be lumped in with the fucked-up stuff rolling around in your brain, biding its time, waiting to pop out in nightmares. I don't want to ever be your nightmare."

I thunked my head against his chest. "Stupid wolf," I said again.

"I know."

I tipped my head back again. "You're not allowed to die. I forbid it."

His lips tipped up on one side. "I promise."

Leaning down, his gaze traveling from my eyes to my lips, he waited. We were still figuring it out. He was a magical null. If I touched him, my magic disappeared. On one hand, amazing! I could have a physical relationship and not hear his thoughts. On the other, who was I if I wasn't the sea wicche? People relied on me. We had a freaking sorcerer in the family. I couldn't take chances with my magic just because he was super hot and I was coming down with feelings for him.

Fuck it. I was pretty sure I knew how to undo Declan's touch. Going up on my toes, I wrapped my arms around his neck, pulling his mouth down to meet mine.

The kiss was sudden and explosive, making me desperate for him. He palmed my ass and then hitched me up so my legs were wrapped around his waist. There was a swoop up and then a thump down.

I opened my eyes, our mouths still fused. "Wha—" I started to say, but he just changed the angle and cut off my words.

He walked us into the barn and then leaned my back against a support beam. When he broke the kiss to nibble on my neck, he said, "Too open out there."

He rotated his hips, hitting me just right, and I groaned. Dropping me back to the ground, he kicked over a crate, put his hands around my waist, and put me on it so our heights were closer. Trailing kisses along my jaw, he flicked the button straps on my overalls, making them pool around my ankles. He took a moment to gaze down at me in my thermal shirt and panties, eyes wolf gold.

His fingertips traced the ribbon of scales that wrapped around my thigh, my waist, before trailing up my back. I'd created my octopus tattoo to cover the scales because I was so horribly self-conscious about them. Ursula, my animated tattoo, must be hiding somewhere. This was all very unusual for us.

I was starting to freeze up, wanting my protective overalls again when he whispered, "So beautiful. My siren."

Squeezing my waist, he brought me close for more heated kisses, making me forget about scales and embarrassment. One large, warm hand went up my shirt to fondle a breast while the other slid into my panties and then into me.

Gasping, I pulled at his belt, getting it undone and his jeans unbuttoned. He stayed my hand, stepping back and swearing.

"Why does the world hate me," he mumbled, pulling up my overalls and fastening the straps over my shoulders.

Then I heard it too. A car was pulling up and parking near the open barn door. I pulled down my thermal and tucked it in while Declan did up his jeans and buckled his belt. A moment later, another car kicked up dirt and pebbles before parking outside the door.

"Work crew is arriving," Declan muttered. He took my hand and walked us out, past the men going in. He nodded to them but kept going to his truck. I'll take you home."

"We haven't cleaned out the toolbox yet."

He shook his head on a growl. "Damn it. All I can smell is you and it's making me crazy." Although clearly worked up, he was very gentle picking me up by the waist and placing me in the truck bed again.

"I need my backpack."

He nodded and went to the cab for it. When he handed it to me, I sat on the wheel well and unzipped the bag, hunting for the honey bottle. Testing things, I flicked my fingers at the tool-box, trying to lift the lid. It was a simple spell and worked well. So Declan only nulled some of my powers. Interesting. We needed to do more research when we were alone and had the time.

I took off my gloves and squirted seawater over my hands and felt an immediate change. Voices and emotions swirled around me until I'd erected my mental walls again. Huh. We needed to figure this out.

He held out his hands before I put the honey bottle away.

"It's not hand sanitizer," I said.

He grinned. "I know, but it might help me get your scent out of my head so I can think straight."

I splashed him with seawater and he rubbed his hands together before wiping them on his jeans. He held them chest high and blew out a breath, shaking his head.

"I guess the ocean isn't a secret weapon for you." I put the bottle away and stood to look in the box.

"I'll be back in a minute. I need soap." He stepped up on the wall of the truck bed and jumped down. Ah, the swoop and thump when we were kissing made more sense now.

Dreading it, I leaned over the box and looked in. First of all, Declan was right. The stench was horrible, and my nose was nowhere near as sensitive as his. Second, the octopus was small and long dead, probably months ago and frozen. I'd guess someone in the pack worked in a restaurant and he took this poor little guy from the freezer for this bullshit prank.

The opossum, though, had been partially eaten. I said a prayer to the Goddess for these two and then used a scouring charm to clean out the box. Without me, he'd have spent the rest of the day trying to clean fur and guts from his very expensive tools and probably wouldn't have been able to get it all out of the gears or the inside of handles. He'd have had to live with the stench for years before he'd finally replaced them all.

Declan came back a few minutes later with paper towels and cleaning supplies. Brow furrowed, he looked into the box. "How did you—oh. Right." He stared at me, eyes still hot as they traveled up and down my body. "So, if you were able to do magic after I had my hands on you, does that mean the water works?"

With a grin, I nodded.

"Well, let's go then." He threw the cleaning stuff in his hands toward the open barn door. "Come on. Get in."

"You've got workmen in there waiting for you," I reminded him.

"Screw them. I have plans for the rest of the day. Come on." He held out an arm to help me down.

Another car drove around the barn, this one holding Kenji and a woman. Declan glanced over his shoulder and dropped his head.

"The world is conspiring against me," he muttered. He pinned me with his gaze again. "Tonight. After work. Okay?"

Kenji was a wolf and I didn't want him listening to us, so I barely breathed, "I can still feel your hands on me. I want them on me again."

"Hey, boss," Kenji said as he and the woman stepped out of a sports car and headed toward us. "I wanted you to meet my sister. She's the architect I was telling you about." Kenji stood for a moment, looking between the two of us. "I can show her around the site for a while if you two need to leave."

I shook my head, smiling at Kenji and his sister. Shouldering my backpack, I walked to the end of the truck bed and hopped off. I held out my hand to the woman. She was beautiful, with short black hair, warm brown eyes, and luminous skin. The woman knew how to moisturize. Wearing black trousers and boots with a terra-cotta blouse, she took my hand and shook.

"I'm Arwyn. I have the gallery across the road, the Sea Wicche."

Looking surprised, she said, "Natsuki. I'm honored to meet

you. What you've done with that old cannery is absolutely amazing. It's the kind of project I would have killed to do. I can't wait for you to open so I can see the inside."

Kenji watched his sister, pride clear in his expression.

"You can come see it anytime," I said. "Just call to make sure I'm around."

"Thank you," she said, nodding happily. "I will."

"Good." I looked between the three. "I'll let you guys do your thing. I need to get back and paint." I started to walk away.

"I can drive you," Declan said.

I waved off his words, still walking. "I'm fine."

"Be careful crossing that road," he called as I rounded the side of the barn.

"I will," I shouted back. Smirking, I thought he had it bad. I turned left at the road and walked along the line where concrete tuned to dirt and grass, waiting for a break in the traffic. Playing the moment over and over when he grabbed me and…Damn. I had it bad too.

FIFTEEN

Stranger Danger

My phone rang just as there was a break in the traffic. Sprinting, I swiped the screen with my thumb. "Hey, Mom."

No response.

"Mom?" I made it to my side before a fancy sedan sped by. *Slow down, you big jerk.* There were pedestrians and cyclists all over around here.

"Darling, why does your voice sound so strange?"

"I was running across the street. All good now," I said, walking the berm on my side of the road.

"That's fine. I wanted you to know that Serena called. That man came in today, made the huge mess, and poisoned her tea. She caught it all on her security cameras, since she knew where to point them. The tea leaves and the surveillance videos have been turned over to the police. No lives were lost."

"That's great. Glad to hear it. She needs to keep an eye out, though. If Calliope tries once, she'll try again." I walked around a guy taking a picture of my mural and went to the back deck.

"Your Uncle John called. He found something of Calliope's in the safe."

"What?" When Calliope disappeared, the first thing we'd done was search for anything of hers I could touch in order to find her, but she'd cleared out her room. Everything, absolutely everything, was gone. The bedroom, bathroom, common areas were scoured clean of her belongings, including furniture. She knew what I could do. She and her demon weren't taking any chances. I'd tried anyway with car seats and door handles but didn't get anything more than a murky afterimage of her.

"Sylvia had kept a framed baby handprint and footprint of each girl in the safe. When I called John about protecting his banking accounts, he checked the safe for some of Syl's jewelry and found the baby things. The poor man is suffering horribly with guilt on top of grief."

"Yeah, I know." I felt so sorry for Uncle John. He was the kindest, gentlest man, and he had to help us hunt down his own daughter. "Can you ask him to get it to me quickly? We don't want him getting into a car accident and the fingerprints burning up." I could try using that new finding spell I'd seen in Sam's grimoire.

"I'll pick it up today and bring it to you. Now, do you remember your Gran talking about a wicche named Bracken?"

"Sure. He's the old alcoholic whose wife and son had to run and hide to get away from him. What about him? And, no, I'm not going to talk his estranged son into giving him another chance."

"Really, Arwyn, that's hardly fair. Your gran got a hold of him and asked him to come after you had that first vision of poisoned tea leaves. He's on his way…"

She was still talking, but I was distracted by the man walking around the side of my gallery and onto my deck. Pocketing my phone, still connected to Mom, I dropped my backpack by the door, freeing up my hands.

"This is private property, sir. You're trespassing."

"It's a business," he said, still moving toward me.

Fingers readying a spell, I said, "Yes, but one that's not open yet. You're trespassing on my property, so it's time to go."

"Are you the sea wicche?" He gave me a long perusal. "With

that hair, you sure look like one." His smile didn't make it to his eyes. "You're a pretty little thing." He tried to peer into the studio, but I'd had the windows treated for just this reason. I didn't want randos from the gallery to snoop in my studio. "Anybody else around or are you on your own?"

"Haven't you heard about sea wicches?" I took a step toward him and could tell he wasn't expecting it. He liked scaring women, liked hurting them. "We're well known for taking lives and stealing souls. Are you sure you want to be standing here right now, leering at me, planning how you'll overpower me?" I smiled my most predatory smile and took another step closer.

Never breaking eye contact, I flicked the fingers at my side and watched the grin slide off his face. His eyes widened in sudden fear. One, two, three, four, five seconds. I took another step forward, my smile widening, before he sucked in a desperate breath, expression now panicked. Had I frozen his lungs for a few seconds? Yes. Yes, I had.

I leaned in, close enough to smell his foul coffee breath and whispered, "Don't fuck with me."

He stepped back and I tilted my head, never breaking eye contact.

"Run along now, before I take an interest in you."

The man turned to take off and ran into a six-and-a-half-foot angry werewolf whose eyes were bright gold. Declan grabbed my would-be rapist by the neck with one muscular arm, picking him up off the deck. I couldn't see it, as he was facing away from me, but given the sudden scent, I'd guess the man had just soiled himself.

Declan gave him a disgusted look. "Tough guy."

"She's—she's a witch," he wheezed around Declan's grip.

Declan nodded. "And I'm something far worse. You should do what the lady says. Run and never come back." He threw the man off the deck and onto the dirt and rocks along the side of my cannery.

Whimpering in a heap, he slowly got to his feet, looked back at us, and limp-jogged away.

Declan stood at the edge of the deck, arms crossed, watching the man retreat.

"How'd you know to come? And I had that covered. He was leaving before you got here."

"I know. He just pissed me off." When he relaxed his body and turned to me, I knew the creepy guy was gone. Gesturing to my pocket, he said, "Your mom's trying to talk to you."

Oh, shit. I fumbled in my pocket and dragged out the phone. "Hey, Mom. I'm back."

"Is the wolf there?" Her voice was angry, but I was pretty sure she was just worried. Probably.

"His name's Declan."

"I don't care about his name. Did he get rid of that man?"

"Actually," Declan began, moving closer and sitting on a bench. His werewolf hearing meant he always heard both sides of a phone conversation. "Your daughter already had it covered. All I did was shove him along."

"Your grandmother and I will bolster your wards. Men like that shouldn't be able to get anywhere near you. Do you have cameras up and running?"

Declan glanced up, looking for cameras.

"You know I do, Mom, but I did have it under control."

"Gran and I will be right over." And she hung up.

Slipping my phone back in my pocket, I sat down next to Declan, bumping his shoulder with mine. "I really am fine."

Nodding slowly, he wrapped an arm around me. "I know." He patted his chest with his free hand. "Got my heart racing when I saw him walk around the gallery. We were standing near the road, Natsuki explaining her vision, and I got a bad feeling. I turned, saw him, and just started running." Shaking his head, he added, "I didn't even tell them where I was going. Kenji was midsentence and I sprinted away."

Resting my head on his chest, I said, "Thanks."

"No problem. You're getting more creeps than I would have expected. The place isn't even open yet."

"Yeah," I sighed. "I've been living like a hermit for so long, I guess I was hoping it wouldn't still be a problem."

"What wouldn't be? And did you know your gloves are still off?"

I stared down at my bare hands and then watched Declan wrap his warm one around one of mine. It was nice. "My mom was probably more panicked than she'd normally be because I've attracted a certain kind of attention from certain kinds of men since I was quite small."

Declan pulled me closer to him.

"They were always trying to lure me away or just straight up snatch me. Because of that, defensive magic was the first thing Mom and Gran taught me. The first time I remember, a man took me before anyone saw."

"First time?" Declan growled. "How many times has it happened?" His eyes were lightening again.

"A few. Anyway, this man clapped his hands around the back of my neck and over my mouth. I dropped into a vision of all the other little girls he'd taken, raped, and killed. When I woke up, I was in the back of his van. Windows blacked out. Duct tape over my mouth and around my wrists. And he was unbuckling his belt."

Declan's hand clutched mine, but he stayed silent.

"My hands were tied behind my back. I needed my hands, but I tried to throw every spell I could think of anyway. I was so scared. I started kicking. Screaming behind the tape. He liked that."

Feeling a jab, I drew my hand away. Declan's hands now had long, sharp claws at the tips.

Blowing out a breath, he shook out his hands and they went back to normal. "Sorry. I'm very angry." He cleared his gravelly throat. "I know there's nothing I can do about something that happened when you were a child, but I want to very badly."

"It's okay," I said, patting his hand. "It has a good ending. After I started kicking, the back doors of the van flew off and there was Mom, like an avenging angel. The man screamed, falling out of the van, curling in on himself and cradling his junk. She grabbed me, spelled the tape so it fell away, and stalked back to our family party on the beach."

"Tell me she ripped off his cock."

"If not off, it was severely damaged."

Declan grunted his approval.

"Anyway, the van was in the beach parking lot, near some bushes, probably where he was going to dump my body when he was done. The next lesson with Mom and Gran was how to get out of duct tape, rope, any binding. So, I know my mom might have sounded more angry than concerned on the phone, but creepy men are a real trigger."

"As they should be."

I smiled, nestling in. "True, but even though she knows I can take care of myself now, she and Gran are racing over. They need to assure themselves I'm not tied up in the back of a van again."

He ran a hand up and down my arm. "You've been dealing with predators all your life?"

I nodded. "Part of why I like to keep to myself. I was also figuring that I'd aged out of the pedophiles' preferred victim pool."

"There are plenty of predators who are just fine with adult women," he growled.

"Yeah, there's that." I wiggled my fingers. "So, I have lots of magic, cameras all around the building, wards that are about to be reinforced by Mom and Gran, and a werewolf down the road."

"Not to mention a selkie guardian that can go get Dad when you need him. Hey," he said, leaning away from me to get a better look, "why aren't you wearing the earrings? They're a direct line to him."

"I know, and after today, I will. I just worried that if I wore them, he could always be listening in, which made me super uncomfortable."

"You got to figure he's a powerful, important guy, right?" Declan said. "He doesn't have time to eavesdrop while you paint, bake, chat with Cecil. He's got stuff to do. Think of the earrings like a buzzer. They get his attention so he can shift his focus to you."

"Hmm. But when we're messing around, stay away from my ears. I don't need my dad hearing any of that."

Declan chuckled and I felt him relax. "Agreed. And whenever possible, before any serious messing around, just take them off."

"Good call."

He kissed the top of my head. "Your mom just parked." Standing up, he pulled me with him. "I'm going to get back to that meeting now."

"Tell Kenji and Natsuki sorry about that."

"Nothing to be sorry about." Taking my hand, he led me to the railing. "Put your hand out. You'll need a reset in a minute." He cradled my face in his big, warm hands, running his nose over my hair, across my temple, before tilting my head up and kissing me softly, thoroughly.

At the clearing of a throat, we broke apart.

"Ladies." He stepped away, his gaze moving between me and the water.

I shot a stream of seawater up, ran a hand through it, and then shook off the droplets. "Hey, Mom, can I have some gloves?"

"I'll leave you three to it. I need to get back to a meeting. It's always good seeing you," he said and then took off at a jog.

Mom opened her bag with a tsk and then handed me a fresh pair of gloves. "I don't like him."

"Hush, Sybil," Gran said. "I like him just fine."

"Besides," I said, "did he not just come at a run to help me?"

"Well, if you're going to have a werewolf lurking around, you might as well put him to use," she said. "Now, let's get to work. Your Gran and I were discussing this on the way over. Your wards are very strong already, but they were built before you were a member of the Council. The Three have a power all our own. We'll build the next ward together."

I wasn't sure there was a ward strong enough to protect me, but it was worth a shot.

SIXTEEN

The Reprise of Stupid Wolf

Once the ritual was complete, my wards strengthened, Mom and Gran on their way, and a frozen pizza consumed, I finally got started painting the interior. My plan was for the walls to be an impressionistic take on the ocean. The wall of windows looking out on the bay would be painted in sea green and foam white. The opposite wall, on the road side of the gallery, would be deep sea indigo and midnight, with small glimmers of bioluminescent jellyfish and sea stars.

Up high on the wall, barely visible, would lurk the gaze of the sea monster tearing the gallery apart. I wanted the walls to be interesting, without taking the focus from the art displayed on them. It was a delicate balance.

I was about four hours in and pleased with the results so far. I kept scrambling down from the scaffold to check the effect from the middle of the gallery. I had to go back over the first section I'd painted when I'd stood back and realized that my brushstrokes were too short. I'd been thinking about Pearl's killer, D with the flashy car. How could I find him, and what did that corridor mean? Would anyone else know or care about my distracted, short brushstrokes? Probably not, but I couldn't handle looking at something I knew was wrong. It didn't look enough like moving water.

I painted over that section using longer, more fluid lines. When I stepped back then, it felt right. I'd been doing ten foot by five foot sections at a time, checking in between each block to make sure the new one flowed with the previous ones. It couldn't look patchy. It had to move like the ocean, ceaseless waves flowing in and out.

Pearl's killer seemed younger. Not as young as Pearl, but maybe midtwenties. He felt entitled, as though it was his right to do with her as he chose. I didn't sense anger or lust so much as joy. Satisfaction.

I was climbing down the scaffold to do a check when my vision began to tunnel and my limbs went weak. Instead of possibly bouncing my head off the concrete floor, I lay down on the plywood platform. As the world went dark, I hoped like hell I didn't roll off.

Growls and snarls fill my head. Paws pounding, pursuing through the thick forest. Declan's wolf stands ready but Logan doesn't step into the circle. He barks, bobs his head, and pads away as the pack descends on Declan, tearing into him. Covered in blood, he fights viciously, but it's too much. On a broken howl, he goes down under almost two dozen wolves, tearing at him with claws and teeth, destroying the one who could have saved them.

The image goes dark and then…

A young girl wakes from a nightmare. Wiping away her tears, she slips from her bed, unsure of who to go to in the night. Her sister is in the bed a few feet away, but this isn't something she wants to talk with Sylvia about. She needs an elder.

Her grandmother is the Crone, the most powerful of the Three on the Corey Council. The girl moves quietly across the room and out the door. Her grandmother and grandfather have rooms at the rear of the house. She avoids the stair that squeaks.

Standing outside the bedroom door, she hesitates. Should she knock?

"Come in, child, and tell me what has you up." The door opens and an old woman with long white hair takes the child's hand and walks her into an adjoining sitting room. The old woman closes the door and sits beside the child.

"What is it, girl?"

In stutters and stops, she tells her grandmother about the nightmare, about a baby that can see the future, can hear thoughts. The baby grows, but is sad and sickly, dark circles under her eyes, patches of hair missing. She wakes screaming in the night and there's nothing to be done to console her.

The babe only lives seven years before she tries to quiet the voices in her head by walking into the ocean.

The grandmother nods, patting the child's hand.

"You've been blessed, Sybil. You will bear a Cassandra wicche. They are very rare and a gift from the Goddess. We must do whatever we can to make her strong. She must live if she is to benefit the family."

Sybil nods, still looking sick and scared.

"Don't worry, child. We'll help. The most important thing—when the time is right—is to find a strong father for her, someone whose gifts match, if not surpass, your own. We must make her powerful enough to survive being a seer."

The image goes dark and then…

A dark, torch-lit stone room, low chanting and heat. My stomach cramps. I want out of this vision now. Head pounding, body sore, the chanting grows louder. Calliope and her demon are going to take me out in a vision. Pulling as hard as I can—

The image goes dark and then…

A man is standing at the top of a dark wooden staircase. Given the proportions of the entry, the art, the antiques, he's in a mansion. He's arguing with someone in the shadows. Shaking his head, one hand cuts through the air. The discussion is over. He turns to descend the stairs and instead goes flying, crumpling at the base, his head at an unnatural angle.

The image goes dark and then…

An older man is walking along the edge of a huge lawn in front of a great house. There are trees between himself and the crashing surf beyond. He checks his watch and again looks for someone. A cigarette flares in the dark. The man goes to the light and is hit in the head with a shovel. His body plummets from the high cliff to the jagged rocks and crashing waves below.

Head pounding, I rolled onto my side. Curled in on myself, I willed my stomach to relax. *Please.* I didn't want to clean up vomit.

There was a knock at the back door. What time was it? "Declan?" If it was him, he'd hear me.

"Yeah? Everything okay?" Concern was creeping into his voice.

Flicking my fingers, I unlocked the door. I heard it open and close as I tried to right myself. I shouldn't have moved so soon. Declan had just walked into the gallery as I climbed down the last five feet of scaffolding and ran past him for the bathroom. And once again, I was heaving into the toilet while he held my hair and ran his heating pad of a hand up and down my back.

Eyes watering, I mumbled, "Sorry," before my muscles cramped again. Stomach already empty, I was flushing foamy bile and wishing I was in my bed.

He held a warm, damp towel in front of me. I took it, thumping back on my butt while I wiped my face, feeling miserable and cold.

"Come on," he said, pulling me to my feet. "Let's get you into bed."

"Oh, sorry. I can't. I feel too sick."

He paused a moment and then chuffed a laugh. "Not that," he said, picking me up. "You need a soft, warm bed, dark, and a cup of tea. I'm not much of a tea maker, but I can google how to do it." He carried me upstairs, pausing to turn off the bright lights. "Can you lock the doors and lower the shutters?"

I nodded and did so. He was about to place me in my bed when I said, "Wait. Can you put me down?"

He did and I toed off my sneakers and socks before dropping the overalls. I crawled under the sheets in my panties and thermal, curling around my abused stomach.

"I'll get you tea," he said, turning back to the stairs.

"Declan?"

He paused.

"I don't need tea. Can you go into my backpack for the honey bottle? Maybe that can help."

He jogged down the stairs and returned a minute later, pouring water onto his hands, rubbing them together, and then gently caressing my forehead, the back of my neck. Almost immediately, I began to feel a lessening of the pain.

"Thank you." I burst into tears and couldn't stop. I was mortified but had no control over it.

He crouched down, brushing my hair out of the way. His big, warm hand was on my face, wiping away tears. "Tell me what I can do?" He held my hand and waited.

"It's not that," I finally choked out. I held up our joined hands. "It's this." I pulled my sleeve with my free hand, so I could mop my stupid sobbing face. "No one touches me. Ever. Not until you."

He rubbed his thumb over my fingers.

"Do you know that study they did on orphanages in the early 1900s?"

He shook his head.

"They were looking into why the death rate for infants in some orphanages was one hundred percent. I'm sure there were too many babies and not enough nurses. Whatever the case, the nurses were told not to touch the babies. Change them, but then leave them in their cribs. What they found is that babies die without love and affection, without touch. They attributed their deaths in the official paperwork to being hopeless."

He squeezed my hand.

"*Hopeless.* I used to think that Cassandra wicches died young because of all the horrible things we see and experience, but maybe it's isolation and hopelessness. You'll never understand what a gift it is for me to experience your touch." More tears slipped over my eyelashes.

He kissed my hand and then leaned in and kissed my lips. When he drew back, he stared down at our joined hands. "I don't understand what it is about me that allows me to do this." He kissed my fingers again. "But I'll thank your Goddess until my dying days for it."

Smiling, vision blurry, I said, "She can be your Goddess too."

"I'll take it under advisement."

Blinking away the tears, I looked into his gorgeous, bearded face, his warm brown eyes, and thanked Her for the both of us.

"Oh," I said, suddenly remembering. "Can you grab my phone out of my overalls?"

He kicked off his shoes, found my phone, and handed it to me before moving to the opposite side of the bed and big spooning me.

I pulled his hand under the covers and rested it on my stomach; the cramping began to ease up. "My own personal hot water bottle."

Kissing my shoulder, he slid his other arm under my head. "Was it a bad vision?"

I thought about that. "Yes and no." I woke up my phone. "I need to make this call and then I'll explain."

"Arwyn?" Detective Hernández said.

"Yeah. Listen, I just had a vision. Most of it I understand, but there were two parts that were a repeat of before. I'm worried the deaths are imminent. They felt...more like Pearl and the teacher in the morgue. I could totally be wrong about the connection, but I don't think so."

I heard paper shuffling and then Hernández said, "Go ahead."

I'd already told her some of this after the first vision, but I filled in the details I saw this time. After giving her as much info as I could, I disconnected, placing my phone on the nightstand and curling around Declan's hand again.

"You think those deaths are connected to your cousin?"

I nodded. "There's something about the energy. It felt familiar. Not exact, which bothers me, but really similar." I blew out a breath. "I'm not positive."

I told him about Calliope's curse that was no doubt making me sick right now and then about my mother. When I got to the dream daughter taking her own life, he pulled me in closer, trying to protect both the me that could have been and the me that was.

"Your mother isn't an easy woman, but knowing that would happen unless she found a father strong enough to keep her child alive…" He shook his head.

"Knowing what's expected of you for the benefit of the family, but fearing it," I said.

"And your family basically trying to breed her with the strongest magical man they could find."

I shivered and Declan's hand rubbed back and forth over my stomach.

"It explains a lot about why Mom is the way she is. The sacrifices she had to make to fulfill her role in the family. Meanwhile, I say no for years, even leaving the country, to avoid the Corey Council."

"For good reason," he said. "Look at you now. You're too sick to sit up. And she didn't have it anywhere near as bad as you. She had it hanging over her head for years. Yeah, that sucks. You've been seeing horrible visions since you were a toddler. You have to cover yourself from head to toe so as to not accidentally touch someone and hear their thoughts, relive their trauma. You feel the pain they've felt. You're not just watching horrible things happen. You take the punch, the stab, the hands around your neck. Don't do that to yourself. You wanting to live doesn't make you selfish."

I rolled over and wrapped my arm around him, resting my head on his chest. "Thank you."

I told him about the Alpha challenge I'd seen, about the ambush. He lay silent afterward, staring up through the skylight.

"You can't go," I said. "They're going to kill you."

He rubbed the arm I had wrapped around him but remained silent.

"Declan."

"I heard you and I'm thinking."

"You can't go." I went up on an elbow so I could stare down at him. "This isn't a fair fight. They're going to kill you."

"We'll see." He tried to pull me back down, so I was resting on his chest.

Headache finally gone, I went up on my knees and glared down at him. "No, we will not see. You are not walking into an ambush." I drilled my finger into his chest to make my point.

Wrapping his hand around my finger, he pulled it away, turning it over and rubbing his thumb in circles on my palm. "I appreciate the information. This is what we'd already been thinking. I'll plan accordingly. You do not, however, have the right to tell me what to do." When I opened my mouth to argue, he added, "Just as I can't tell *you* what to do."

On a huff of annoyance, I slid out of bed and stomped to the bathroom. I needed a minute to pee, strategize, and brush my teeth.

SEVENTEEN

If You Don't Like Reading Sex Scenes, You'll Want to Skip a Lot of This Chapter

When I went back in a few minutes later, I had a plan. "Okay, hear me out. I know you don't want me there—which is just wasting your best secret weapon—but you absolutely need to take Kenji and Daniel with you as backup. Get them to tell you the guys who can be bribed to sit this one out. I've got money. I can help bribe people."

He'd already started shaking his head.

"And I know a lot of wicches. They can go and keep the noncombatants out of the ring. If they try any underhanded stuff, my family can hex them, leaving Logan for you to deal with. We won't interfere with the challenge itself. We'll just keep the others from jumping you."

"No."

I waited for an explanation but got nothing more. "Why the hell not?"

He patted the bed beside him.

"No. Tell me why you won't accept my help." It didn't matter what he said. He didn't own Big Sur. He couldn't keep me from saving his stupid life.

Sitting up, he held out a hand. "Come on. I don't like it when you're so far away."

I thought about smacking his hand but then took it, climbing back on the bed. He tried to pull me down with him, to tuck me into his side, but I wasn't giving in that easily. I sat on his thighs, crossed my arms, and stared down at him.

"Well?" I waited.

"I've had this fantasy so many times. Except you weren't wearing the top. I'm not complaining. You're keeping it interesting."

I balled a fist. "I will punch you in your junk right now if you don't explain why I'm not allowed to help you. You raced over here this afternoon to help me, but I'm not allowed to return the favor? Why the hell not?" I might just punch his junk on principle.

The charming smile dropped and he sighed. Scrubbing his hands over his face, he said, "No threats of violence between partners."

"Okay, fine, whatever. I wasn't really going to do it."

"You punched me in the truck."

"Only because you were pissing me off."

He pinned me with a glare. "Arwyn."

I absolutely agreed with him, and I was ashamed of the threatening and the hitting, but I also really wanted to smack him for not letting me help. "Sorry," I said in a voice that clearly indicated I was not at all sorry.

"It can't always be your way. I'm a pretty easygoing guy, but that doesn't mean you can order me around." He rested his hands on my thighs. "Tell me you understand that, Arwyn, or this ends right here. I'm not your lap dog."

My arms dropped and I squeezed his hands. "I don't want a lap dog. I just don't want you to die." My eyes filled with sudden tears. Looking up, I blinked rapidly. "You've got a secret weapon in your pocket. Why won't you use me?"

He patted his chest again. "Come down here and we'll discuss it."

"No." I wasn't letting him lull me into agreeing with his stupid scheme.

"So stubborn," he muttered, his thumbs brushing back and forth over my inner thighs. "Okay, Arwyn. Are you listening?"

I locked eyes with him and he sighed, no doubt seeing the hurt in mine.

"It has to be a clean fight."

When I opened my mouth to argue it would never be a clean fight with Logan involved, he held up a finger.

"There can be no question who the stronger wolf is. We don't recognize the authority of wicches, vampires, fae, humans—anyone—over us. If your family comes to interfere in the fight, it will never be viewed as a valid challenge and I won't be seen as the rightful Alpha. Daniel and Kenji have no place in the pack at present. They'd be attacked the moment they set foot on pack land.

"If I am to ascend to Alpha, to whip this pack into shape, I can't plot and bribe. The only way I earn their respect and loyalty is through honor and strength. I won't cheat for the greater good. I can't control what others do, only what I do. And I don't cheat."

Stupid, noble wolf was going to get himself killed. "So I just sit back and wait to be informed you *left town*," I air quoted. "Is that it?"

He squeezed my thighs. "A little more faith in me would be nice, but essentially yes."

"Well, I have to say, I hate everything about that. Except the righteous anger. That was kind of hot."

His gaze softened as he gripped my hips and dragged me forward, so I was perched on the bulge in his pants. "Only kind of?" The thumb that had been caressing my inner thigh slipped into my panties, and then slid up, down, and around. Shuddering, I tilted back and braced myself on his legs. I felt a claw at my waist and then my panties were gone, and he had a finger in me while his thumb continued its relentless pursuit of my orgasm.

It didn't take long and then—I don't even know how he moved me so quickly—he'd slid down on the bed, my knees on either side of his shoulders while he gripped my hips, keeping me in place and wrecking me with his mouth. I might have moaned. There was undoubtedly shouting. It's possible I left my body.

Still quivering, I was tossed back on the bed while he peeled my thermal and bra off. I reached for his shirt, still not believing this was happening. A man I cared deeply about—with a ridiculously hot body—was able to touch me. But it wasn't even about that. I mean, yes, it was, but mostly it was about my being able to touch him, to run my hands all over him, and not experience pain or horror or fear. He was a gift I would never not be grateful for.

Kneeling between my legs, he lifted my knees. His gaze drifted over every inch of me before his lips followed the same path.

"So beautiful," he murmured between kisses.

Desperate, mindless, I wrapped my legs around, him, tilting up, needing him.

"Soon." His tongue swirled around my breasts. While his mouth ravaged one, his hand plucked and rolled the other. Head thrown back, hands kneading his shoulders, I couldn't get enough of him, couldn't feel any more. And then I did.

He slid in, and we both groaned. I had a moment of panic. "Condom?"

"Yes." And then he pulled back, slammed home, and all thought was gone.

The orgasm shattered me, but he wasn't done. He slid out, flipped my liquid body over, lifted my hips and slid back in. One hand at my waist, keeping me in place, the other at my breast, he gave me one more life-altering orgasm before finishing with me.

Breathing heavy, still joined, he wrapped an arm around my waist and repositioned us so I was once again the little spoon. Keeping one arm under me, around my middle, he rested the other on my breast, kissing my shoulder.

"I may never walk again." My heart was still hammering in my chest.

"It's overrated."

"That made up for many years of nogasms."

"Nogasms?" His fingertips swirled lazily on my stomach. It should have tickled but didn't.

"No partnergasms." Sex was miserable when you could hear every thought and experience every sex-related issue. I used to drink to dull the voices. The sex was still horrible, but I had the added bonus of heading down the alcoholic path in life. Deciding it wasn't at all worth it, I gave up partnergasms.

"Ah. Happy to help in any way possible," he growled, his beard tickling as he kissed a trail over my shoulder.

Still joined at the happy place, I realized I was feeling full to bursting again. "How?"

Chuckling, he moved my leg, opening me up, resting it on his own. Slowly, very slowly, he began to rock while the fingers on my stomach moved lower and the one at my breast brushed over my nipple.

It didn't take long before exhaustion was forgotten and there was only Declan. Writhing, I tried to feel every inch of him, be felt by every inch of him. The tremors were gaining strength when I felt his teeth on my shoulder. It didn't hurt. If anything, it seemed to intensify the orgasm for both of us.

Panting, spent, I rolled away from him. "Don't even think about it. I need sleep."

"Me too. Let's get cleaned up first, though." He was already up and dragging me from the bed. "Come on. Quick shower, sheet change, and then we sleep. Okay?"

I stumbled after him, legs weak. When he turned on the water and tried to pull me in with him, I squawked. "Dude, if I get this hair wet, it's at least an hour of drying and conditioning." I began coiling it all up, and he took advantage of my arms being over my head to use both his hands all over my body.

"I'd like to remind you about how those long, sexy curls of yours might have brushed over a lot of me while parts of me might have been covered in bodily fluids."

I stopped what I was doing and dropped my arms, my hair

cascading down my back. *Damn*. He was right. "From now on, hair gets tied up before any messing around commences."

"Noted." He pulled me into the shower with him.

An ancillary benefit of all this hair was that he wanted to wash it and he gave a great scalp massage. Although the scalp massage did lead to other water sports, we were finally back in a clean bed, my damp hair in a special towel. Snuggled into his side, we were both out within minutes.

EIGHTEEN

The Vibe Has Changed

I woke to knocking and my phone buzzing. Reaching for the phone, I knocked over a handwritten note. Detective Hernández was on the phone. I swiped and answered. "Yes?"

"Oh, good. Are you home now? I'm on your deck."

"You're—um." I looked around. I was alone in bed and naked. "Okay. I just woke up. Give me a few to get up and ready."

"Sorry, Arwyn. I didn't mean to wake you." The roar of the surf almost drowned out her words.

"S'okay. Give me a few and I'll be down." I ended the call and read the note.

Good morning. I put drops of seawater on all the parts of you I could see. You should be good to go after last night. Call me when you wake up. D

I went to the bathroom to take care of necessities and deal with my hair. I didn't usually sleep this long, and I went to bed with it damp. "Oh, come on!" We'd conditioned it, so the curls were glossy and healthy, but one side was matted down and the other bouncy. Could I spell it? Sure. I'd done that a lot over the years. Spelling made it frizzy, though. Damn it.

Slipping on a robe, I went back out and leaned on the half wall overlooking the studio. Flicking my fingers, I opened the shutters and blinked in the too-sudden brightness before unlocking and opening the back door.

"Detective Hernández?" I called.

She appeared in the doorway a moment later. "I like the new benches."

"Thanks. Declan made them. I need to deal with my hair. Why don't you come in and sit down?"

"Sure. Go ahead." She moved to study the corridor painting while I ran back into the bathroom. After sending Declan a quick text, thanking him for the seawater droplets and letting him know Hernández was here, I hopped into the shower to wet my hair down again. Could I have just worked on the flat side without going back in the shower? Sure. But it would have taken longer. After lightly conditioning, I began the drying process again. As it was daytime, I'd dry it until it stopped dripping and then let the air and sun do the rest.

Dressed and ready, I finally went down to find Hernández texting on her phone.

"Sorry about that."

She stood, shaking her head. "I'm the one busting into your day." Pointing at the painting, she asked, "What's this?"

"Just something I keep dreaming about. I'm not sure why yet." Grabbing the container on my kitchen counter, I popped the top off and offered her a strawberry banana muffin.

She took it while still staring at the painting. "There's something sinister about it, isn't there?"

Nodding, I looked down at a muffin and decided against it. "I hear whispering when I see that. Two people—I'm pretty sure it's two—plotting behind one of those doors." I put the container back on the counter and chose the kiwi yogurt in my fridge. I grabbed a spoon and went to my chair.

"The dark wood walls, the rug; it reminds me of where I was

this morning." She broke the muffin in half. "Where I'd like to take you, if I can."

I gave her a look as I continued eating my breakfast. "Do you really need me, or will this just make life easier for you? Because I have a shit ton to do here."

Heavy treads sounded on the deck. Declan came into view and then in through the back door. He nodded to Hernández and then came to me, leaning over and giving me a kiss.

"I thought you'd sleep later." He crouched down by my chair, his brow furrowing as his gaze slid to my hair. He reached out and coiled a curl around his finger. "I thought this was dry."

"There are three people in this relationship and one of them is my hair. Just so you know, she's a high-maintenance bitch."

His phone buzzed and he stood. "I look forward to learning all about her. I need to get back. The crew is arriving." He slid his fingers through my hair, rubbing them against my scalp.

It took everything in me not to shiver, remembering last night.

"You're painting the gallery today. Right?" he asked, starting to move away. "Remember to open all the windows."

"That was the plan until this one showed up," I snarked, eating more yogurt.

Pausing, he looked between the two of us, his hands on his hips. I could see it. The poor guy was torn. On one hand, he wanted to get rid of her for me but on the other, he knew it wasn't his place to step in and that if she was asking for help, someone was probably dead.

"That's what I was explaining when you arrived," Detective Hernández said. "The dean at a very wealthy private school fell down the stairs and broke his neck sometime early this morning. The school has a lot of influence, and it wants the incident to go away as soon as possible. There's nothing to indicate foul play. Nothing *except* Arwyn's vision."

"Which isn't evidence," I said, getting up to clean out the cup and put the spoon in the washer. "Is this dean connected to the teacher Osso had me read at the morgue?"

"Yes. Same school," Hernández responded. "They want to chalk it up as an accidental death, but we both know it's not. I was hoping if you came to the scene, you might pick up on something that I could use to keep the investigation open."

"You'd think two deaths in the same school would be enough to cast suspicion. And how long are we talking here?" I leaned against the counter, calculating how much work I had to do versus how many hours were left in the day.

Declan glanced around. "The bottle needs to go in your backpack."

Nodding, I said, "I'll get it in a minute. I should probably change the water every day, while I'm at it."

He jogged up the stairs to retrieve the honey bottle.

"You'd think, but schools like this have lots of pull. It looks like a fall, so they're pushing for me to close it," she said.

Declan came down a moment later and handed me the bottle. I went up on tiptoes and kissed him. "Go ahead. You've got people waiting. I'm fine."

"Okay." He gave me a longer kiss that scattered my thoughts. "Dinner tonight?"

Embarrassed, mind now in my bed, I said, "Uh huh."

Grinning, he nodded to Hernández and left.

"So," Hernandez said, leaning back on the couch. "The vibe seems a little different between you two."

"Huh," was all the response she got to that. "Back to timing. How quickly can you get me back home?"

She stood up. "As quickly as I can. If I have to stay, I'll have a patrol car bring you back."

"Yeah. Fine. Let's go." I shouldered my backpack and went out to the deck with the honey bottle in my hand. "Good morning, Cecil!"

Hernández quickly looked over the railing to watch the tentacle slap the water.

"It's good to see you, Charlie. Herbert, you're looking quite dapper today." The starfish really were looking fully recovered after the deck fire a few weeks ago. I glanced around for a tennis ball but didn't see it. "Wilbur, where are you?" I grumbled.

Greetings complete, I emptied the honey bottle first and then drew up a jet of seawater, catching it in the plastic bear. Hands wet, my body reset after kissing Declan, I returned the bottle to my backpack and slipped on a pair of gloves. Flicking my fingers, I locked the door and then followed Detective Hernández to her car.

She drove us away from the city, toward the hills and forest.

"Which school?" The road was narrow, and I was seeing fewer and fewer buildings.

"Cypress Academy."

Huh. "My mom wanted to send me there."

Detective Hernández looked over and then back at the road. "Wow. Okay. Horse stables, a polo field, Olympic-sized swimming pool, cutting edge tech in every room, a French chef in the kitchen. Senators and Fortune 500 CEOs went to school there. I assume that means you come from serious money."

"Yes and no. Mom would have had to ask my grandparents for the tuition. She was worried about protecting me." I turned to Hernández. "I'm quite valuable to the family, you know. If Mom said the only way to keep me safe was this Richie Rich school, the grandparents and aunts and uncles would have had to chip in."

Hernández glanced over again. "And they would have resented you for it."

Rubbing my forehead, I said, "They already resented me. If I'd cost them money too?" I shook my head. "No. I told my mom that wasn't the school for me. It didn't feel safe. She believed me and I went to the local public school."

I fiddled with the straps on my backpack. "I think I had a cousin go there, though. Once Mom had told them what an excellent school it was, one of her brothers or sisters had to actually send their child there—something Mom couldn't do—just to show her and the rest of the family that they were better."

Crossing my arms over my chest, I slouched in the seat. "There's so much competition and jealousy in my family. We're an old and powerful line of wicches. Our names are whispered with apprehension and fear in the wicching community. Mom is the most powerful of her generation and she was the one who bore me, the first seer in a couple hundred years. She's been on the Corey Council since she was a teenager."

The road had widened, taking on a more stately feel as we wended our way through the woods. "Mom's siblings and cousins —I'm not sure how to explain this. She was always the special one. Even if you love someone, it can be hard to deal with favoritism. My mom works her ass off and no one feels duty more acutely than her, but growing up surrounded by resentment can make you brittle.

"And then, in a family that prizes our wicche blood, the fact that she bore a half fae daughter and is *still* the favorite? They never outwardly went against her—she and Gran are magical titans—but the whispers amped up and became meaner."

"I would imagine," Hernández began, "that the mixed blood child took a lot of grief herself."

I shrugged one shoulder. "It's all the same thing, isn't it? Like my mom, I've been shown favoritism in the family, even though no one even knows who my father is, other than fae. It can be hard for people who follow all the rules and expect a reward only to find that people who ignored the rules were the ones rewarded. For a certain kind of person, one who keeps track of every infraction, that can be tough to accept."

She pulled through tall wrought iron gates. "Families can be rough. Someday, I'll tell you all about mine."

We'll pulled up to a small guard house. Hernández stopped and showed her ID to the uniformed guard.

"Detective, you can go through. I'll alert the headmaster you've returned."

Hernández nodded and continued down the drive. The trees opened and there stood the very impressive Cypress Academy.

"Holy crap," I muttered. "This place is ridiculous." The Gothic Victorian mansion seemed to go on forever. The pitched roofs, the ornate gables, the canted bay windows, the octagonal turrets on the end of each wing; it was an architectural masterpiece. Three stories high, red brick with a charcoal gray trim, it seemed to be aiming for powerful and elegant. And while I agreed those descriptors served, it was also ominous and vaguely threatening. I appreciated its beauty, but I didn't want to go in.

NINETEEN

I Can Punch People I'm Not Dating, Though, Right?

Hernández parked next to a patrol car. As we got out, a pinched-faced man with dark eyes, a receding hairline, and a considerable stick up his butt came down the marble stairs from the oversized double doors.

"Really, Officer. I thought we were through. I don't appreciate having police cars in front of my school." He stood with his hands on his hips, taking up space with his Wonder Woman pose.

I ducked my head, not wanting to laugh in his face. He looked like his next move was to tell on us.

"Mr. Whitmore, need I remind you that a colleague is dead? It's my job to investigate." Hernández walked up the stairs.

"I thought we'd decided it was an accident," he said, stepping in front of her.

"Sir, I understand this can be difficult for a man used to being in charge, but this isn't your decision. I'm *Detective* Hernández, not Officer. This is my case and I'll be investigating until I'm sure of what happened. Now, if you could excuse me, I need to study the crime scene."

"There's no crime," he insisted.

Hernández stared him down. "Are we going to have a problem here, sir?"

He broke first. "I suppose I'll need to put in a call to the mayor about this. I'd appreciate when you girls are done that you clear out these cars and that horrible yellow tape. The children don't need to see that."

His gaze finally moved past Hernández to me. Looking me up and down, his face darkened as he took in the paint-splattered sneakers, overalls, and hair. "You're a police officer?"

I shook my head, desperate to hex the pompous pusbag for referring to us as *girls*. I hated petty little men like him.

"Ms. Corey is a consultant," Hernández said.

He turned on his heel and walked back through the main doors, neither holding them open for us nor giving the detective any more of his attention.

I caught up with her in the huge entry. "Are we sure that weasel didn't do it?"

One side of her mouth tipped up. She looked up and down the now empty hall and then pointed me to the right. "It would make my year if I got to slap my cuffs on him," she muttered. "*Girls.*"

The wide hall had a thick rug in muted colors running down its center. The walls were a dark wood with carved details. Large, ornate pendant lights hung from the ceiling and every fifteen feet or so, there was a break for a classroom door. There were no glass panels in the doors, like the ones at my old schools. These were solid carved wood with brass plates in the center, giving the room number and the teacher's name.

The bright yellow police tape at the end of the hall stood out against all this darkness. This school clearly eschewed the use of brights and pastels.

Hernández checked her watch. "We have about twenty minutes until the next bell and the halls fill with students." She pointed to the base of the stairs. You can see the bloodstain."

I ducked under the tape and stared up the steps. Yep. This was what I'd seen. Stuffing my hair down the back of my top, I crouched and slipped off a glove.

"Do you want me to hold your backpack?" she asked.

Moving my shoulders, I gauged the weight and my balance. "Nah. I'm fine." I touched the bloodstained carpet with one finger.

"This discussion is over. Every student here signs an honor code. You know that better than anyone. Plagiarism is a clear violation of that code." The Dean of Discipline walks down the hall, angry he has to deal with the student's parent. Again. This is what's wrong with these students. The parents are always defending their children's poor behavior, all in pursuit of an Ivy League acceptance. Well, the student has already received a warning. He squandered it and now he'll have to deal with an F in his Government class. They're already bending rules, letting him retake a portion of his class, allowing him to resubmit his final research paper. His low C just became an F. There goes Harvard.

"It was an accident. I was working with him, tutoring him. We'd printed pages and pages of research so he could defend his argument. It was late. He was tired. I'm sure he didn't even realize he'd done it."

"Don't be ridiculous. He's seventeen years old. He understands what plagiarism is. He did the exact same thing in his World History class as a sophomore. Enough, now. I don't even know why you're inserting yourself into this. You're tutoring. Fine. The next time you tutor, make sure they know that stealing someone else's words and ideas without proper citations will earn them an F for the semester. Now, I'm done with this. I have work to do."

He turns to descend the stairs and a hand holding a large chunk of glass slams against the back of the dean's head. He pitches forward and goes flying down the stairs, breaking his neck.

The one who stands at the top of the stairs slips back into the shadows.

Opening my eyes, I saw Hernández holding out an alcohol wipe to clean the sticky blood from my fingers. Something pulled my gaze up and I found a pair of blue eyes staring down at me from floors above. Hopping over the bloodstain, I ran up the stairs, popped the police tape on the railing of the second-floor landing, and then ran up another flight. Classes were still in session. Who was watching me?

As I hit the top stair, I heard the soft shush of leather-soled shoes and the quiet snick of a door closing. I looked in every direction. The third-floor landing was empty.

Hernández came up the stairs right behind me. "What? What did you see?"

"There was someone up here watching us."

A tone sounded and doors opened, feet pounding in the halls, up and down stairs, though it remained quiet on the third floor. I moved away from the banister to look down the hall. Perhaps the faculty offices were up here. Looking to the left, I froze.

"What is it?" she asked.

I pointed. It was the corridor that had been haunting my dreams and finding its way into visions.

Hernández had a moment too before she began to walk down the corridor. "It's exactly as you painted it." She opened her phone and pulled up a photo she'd taken of my painting. She, no doubt, was comparing my painting to the real corridor, looking for differences that could be meaningful. She'd done the same with my painting of a path in the woods where a child had been taken on a previous case,

She hadn't gone more than a few steps when we heard a familiar voice.

"This area is off-limits. The accident was on the first floor. You can't wander around this institution without a warrant, and you won't get one. The mayor is even now talking with the chief of police."

"Are these faculty offices up here?" I asked.

"No. These are student residences. Cypress Academy serves as a boarding school for sixty percent of our student body. Really, I must insist. This officer—"

"Detective," Hernández reminded him.

"—may have the credentials to enter our campus, but you, as a consultant, do not. We don't allow strange adults to wander our school and certainly not in the residences. Now if you'll please follow me out."

Hernández had already said that her captain was pushing her

to close the case as an accident. That was why I was here. So far, I hadn't found anything concrete to keep it open, so we followed him down.

On the second-floor landing, right where the conversation and bash would have happened, there was an antique table displaying various awards for students who had long since graduated.

"Headmaster?"

He paused on the first step down.

Pointing at the clean spot in the very light layer of dust, I asked, "What was here?"

Sighing, he came back up and looked where I was pointing. "I have no idea what you're talking about. It's time to go now."

"She's right. I see it," Hernández said, taking out her phone, leaning down, and photographing the spot.

"The cleaning staff may have moved one of the awards or a student took it as a prank," he said, turning toward the stairs again.

"Sir," Hernández said, "this is why you're a headmaster and not a detective. All of these awards are weighty. They're substantial blocks of wood, metal, and glass. And this is where the dean went tumbling down the stairs." She pocketed her phone, then took out her notebook and began scribbling.

"I'm sure there's a perfectly reasonable explanation for—"

"Sir, I'm going to stop you there. Can you please find any custodians currently working and send them here to see me?"

"The staff is very busy," he said, bristling at the interruption.

"I'm sure they are." She looked from her notebook and shot him a look that would have had me backing up. "So are we. Is it your intention to obstruct this investigation?"

He blew a sharp breath out of his nose and then went down the stairs without another word.

"Ooh, he does not like you at all." I snickered, looking over the railing as the headmaster stalked out of sight.

"Color me surprised." She added notes to her book. "A Latina telling him what he can and can't do?" She looked up at me, eyebrows raised. "I will bet you five dollars that when he gets around to sending a custodian or two, they will look more like me than you."

"Do you think it's your gender or ethnicity that has him more worked up?" I asked, leaning on the railing and watching the stragglers run to beat the bell.

"Both, especially in combination. Men like him base their worth, their identity, and place in society, on being able to pee standing up and having skin too sensitive for the sun."

Laughing, I said, "We can pee standing up too. It's just messier."

Her perpetual poker face broke and she grinned, her brown eyes sparkling.

Shaking her head, she walked over and leaned on the railing beside me. "This place is another world." Gesturing with the notebook in her hand, she said, "And *his* problem is he's forgetting he isn't a part of it. He works here. His students may come from influence and money, but he's just a jumped-up school principal who believes he's gained power through proximity."

"Would you have wanted to go to a school like this?" I asked.

She shook her head. "Not even a little bit." We both heard footsteps and looked down the hall to see two Latinas in matching black dresses walking our way. "You can give me the five on the way home."

"I don't believe I took that bet because I'm not stupid." Whispering, I added, "The killer hit him with a block of glass."

She nodded and then lifted her voice. "Hello. Sorry to interrupt your day. I'm Detective Hernández and I'm investigating the dean's death this morning. I assume you both heard about that?"

The women shared a glance and then nodded nervously.

"I just need to ask you a few questions. Can I get your names?"

The first woman cleared her throat and said, "Sofia Rodriguez." She wore her hair pulled back tightly in a bun and had small pearls at her ears and a gold wedding band around her finger.

Hernández smiled, trying to put the women at ease. "My name is Sofia too."

Tension in the woman's shoulders seemed to ease.

"Isabel Alvarez," the other woman volunteered. She wore no jewelry, save a cross at her neck. Her dark brown hair was short and threaded with gray.

"Can you both come over here?" Hernández led them to the top of the stairs. "I want you to look at the awards on this table."

The women did and then exchanged a concerned look.

"What did you notice?" the detective asked, her voice gentle.

Isabel pointed to the end of the table. "One's missing."

Sofia nodded. "It's glass and very heavy."

Isabel looked at Sofia with irritation. "Rosa didn't dust yesterday."

"That's good for us," Hernández said. "The clean spot tipped us off that something was missing."

Sofia's hand flew to her mouth. "The dean was hit with the award?" Whispering behind her fingers, she added, "He was murdered?"

TWENTY

Sofia & Isabel

"I'm still investigating. Do either of you remember the last time you saw the award on the table?"

"Two days ago?" Isabel said, turning to Sofia. "Didn't I work on the third floor two days ago?" She shivered and then crossed herself. "Ay, Dios Mio, murdered."

"Yes," Sofia responded. "Rosa was yesterday."

"I cleaned it two days ago," Isabel confirmed.

"Thank you," Hernández said, making a note. She looked up the empty hall and lowered her voice. "I think we all know that some people don't notice the ones who provide services for them. The help, right?"

Both women nodded.

"And because of that, you often hear and see things they don't intend anyone to know about. Secrets they'd rather keep hidden."

The women glanced at each other and reluctantly gave what could be construed as a nod.

"Now, if the dean was in fact helped down those stairs, it would have been by someone who was upset with him. Can you think of anyone who's been upset with Mr. Grimes? Or perhaps a time you saw him very angry himself?"

Sofia glanced over her shoulder and then leaned in to whisper. "The dean is always angry."

Isabel nodded.

"He's the disciplinarian of the school. These children—" Sofia stopped and shook her head.

Isabel patted Sofia's arm.

"Most are good kids," Sofia continued. "They can be bratty, but they're here, not home with their families, so we understand some brattiness." She paused when we heard someone walk by the bottom of the stairs.

"Others," Isabel continued, "I think were sent here because the parents didn't know what to do with them anymore."

Sofia took up the explanation. "They throw money at the school for the people here to raise their children. But these people aren't their parents. They're teachers and administrators, coaches. This is a job, and then they go home to their own families."

"They try," Isabel said. "The teachers work long hours to help any student who needs it, but they're not parents. And some kids are just…"

"Bad," Sofia finished.

"Yeah, but everyone coddles them because they don't want to deal with the rich, powerful parents who put them here. The dean is the one who upholds the rules. He gives the demerits. He calls the parents," Isabel explained.

Sophia took over again. "He and the headmaster fight a lot. The dean wants students punished for breaking rules. The headmaster wants them given more chances and ways to get out of trouble because he doesn't want to deal with angry parents. The dean calls to tell them what their child has done and what the consequences will be. Then they call the headmaster to yell and threaten that the consequences better go away or they'll pull their school funding and get him fired."

I interrupted. "Hi. I'm Arwyn. I'm a consultant for Detective Hernández. I had a question. When you say they threaten to pull funding, I don't understand. Don't they have to pay a tuition to have their student attend this school?"

Even though I'd been standing there the whole time, the women seemed nervous about responding to me.

Hernández must have noticed the same thing because she patted me on the shoulder and said, "Arwyn would never do or say anything to jeopardize your jobs."

They didn't look entirely convinced, but Sofia said, "Yes. They all pay tuition, but some parents contribute more for the building fund."

"The parents of students who get into trouble pay more to keep their kids here?" the detective asked.

Sofia shrugged. "We don't know who pays extra and who doesn't. We've just heard the threat to stop the extra money."

Hernández jotted down some notes and then used her pen to gesture up and down the halls. "What about the residences? Who's here nights and weekends with the students? The headmaster said about sixty percent of the student body boards here."

"The numbers change," Isabel said. "When I first started working here—almost twenty years ago—only, maybe, forty percent of the students lived on campus. Now, it's much more."

"The housemasters chaperone the students," Sophia said. "One male, one female. One lives at this end of the third floor. The other is at the far end."

"Good," Hernández said. "And their names?"

Sophia looked at Isabel, her brows furrowed. Isabel shrugged.

"In this school, they call each other their job title," Sophia explained.

"The teachers use names," Isabel added.

"Downstairs, the teachers and administrators have plaques by their doors," Sophia said. "Like Headmaster, Mr. Whitmore. We clean those so we get to know everyone's name and where their rooms are."

"Up here," Isabel continued, "it just says Housemaster by the door."

Isabel tapped a finger over her lip and stared down the far end of the hall. "I think I heard a student call the woman Ms. Collins, but I'm not sure. The man is new. He's only been here for maybe a month. Mr. Reed, though, he worked here almost as long as me. He just retired, said he wanted out before finals because exam weeks were always crazy in the residence." She shook her head. "The things the kids get up to, trying to cheat their way into better last-minute grades."

"Do you remember Mr. Reed's first name?" the detective asked.

"Harold," Isabel said.

Hernández made more notes. "Back to the dean. Did you see or hear him argue with anyone in the school beside the headmaster?"

"There'd be too many to count," Sofia said. "He just ran angry."

"Not with us," Isabel clarified.

"No." Sofia shook her head. "Some can be very high and mighty."

"Blaming us for dumping the garbage because they'd accidentally thrown something out they needed," Isabel said. She elbowed Sofia. "Remember Dr. Marcel? He told me to go get in the dumpster to find his computer thing."

"Thumb drive," Sofia said. "It was the dean who told him to jump in the dumpster if he needed it so badly, that it wasn't Isabel's job to fix his mistakes."

Isabel nodded. "Then the dean dismissed me and stayed to deal with Dr. Marcel's screaming. I really appreciated that."

"Like you said before," Sofia said to Hernández, "a lot of them ignore us. We go in, clean, and leave, and they never look up from their work. Others, though, will stop what they're doing to ask how my day's been, how my kids are doing, what my plans are for break. There are a lot of good people who work here, but not all."

"That sounds like just about any job," Hernández said, and both women nodded.

There was a buzz and they both looked at the bands around

their left wrists. "Sorry," Sofia said. "It's the headmaster. We need to get back to work."

"Of course," Hernández said, pulling business cards out of the inside pocket of her blazer. "I don't want to get either of you in trouble. Thank you so much for speaking with me. If you think of anything—anything at all—that might help my investigation, please contact me. Okay?"

They both studied the cards, nodded, and slipped them into their pockets.

"It was nice meeting you," I said.

Sofia smiled but Isabel gave me a wary look before they both hurried off down the long hall.

"Let's head out. I've already kept you longer than I intended," Hernández said, letting me go first down the stairs while she tied together the ends of the police tape I'd snapped.

On the drive home, I rolled down the window. It was a beautiful warm day, and I was very happy to be out of that building. "So, do you think you'll get to handcuff the headmaster after all?"

The corner of her mouth kicked up. "I'll look into it, but he doesn't strike me as someone who wants to invite scandal into his precious school. Firing the dean gets the job done."

"If he's allowed to fire him," I said. "Schools like this have boards or trustees or something. It may not be his call to can the dean."

"I'll look into that too. I also really want to talk to Mr. Reed. He's no longer affiliated with the school and worked there going on twenty years. Hopefully, he can tell me about the power dynamics in the school: grudges, scandals, affairs, bribes. All the things that make people kill."

"And that building fund," I added. "What were they really paying for? In the vision, the killer was arguing on behalf of a student the dean was suspending for plagiarism."

Hernández shook her head. "I've got so much bouncing around up there, I forgot to ask you what you saw. Can you run through it for me?"

I did and she pulled over to take a few more notes.

"The dean said, *You should know that better than anyone.* Is that right?"

"Yup." I checked the time on my phone and groaned internally. This was taking way too much of the day. I also had a missed call from my mother. Maybe she had the fingerprints for me.

"Odd phrasing, don't you think?" she asked.

"Yes. He was dismissive of the person—who feels male—that he was talking to. But from what Sofia and Isabel said, he was a pretty cranky guy. The fact that he wasn't rude to the cleaning staff, and instead defended them, makes me think well of him."

Hernández nodded. "Can you imagine working at a place where every time you busted a kid for doing stupid kid stuff, instead of saying sorry, they hit you with, *Do you know who my father is?* You could not pay me enough. If I had that job, I'd be pretty cranky too."

She turned off the long road from the school and buildings began to pop up again. "Tutoring. Do teachers tutor on the side to make extra money or was this not a teacher? I need to find out who the new housemaster is, see if he also tutors. You keep seeing that corridor and they said the male housemaster's room was down there."

"In the vision, the killer attacked when the dean refused to listen. He was on his way to call parents. So, was the point of the killing to keep the dean from talking to a parent? To keep the kid from getting in trouble? The dean might be gone, but the teacher who discovered the plagiarism is still there. Killing the dean doesn't make the cheating disappear." I had a horrible thought. "Then again, we have a dead teacher too."

"We do. I'll talk with Arthur, see if we can find a connection beyond working at the same school." Hernández tapped a finger on the steering wheel, thinking. "These places are seen as a pipeline to the Ivy League. We hear about parents and schools doing shady stuff to make sure junior gets into his school of choice.

Grease the right palms, do well on the right tests, their future is set."

I nodded, considering. "And paying people to take those tests and ace them for you is not unheard of. Maybe that was what the tutor was freaking out about. He wasn't tutoring. He was writing the paper, for a fee, and he screwed up and plagiarized. Can't have Daddy know the money he spent for an A ended up getting the kid an F. That's going to screw up his transcript."

"Hmm." She put on her sunglasses. "I like that. Another avenue to investigate."

"Will they let you, or will they shut it down?"

"I have enough. I can convince my captain to keep working. After I drop you off, I'll head to the coroner. I need them to confirm blunt force trauma that's inconsistent with a fall. We'll see."

TWENTY-ONE

Untwisting Curses

When Hernández dropped me off, I saw that same middle-aged man was back, parked on the side of the road, staring at the mural. *Shit.* His car door opened as I walked past him.

"Excuse me," he said.

I turned, fingers twitching, readying a spell. "Yes?"

"Are you hiring?" His eyes kept darting to the mural over my shoulder.

"No," I lied. "I already have a full staff." He was right, though. I really needed to get on that. Part of me was hoping Hester would work here part-time. I wanted her away from all the memories, all the photos of her dead daughter. Forcing herself to leave the house and interact with others a few hours a week might be healing for her.

I'd also been considering asking my Aunt Elizabeth's kids, Frank and Faith, if either or both wanted a job. They were still teenagers and, like their parents, kind people. Which was very uncommon for cousins of mine.

"I can do all kinds of work," he said. Sweat was beading on his forehead.

"That's nice. There are lots of other galleries around town and

Carmel has tons." I was having a hard time telling if he was just socially awkward or menacing. Declan hadn't liked him being near me, but that could've been a wolf thing.

"Those places aren't the same." He rubbed his wispy mustache. "I'm supposed to be here, with you and the tentacles. I just know it." His vehemence had me taking a step back.

"I see," I said, flicking my fingers.

He checked his watch. "I have to go."

"That'd be good. And just as a reminder, this is private property. Do you see the signs posted? You can't park there, okay?"

He rushed off without answering, which was fine. I was happy to have him gone.

My phone buzzed. Declan.

"Hey, how's construction going?" I asked.

"That obsessive guy's car is back. Be careful when you get home."

"Already here." I watched while the sweaty man got behind the wheel and started it up. He pulled out without checking traffic, causing a minivan to slam on the brakes.

"I sent him on his way," I explained.

"Good. There's something off about that guy."

"No argument," I said, rounding the gallery to the deck. "By the way, I need tall gates on either end of the deck to keep weirdos from sneaking up on me."

"I was thinking the same thing," he said. His voice had become easier to hear. He must have walked outside, away from the construction noise. They were still in demolition mode over there. They were being careful, though, as the building had a light smattering of structural damage. "I sketched out some ideas. I'll show you tonight. Are you still up for dinner?"

"You bet." I glanced around. Still no tennis ball. Hmm, maybe something happened to our ball.

"Great. I'll see you later."

"Have fun tearing stuff apart." I opened the back door of the studio.

Laughing, he said, "Always."

After disconnecting, I dropped my backpack and got a new tennis ball from the canister. I found the orange flippy thing to make the ball sail and went back out. The sun was so bright, reflecting off the waves, I wished I had sunglasses.

"Wilbur! Are you around?" I flung the ball, waiting for him to arrow out from under the deck. When he didn't, I drooped. Where was he? Maybe I'd go swimming later. He always seemed to find me when I was in the water. I couldn't do it now, though. The field trip to Cypress Academy had put me behind schedule.

Weaving my hair into a loose braid, I went in and got back to work painting the gallery.

Hours later, I felt my phone buzz in my pocket. I peeled the rubber gloves off my regular ones and fished the phone out of my pocket. Mom.

"Hey, Mom." I put her on speakerphone so I could keep going.

"Darling, are you at the gallery?"

"Yep. I'm painting the walls."

"Oh, good. I'm on my way to pick you up. We need to go to your Gran's. She says she feels a dark presence circling the house."

I sealed the paints, cleaned the brushes with a spell—which I hated doing, as it often left the hairs of the brushes in a sorry state. Climbing down the scaffolding, I said, "I'll be out front in a minute."

I studied the wall so far and felt like I was making good progress. It wasn't there yet. I needed to think about how to amplify the illusion of ocean water.

Grabbing my backpack, I locked up and jogged around the side of the gallery. Damn Calliope. Why wouldn't she leave Gran alone?

Mom wasn't in front yet, so I paced. I did, of course, know why. Gran was the matriarch. She held the family in check. Cal and her demon wanted us in shambles so we'd be easier to pick apart. Was the goal money? Power? It wasn't as though Gran's power could be transferred upon her death.

I kicked a rock. Maybe laying waste to the family was the point. Tires kicked up pebbles behind me. I got ready to jump out of the way in case it was Sweaty Guy again. Thankfully, Mom's tasteful sedan pulled up beside me.

"I was with John and Roger at Hester's when your Gran called. John gave me the baby prints. They're in the back seat. We need to have you look for Calliope when we're done building wards," she said.

I glanced over my shoulder at the bag on the back seat. "Okay."

Gran didn't live far away, so we were there in no time. Mom slowed as we neared, turning through a narrow break in the foliage. Pacific Madrone and Monterey Pine created a canopy over the hidden driveway, with white camellia bushes, elderberry, hostas, and hydrangea filling in the pockets around the circular cobbled drive.

She parked by the glossy wooden front door, carved with protective sigils. Gran's house was like a bag of holding. It appeared to be a tiny forgotten stone cottage, clinging to the edge of a cliff. When you walked in, though—over polished wood floors, laid in intricate patterns mirroring the sigils on the door— the ceiling rose higher than the roof. A one-room hovel became a three-bedroom, three-bath showplace, with every room boasting huge windows overlooking the ocean.

Gran opened the door as we got out. "It's gone now. It was poking at the windows and doors, trying to slide past the wards."

I was happy to see anger and not fear on her face. "We'll bolster the wards, just like we did at the cannery, to keep it away."

Nodding, she waved us in.

When I walked through the door, I felt something off. Stopping short, I caused Mom to run into me.

"Really, Arwyn, what are you doing?" Bumping into people was rude and undignified. She wasn't happy I'd made her do it.

"Sorry, Mom." I stepped out of the way. "Could you two go in? There's something around the door that's bothering me."

They got out of my way and I moved in and out of the door,

pausing on the porch. Like a divining rod, I was trying to find the smudge of darkness attached to Gran's home. My head started to pound. "It's the door itself."

Taking off a glove, I touched the door.

Smoke hangs in the flickering torchlight. The heat is oppressive. Delicate hands work a mortar and pestle, grinding something into a paste. My head begins to throb in time with low chanting. I recognize the voice. Calliope is twisting a spell, doing black magic. On the large wooden table is a headless chicken and an open book, a grimoire.

The ancient spell book is bound in cracked, peeling leather. I can't read the open page, but it contains cramped handwriting and stains that have amassed over the ages. She picks up an athame, a wicche's ceremonial dagger, and slices her palm, dripping blood into the concoction. Next, she tips in the contents of a small vial and then circles the pestle counter-clockwise, the chanting getting louder and faster.

Outdoors now. In the night. Gran's house. That same delicate hand dips a small paintbrush into a jar holding the cursed potion and she begins to alter the blessed sigils on Gran's door, unwinding, one by one, the protections.

Blinking, I caught myself before I hit the ground. Touching those damn curses was what was making me so sick. "We need a nulling draught," I told my mom as I slipped my glove back on.

"What is it?" Gran asked.

I explained what I'd seen. "We need to wash all the sigils, null all the spells, protective and cursed, and then we need to build the wards again."

Mom and Gran stared at me. "It took days for us to create those wards. A nulling draught won't undo our work."

"No," Gran admitted, "but the three of us working together can strip it down and build it back up. Good," she said, rubbing her hands together. "We know what she did, and we know how to fix it. Let's get started."

We worked well into the evening, hands held, as the Three touched each sigil with our magic, purifying it and then rebuilding the ward. As each mark was stripped and again blessed by the

Goddess, a part of the door burned bright and then went out. When we were finally done, the door was filled with scorch marks, but all the protections and then some were back.

I hadn't been one of the original ward makers. That had happened before I was born. Now, though, there was fae magic threaded through, making it far more difficult for a sorcerer to dismantle.

Since Gran had felt the presence circling her house, we did the same, looking for weak spots. I found two more areas where Calliope had corrupted the wards. Afterward, exhausted, we went in and collapsed in the living room, Gran in her rocker by the fireplace, Mom on the couch, and me in the chair to the side.

My phone buzzed. When I pulled it out of my pocket, I saw I had missed calls and texts. Groaning, I got back to my feet and went out to Gran's patio, overlooking the ocean.

"Hey. Sorry I missed your messages."

"Oh, thank God." Declan's voice was grumbly and concerned. "I thought that creep had come back and taken you."

"He's human. He can't hurt me."

"Except if he touches your skin, puts you in a trance, and steals you while you're out. A lot of damage can be done to an unconscious person."

"That's the stuff I try not to think about or I'd isolate myself even more. I'm sorry you've been worried, though. I'm at my gran's. Mom called and said Gran was feeling a dark presence lurking around her home." I explained the rest, including the fact that we'd just completed our work here.

"Are you safe outside?" Poor guy. I'd really scared him.

"Sure. When we create the wards, we're not just creating a magical seal on the house. We're extending the protections to her property. All bets are off out on the main road, but on Gran's property, we're fine."

"I can run it for you, see if I pick up her scent anywhere. She may have planted curses in other spots."

I was about to say we had it, but this was Gran we were talking about. We needed her protected. "Yes. Thank you. That would settle our minds."

"Good. I'm on my way."

I went back in and explained that Declan was coming to check the grounds. Mom thought it unnecessary, but Gran was grateful.

"Don't be ridiculous, Sybil. We need to know if she and her demon planted more curses on my property, and we have a Quinn in the family who can check. You say thank you when he arrives," Gran said.

"He's not in the family," Mom protested.

Gran pushed back and began to rock in her chair, seeming to catch a second wind. "You keep telling yourself that, if it makes you feel better."

The next few minutes were tense, but when I heard Declan's truck, I headed out to the drive. The first thing he did was pull me into a bruising hug, kissing the top of my head.

"You had me worried."

"Sorry. I know we had a date. I forgot to contact you before we got started." I shrugged in his arms. "I'm not used to anyone besides Mom and Gran looking for me."

"That's something we'll both need to get used to. And it's not your fault. I was the one letting my mind run away with what could have happened." He kissed my lips. "I'm glad you're okay."

"Thanks." I grinned into his chest. This was nice.

He gave me one more squeeze and then let go. "Let me get undressed and I'll shift." He went back to the far side of his truck, opened the door, and started to strip, dropping his clothes on the seat.

"Gran's getting her security checked and I get a show. Win-win." I was trying hard to play it cool and not ogle him, but he was built like a god, so it was tough.

He bent down to unlace his boots, step out, and then lose his jeans and boxers. He gave me a wink and then shifted. Just like that. In the span of a blink, a huge black wolf was shaking out his fur and rounding the truck to me.

TWENTY-TWO

Clearing the Air

Goddess, he was gorgeous in either form. "Can I?" I held out my hand. He chuffed and then ducked under my fingers. He'd been standing there talking to me two seconds ago and now he was this incredible animal, letting me pet him. He rubbed his head against my leg and then trotted off, around the side of Gran's house.

Eventually, the front door opened and Mom and Gran came out.

"Declan's checking the property."

Gran nodded and then they both sat on the bench at the end of the porch. "Tell us about this grimoire you saw on Calliope's table," Gran said.

I walked over and waved my hand—a small spell to clean off any dirt or pollen on the porch—and then sat, leaning against a thick wooden pillar.

"Oh, don't sit on the ground," Mom admonished.

"I'm fine and I'm wearing work overalls." Folding my legs up, I thought about what I'd seen. "It was about the size of the family grimoire. There was something about it, though. My head was pounding from the chanting, but when I looked at it, I felt the shove to look away." I closed my eyes, trying to remember everything.

"Picturing it is causing my head to throb again." I looked up, trying to shake off the pain. "Did I tell you Dave thought there was another Corey family grimoire, one containing black magic that's passed down from sorcerer to sorcerer?"

Mom rubbed her forehead, clearly frustrated. Gran, on the other hand, stared out into the night, barely nodding.

"That sounds right to me," Gran finally said. "There are too many of them in our family. A cursed grimoire, luring in the cruel, the weak, the power hungry. That sounds right."

"How do we destroy it?" Mom asked.

"We can't," Gran said just as I said, "What would be the point?"

Mom looked between the two of us.

"It's an ancient book, oozing black magic," I explained. "And although I've never seen one or thought about it before this moment, I'm getting this pain in the pit of my stomach. I think it's one of those books bound in human skin."

Mom looked as queasy as I felt.

"I couldn't read the page that was open. I'd thought the handwriting was too spindly or I was viewing it from too far away, but now I think it was another language. Some kind of demonic script. I wish Dave could see what's in my head so he could tell us if that's right."

"Contact this Dave," Gran said, "and explain what you saw. Your description might be enough for him to identify a demonic grimoire."

I brought my knees up and rested my sore head. "I will."

"I'll get the fingerprints while we wait," Mom said, going to her car.

My head was killing me and she's all *dance, monkey, dance.*

Handing me the frame, she said, "I know you're in pain right now, but we're also all together, which might strengthen you." She sat beside Gran again. "At least try, Arwyn."

"What is this now?" Gran asked.

"Sylvia had her girls' hand...."

I stopped listening, trying to quiet the pounding in my head so I could see something. I undid the brackets at the back of the frame, taking out the sheet of thick paper holding Calliope's baby handprint and footprint. Head bowed, breathing slowly, I recited the finding spell from Sam's grimoire and slipped off my glove, touching the fingerprint.

Images flash through my mind, a strobe light of Calliope's life. Being held and fussed over, crawling and then walking, running to keep up with her sister. The cousins. Being left out of big kid games. Watching Serena learn to harness and use her magic. Resentment building. She tries in secret to duplicate what her sister has done, but it doesn't work. She's too young, just as Mom keeps telling her, but everyone knows Arwyn could do magic as a baby.

The flashes continue in my head: school, report cards not as high as Serena; mirror, not as beautiful as her mother or sister; magic, not as powerful as the rest of the cousins. They treat her like she's still a baby but she finds she enjoys the coddling, enjoys that Serena often gets yelled at for not being nicer to her baby sister.

What she used to hate, she now understands is an advantage. She's small and looks young and innocent. She uses it to throw suspicion off herself, usually directing it at her sister. She loves that her father still picks her up and refers to her as his Little One while he only holds Serena's hand. She often squirms so he has to use both arms to hold her, dropping Serena's hand. Calliope loves smiling over her father's shoulder at Serena, who now walks alone.

Aunt Abigail, though, she sees Calliope as special. She singles her out for advanced magical training. Eventually, she introduces her to her shadowy helper who makes her magic stronger, and Calliope wants it all. She wants her own helper and all the power.

She wants them to stop talking when she moves into a room, to cower if she's angry. She wants a seat on the Council so she can learn all the secrets and use them to her advantage. She's smarter. They should be listening to her. But, no, they want to wait for that stupid half-breed

Arwyn on the Council rather than her. Years, years they wait for the bitch when she's standing right there, being the dutiful daughter and sister, chauffeuring that old bag around. They all take it as their due, never really looking at who Calliope has grown into, never respecting the power at her fingertips.

Well, she's showing them now, isn't she? They fear her and she delights in it. Her greatest joy, though, is in finally getting even with all the people who have slighted or belittled her over the years. Mom, beautiful, powerful, beloved Mom, was starting to look at Cal strangely, starting to ask questions. Mom had Sybil's ear. It wouldn't be long before she shared her suspicions about her daughter.

Cal had to move sooner than she'd expected, but it was okay. Freeing, even. Her friend had told her it would be, and he was right. How could she fulfil her destiny as the head of the Corey coven with her babying mother still around? Her mother wasn't a bad person. Her death, though, was needed in order to lob a grenade into the family and then step into her place. The more Sybil relied on Cal, the more she'd realize she couldn't do without her. She and her friend would see to that.

Gran is old. She'll be easy to dispose of, especially since Cal has never liked her anyway. The old biddy always watched her a little too closely. Burn down the gallery with Arwyn in it and Cal rises as the head of the family, with lots of inheritance money coming her way.

Torchlight flickers in a stone room as Calliope ascends the stairs to the main floor. The rooms are empty and her footsteps echo throughout. She goes to the back window, arms folded, and watches the waves. There is a small, bare patio and boulders at the water line. Spray plumes up as wave after wave hits the rocks.

She smiles, walking to the kitchen. Soon the favored one will get hers and Calliope will laugh, finally rid of the half-breed.

Eyes fluttering, I heard a sharp intake of breath and then a big furry head was on my shoulder, rubbing against my cheek. He sniffed and quietly whined. Following his gaze, I saw the finger that had touched the handprint was blackened. Mom and Gran began to recite a healing spell and I joined in. On the third repetition, the black was gone and my finger no longer felt numb.

Lifting my other hand, I scratched under his chin a moment before he slipped away, padding through Gran's front door. Mom sat up straight, her expression alarmed. Gran patted her daughter's knee and we waited.

"Well," Mom said. "What did you see?"

A moment later, he came out with my backpack, dropping it beside me.

"What?" I asked.

He nudged it closer to me and then trotted to his truck.

Did he want me to leave? Ugh. Dumbass. I unzipped the backpack and pulled out the honey bottle, pouring seawater on my hands and then patting it on my forehead, my cheeks, the back of my neck.

"Oh, that's right," Mom said.

"Dad's DNA to the rescue," I mumbled.

"Better?" Declan asked from the far side of his truck.

"Yeah. Thanks for reminding me." The pounding was no longer making me nauseated.

"What did you see?" Mom repeated.

I explained as best I could. "The flashes made it difficult. Those are my impressions of what was happening. My interpretations could be off."

Mom and Gran sat silently, thinking.

"She was right," Gran finally said. "There was something about that child that always seemed off to me." She stared out at the trees surrounding us. "Of course, I hadn't thought sorcery. I thought maybe drug addiction or kleptomania."

"I didn't see it," Mom said. "She was Sylvia's baby, and I didn't see it. I thought she was a sweet little thing. Not as powerful, sure, but a good girl." She blew out a breath. "I never saw it."

"And we still don't know where she is," Gran said, "other than in an empty house on the ocean."

"It was large. The rooms she walked through were huge and the view was amazing. This wasn't a hut in the woods, which is what I was afraid of. At least oceanfront property gives us a place to look. Maybe we should rent a boat and sail along the coast until we see or feel something dark."

"Yes," Gran said, patting my mother's knee again. "Let's set that up."

"I will." Tapping my leg with her foot, Mom gestured to the bear bottle. "Is it working?"

"Mostly. The ocean always makes me feel good. I was helping on that child killing case last month and was struggling. Declan thought to go out to a stream in the family's backyard and pat fresh running water on me. It helped. Visions often make me sick, so I tried bottled ocean water to see if it would ease the pain, and it did."

"Good," Gran said. She looked up at the sound of Declan's boots on the cobblestones. She turned to her daughter. "I don't know why that never occurred to us."

"Probably because we never talk about my dad and try to hide the things that are different about me because of him."

When I felt Declan's hand on my head, I realized I'd said the quiet part out loud. I dropped my wet hands from my face just in time to watch my mother walk into the house.

Gran sighed, watching her daughter disappear.

I wanted to talk with her about the other vision I'd had about her and her own prophetic dream of a Cassandra child, but now wasn't the time—or maybe it was. This had always been the pattern. I asked a question, make a reference to Dad, and she got angry or sad or something and walked away.

I raised an arm and Declan pulled me to my feet. "You two stay here. I'll be back." I stopped at the door, remembering. "Wait. Did you find any curses on Gran's property?"

Declan shook his head and sat beside Gran. "All clear."

"Well, that's a relief," she said, but I was already walking through the door, looking for my mom.

I started for the kitchen and then saw movement out the back window. Mom, silhouetted against the night sky. Detouring to the door off the living room, I startled her when I stepped onto the patio.

"Arwyn, I thought you'd be leaving with that wolf." It wasn't cold out, but her arms were crossed tightly.

"I didn't mean to upset you." I moved closer but she walked to the edge of the cliff, overlooking the roaring ocean.

"I'll try to stop by tomorrow to see your progress. I know you're tired. You should go home and try to get some sleep. I'd like to be left alone now," Mom said, her face tipped up to the moon.

"I hear the dismissal loud and clear, Mom. I've heard it most of my life. I need to tell you something, though."

"Oh, darling, I'm not up to hearing about what a horrible, cold mother I am."

"I never said that." I've thought it plenty, but I never said it.

"You didn't need to. Lots of family members over the years have felt the need to inform me." She closed her eyes, her face still lifted to the wind.

"They're just jealous and more than a little afraid of you."

She barked out a harsh laugh and shook her head. "I'm fine. You should get back. I know you have lots of work to finish."

This was when I'd normally take off, happy to get away from the crushing expectations they had for me. "Not this time, Mom."

Opening her eyes, she glanced over and sighed. "All right. What is it you need to say?"

"I saw you in a vision."

She waited, brow furrowed.

"You were little and had had a nightmare about having a Cassandra daughter who would live a short, miserable life before walking into the ocean."

Mom's eyes filled with tears, but she didn't look away.

"Great-Gran told you the Goddess had blessed you and that you needed to find a father for the child who was powerful, maybe even more so than you, so that I could live."

She didn't speak.

"And you did, because here I am. It hasn't been an easy life, but you made me strong enough to survive it. Thank you."

The tears finally slipped over her lashes.

"Did you hate him? Was he cruel?" I paused, not wanting the answer but needing to ask. "Did he hurt you? Is that why we never talk about him?"

She lifted one hand to her mouth, as though trying to keep it all in, and then shook her head. Finally, behind her fingers she whispered, "I loved him."

"What?"

Wiping at the tears, she nodded. "I did. I loved him so much and he loved me."

"But then…"

"I wanted to be with him all the time, but I had responsibilities to the family. I was on the Council and missing meetings. People relied on me, and I was letting them down."

"Mom, you're entitled to a life. Your siblings didn't give up their partners for the sake of the family."

She shook her head. "It's different for me. I had been gifted by the Goddess, chosen to be the next to lead. Like your great grandmother and Gran, the health, welfare, fortunes of this family have fallen to me to protect."

"Okay, but you could do that with a partner. Gran and Great-Gran had husbands."

"They had wicche husbands." Anger underlined her words. She turned back to the ocean. "I was young. The elders set the expectations and held me to them. It was one thing for me to bear a half-fae child who could help the family and an entirely other thing for me to bring that fae man into the family, for there to be other half-fae children sullying the Corey line."

"This family is lousy with sorcerers and they look the other way, but bring in a fae man and they hold the pure bloodline? That's it, Mom. We're going scorched earth on this whole fucking family."

She let out a breath and smiled through the tears as she pulled me into a hug. "I wish I had your strength."

"You're the strongest person I know," I said, hugging her back. This was so unlike her, the tears and hugs.

She stepped back. "My darling girl, don't confuse strength with good posture."

"And don't you run yourself down. You stand up to everything thrown at you," I insisted.

"Not everything. They told me I had to give him up and I did." She shook her head. "He was so angry with me, so disappointed."

"I'm sorry. I wish we both could have had him in our lives."

Reaching out, she tucked a stray curl behind my ear. The gusts off the ocean were gaining force. "I'm sorry my actions kept you from having a father. I knew you needed him, but I also knew I wasn't strong enough to turn him away again."

"I don't know if this will make you feel better or worse, but he's been keeping an eye on me."

Her expression went blank. "What?"

"Do you remember the seal I play fetch with?"

"Wilbur, yes." She *was* paying attention.

"Turns out he's a selkie. He introduced himself to me a few weeks ago. In his human form. He said he was there at my father's orders to keep an eye on me. And when Cal and her demon sent someone to burn down my gallery, a huge wave doused the whole building."

She walked closer to the edge, hugging herself in the cold wind. "When you were little, I used to take you to the beach to play so he could see you if he wanted."

I smiled. The image of Mom basically holding me up to the ocean to show me off was so odd and yet sweet. "And why you took over Great-Gran's house a stone's throw from the water?"

She nodded. "And why I always scheduled family get-togethers on the beach."

I laughed and she turned to look at me. "When I was little—I don't know, three or four—we were at the beach. I was sitting on the sand, playing with a shovel and pail. The waves sometimes touched me, like a kiss. Colin was being a jerk. Naturally. He took the pail and threw it into the surf and the very next wave brought it back to me."

Mom chuckled, her gaze avid.

"Well, that ticked him off, so he took both the shovel and pail, walked out farther, and threw them again. And the next wave returned them to my lap."

I hadn't seen a smile like this on my mother's face for far too long.

"He wasn't having that, so when the next wave came in, he kicked me over so I went face first into the water."

Mom's expression turned thunderous.

"I was fine. The water's never scared me. I felt a hand right me, so I was sitting again with my shovel and pail. At the same time, Colin was stung by a jellyfish."

Mom stepped forward and grabbed my elbow. "I remember that. It was chaos and he was screaming his head off. John was trying to get him to settle down so he could heal the sting."

"I guess. I wasn't paying much attention to him. I was looking in the water, trying to figure out who'd helped me."

She looked down at the ground, shaking her head. "He's been keeping an eye out for you all this time." Wistful, she looked out to sea.

I was about to leave her to her memories, but stopped myself. "Since we're finally talking about important stuff, can I ask something else?"

She turned and hesitantly nodded.

"I know I really let you and Gran down by not accepting a spot on the Council when I was a teenager. And seeing how hard it's been for the two of you because of that, I get the anger, but your—I don't know—coldness toward me started long before that."

She turned away from me, shaking her head.

I started this, so I was going to finish it. Talking to her back, I said. "I recently remembered when it started. I was young, still in the bedroom beside yours, and I'd had a horrible nightmare. I was crying inconsolably, and you came to hold me and hear what I'd seen. I'd told you about Aunt Sylvia's death, and you shut down, moved me to the turret room, and everything changed between us.

"I was ashamed of what I could do after that, tried to hide it. When I woke every night, I stayed in my new room, far from you, and learned to deal with it on my own. I know you loved Sylvia, probably more than anyone else in the world, but I don't understand why you've been so angry with me. I didn't *wish* her dead. I loved her too."

She was silent for so long, I didn't think she was going to answer me. I should have left before, when she was happy knowing Dad had been watching out for me. I shouldn't have upset her again. I guessed it didn't matter why. She was entitled to her own feelings.

I blew out a breath, ready to walk, but I saw that her shoulders were shaking. "Mom?"

"Is that really what you remember?" she finally choked out, still turned away.

"Yes."

She walked back to me, wiping at her tears, and gently cradled my face with her wet hands.

Mom hurries into my room and sits on the bed, rocking me. "It's okay, my love. It's all going to be okay." She rocks me, whispering assurances. "Do you want to tell me about your nightmare?"

I shake my head against her chest. "It's bad."

"I know, angel. They're always bad and I'm so sorry. We'll get through it together, though. You're not alone."

She rocks me for a long time, eventually singing softly to me, as I get sleepier and sleepier.

"The man hurt me, hurt me so bad."

Mom rears back. "What man? When?"

I stare into space. "He rips at my clothes. Crushes me—I can't breathe. His hands are around my neck. I was calling for you, over and over, but you didn't come. I was so scared and you didn't come." I looked up at her. "Why didn't you come?"

"I will," she says fiercely. "I'll always come."

I shake my head and sigh. "You don't." I extricate myself from the hug and roll over in bed. "You can go."

She stands, tears streaming down her face, clearly torn.

"Auntie Sylvia died," I mumble into the pillow. "Whispers. Something heavy is crushing her. She can't breathe too. I'm tired now."

Shellshocked, she slowly turns and walks from the room, closing the door quietly behind her.

I blinked my eyes open and Mom stood before me.

"You pushed *me* away. The next morning, you started moving your things to the turret room. I told you I wanted you close to me, and you'd sadly patted my hand and kept moving your clothes and toys."

She wiped at her wet face again. "I didn't know what to do. I was already worried about being a failure as a mother, trying to keep my little Cassandra healthy and happy. The visions were so hard on you. It was like your whole world shattered every time."

Wiping again, she said, "I was in my twenties, and I had this amazing little girl who saw so much, took all of it on her shoulders, and I didn't know what to do or how to help. And my baby, my little girl was dismissing me. My child knew I was failure and dismissed me."

"I'm sorry. I never felt that way. Not once," I said. "I thought you were angry with me for telling you about Sylvia."

Shaking her head, she looked down at my hand, which she had clutched tightly in her own. "I worried about Sylvia, of course. I talked with John and we both did whatever we could to keep her away from heavy things. We assumed her being crushed meant something heavy was going to fall on her. When she was in that car accident—what—sixteen years ago, John and I thought that was it. That was your vision and she'd survived it. We always made sure she drove the safest cars on the road, and she'd survived the vision.

"No. It wasn't Sylvia. You told me you were going to die horribly, in pain and alone, and I was going to do nothing to help. I was horrified. The Goddess had gifted me with you, and I'd screwed it up. I'd tried so hard to take care of you and I'd failed. You were going to die anyway."

Sniffing, she wiped at her face again. "You'd moved away from me. We were the only two people in that big house and you distanced yourself from me. Oh, how I cried. I couldn't sleep, knowing my baby had seen her own death, knowing I wouldn't be there to save her. It felt like you were trying to get used to dealing with the hard on your own. And after a while, I learned to harden my heart to the pain."

She squeezed my hand. "I've always loved you and been so incredibly proud of you. I know I can be hypercritical. I don't know why I—" She sighed. "I love you so much and I live in constant terror that something horrible is going to happen. That anxiety became anger with you for scaring me. I've missed so much time with you, fixating on losing you."

Rubbing her forehead, she said, "It makes no sense. I know. I was angry with you for going to Europe, not because of the Council—though some of that was there—it was mostly because you were across the world, putting yourself somewhere I couldn't run to help you. I worried every single day you were away that this is when it happens. I wouldn't be there to help because you were on another continent."

I pulled her into a hug. "I'm sorry, Mom. I've always loved you. All these years, I thought you didn't like me very much."

On a sob, she rocked me back and forth.

TWENTY-THREE

Otis Racoon's Jug Band

It was late and I was exhausted, but I did my best to stay awake while Declan drove me home. "So, it turns out my mom and dad loved each other."

He reached over and held my hand. "That's always the hope. What happened?"

"The family. Mom was expected to step into her role as next in line to lead. She missed Council meetings, let some things drop. You know, had a life. If he'd been a nice wicche, I think there would have been more leniency and understanding. Fae blood sullying the Corey line was a problem, though."

Declan's hand squeezed mine. "So it's okay for you to be half fae, as they need a Cassandra wicche to live a long life in order to help them. But any other little half-fae-ling running around is a threat to the supremacy of the Corey line?"

"Something like that."

"I'm surprised she didn't tell them to go fuck themselves." He turned onto the coast road.

"She was young—eighteen or nineteen—and had been groomed since birth to take the mantle when it was time. Telling them to fuck themselves would mean walking away from her family, from her whole world."

"They wouldn't have let her leave with you. She had all the power," he said.

"Maybe, but you don't have it if you don't know it. And she didn't." I blew out a breath and crossed my arms, staring at the moonlight dancing on the waves.

"What's wrong?" he asked. "Your scent changed."

"My—" Right. Wolves could smell emotions. Cool yet creepy. "It's just that I've always seen Gran as the one on my side. Great-Gran didn't care for me. I remember catching looks from her when I was little. She scared me. I don't think she trusted a half-fae seer. Gran, though, once she took over as the crone, always backed me up. Mom wanted me to stop playing in the abandoned, horribly dangerous cannery. Gran tells me to go have fun."

Declan gave a chuff of annoyance.

"What?"

He shook his head. "Finish your thought." He parked in front of the gallery and cut off the engine.

It felt so wrong to say anything against Gran, but... "Her daughter was happy and in love. She was pregnant and Gran didn't step in to stop the rest of the family, to defend her daughter." I scrubbed my hands over my face. "Now that I know the story, all the times Gran rolled her eyes at Mom, sided with me against her—damn, those were such dick moves."

I started to tear up. Saying anything against Gran hurt my heart. "What? Her daughter was just a tool, the conduit to a healthy Cassandra wicche? If she meant so little, let her be with her love. If she's powerful—and she is—and next in line, then show her the proper respect. Recognize her choices as her own, not subject to committee approval."

"Yes, but like your mother, your Gran was also conditioned since infancy to follow the word of the elders. And given your memory of your great grandmother, she might have tried but was shot down."

"Yeah. There's that. I just wish she could have been more obviously supportive of her own daughter, the way she was of me. It makes me question…"

"If she was indulgent of you, her granddaughter, or of you, the Corey's Cassandra?"

I unbuckled and leaned into him. "Yeah."

Tapping my forehead gently, he said, "And what are you really thinking in there?"

Grinning, I looked up at him. "Getting my mom and dad back together."

"And there she is." He unbuckled his seat belt, grabbed my backpack, and stepped out of the truck. "Step one in your quest would seem be to be meeting him."

I slammed the door, and he caught my hand in his as we walked around the side of the gallery. "Yes. That seems like a good step one."

"It occurs to me," he said, "that someone has a big grand opening of her new art gallery coming up. Maybe your dad might want to attend."

Declan and I were talking quietly and the ocean was loud, so it was odd when he stopped walking and put a finger in front of his lips to shh me. Grinning, he motioned me forward.

As I was sure he wouldn't blithely send me into danger, I ran around the corner, setting off the security lights, and found three little raccoons on their hind legs, front paws out, like they were warding off velociraptors, completely frozen in the sudden light. All three were crowded around the back door of my studio, no doubt trying to figure out how to break in and steal baked goods.

"I can see you, you know." Two of them went down to all fours and backed away. The third was still frozen. I crouched down. "Aww, buddy. It's okay." I realized he was looking over my shoulder at Declan. "Squat down, scary wolf."

He did, handing me my backpack. "I smell a muffin in there. That might help."

"Ooh, good idea." I unzipped the top and pulled out the

muffin from yesterday that I'd wrapped in a paper towel. I broke it into three pieces and tossed them out for Otis and his siblings.

The nervous one by the back door finally relaxed and reached for the muffin. The other two scampered back and grabbed their own. Declan stood, pulling me with him, and we sat on the nearby bench, watching the raccoons nibble away. The nervous one stuffed the whole piece in and then moved back to a safe distance to chew.

"She's scared of me," Declan said. "The closer I get to the full moon, the stronger the wolf scent."

I turned and sniffed his shoulder. "I just smell laundry detergent and warm Declan skin, not wolf. Of course, I'm not sure I'd be able to identify wolf smell. I didn't notice a different smell when you were in your fur."

He tapped my nose. "That's because this isn't as sensitive as theirs. They see human but they smell wolf."

"Oh." I nodded, watching my little friends. "If you guys are still hungry, I can get you more." I turned to Declan. "I don't know how healthy it is for them to just be having muffins, though."

He laughed, causing the nervous one to move farther away. "They're raccoons. They eat garbage. They're fine."

"Okay, good. Wait right here, guys." I unlocked the back door and went in, closing it behind me. I didn't want to chase baby raccoons around the studio. Balancing four muffins, I went back out, placed three on the deck, near each of the raccoons, and gave the fourth to Declan.

"Thank you. I'm starving."

"I'm sorry I screwed up our dinner date." Watching the three, I decided Otis' siblings needed names.

"Not your fault."

I knew which one was Otis. Don't ask me why. I just did. They looked identical, but I knew he was the one in the middle. "Can you tell if the ones on the right and left of Otis are male or female? They need names."

Declan lifted his face, scenting the air. "Female by the door and male by the railing."

Studying the nervous one, I said, "You, I shall name Daisy." She paused midbite and then continued eating. I watched the third for a few minutes. "It's got to be Jasper."

"Otis, Daisy, and Jasper, huh?" Declan tugged on my braid. "Do they play banjos?"

"Otis is on the banjo. Daisy plays the washboard. And Jasper… has one of those moonshine jugs he blows into."

Declan kissed the back of my head. "I think you need to paint that."

"I don't paint that kind of—" I mean, I could. It might be a nice change from some of the other paintings I do. "Maybe a collection geared toward children and nurseries. That's a thought. Maybe watercolors or line drawings. I'll think about it and experiment. But not now. I have a gallery to get ready."

Declan's stomach grumbled loudly. "Sorry. Werewolf metabolism and I shifted tonight, adding to the need to eat soon. I have to ask. Do you have any meat I can cook? Otherwise, I'll run out and pick us up some dinner." He put a finger under my chin and tipped up my face so he could see me in the moonlight. "Or are you too tired for company? I can head out, if you are."

Leaning into him, I said, "I'm very tired and emotionally wrung out, but I would love for you to stay, and I have a beef stew in the freezer I can heat up. I also have some smoked salmon you can have while the stew is heating."

"Perfect," he said, putting me on my feet and ushering me to the studio door.

"Good night, Otis, Daisy, and Jasper!" I called. "Sweet dreams, Cecil, Charlie, and Herbert! Oh." I stopped Declan before he followed me in. "Can you see if Wilbur's tennis ball is on the deck? I haven't seen him for a little while. I'm getting worried."

"Sure." He stepped back out and I went to the kitchen.

If I was going to date a werewolf, I needed to up my meat

game. I should probably get a barbecue. No. Better yet, he gets one and all barbecuing happens over there. Yeah. That works.

I plated the salmon and left it on my worktable with a fork, napkin, and beer while I went into my freezer, looking for the container of stew. I'd just turned around when I bumped into Declan with an empty plate.

"Dude, chew your food."

Grinning, he rinsed off the plate and put it in the dishwasher. "That helped take the edge off. Thank you. It was getting painful."

I gave him the container on my counter with four muffins. "Have at it. This will take a few minutes."

He took them and sat on the couch, polishing them off in eight bites.

After defrosting it, I finally had the stew on the stovetop, heating up. I turned and found him watching me. "In the truck, when I was talking about me playing in this abandoned cannery, you got angry, but then told me to finish my thought. Why did you get angry?"

"It doesn't matter." He shook his head, placing the empty muffin carrier on the coffee table.

"Why?"

He sighed. "I don't want to say anything negative about your family. You have one and it's large and complicated. Some are evil, others incredibly kind. I don't have that, have never had that. It was just my aunt and me, so my perspective is probably skewed."

Stirring the stew, I considered his words. "I'll take all of that into consideration, but I'd like to know what was going on in your head. I've shared a ton about me, and it hasn't been easy."

"Okay. I like your gran. I do. But undermining your mom, always being on your side, even when you wanted to do something dangerous—your mom was right. You shouldn't have been playing in an abandoned cannery—it feels manipulative. She was keeping the Cassandra close and loyal while freezing out her daughter. It rubs me the wrong way." He paused a moment. "But maybe I'm just pissed that they don't want mixed blood in your family."

I turned back to the stove and continued stirring. It was starting to bubble. "Almost ready." Ignoring the tears running down my face, I pulled one of my mixing bowls out of the cupboard and poured the contents of the pot into it.

"Arwyn?" His voice was deep, grumbly, and too sympathetic. I didn't want to cry, didn't want to think about this at all. If I could have gone back in time and unasked the question, I would have.

I did a quick glamour spell so my face looked normal, and brought Declan his dinner.

He put it aside and held out his hand for me. "I'm sorry. I shouldn't have said anything."

"No. I'm fine. You eat, okay. I'm just going to run upstairs to the bathroom. My stomach is off." I climbed the stairs quickly, went into the bathroom, and closed the door. I tried to hold it in. My stomach hurt from trying to hold back the tide. When a gasp escaped, I turned on the shower to mask it.

Crying into a towel, I rethought a million interactions with my mom and gran, recasting the villain. I tried to convince myself there were no villains, just different levels of love and loyalty, but after hearing what my mom had been going through, to have her own mother rolling her eyes and indulging me hurt my heart. I'd spent most of my life misunderstanding my mom's fear of losing me, but Gran knew. She never pulled me aside to explain why my mom was the way she was. She let me disrespect her. Mom ended up with no love and a daughter that was a hostile brat.

I'd been too young to understand why my mother seemed cold and distant. As a child, I'd decided she disapproved of me, and I'd held onto that belief my whole life. All the years lost because I couldn't see her clearly.

TWENTY-FOUR

I Think You Need a Day Off from Evil. It's Really Affecting Your Mood

A soft knock sounded at the door and then Declan walked in, pulling me into his arms and turning off the shower. "I'm sorry."

I shook my head into his chest. "It's stupid."

"It's not. They're your family and you love them." He squeezed his big arms around me, kissing the top of my head. A moment later, his stomach rumbled.

I wiped my face and leaned back. "Let me see what else I can find you."

"No. I still have the stew downstairs. I haven't eaten it yet."

"Why not? You're starving." I broke away from him and snagged a wad of toilet paper to dry my face.

"Did you think I was just going to sit down there eating while you were up here crying?"

"Kind of. Yeah." I threw the wad in the trash and went for the door. "Come on. Enough of that. Time to eat."

Declan reached for me as I walked by. "Arwyn."

"Nope. Let's go." I went downstairs and checked his bowl. "Still hot. Let me know if you want it hotter." I went to the kitchen. "In fact, I have some sourdough rolls you can eat with it. Give me a minute." I defrosted them with a spell and then popped them in the oven. "They won't be exactly like coming out of their first bake, but they heat up pretty well." I turned to him and found him watching me again. "Do you like butter with your bread?"

"Sure, but how about if you sit with me and we'll watch a British mystery again? Something to take your mind off everything else." He ate a large spoonful. "And this is delicious. Thanks for dinner."

"I'm glad you like it. My mom made it. I bake. I don't know how to do all the other stuff." I took the rolls out, split and buttered them, and then brought one to Declan and bit into the other. The warmth was nice. What I needed.

"You should eat something besides a roll." He held out a spoon of stew again and this time, I took it. "Why don't you finish it? You gave me four servings."

"Six. This roll is good for now. I'm not up to eating a lot." I took another bite and enjoyed the crusty, buttery-ness. "Tea. I could use some tea." I went back to brew myself a pot before returning to Declan and the couch. By then, he had the screen down and the guide up.

I don't have a standard television. I had a screen built into the ceiling that comes down on a remote, with a mounted projector and some streaming services. I don't watch shows very often, usually reading in the evenings. I used this side of my studio as my living room, but it was still a huge open studio space. I had storage closets across the room from the couch and didn't want to mount a screen on a closet door, and I had no desire for a free-standing screen at the edge of the lounging area. I would have knocked that thing over a dozen times when I was moving around thirty-foot tentacles in here. Phil, my contractor, suggested this setup and it'd worked well.

"Are we sticking with the vicar solving crimes in his sleepy yet murderous village? Or should we watch some baseball?"

"Murderous villagers, please." I slouched down, put my feet on the coffee table, and held the mug of tea over my stomach, soothing the squirmy feelings writhing inside me.

Later, after the body had been discovered and the vicar had begun his investigations, I felt the mug tip and woke with a start.

"You were about to spill." Declan put the mug on the coffee table and then patted his chest.

I snuggled in and was out.

I awoke in darkness, confused. No nightmares had ripped me from sleep, though I vaguely recalled whispering. Then I remembered last night. What time was it? Patting my pockets, I looked for my phone. Nothing. Flicking my fingers, I turned on the lights and instantly regretted it. Too bright.

My phone was on the end table, plugged into a charger. Aww, that was sweet of him. Two texts and two missed calls.

Declan: Good morning! Hopefully you slept a good long time. Call me when you're up.

I would.

Mom: Are you okay? Call me right away.

Great. I checked the phone messages and sure enough, they were from Mom. I hit call back.

"Where have you been?"

"I was asleep. What's the matter?" I went upstairs to get cleaned up.

"Asleep? Since when do you—never mind. My tea shop was broken into last night. I want to pick you up and bring you here. We need to know if it was just humans causing trouble or if Calliope sent someone here to poison my tea leaves and who knows what else."

"Okay. I just need to get ready. I'll be out as soon as I can."

"Good. I'm on my way."

Tying my hair up, I turned on the shower. There was no time to deal with my hair, so a body shower it was. Knowing how my mother felt about overalls, I put on my black jeans, black slip-on sneakers, and a teal, long-sleeve top. Mascara, lip gloss, and I was ready to go. I even had gloves the same color as the top.

Grabbing my backpack, I walked through the gallery and headed out the front door. With a flick of my wrist, I locked it up tight and jogged down the steps to Mom's waiting car.

"Thank you, darling." She found a break in the cars and headed down the road to Pacific Grove, where her home and the tea shop were located. She and Sylvia owned two tea shops, one in Carmel and one in Pacific Grove, but Mom worked in the Pacific Grove location, closer to home. We crossed the city line not far from the gallery, but her business was downtown.

"We should have updated the wards when she hit Serena's shop." Shaking her head, Mom stopped to let pedestrians cross the road to the beach.

"We need to do your house first," I responded. "Yes, we'll reinforce your business, but I'm more concerned with where you live. Have you spoken to Gran yet? Is she up for doing ward work today?"

"Yes. I called her first."

The road along the coast was narrow and curvy. Add in dog walkers, joggers, and cyclists and it became a drive that required all of Mom's attention. Thankfully, I got to stare out the window at the surf.

"How much damage is there?" I asked.

Mom, stiff behind the wheel, pushed out breath. "As far as I can tell, the building itself is still sound. The tables and chairs are mostly intact. The rest—There was glass everywhere. I only saw the front room and then stepped back out. I didn't want to accidentally walk through a curse. That's why I need you." She stopped again for a mom and two little ones in a wagon with a mountain of beach toys and towels.

"So, you were thinking, if someone needs to walk through a curse, it should be Arwyn?" At her look, I quickly said, "Sorry. It's a bad habit."

She nodded. "We both have bad habits to break."

The Sisters' Tea Room sat on a corner near the Marine Gardens Park and Point Pinos Lighthouse. It was incredibly valuable real estate, but as Coreys had been living here for generations, this storefront—and a few others around town—had been purchased long ago, before this area had become the tourist spot it was now.

Since Aunt Sylvia had been killed by Calliope, there'd just been one sister running the tea room.

Mom pulled right in front of the broken glass door. "I already called my insurance. They said they'd send someone out today. I can't make any fixes until they show up."

A customer parked, walked almost to the door, and then stopped. Mom got out and explained the tea room was closed for repairs. The woman was sympathetic but also in a hurry, now needing to find somewhere else to get her tea fix.

There were coffee places everywhere but finding a good tearoom could be quite difficult. One like Mom's was extremely rare. Not only did she stock difficult to acquire tea leaves, but she also was a master brewer.

She unlocked the broken door and held it open for me. I should have worn thick-soled boots, with all the glass on the floor. A couple of the tables were knocked over, some chairs upended, but it looked more like an afterthought.

"Did you call the cops?" I asked.

"Not until we know it's safe for humans to be wandering around in here," she said.

The glass case displaying scones, muffins, and quiche tartlets was smashed, the food strewn about. The glass jars holding her most popular teas had been thrown across the room, adding tea leaves to the glass everywhere.

"Did you already take pictures? I need to slide through the glass and leaves so I don't cut my foot open."

"Give me a minute." She took out her phone and started snapping away.

"Take a panoramic while you're at it." While she took pictures,

I studied the shop, looking for what to touch, what would hold the story. "Were you robbed or was it all destruction?"

"The till was open. I keep about three hundred in smaller bills for the customers who still pay in cash. I don't know about the safe in back."

"This feels like rage to me," I said. "Each of these jars of tea leaves is worth real money. You have a few in back that are worth, what, about a thousand each?"

Mom nodded.

"This wasn't about a couple of hundred dollars." I went back to the glass on the floor by the shattered front door. Crouching, I slipped off a glove and touched a large shard, thinking about the break-in.

"Destroy it all," she whispers to the dazed man. "But I get to go first." She swirls a fist, disarming the security system and muffling the coming sounds of destruction. Reaching back, she slams a shiny, new hammer, purchased just for this, into the glass door.

Stalking through the shop, she shatters every piece of glass she can find, enjoying the power. The dazed man follows behind, tipping over furniture. With a wave of her hand, the cash drawer pops open and the man collects the bills.

"Come on. The good stuff is back here." She walks straight to the most expensive tea leaves, slams the jar with her hammer, and then stomps on the leaves in her combat boots. In a frenzy, sweat beading on her forehead, she smashes every one of the thirty-odd jars and then starts on Mom's collection of fine bone china tea cups and saucers. Sybil and Sylvia spent decades scouring antiques shops to find each and every one. It's another connection to her sister that Mom has lost.

Calliope goes to the safe and again tries a spell. It doesn't work this time. She spins the wheel, trying a combination she knows. It doesn't work. Frustrated, she kicks it and orders the man to pick it up. He tries, but it doesn't budge. Screaming, she hammers every framed photo of our family on the wall.

Grinding glass with every step, scarring the polished floors, she heads to the front room. "Keep going. I want it all destroyed. Fucking bitch can't keep the money from me. It's half mine." She throws the hammer, end over end, at the front window. Instead of shattering the entire pane, the hammer bounces off. The window is warded against vandalism.

Eyes blinking, I stood. Mom was waiting for me with her arms crossed. I explained everything I'd seen, including the fact that I hadn't seen Cal plant any curses. She hadn't been carefully planning. She'd been in berserker mode.

Mom turned her head and studied her front window before picking up a chair and finding the hammer. "We'd warded the exterior when we bought the business." She shook her head, arms wrapped around herself again. "Stupid." She walked around an overturned table. "So sure of myself and my power."

She started to pick up another chair and then, remembering, put it back down. "I hadn't thought to ward again when Sylvia bought the new door. So much of this could have been avoided if I'd secured our business properly."

"This isn't your fault. It's that psycho Calliope. She destroyed the place. Her little hissy fit does tell us something, though," I said.

Mom nodded. "Money again. She's still trying to get her hands on it, which means no one else in the family is helping her, thank the Goddess."

We heard a noise in the back room and we both went on alert, prepping spells. Mom got to the door first, one hand reaching for the knob while the other was raised, a spell ready to be lobbed at whoever was still here.

She flung it open and then quickly fisted her hand, catching the spell. "Bracken. You startled us. I hadn't realized you'd arrived."

TWENTY-FIVE

Island of Misfit Toys: Population 1 More

In the darkened hall, I got my first glimpse of Bracken around my Mom's shoulder. He was older than I'd been expecting. When Gran wanted me to find his son and talk him into seeing him, I'd assumed the guy would be Mom's age. He looked more like Gran's age.

Shoulders hunched, shuffling through the broken glass and tea leaves covering the floor, he mumbled to himself. "One and a half. Two. Three. Inconsistent. Subpar materials." He had a shock of white hair that glowed in a beam of light coming from a high window. He wore a brown tweed blazer that was too big for him. The leather patches at his elbows were worn. His tan trousers were creased at the back of his knees, as though he'd been sitting for quite some time. Incongruously, on his feet he wore charcoal Vans, the slip-on sneakers normally favored by skateboarders.

Shuffle, shuffle, eyes trained on the ground, the muttering got louder. "Sybil, I hope you didn't pay the same price for each of these jars. The thickness of the glass is alarmingly dissimilar. If you did, you've been cheated. Some of these jars are only one and a half, perhaps two millimeters thick at most. But these others over here are a much hardier three millimeters."

His shuffling feet had created meandering lines of uncovered wood floor in the utter chaos. "Of course, the thicker glass has broken into far more dangerous shards, but it's the workmanship I take issue with. Some of this glass has a slight tint to it as well, which makes no sense at all. You need to be able to see the tea leaves properly to ensure freshness. Which may be why the leaves over in this corner are in bad shape. Perhaps the seals weren't tight enough because of thickness variations. Moisture got in. The scent should have tipped you off, though. You really need to sniff each and every jar every day to make sure you're brewing the best teas. None of this was poisoned, by the way. Mary told me you were concerned and that I should come right away to check, so I did. No poison, but there was mold starting in the jar in the corner, bottom shelf. Not that it matters anymore. It'll all need to be thrown out. When you purchase new containers, though, you have to use a reputable company. The thicknesses should be consistent. Unless you intentionally purchased cheaper glass, in which case, I suppose you got what you asked for. Also, did you know the floor has a four percent incline toward the door? You've been walking up and downhill every time you came into this storage room. You need to pull up the wood and have the subfloor leveled. And these shelves—no doubt as a result of the floor not being level—are themselves about four to five degrees off. I'd venture to guess these jars, over time, have begun to slide ever so slightly to the right. I also noticed—" He finally looked up from the floor, his gaze going right past Mom before locking on me. A sigh escaped on an, "Oh."

She looked over her shoulder and moved out of the way. "Bracken, this is my daughter Arwyn. Arwyn, this is Bracken."

I stepped into the room and watched his furrowed brow relax, his Corey green eyes soften. How odd. They'd told me he wasn't one of us. He wore gold-rimmed round glasses perched on his long, thin nose. Pale, as though he spent little to no time in the sun, his concerned expression turned dreamy.

"Beautiful." He shuffled toward me.

I took his hand and led him from the chaos that seemed to be making his mind spiral. "Hi. Let's come out here, where it's not so bad."

He nodded, following like a trusting child.

Once back in the main room, I took him to a table by the large window, moved a chair so he could look out at the park, the huge tree, and the lighthouse. I moved a second chair, ignoring my mom's throat clearing of annoyance that I was altering the crime scene. I sat across from Bracken and his gaze shifted from the park to me.

"I know it's impolite to stare," he said, "but looking at you is restful for me." Lowering his voice, he leaned in, his gaze traveling over me. "When there's too much, it's like all the musicians in a symphony testing their instruments. Discordant. Cacophonous."

He lowered his voice even more. "I was building to a panic attack. I felt it coming, but everywhere I looked, there was more disorder." He swallowed. "And then I saw you and my mind cleared. Your face is perfectly symmetrical. Your hair is a harmonious blend of brown, red, and gold." He shook his head. "Extraordinary. Now, with the light from the window behind you, there's almost a halo of blue around it."

He took another deep breath. "I'm sorry, but I find your perfection relaxing. Thank you."

Grinning, I said, "Well, thank *you*." Mom was puttering behind the counter, paying little attention to us, until I asked, "Do you have a place to stay? Mom and Gran have guest rooms, if you need one."

Mom looked panicked for a moment.

He shook his head, still staring. "No, thank you."

She relaxed and went back to taking photos with her phone. When another customer came to the door, alarm and confusion clear on her face, Mom walked to the shattered door, explaining she'd be closed for a couple of weeks to make repairs. The woman said she was sorry and left.

"I'll make you a sign, Mom." Going through my backpack, I

pulled out a sketchbook, a black chisel-tipped marker, and a set of colored pencils.

CLOSED due to unforeseen and extraordinarily rude vandalism. We'll open again soon!

I drew a tea pot in one corner and a steaming cup of tea in the other, with a few tea leaves around the page.

"*Closed* is probably enough, darling." Mom had moved closer and was watching.

Before I could respond, Bracken said, "Nonsense. She's creating art while telling a story. Your customers will understand why you're closed, and they'll return happily when you reopen, buying more than they need to show their support."

She patted my shoulder in apology. We probably both heard the unspoken *bad habits*.

"That door needs to be boarded up," I said, finishing the sign and handing it to her.

She taped it in the front window. "Your Uncle John is on his way with plywood, screws, and a drill."

"Good." I put my things away, returning my attention to Bracken, who had yet to take his eyes off me. I know that sounded creepy, but it wasn't. I recognized the desperation in his eyes. I could see what he was going through. If staring at me helped to settle his mind, so be it.

Mom gave Bracken a wary look and then answered her phone. It sounded like she was talking with Gran. Her gaze kept shooting to Bracken as though he were a problem she was trying to figure out how to deal with.

I understood my mother better after last night, but that didn't mean I gave her a free pass. Bracken had come right over to check on her business and she was treating him like he was unwanted. I loved my family. Many of them annoyed the crap out of me, but I still loved them. Well, not Colin.

This was the problem, though. They didn't understand or sometimes even try to accommodate those of us who were often viewed as weirdos.

They wanted us to hide what made us unique. Intellectually, I understood it was probably because wicches had been hiding their existence since the beginning. Anyone who drew attention was a danger to the coven. No one wanted to die by fire or at the end of a rope. While I might understand the origin of the impulse, that didn't make it any easier to deal with.

"I think Gran said you're a writer. Is that correct?"

He nodded. "Historian, actually, though I do write books." His hands were clasped on the table but his knuckles were no longer white, so he was easing down.

"Which historical period do you study?"

Shoulders straightening, he said, "All of them. It's fascinating. All of human—and magical—history unrolls in every direction around us. I like to follow the lines."

"Lines?" I asked.

He shrugged. "Whatever interests me. Sometimes I follow the history of one family. Sometimes it's a country, a political movement, a type of weapon. It could be an abstract emotion like love or loyalty. I trace how different cultures in different ages viewed and expressed that abstract idea."

"And you write books about the things you study?" I pulled out my phone and looked up Bracken Corey.

"Yes. Exactly. If it's a topic I find particularly interesting and few, if any, have written on it, I write a proposal and my agent sells it."

I scrolled the results. "You're a best-selling author. How did I not know this?" I gave my Mom the stink eye but she was still busy talking with Gran and therefore wasn't paying any attention to me.

"Yes. Thankfully many of my books have sold well. I don't know how I'd support myself if they didn't. I'm not suited to doing anything else."

I couldn't even think about a life without my art. "I understand completely." I considered a moment. "You said you wrote magical histories. Those can't be traditionally published. How do people—members of the magical community—read them?"

The way he regarded me changed. Instead of staring at a painting, he was looking at the person he was speaking with. Hopefully, that meant the chaos swirling in his brain was slowing down and dissipating. "There are wonderful tools created for nontraditional authors, programs that allow me to do the formatting for ebooks myself. And there are other services that enable writers to upload their digital books and distribute them. Thankfully, I make enough from my human histories that I can distribute my magical histories free of charge."

"I'd love to read them," I said. Coreys were all about secrets. I wanted to know the whole truth, not what had been cherry-picked and fed to me in order to gain the desired result.

"Of course." He patted his pockets and came up with a business card. Sliding it across the table, he added, "Go to that address and use that password. You'll see all the magical histories and can download whichever you want."

I glanced over the directions on the back. "Perfect. Thank you!"

Nodding, his focus shifted to the window. "Lovely park. It looks as though two of the trees needed to be removed. I wonder why."

Glancing over my shoulder, I studied the tall trees but didn't see the pattern break he had. "Is that what puts you on a research path? Noticing a pattern, or a break in one, and wondering why?"

He laughed. "Yes."

"I have a question for you then."

His gaze became intent, but not in the desperate way it had. More, the idea of a research question excited him.

"I'm not sure if Gran explained, but we're dealing with another sorcerer."

"Sylvia's child. Yes."

"A man—a half demon, half Corey—suggested there might be a black magic family grimoire that was passed down from sorcerer to sorcerer. Have you ever heard of anything like that?"

Mom had stopped and was listening avidly.

Bracken had begun nodding before I'd finished the question. "Oh, my, yes. I told your grandmother Mary—or was it her sister Margaret—all about it years ago. I believe there to be a correlation —I won't say causation because there are too many factors—but a correlation between the preponderance of sorcerers in this family and what is essentially a black magic training manual with instructors dedicated to passing along the secrets."

He leaned forward, hands flat on the table. "You say you know a demon, a Corey demon at that. How in the world did you meet him, and do you think he'd speak with me?" Bracken pulled out a small notebook, like the kind Detectives Hernández and Osso favored, and began scribbling notes in what looked like shorthand. "I have so many questions."

TWENTY-SIX

A Black Hole

"His girlfriend Maggie, a banshee, had been kidnapped and he came to me for help in locating her."

Nodding, he scribbled something and looked up. "Why you?"

Head tilted to the side, I stared back, confused by the question. "Because I'm a—"

Mom dropped something and came rushing over. "You can get back to work, darling. I'll drive you."

"Cassandra wicche," I finished.

Bracken blinked and then stood abruptly, expression stricken. He began to turn to my mother, seemed to remember the chaos, and turned back to me. "Sybil, a new Cassandra emerged, and no one told me? Was her existence hidden from everyone or just me?"

Furious, he glared at me, but I knew the anger was directed at Mom, at Gran, at whoever had kept yet another secret.

"Bracken, no one kept her existence from you. We were trying—"

His fist hit the table. "My child has been missing for twenty-two years. I have agonized for—and all this time you hid the one person who could have told me if he was dead or alive. The hole in me..." He swallowed and then stalked to the door, flung it open, causing more glass to shower the floor, and went around the side of the building.

Mom patted my shoulder. "I can ask John to drive you home. I need to wait for the appraiser."

"Mom." I gestured to the open door.

"I know. More glass, but I can explain that to the insurance person." Her phone rang and she answered it.

I, on the other hand, grabbed my backpack and went after Bracken. I found him pacing and muttering in the parking lot next to a fancy, streamline RV. "...and they wonder why there are so many sorcerers in this family when..."

"Can I ask you a question?" I shouldered the backpack.

The muttering wound down and he stopped his pacing, waiting for me.

"I was told a couple of weeks ago about your wife taking your son and leaving. Gran thought you might be willing to help us with Calliope if I talked your son into contacting you."

Face hardened, he stood silently.

"I told them I wouldn't because I'd been told you were an abusive drunk."

He blinked, the color draining from his face.

"I refused to talk a victim into reuniting with his abuser, no matter how much they said we needed you." My phone buzzed in my pocket, but I silenced it with a thought.

"I was never abusive," he finally said.

"Would your wife and son agree with that?"

Shoulders slumping, he walked back to the RV. "I loved them but—you see what I'm like. I tried to mask it, to shut myself away in my office when the chaos was too much. I tried explaining, but she didn't understand. She said she did, but she didn't. She thought it was a sign of weakness to lose control of my own mind. I agreed, but I couldn't fix myself. I spent more and more time locked away. I wasn't a drunk, but I did try using alcohol to numb my brain. I wanted to be with them, to sleep with my wife and play with my child, but the house was disordered. The alcohol didn't help me not see it, so that was a failed experiment."

He rubbed his forehead. "While they slept, I cleaned and put everything back to rights. If I could impose order, calm my thoughts, I hoped to spend time with my family, but then morning came and there were shouts and squeals and toys appearing and questions about food and pots and pans clanking and spilled drinks and…and I moved back into my study, into the quiet and order."

He took off his glasses and cleaned them with his handkerchief. "Did I ever yell? Yes. But never in anger. I was trying to talk over the screaming in my head. I hadn't realized I was yelling until I saw I'd frightened them, that they were clinging to each other, eyes big as they stared at me."

"I'm sorry." I knew exactly what it was like to desperately try to mask your true self.

Heartbroken, he nodded. "Me too."

I moved closer. "Would you like me to look for him?"

"Yes."

"Is this yours?" I pointed to the RV.

Nodding, he patted his pockets, unlocked the door, and held it open for me.

"Arwyn? Can you come back?" Mom called.

"Don't worry. I'm fine," I said, stepping up into his home on wheels. Neat as a pin, it looked like a demonstration model. "This is really nice." Granted, I'd never been in an RV before, but I hadn't expected them to look so cozy and apartment-ish.

There were two big leather captain chairs for the driver and copilot at the front, but the living area was beautiful. A wingback reading chair and ottoman in a tufted green leather sat under an antique lamp. There were compact coffee and side tables in a warm dark wood and under the window across from the chair, a matching green leather bench butted up against bookcases. All the way down the length of the RV on one side were glass-fronted mahogany bookcases with latches at the handles.

"Is that how you keep the books from falling when you drive?"

He nodded. "That and a spell." Floor to ceiling, the shelves were filled with books of every age and condition. In fact, he'd begun to double shelve.

"How do you keep track of which books are in back?" This collection was incredible.

He gave a barely perceptible shrug. "I remember."

I paused, worried I'd overstepped. "Is it okay that I'm looking around?"

He thought about it. "Yes. I normally don't like people in my space, but you don't seem to be setting off any alarms in my head."

There was a small galley kitchen that gleamed.

"Go ahead," he encouraged.

The bathroom was perfectly appointed with a decent-sized shower. At the far end of the RV, in what was probably intended to be a bedroom, was a study. Bookshelves continued, wrapping around the room. There was a sofa in the same green leather and a dark wood desk.

Turning in a circle, I grinned. "It's beautiful and perfect." There were benches under the windows on either side of the room. I sat and pointed at the couch. "Is that where you sleep?"

He nodded.

"I do that too. I'm a horrible sleeper."

He made a sound of agreement in the back of his throat.

"I understand why you don't do guest rooms. This is much better." I'd never thought of myself as an RV person, but being able to travel with your home was amazing.

"I tried to visit your grandmother once, but the sigils on her door and floor were overwhelming." He scratched his head, walked around the desk, and sat.

"The ward was?"

"Hmm? Oh, no. The sigils themselves. They were just enough off to make my neck itch. I need uniformity and pattern. The sizes were different. Some were straight lines and right angles. Others were loopy. I could have kept my back to the entry, but the pergola on the patio is settling. The left side is now about six degrees lower than the right. I tried to look out the window at the ocean but my eyes were drawn to the edge of the pergola visible on the left-hand side of her picture window."

I nodded. "I've noticed that too."

He opened a drawer, touched his perfectly organized pens and uniformly sharp pencils, and then closed it again. "The difference is that you can notice and let go. I cannot. And yes, I'm aware that this"—he gestured all around him—"is just making my world smaller and smaller." His eyes found mine. "I fear I'll soon be condemned to a single room for life because I can't handle the world."

Recognizing the naked truth of that statement, I shared my own truth. "I'm afraid the visions and nightmares will drive me insane, just like all the other Cassandras. I feel like I'm already on borrowed time. Most of us don't live long enough to make it to double digits."

He suddenly smiled, and it lit up his face, making him look twenty years younger. "Quite a pair, aren't we?

Grinning back, I said, "We are." I glanced around again. "Do you have anything of your son's?"

"Yes." The bookcases in this room had solid door cabinets at the bottom. He went to the one closest to his desk, unlocked it, and pulled out a pristine baby giraffe. He placed it on the bench beside me and then went back to his desk.

"Okay. Was your wife a wicche as well?"

He nodded. "She's a Booth."

They were another old, respected line of wicches. They didn't pack the power of a Corey, but neither did they have our propensity to produce black wicches and sorcerers. Which reminded me…

"Do you know why Gran—when she first mentioned you— told me you weren't a Corey?"

Confusion gave way to affront. He shook his head. "My sister believes in loyalty and duty above all else. I tried to live up to the expectations, but it was too much. I walked away and apparently in her mind that meant I was walking away from the family." He stared at his desk. "Her responsibilities haven't been easy, but neither does she make allowances for another's"—he shrugged—"capacities."

True. I loved her but true.

"Sometimes, when I'm reading family, it can get muddled," I said. "Hopefully, the Booth side is strong enough for me to see him as an adult." I slipped off a glove and picked up the toy.

"What is the matter with you? You said you were happy about the baby. I have to do this all myself and I'm exhausted! Do you hear me? I can't think straight. He's colicky and it's always me around the clock I'm on duty for feeding and changing and rocking. I need help!"

The poor woman is dressed in a stained t-shirt and sweats, her hair tied up, dark circles under her eyes, red blotches on her cheeks, as she paces with a crying baby and his giraffe.

A much younger Bracken, his dark hair beginning to gray at the temples, stands like a deer in headlights.

"Well? Can you at least take him so I can pee?"

Bracken stands frozen. I can see exactly what's happening, but she can't. Too bone weary to pick up on nuance, she interprets his lack of response as a lack of caring, when it's quite the opposite.

On a scream of frustration, she places the crying baby in his swing and stomps off to the bathroom. The door slam seems to startle the infant into momentary silence. Bracken approaches his son as though he's a highly unstable bomb.

Crouching, Bracken reaches out to touch Ben's hand. His son wraps his whole tiny fist around Bracken's finger and holds on.

"Hello," he whispers. "I'm sorry your tummy is so upset. I researched colic and it sounds dreadful."

The child stares wide-eyed, one hand still clutching Bracken while the other plucks at his giraffe.

"The good news is that it doesn't last forever. Of course, a baby probably has a different understanding of that word. As far as you're concerned, it has lasted forever. But, as someone who is much older than you, I can confirm that it will be of short duration. Unfortunately,

you're still in the thick of it right now, so that's probably not of much comfort.

"You have Corey eyes. Did you know that? I thought perhaps you'd have your mother's Booth brown, but you have mine." He paused, studying his child. "It's quite odd to recognize my father's chin on a brand-new face. He's passed now, but I can tell you about him. He was a good man."

The flush of the toilet breaks the spell. Ben takes a breath and then resumes his squalling. When the door opens, Bracken is backing away to the door of his study. His wife won't look at him. She picks up Ben and resumes walking laps around the living room. Knowing he's failed miserably, Bracken retreats to his magically soundproofed study and his books that quietly wait for him.

The image goes dark and then…

Bracken opens his study door. Different day. Different clothes. His expression more worn. The house is quiet. He remembers a pediatrician appointment and wonders if that's where they are. He'd thought it was the following day, but perhaps he's gotten his days confused again. He walks into the kitchen to check the calendar and is surprised to find the usual mayhem of breakfast missing. It looks as it did when he finished cleaning last night.

He can't say why, but a stone begins to form in his gut. Feeling sick, he walks down the hall and looks in the baby's room. It's been stripped. The crib and changing table remain, but the toys are gone, save for the giraffe forgotten in the crib. He checks the closet and finds it empty.

White noise roars in his head as he walks to the bedroom he sometimes shares with his wife. The closet is empty. Suitcases are gone. His knees give out and he collapses onto the bed. He fumbles in his pocket for his phone, tapping his wife's contact. There is a high-pitched beep and then an electronic voice is telling him that the number has been disconnected.

Like a zombie with a black hole where his heart had been, he retraces his steps to his study and shuts the door.

When the image begins to go dark, I think, Show me Ben now.

A young man with dark hair and Bracken's eyes shelves books in a dim, quiet shop. A bell rings and he walks to the aisle and greets the man entering, asking if he can help him find what he's looking for. The man explains he's looking for a first edition of an American Renaissance writer for his grandfather. He doesn't know much about the topic and is looking for recommendations, so Ben walks him through the shop, explaining what they have that his grandfather might enjoy.

When the man leaves, he steps out onto a bustling street. The brass sign above the door reads Chadwick & Sons, Rare Books.

Blinking, I found Bracken watching me, expression intent. "Is he all right?"

TWENTY-SEVEN

Did You Say a Shark?

I nodded. "Yeah. He's good. He takes after you."

He let out a slow breath and stared down at the desk. "He's alive," he said to himself.

I brought him the giraffe and explained what I'd seen. I wasn't sure if he was aware of how tightly he was clutching his son's toy.

"He likes books?" He gave his head a little shake and took in all the books surrounding him. "I could show him all… but, no. He doesn't know me. Probably doesn't want to know me."

"Only one way to know for sure," I said.

He slid out his bottom drawer and lifted a laptop computer. He opened it and began typing. "It wouldn't hurt to look up the bookstore, would it?" And then he paused and checked with me. "This is all right, isn't it? This isn't invading his privacy?"

My heart broke for him. He wanted so much to have the life his brain wouldn't allow. "You are a man who collects books. He works in a rare bookstore. You could have just stumbled upon him while searching for a book."

He lifted one eyebrow.

"Well, it's true. Besides, I don't think looking up a business name to know what city your son works in would be considered stalking."

He considered that and then resumed typing. "Boston." He sat back in his chair. "My son lives in Boston." He closed the laptop. "I think that's enough for now. My son is living in Boston and he's a bookseller." Tears filled his eyes. "That's enough."

"Listen. Since I don't know what Gran and Mom have told you or asked you, let me ask: Do you know where Calliope could be hiding? Maybe where previous sorcerers have lived?"

He was silent for quite a while. "No one asked me, but now that you say it, I believe I saw a reference to a home owned by a dark wicche we later learned was a sorcerer. Hmm. Let me think and go through some books. It wasn't an address, in any case, but I believe there was a description…or perhaps the house was named. I remember thinking that might be enough to locate it, but I was researching something else and therefore didn't—oh, that means I would have added a note about it in one of my journals."

He tapped his chin. "Give me time to think and search. If I have anything, I'll let you know."

"Thank you. Now, more immediately, do you need somewhere to park this?" When he nodded, I continued. "My gallery is on the ocean. It's a converted cannery. You can park on my property and have a view of the ocean." I gestured to the large back window behind him. "I should warn you, though. My gallery isn't sedate."

He returned the laptop to the bottom drawer and then got up and went back through the RV. "Let's go see. I'd prefer not to stay here longer than necessary." He got into the driver's seat, waiting for me to strap myself in beside him before turning on the engine.

I pointed in the direction of Monterey. "It's near Cannery Row."

He drove the behemoth with the ease of a sedan right back onto the narrow twisty road Mom and I had taken here. "I know the one. I remember when Mary bought it. The rest of the family thought she'd tear it down and build a hotel or something, but she let it sit, saying she had plans for it."

I turned to him. "Really? How odd. I'd never considered why Gran purchased it and let it sit before." I watched a couple of surfers bob in the water, waiting for a wave. Out of nowhere, a memory surfaced. "We often had family get-togethers on the beach. When I was five or six, I'd wandered away from the group to go see this building hanging over the water. I'd thought it was a house and wanted to live there."

"No one was watching a five-year-old Cassandra by the ocean? Goddess, you could have been swamped by a wave and drowned." He shook his head, angry on my behalf. "The carelessness with one so precious."

"Aww, thanks." I patted his shoulder. "I'd have been fine, though. Dad wouldn't have let me drown."

He turned to me quickly and then back to the road. "I was under the impression your mother had never shared the identity of your father."

"Oh, she hasn't, but he's water fae."

Bracken's foot came off the accelerator. At a honk behind him, he continued driving. "She chose a fae father for you?"

"Or they fell in love and nature took over. I'd prefer not to think about that part, though."

He was silent for a few minutes. "You're right. Cassandras do, almost exclusively, die as children, either at the hands of humans for being demon possessed or by their own hands because what they see is more than their little minds can process. You, though, being half-fae, have a strength and resilience they didn't, which is no doubt how you survived to adulthood. Fascinating."

He paused. "Multicolor hair with a blue halo in the sun." Laughing, he tapped the steering wheel. "Utterly fascinating."

"Thanks. All these books you have here, do you have anything about Cassandra wicches?"

"Hmm, perhaps anecdotally. As I'm sure you know, you're quite rare and while we know Cassandras are a blessing from the Goddess, we also know in times past, anything that drew attention to us could cause our torture and death. And so it happened, sadly, that it was sometimes the child's own family that took her life."

A cold chill ran down my spine. I couldn't imagine fearing my mother as well as the near constant psychic assault. Those poor girls. They'd had no chance.

"I'm sorry," he said. "I interrupted. Please continue. You, as a small child, went on an adventure, marching across the sand to visit the abandoned cannery. I have no idea if you marched, but in my head, you are. Please, go on."

"I might have marched. I could have skipped. I was, I'm sure, trying to escape my cousins. Anyway, I climbed the rocks, squeezed through a fence, and walked along the rotting deck. I remember a man appeared out of nowhere." I tried to piece the images together in my head. "He came around the far end. Thinking about it now, he didn't look as though he'd been squatting there or anything. He was just a man, jeans and a t-shirt. He smiled a razor-sharp smile and I peed myself.

"I remember being ashamed. I wasn't a baby anymore. But that was in the back of my mind. I was paralyzed. I wanted to run but I couldn't move. I didn't understand what he wanted, but I saw violence in his eyes. I saw my death and his euphoria at finding a little girl all by herself. I tried to scream, but nothing came out.

"And then this massive wave came over the railing and slammed the man into the wall of the cannery. It felt like one of my visions. It didn't seem real. I wasn't wet, but the man was washed off the deck and into the ocean. Finally able to move, I went to the edge and watched as a shark—*a shark*—swam up and bit him in half."

"I'm sorry," he said, his voice quiet.

I blew out a breath. "I'm okay. Dad saved me."

"And that's wonderful, but you saw what he intended to do to you. No one, especially a child, should have to experience that kind of evil."

It was one of a million horrible things in my head, the fodder for endless nightmares. "Anyway," I said, "I realized, once the fear was draining away, that my foot hurt. I looked down and saw a sliver—No. That sounds too small. The deck was rotting and a shard of wood was sticking out of my bloody toe. I had a moment of a different kind of horror before the tears began to fall but then, up from the water came a tentacle. It shocked the tears away. The tentacle gently wrapped around my foot and when it slipped back into the water, the sliver was gone and my skin was smooth and unbroken."

"An octopus and a shark." He shook in head in wonder. "What I would have given to see that."

"Welcome to my world. The Sea Wicche is coming up here on your left." It was a good memory and probably explained my love of octopuses.

When he got close, he slowed again, coming to a standstill in the road. Cars honked and drove around him, but he was transfixed. Hopefully not in a bad way. If the gallery short-circuited his brain, I couldn't drive this thing. I could probably just call for Declan, though. He'd hear me.

Bracken began driving again. "I need to turn around, which is tricky on these narrow roads."

I pointed to Declan's property. "You can use his parking lot to turn around. I know the owner. It's okay."

Bracken turned on his signal, slowed, and went through the open gate. He was doing a three point turn when Declan walked out of the construction zone to watch.

I rolled down the window and waved. Declan's expression lightened immediately. We were no longer trespassers to be dealt with. His grin made my stomach flutter.

"Bracken, can you stop for a minute so I can say hi?"

He did and Declan came over.

"What are you doing up there?" he said. "I thought you were still sleeping." He stepped up on something. Running board? Wheel? He rested his arm on the window frame and then leaned in to kiss me.

Every time. He made my insides go funny every time. "Sorry. I meant to call but I had multiple messages from my mom. Her teashop was broken into, and she needed me."

"I'm sorry to hear that. Is everyone all right?"

I nodded. "It happened in the middle of the night. You know, now that I think about it, I'm not sure what happened to the possessed man who helped her trash the place." Damn, Calliope was wrecking lives left and right. "Declan, this is my Uncle Bracken. Bracken, this is my boyfriend Declan."

Declan nodded and Bracken returned it.

"We just met this morning. He needs a place to park his motorhome and I suggested the parking lot on the far side of the gallery."

"Good idea." Declan didn't make it obvious but his nostrils flared and I knew he was scenting Bracken, probably trying to figure out why we'd only just met and why Bracken wouldn't meet his gaze for more than a second. "You know, if that doesn't work, you can use my property as well. You have options."

I knew what he was doing, and it made my insides flutter more frantically. Bracken was an unknown and he wanted him closer to himself than me.

"Thank you." Bracken's voice sounded strained.

"Bracken, Declan is a Quinn. His father was Alexander Quinn. Did you ever meet him?"

That did it. Bracken turned to study Declan. "Yes. I see. You favor your father. I did meet him. Many years ago. I was researching the history of lycanthropy. I have a book here—" He started to get up, but the seat belt kept him in place. "Oh, of course." He fumbled with the belt, but I rested a hand on his arm.

"Perhaps another time."

He stopped struggling and nodded.

"I'd be very interested in anything you could tell me," Declan said. "My father was killed when I was young. I'm afraid I don't remember much about either of my parents."

Bracken seemed to be trying to settle himself. "I can locate the book for you."

"How's construction going today?" I asked.

"Good. We're done with the tearing down and are about to start building new." He played with a coil of hair that had blown out the window. "How about if I bring over dinner when I'm done for the day?"

"Sounds great."

"Good." He looked over at Bracken. "Will you join us?"

Bracken shook his head while he continued to stare out the windshield at the ocean across the road.

"Okay. We need to go," I said. "We need to see if my place works for Bracken." I kissed him. "I'll see you tonight."

Declan hopped off the side of the motor home and waved as he walked back toward the barn. He stopped and turned. "Oh, remind me I need to ask you a favor."

"What is it?"

He waved away my sudden concern. "Nothing we need to worry about now. Logan's people are making a habit of slashing my tires and smashing my windshield. It's getting expensive." He wiggled his fingers. "I was hoping you could do something to—I don't know—make them harder to cut and break." He pointed to the poles around the property. "I have cameras up, but they're waiting until I'm parked at a grocery store or outside your place."

"I'm sorry and, yes, I can do something."

"It's more irritating than threatening." He shook his head. "Anyway, let that go. Have a good afternoon and I'll see you this evening." He waved and headed back to the sounds of construction.

I turned to Bracken. "Okay?"

Bracken let out a breath. "Yes. He's very large."

I laughed. "He is. He's also incredibly kind and protective."

"I sensed that. Some wolves are quite aggressive. Alexander had a commanding presence. There was never any doubt who was in charge. He wasn't as easy as his son seems to be, but neither did he have the hair trigger some wolves do. He was the most powerful wolf I interviewed, but I was never concerned about my safety. In fact, I've never felt safer. I knew if anything attacked, he'd have it sorted out with minimal effort."

Declan was indeed like his father. When he'd met soon-to-bedeposed Alpha Logan, there was no aggression and no fear. Logan had been doing everything he could to try to intimidate Declan, while Declan ignored the posturing and instead tried to finagle a brownie from me. It made Logan go all wolf-eyed, but Declan wasn't the least bit concerned. He knew he was the strongest, the most dominant, and therefore didn't need to engage. Besides, he was interested in me. And my brownies.

I pointed toward the road. "Let's head back. The gallery is even more chaotic from this side. Let's see if it's doable for you."

TWENTY-EIGHT

He Just Looks Crazy. He's Okay. Mostly

Bracken maneuvered back out onto the road and once again stopped when he saw the mural and tentacles. This time, though, people just drove around him without the honking. Maybe locals were used to people slowing here. I really hoped the gallery didn't get a public safety citation.

He started driving again, went past the gallery, pulled to the side, and then backed onto the newly paved parking lot. His precision was impressive. The rig was less than a foot from the outer wall of the gallery and he was backed up to the water.

"Would you like a tour?" I unbuckled and moved into his living room.

"Very much."

We got out and he stopped to watch the waves a moment before stepping onto the new deck. His fingers trailed over the edge of one of Declan's curved benches. They'd been built to fit perfectly with the curve of the deck itself.

"Beautiful," he murmured.

"Declan built the deck and benches. That's how we met."

He nodded absently as he approached one of the tentacles rising up out of the water, seemingly poised to rip apart the gallery.

He reached out and then stopped himself. "May I touch?"

"Of course. They were pretty strong to begin with, but I added a spell to protect them. Once I open, people will be grabbing them and taking selfies, so I needed them close to indestructible."

"Extraordinary." His fingers ran over the tentacle and suckers. "It looks so real, I expected it to feel fleshy." He turned to me with wonder in his eyes. "Truly extraordinary."

"Thanks." I waved him forward. "Is it too much for you?"

He shook his head. "It doesn't seem to be. Perhaps because it's art." He gestured to the water. "The ocean is chaotic, but that doesn't bother me either. Nature has rules and forms that it adheres to in its own chaotic fashion. Art must be the same to my brain."

"Come see the rest then." When we got down to the studio door, I pointed to the railing. "Wait. I want to introduce you first."

I leaned over the railing, and he mirrored me. "Cecil! This is my Uncle Bracken." Cecil did more than just tap the surface this time. He rose up, right below the surface, and eyed Bracken.

"Charlie, Herbert, you're looking quite dapper today." The starfish were a gorgeous orange against the vibrant purple of the algae on the pilings they clung to.

A tennis ball rolled to a stop by my foot. "Hey, they all decided to say hi. Give me a sec." I opened the studio door and grabbed the whippy ball thrower, sending the tennis ball sailing over the water. With a bark, a seal went racing after it. "That's Wilbur. He's a selkie, but when he's in his seal skin, we play catch."

I put the ball thrower back inside the door and waved Bracken in. "This is my studio and apartment."

He smiled, studying it all. "You live where you work. Like me." He stopped in front of the corridor painting. "Ominous. I'm not sure what's going on behind that door, but it feels deadly."

I stood beside him. "Which door?"

He pointed to the last door on the right. "The angle of the door is a hair different from the other doors. That one is ajar."

I studied the door angles, and he was right. Pulling my phone from my pocket, I swiped through and called Detective Hernández.

"Arwyn, I was planning to stop by and see you today. Actually, Osso and I both were. Are you available?"

"Uh, yeah. We can do this in person. I should be around, sure." It was like the whole world was conspiring to make sure I couldn't work and open this gallery on time.

"Great. It probably won't be for a couple of hours. See you then."

I disconnected and pocketed it. Bracken was wandering around the studio, stopping to check out one piece of art and then another. When he gestured to the painting facing the wall, I nodded.

He turned it around and then stepped back, one hand out in front of him, warding it off. "Did she die?"

"How in the world did you know that?" I'd never sell the painting of Pearl's murder, but it honestly just looked like churned-up seawater and the possible silhouette of someone above the water.

"It has a feminine feel." He pointed to the silhouette. "And this is malevolent. Did he hold her under the water? Drown her?"

"Yes."

He turned the painting back to the wall.

"Are you sure you're not a little psychic?" I asked. His perception was uncanny.

He shook his head. "Just observant."

"The gallery is through here." I opened the adjoining door and stepped back. Construction was done. The display cases and pedestals were in place. Nothing sat atop them, though, because I was still painting.

He walked to the wall I'd been working on. "I see. The sea monster that's attacking the gallery is waiting here in the depths of this water."

"Yes. Exactly. This is the darkest wall, the deepest part of the ocean. The walls will get lighter as the eye travels around the room, closer to the surface. The windows are the light, the air."

"I believe," he said, quickly looking from the windows to the cross beams forty feet above us, "that I've had enough new experiences today." He turned his back to the window wall.

"These are the original cannery windows. Are they misaligned?"

He nodded. "Perhaps through time. As this was a cannery, it's also possible there hadn't been a strong concern for right angles. I would imagine they just needed the people chopping off fish heads and tails to be able to see what they were doing."

He patted his pockets, which I was beginning to think was a soothing tic. "I think I should retreat to my home now. I need familiar sameness to rest."

"Of course. Let me get you some muffins and tea to take with you, though. Okay?"

He nodded, and I went back to the studio. A few minutes later, I sent him off with two muffins and a thermos of tea.

I checked the time on my phone. Half the day gone. I ran upstairs to change into work clothes and then climbed the scaffold to paint.

A few hours later, the main wall complete, I was working on the far wall when I heard knocking on the front door. Odd. Most people knew to come around the back.

I climbed down and answered the door, finding Detectives Hernández and Osso. "Hey. How did you guys know I was in the gallery?"

"We didn't," Osso said. "Hernández wanted me to see the glass tentacle you have out here."

"He took a picture with it," she said, grinning.

"For my kids. They both love the glass octopuses you gave them," Detective Osso said.

There was something so surprisingly sweet about a giant of a man, who could shift into a bear, being delighted by a glass tentacle, but I kept that thought to myself. I didn't want to wreck his grumpy hardass reputation.

"Good. I'm glad they liked them." I waved them in.

"Aren't you concerned about idiots breaking that thing? It's glass," he said.

I led them into the studio, where we could sit down. "I know, but I have security cameras up and the tentacle is spelled. It's the best I can do to protect it." I went to the kitchen and looked in my refrigerator and then freezer. "Are you hungry?"

Osso said, "Yes," at the same time Hernández said, "That's okay."

I turned and stared at her.

"I mean, I wouldn't say no. I just didn't want you to go to any trouble," she said.

"It's not trouble," Osso said, glaring at Hernández, who was getting between him and food.

"I think that's supposed to be *my* line, but it's true enough." I washed my hands and then, given who one of my guests was, pulled a honey pound cake out of the freezer. After defrosting with a spell, I cut it into pieces, grabbed napkins, and brought them the plate. "Drinks?"

"Tea," Osso said, and Hernández nodded her agreement.

"You got it." I was walking back with three mugs of tea a couple minutes later to an empty plate. I passed the cups to the detectives, dropped mine off on the little side table by my chair, and then picked up the empty plate and defrosted three blueberry lemon muffins because I was hungry and that sounded good. I added a bit of toasty warmth to them. It wasn't as good as an oven, but it was far faster.

Osso had already eaten his muffin in one bite and was currently eyeing the second one as I sat down.

"Stand strong, Hernández. If you want it, it's yours." I split mine in half, taking a bite of the bottom, saving the top for last.

Mirroring me, she broke off the top, kept it and offered him the bottom, which Osso tossed in his mouth.

"So, what's up? Why are you both here?" I took a sip of tea.

Hernández swallowed a bite. "We've been talking. We're wondering if our cases are connected."

I shook my head. "Different killers."

"Right," Osso said, taking over, "but are they connected?"

I thought about it a moment. "Like Leopold and Loeb?"

"And Abel and Furlan," he said, "Lucas and Toole, Bianchi and Buono. There are too damn many to list."

I kicked off my shoes and pulled my legs up, crossing them. Was this why I'd originally thought the murders were done by the same killer? "I keep hearing whispering." I pointed at the corridor painting. "There's whispering behind that door. That was why I called earlier. The angles of the last door on the right are off. The door is ajar and I hear whispering, so…yes. It could be two killers working together."

Osso and Hernandez both stood to get a closer look at the painting.

"And it can't just be a mistake you made drawing the line?" Osso asked.

"It absolutely could, but look at all the other doors. It was my Uncle Bracken who saw it. His brain identifies patterns—or breaks in them—immediately. He asked what was going on behind that door because it felt evil."

Hernández nodded. "It does. This is like the yellow dress in the forest painting." She was the one who'd caught that. I'd been helping them with a child abduction case. I'd painted what I'd seen in a horrible nightmare, but I hadn't remembered painting the yellow sweep. Hernández noticed it under a tree in the painting. That bit of yellow was the dress Ana was wearing when she was killed.

"Can you contact the school? Find out who's lived in that room? I don't think they're current students. They feel older. Maybe the school could give you a list. I know one or both of them were in that room."

Osso was already shaking his head. "Fancy, private school like that? They don't give up information without a court order and multiple calls to judges and senators."

"You met the headmaster," Hernández said. "We don't have enough for a warrant and he's not the type to help us out, even if it is his dean at the bottom of the stairs." She turned to the back door and flinched. "Arwyn, are you aware there's a crazy-looking old guy on your deck?"

TWENTY-NINE

Back to Murder

I followed her gaze. "That's my Uncle Bracken. I mean, yes, he's a crazy-looking old guy, but he's also my uncle."

Hopping up, I slipped into my shoes and met him at the door. "Hi. I'm just talking with a couple of detectives. Would you like to come in and meet them?" He shook his head and turned back in the direction of his RV. "I wanted you to know that a strange man was lurking, staring in the gallery windows and trying the back door."

Stiffening, I looked left and right. Was it the sweaty man who'd been parked in front waiting for me or a new one?

He patted my arm. "I got rid of him. I didn't like the look of him. I think he was like the man who'd cornered you as a child."

Unfortunately, I thought so too. "Thank you. I appreciate you keeping an eye out for me."

Nodding, he went back toward his RV. "I liked the muffin."

Good. I should make quiches later today. He needed protein. And I needed eggs. As I composed a shopping list in my head, I went back in to find the detectives gone.

"Hello?"

"We're in your gallery," Hernández called. When I walked in, she asked, "Everything good?"

"Creep, possible stalker. My uncle got rid of him for me."

Osso gave me a look. "Permanently?"

I rolled my eyes. "He's a historian, not a hit man. He just gave the guy a magical shove."

"Why do you say he's a stalker?" Hernández asked, expression concerned.

"I've had to do the same kind of magical shove a couple of times. He's fixated. I can feel it. Declan even gave him a big, scary wolf glare and it didn't register at all. I'm deciding how to deal with it."

"You could make a report with us," she said.

Osso shook his head. "What are we going to do that she can't do better and faster?"

"But." Hernández was at a loss.

Her fear for me was palpable and it warmed my heart. I patted her elbow. "I'll be okay. I've had to deal with creeps my whole life."

Osso grunted, apparently agreeing with Declan's anger. He shook it off and then studied the walls. "I know you're busy here, but can you come with us?"

I sighed. "Why?"

"Dead man. Luis Garza. He fell or was pushed off a cliff onto rocks, just like in your vision. We probably wouldn't have found him, but a sailboat saw him and called it in before the tide washed him away. I want to take you to the estate. It's on 17-Mile Drive."

"That's Carmel," I said. "Isn't that a different police force?"

He nodded. "It is, but we cooperate. They agreed to give us the case because Luis Garza used to be the groundskeeper at Cypress Academy. That means this death wraps into our cases. Garza was fired or quit—we'll find out—five years ago."

"Five years, huh?" I stuffed my hands in my overall pockets. I had work. The problem was, I also had nightmares about this.

"Yeah. We're wondering if it had anything to do with a couple of former students," Hernández said.

I headed back to the studio. "Let me get my backpack."

On the drive, I sat in the back seat and texted Dave.

Me: Do demons write grimoires?

Dave: Not as a rule but a few exist.

Me: I had a vision about Calliope using one, building a spell. I couldn't read the words on the page. Just looking at them made my head pound and my stomach want to hurl. I wondered if it might be a demonic language

Dave: That's an interesting idea. Let me see if I can find out who the original Corey symbiot was. If I don't know the demon, my father will. That would explain a lot and it might make her easier to find.

Me: How?

Dave: If the grimoire is demon made and we know who the demon is, I might be able to locate it. MIGHT. Let me look into it.

Me: Great. Thank you!

Dave: Yeah and Maggie says thanks for the hedgehog.

Osso badged his way through the gate at the entrance to the 17-Mile Drive. The road led through some of the most beautiful properties in Carmel and Pacific Grove. It hugged the ocean and included Pebble Beach, the Lone Cypress, huge mansions, the Del Monte Forest.

"Why was a former groundskeeper on an estate around here?" I asked.

"We had the same question," Hernández said. "Turns out the

couple that owns the place, the Masons, have a kid who went to Cypress Academy."

"Interesting," I said.

"We thought so too. The owners are in Europe and told us their son lives in New York now. He went to Harvard and works in finance. We'll check his whereabouts, but we doubt he's taking a red-eye back and forth across the country to kill people from his old school. From what Mom says, he loved Cypress. We haven't been able to reach him yet."

"Very important meetings," Osso sneered.

"Yes," Hernández confirmed, "but the secretary says he's there. We'll reach out to the local PD and see if they can check for us."

"So was Garza working as their groundskeeper?" I asked.

"No. He has his own landscaping business now. Had. It's quite successful. *But,* Mom did let it slip that junior liked to throw end-of-year parties at their estate when they were away."

"Meaning," Osso cut in, "all of his classmates would be familiar with the estate and that his parents went to Europe every year around this time."

"If they'd been invited," I said.

Hernández turned around to look at me.

"I doubt he invited everyone. This wasn't a kindergarten birthday party. If the murderers felt comfortable enough to use it to kill Garza, they'd probably at least attended the parties, meaning they were part of the popular crowd or—"

"Had a grudge against the kid and wanted to cause some trouble," Osso finished.

I nodded. "Exactly."

"We were thinking friend," Hernández said, "but maybe enemy. These two probably knew how to hang with the crowd. The Masons' son"—she checked her notes—"Edmund might not have even known they hated him. Your cousin thought he was charming, right?"

"Yeah. She did." It was so much easier thinking of these two in the abstract. When I had to consider Pearl's death, her mother's grief, it hollowed me out.

The car went silent and then Hernández said, "Sorry. That was thoughtless of me."

"No. You're working. This is what you need to do to figure out who the killers are. Do what you do. I'm fine."

Osso turned off the 17-Mile Drive, which was always slow with tourists stopping to take pics. He used back roads to get us to the Masons' seaside estate. There was a tall, wrought iron fence at a break in a high stone wall. You couldn't see the house through the bars of the gate. The narrow drive curved out of sight, hiding the estate from random sightseers.

Osso got out and punched in a security code on a keypad to the left of the gate. When the gate rumbled open, he got back in and drove through a grove of trees before the road opened to a rolling lawn leading to a French Provincial mansion. The trees seemed to surround the entire estate. It went on so far, though, it was hard to tell for sure.

"Stables? Am I seeing horse stables way back there?" I asked.

"Sure looks like it," Hernández said.

"I wonder who takes care of the horses when the family's away," I said. "I mean, who's mowing this perfectly manicured lawn? There must be tons of people with that code to get in here and maintain this place."

"Yeah," Osso said. "Hernández has a list of—what—almost twenty service people who come to the estate regularly. The house-cleaning service comes twice a week, regardless of whether the family is home." He shook his head. "Something about dust and musty smells. I don't know. Rich people problems."

"Okay, so are we sure—" I stopped. What the hell was I doing? I wasn't a detective. Why was I acting like I was on their investigative team?

Osso looked at me in the rearview mirror as he pulled to a stop in front of the main house. "What?"

"Sorry. I'm not a cop."

Hernández got out and opened the back door for me. "It's okay. Most of your questions we've already asked ourselves and have done the digging, but not all. Sometimes you bring up ideas I hadn't considered."

I grabbed my backpack.

"Besides," Osso said, "you do all this for free. We can put up with questions and theories for free psychic insight."

"Okay. I'll finish the thought. Do any of those service employees or their families have ties to Cypress Academy? Like the women we met, Isabel and Sofia. They've been at the school a long time, but I'm sure others had a hard time and left and now maybe work for the company that cleans here."

"You're losing the thread," Osso said as he led us toward the cliff at the edge of the property. "The killers aren't a couple of disgruntled cleaning ladies. You said we're looking for young men, previous students of Cypress, right?"

"Good point." I followed in his wake.

"You're not wrong, though," Hernández said. "That is what we check. Maybe one of them has a nephew who's brilliant and got a scholarship to attend. Lots of possibilities."

Osso snorted a laugh. "You really see these people inviting the little Latino charity case to their millionaire parties?"

"Depends," I said, and Hernández nodded. "If the scholarship kid was a star at the school or just friends with this couple's son, yeah, he'd be invited."

"This isn't a school that accepts a bunch of poor kids who work hard. We checked. There are only one or two scholarships given every year. Maybe I'm jaded, but I'd guess those scholarship kids are treated like the help by the rest of the students." He stopped at the edge of the lawn.

"Huh," I said. "I would have thought they'd at least put up one of those short corral fences, so people didn't accidentally walk over a cliff to their death." We all walked to the edge and looked over. The water barely broke over the rocks. I checked the time on my phone. "Low tide."

Osso nodded. "If Garza went over at high tide, the killer may have thought the body would be washed out to sea."

"Body gets caught on the rocks, ebb tide, and sailboat passes," I said.

"We were lucky," Hernández agreed. "The coroner says his death was last night. If the tide hadn't been receding, we might not have found the body for weeks."

"If at all," Osso said.

"Are we sure this is where he went over?"

Osso shook his head.

"Okay." I handed my backpack to Hernández. "You two move back. Let me wander around a bit."

THIRTY

A Spring in His Step and a Song in His Heart

I shook off the conversation and centered myself. Closing my eyes, buffeted by the wind, I lowered my guard and thought about the man's death. Immediately, I felt emotions coming at me from Hernández and Osso. "Could you guys move farther away? I don't need to know someone got into a fight with their significant other this morning."

"Don't look at me," Osso grumbled.

"It wasn't a fight. Just a misunderstanding about who said they'd stop at the market yesterday. We're out of coffee," Hernández explained.

Thankfully, their voices and emotions were quieting as they moved farther away. I tried again. No. This wasn't the place. "A man shoved his elderly mother over right here. He wanted to inherit the family fortune, but—based on the clothing—it was probably a hundred years ago."

I walked along the edge. The murder had taken place last night. I should feel something. Since I didn't, I kept walking. When I reached the tree line, I almost turned back, but I felt a pull ahead. Yes. This felt like the one who'd killed the teacher at the country club.

When I passed a large pine tree, the buzz became painful. I slipped off my glove and touched a finger to the bark.

He checks his thick gold watch again. The stupid old man is late. He looks up at the big house and steps out of the moonlight, leaning against a pine tree. The family never used to have cameras pointed in this direction. Hopefully, that's still true. He pulls down the brim of his ball cap and tugs up the collar of his jacket.

That's all he needs. He'll never hear the end of it if he gets caught trespassing. He checks his watch again, anticipation building. Is it fear? No. It's excitement.

The nosey old man had no right questioning us or going to the headmaster. A nice fat donation to the building fund, a gardener is fired, and suspicions fade away. That one wasn't on me, anyway. It wasn't my idea to kill the stupid cat.

He takes out a cigarette and lights it, feeling like a tough guy in an old movie. His fingers are trembling. He takes a long drag and then coughs horribly, feeling stupid and belligerent with it. He drops the cigarette in the pine needles and crushes it under his shoe.

"Hello?"

Finally. He sees the old man looking around, so he turns on the flashlight on his phone.

The old guy moves forward. "I almost turned around," he says. "I don't understand. Why are you contacting me now? I tried to help you years ago and you got me fired."

"That wasn't me. You were right about him. I didn't want to do that stuff. He made me."

"Okay," Garza says, moving closer. "But why all this mystery?" He gestures to the dark, empty estate. "You're a man now. Do what you want. You were done with school bullies years ago."

"I wanted to apologize for how we treated you." The excitement is growing as he grips the wooden handle tighter.

Garza looks around, brow furrowed. "Yes, but if you want to apologize, you go to the person. I had to pay to get into this community, so I could drive here, and then wander around this fancy place. If cops show up, guess who's getting arrested? This isn't how you apologize." He says it as though he's speaking to someone who's missed quite a few life lessons along the way.

"Don't worry," the killer says. "This won't take long."

Garza checks his watch. "I need to go. My wife is waiting for me."

"Here?" He can't keep the panic from his voice.

Garza squints into the dark, trying to read the young man's expression. "No. At home."

"Oh," he sighs. "That's good then."

The shovel comes up so quickly out of the dark, Garza barely registers a glint of metal before it bashes in the side of his head. He drops like a stone and the young man giggles.

Almost done. He takes out his phone, snaps a pic, and texts it away. Another one checked off the list. His father always complains that he never finishes what he starts. He almost wishes he could show his dad the list they started seven years ago. He's finished quite a few things.

He throws the shovel into the brush and then tries to lift Garza. He can't do it. He grabs the old man's wrists and tries to drag him, but it's harder than he anticipates. He should have made the old man walk closer to the edge before he hit him. Now what is he supposed to do?

His phone pings with a new text. He looks. It's a screenshot of the old man's name with a line through it. A zing of pride races through him.

Looking around, he tries to figure out how to move the trim man who couldn't be taller than 5'6". Embarrassed, he's glad he's alone right now. He'd be mocked for this for years. The shovel! He picks up the shovel and sides it under the gardener's butt. He grabs one arm and the shovel handle, slowly dragging Garza over pine needles, roots, and branches to the edge of the cliff.

The young man is sweaty and wheezing, but he did it. Rolling the body to the drop-off, he pulls out his phone, opening the camera function. With his foot on the gardener, he gives it a quick shove and then snaps a few more pictures as the body falls and splashes into the water.

Done, he strolls back through the estate, a new spring in his step, swiping through images, looking for the best to send. Once he has, he gets *in his car and drives home. Maybe he'll treat himself to an ice cream. He finished what he'd started, after all.*

Blinking, I found Osso and Hernández hovering. "What?"

"You what," Osso grumbled. "What did you see?"

I explained as I made my way through the trees to the cliff. Pointing at the discarded shovel, I said, "There's your murder weapon. He wasn't wearing gloves, so his prints should be all over it."

Osso took a glove out of his pocket and used it to pick up the shovel.

"I'm kinda torn right now," I said.

The detectives looked at me.

"I was going to ask you to take me to Mr. Garza's body so I could read him. He knows something about these two. The thing is, that's his blood, hair, maybe some scalp right there. I don't want to touch that, but if I do, it'll save us a trip to the asshole coroner's place."

"And she would be there," Hernández said. "This is a normal working day for her."

Great. Sighing, I took off my glove again and—as I didn't want my fingerprints on a murder weapon—touched the back of my hand to a bloody clump of hair, thinking about how he knew the killer.

He's younger. Wearing a long-sleeve olive green shirt and matching pants. A patch on the pocket reads **Garza**. *He's in a forested area, sawing through a tree branch that cracked in last night's storm. The students aren't allowed in the grove on their own, but still. Can't have a heavy branch fall on a kid chasing a soccer ball.*

He pauses to answer a text from the headmaster and hears whispering. He turns his head, trying to determine where the sound is coming from.

He follows the whispers and giggles through the trees, hoping he's not going to find students having sex. He hates that.

When he finds two teenagers not touching each other, he breathes a sigh of relief. He's about to bark at them about getting back up to the school when he hears a weak, pitiful mewing sound.

He circles around behind them, a sick feeling in his stomach. The boys haven't noticed him. They're too engrossed in what they're doing.

"What—" It's all he can get out. The tall one's hand moves so fast, Garza almost misses it. Something shiny and bloodstained just went in his pocket. The stick he'd been using to hold the wounded cat in place drops to the ground.

The other boy, shorter, looks scared. "We found him like this. We were going to bring him up to the school."

The tall one nods. "We heard him crying and came to help. We were trying to decide the best way to pick him up so we didn't injure him further."

"Get back to the school," Garza orders.

The short one doesn't need to be told twice. He takes off running. The tall one looks down his nose at the groundskeeper. "You shouldn't talk to us that way. We came to help. Our actions are laudable and you should remember your place." With that, he turns and walks back through the forest, leaving Garza with a tortured cat.

The image goes dark and then…

Garza is walking down the school hall. He's uncomfortable in here, much prefers to stay out on the grounds, but he's been thinking about the shorter one, the scared one. He hasn't been able to sleep, thinking about the two of them, what he's sure they did. He spoke to the headmaster, but that was a waste of time. The headmaster assured him that they were good young men from fine families and he was positive Garza had misinterpreted the situation.

He'd even gone to the dean, but he kept asking Garza if he'd actually seen the students hurting the cat. He hadn't, so the dean said he'd make a note of it in his files and dismissed him.

His wife told him to let it go. He'd done what he could. It was up to the school now. He knows she's right, but the shorter one looked scared and he needs to check on him, maybe help him get away from the other one. His own son had fallen in with the wrong group of boys when he was in school. Garza knew how hard it could be to break away from so-called friends at that age. Maybe the scared one just needed some help, an adult to blame that allowed him to save face.

He knows when the shorter one has PE, has seen him out on the field, and so is waiting outside the boys' changing room for him. When the student emerges and sees Garza, he quickly looks around. Garza waves him over and the boy goes reluctantly.

"Are you okay?" Garza asks.

He shrugs, still seeming to look for the dean.

"Listen," Garza continues. "You're a decent kid, right? You didn't want to hurt that animal, did you?"

"We told you. We found him like that." He looks over his shoulder. "Maybe a mountain lion attacked him." He shrugs again. "I don't know. We were just trying to help."

"I saw what the other one had in his hand. I saw the knife. Do you need help? The headmaster can keep you safe. I can talk to him for y—"

"No!" he whisper-shouts, looking over his shoulder again. "I told you, you're wrong." He turns back to Garza, his expression cold. "Unless you'd like me to tell the headmaster how you make me uncomfortable, always trying to talk to me and touch me, I suggest you leave me the fuck alone," he hisses.

Garza recoils. "I'm only trying to help."

"That was your first mistake." The one-minute chime is heard over the loudspeaker and the student jogs to his next class.

When the image dims again, I think of his death.

He knows his wife will be annoyed with him, but when the young man contacted him, he couldn't say no. He should have. He sees that now, but he keeps thinking about the fear on the kid's face when he'd caught them with the cat. The kid told him to park on the road, so he does. Why they couldn't meet at a coffee shop is beyond him. The big house is dark and the grounds deserted. He's got no reason to be on this property. If this is some stupid prank, he might be calling his very angry wife to bail him out tonight.

He sees a flare of light at the tree line, so he goes in that direction.

The same scene plays out, but this time I have a better look at the killer as an adult. *It's dark and Garza's eyesight isn't as good as it used to be, but still. The killer was right. Garza doesn't see the shovel until it hits him.*

What the young man doesn't realize is that the hit didn't kill him. Garza comes to, groggy and sore, as the killer rolls him to the edge. He sees a series of flashes and then is kicked over the edge, freefalling into the ocean and rocks below…

"What the hell was that?"

I opened my eyes at the bear's snarl as I dangled over the cliff, hanging from the arm around my waist. At the same time that I processed what a strange predicament I was in, a huge wave hit the cliff, a good thirty to forty feet higher than normal.

I waved at the water. "Thanks, Dad! I'm okay!"

Osso moved away from the edge and put me down. Hernández had a hand on her chest, her eyes wide.

"What?" I asked

"You walked right to the edge and stepped off. I don't know how Arthur got there in time to catch you." Hernández was shaking her head. "We thought you were out of the trance. I'd just asked you what you'd seen and you walked straight over the cliff."

"It was like watching Wile E. Coyote," Osso said. "I thought you were fine, just wanting to look where Garza would have gone over, but there was no hesitation." He rubbed his hands over his face. "You gave me a damned heart attack."

"Sorry about that," I said. "Garza didn't die when the shovel hit. He was waking up as the killer rolled him to the edge. He felt the kick over. The poor man was terrified as he dropped. And his last thoughts were of his wife and kids."

Hernández took my arm. "Can you move farther away from the edge, please." She blew out a breath. "I think I aged twenty years in that moment. If my hair turns gray, it's on you."

"I really am sorry. I don't usually move around like that."

They both looked like they might be sick.

"What do you say we head back? I'll buy you both dinner on the way home. Wait. No." I checked my phone. "I'm supposed to be meeting Declan for dinner. I'll bake you guys a thank-you-for-saving-me-and-I'm-sorry-for-scaring-you surprise."

"With honey," Osso said as he pulled another glove from his pocket and picked up the shovel again before heading back toward the car.

THIRTY-ONE

Wicche vs. Gun

Once in the back seat, I went into my backpack and pulled out a sketchbook and pencils. "If you can keep the ride as smooth as possible, I'd appreciate it."

Hernández turned in her seat. "You have a face for us?"

I nodded. "I've got both of them as teenagers. At a guess, I'd say they were fourteen or fifteen. And then I have one as an adult. He was standing in the dark, but I have a feel for his adult face."

I started working on last night's killer as a teen and had a thought. "Can you guys get yearbooks for the school?"

"We're already working on it," Osso said, "but the school loves nothing more than to deny requests and line up lawyers to shout about privacy."

"Is there an assumption of privacy for a yearbook?" I asked.

"You wouldn't think," Hernández replied. "It's filled with pictures and names and handed out to the entire student body. We got a judge to sign the warrant, but they're fighting it."

"All their damn stalling stunts are getting people killed. If they'd cooperated from the jump, we might have a line on these bastards, and maybe Luis Garza would still be alive."

We were all frustrated into silence. Closing my eyes, I found the face again and drew.

By the time I was finishing the third face, I looked up and realized no one was in the front seat and the car was parked in front of the gallery.

Hernández, Osso, and Declan were sitting on the steps chatting. I put my pencils away and tried to open the door, but it was locked. All the windows were open, so I called, "Am I under arrest?"

Declan laughed and Osso took out his keys and hit the unlock button. I walked over, handed Hernández my sketchbook, and sat beside Declan. He wrapped an arm around me and kissed my head.

"Sorry I'm late," I said, resting my hand on his knee.

"We didn't set a time and you were busy." He looked over Osso's shoulder at the sketches.

"Oh, here," I said, taking back the sketchbook and ripping out the three pages. They were trying to be careful with the images, gently flipping the sheets back and forth. Now they could study them all at once.

Osso tapped the adult portrait. "This one killed the teacher and the groundskeeper."

Hernández shook the taller teen's portrait. "And this one killed your cousin and the dean."

"Yes," I said. "That feels right."

"Okay," Hernández said, standing up. "We'll let you have your dinner. Thank you, Arwyn."

Osso stood as well. "We'll get started trying to identify them through the images. You two have a good evening."

They drove away, leaving Declan and me on the steps.

"What's for dinner?" I asked.

"Mexican food. I went back to Mariana's and ordered a little bit of everything." He stood. "It's still in my truck. I'll go grab it and we'll heat it up," he said, heading around the far side of the gallery.

"Wait. You actually parked in the parking lot?"

"I decided I was setting a bad example. If people keep seeing cars parked in front, they'll think it's okay." He rounded the corner and was out of sight.

Returning the sketchbook to the backpack, I looked up when a car skidded to a stop, kicking up pebbles. The passenger side window rolled down and the sweaty man lifted a gun.

"Get in now," he snarled.

Declan raced back around the corner, but I held up a hand, asking him to stop. I knew it was probably killing him to do it, but he waited.

Was this what Calliope had planned for me? "I'm not going to do that." I kept eye contact while searching for the honey bottle. I knew some very basic spells still worked after touching Declan, but I wasn't taking any chances with this one.

His eyes darted to Declan once and then they were trained on me. The fervor, the obsession, were shining in them.

Finding the bottle, I squirted it on my hands, and I saw, as clearly as a movie, exactly what he wanted to do with me. I almost lost my footing on the step, but I had to put it aside. He'd never get control of me and therefore none of what he dreamed of would happen. At the bottom of the steps, I flicked my fingers and jammed his gun. "I need you to go and never come back. Do you understand me?"

"No."

I gave him a magical shove, but still he stayed, staring, willing me to get in his car. And then I felt it. Calliope was in there, pushing him. "You again?" I said, adding more of a punch this time.

Shaking, blood beginning to drip from his nose, his focus never left me. Jaw clenched, eyes wild, his free hand wiped at the blood. "Get in," he ground out, but there was a petulant whine to it.

"That's never going to happen, oh cousin of mine. You want to truck with demons, give up your soul, that's on you. Why, though, are you dragging all of us into it? Go be evil somewhere else."

"Fucking bitch," he spat out, pulling the trigger.

Declan dove on a roar as a concussive bang had my ears ringing. He twisted us, mid-tackle, so he was skidding on the asphalt and I was on top of him. His hands were all over my head, checking for a wound. "Are you hit?"

I kissed his nose.

Sitting up, confused, he checked my body, no doubt looking for blood.

"I'm fine."

His squeezed my hips. "How are you fine? It was pointed right at you when he fired." He wrapped his arms around me tightly and leaned back so he was lying on the pavement again. "God. I was so scared. I can't remember ever being that scared in my life. I'd just found you and he took you away."

"Nope." I snuggled in. "I'm right here. We're both okay, but he's not."

"I smell blood."

"Yeah. That's because his gun jammed and exploded in his hand." I climbed off and gave him my hand, yanking him to his feet.

"I keep forgetting how strong you are."

"You should never forget that," I said, pulling my phone out and tapping on Hernández.

"Hello," she answered.

"I'm going to need you to come back." I looked in the window. "My stalker returned and tried to abduct me at gunpoint—"

A loud roar had me pulling the phone from my ear. It was followed by squealing tires.

"Tell Osso to slow down. He's dead. I think his gun jammed and blew up in his face."

There was a loaded silence and then Osso said, "Yeah. That'll work. Call 911 and tell them you just contacted us. You were scared and not thinking, so you called the cop you knew before them. We'll be there in a few."

I did as I was directed and then Declan and I resumed our seats on the steps and waited.

Declan wrapped an arm around me. "If it makes you feel any better, you didn't have a choice. He was never going to stop."

"No. He wasn't, especially with Cal pushing him."

"Still sucks, though," he said.

"It really does. Remember when Dave told us that having a sorcerer working in a particular area causes all kinds of problems that aren't related but are? The evil seeps in and causes people, who might normally have been able to control their urges, to indulge in their most wicked desires?

"This one," I continued, "might have always been obsessed—I think some people are affected by the fae blood—but it would have taken the form of visiting the gallery too often and staring, the fantasy staying trapped up here." I tapped my forehead. "Instead, he bought a gun today so he could kidnap me and act on all those dark fantasies."

"You think your cousin sent this guy?"

"I know she did. I felt her. She found some guy teetering on the edge and pushed him over it. When he was sitting in his car, watching me paint the mural, I didn't feel her. You sensed the obsession, but he wasn't homicidal until she twisted the obsession, making it dark and violent."

"I'm sorry," he said.

"Me too. She knows I have stalker issues. She's probably laughing her ass off right now. She was there for one when I was a teenager. We were at a family picnic on the beach. I was sitting on the rocks, away from the group, trying to decide if I should go swimming. The ocean always made me happy, but I was in maybe eighth grade. The boobs had developed, and certain cousins enjoyed teasing me."

"Fucking Colin," he said.

I kissed his cheek. "Exactly, although not just him. Anyway, this guy showed up—late twenties maybe—and sat down next to me, trying to get me to engage, asking all these questions. I knew I could get rid of him, but it was scary, you know?"

He nodded. "And all the spells you know to make strange

people go away are useless if he touches your skin and you're out, lost in a vision."

"Yes." I tipped my head onto his shoulder, amazed every time I was able to touch him. "Anyway, I looked and thought I saw Calliope watching. Everyone else was in the water, eating, talking, not paying attention to me. Cal walked over to the adults, and I hoped she was going to get my mom. Nope. She got a cookie, sat down, and started chatting. No one looked my way. At the time, I assumed I was wrong, that she hadn't seen the guy. Now, well, lots of memories have had to be altered.

"Anyway, the guy kept asking me my name and if I wanted to go for a walk. He knew a great place just down the beach. I hit him with a go-away spell, and he stood for a moment, but then sat back down and launched into his *you're so beautiful* spiel again. I hit him with a spell, he stood, and then sat back again.

"I heard familiar laughter and turned back to the group to see Cal watching us, one hand fisted on the table. She was spelling the guy to stay."

"I don't understand," Declan said. "How did you know?"

"The fist. You know when I do spells, my fingers are moving?"

He nodded.

"Cal uses a fist. When she saw me looking, she quickly got my mom, who stormed over, yelling and spelling as she came. The guy took off at a run and then Cal came over, saying she was trying to help me get rid of him, but her magic wasn't strong enough yet. My mother patted her shoulder and thanked her for helping me, reassuring her that her magic would strengthen as she got older. Remember, Cal is only a little younger than me, but she's petite and likes to play on people's impulses to take care of her. She went back for another cookie, all smiles, and I got yelled at for being away from the group and not practicing my spells well enough to get a creep to leave me alone."

"Fucking Calliope," he said, making me laugh.

I hugged him around the middle. "Thanks for being on my side."

"It's my favorite place to be."

A patrol car arrived, skidding to a stop. The officer got out of his vehicle and drew on us. Declan raised his left hand, and I raised my right. Our other arms were wrapped around each other.

"Dude," I said. "He's the bad guy, not us."

"I'd appreciate if you lowered your weapon," Declan said, not doing the best job of keeping the growl out of his voice. "She's already had one gun in her face today."

Thankfully, Osso pulled up a moment later, jumped out of the car, and stood between the patrol officer and us, so we put our hands down. Osso kept his voice low, but from the way the man wilted, I'd guess he'd been dressed down quite harshly. The cop quickly got back into his car and pulled away.

"Idiot," Osso grumbled. He gave Declan and me one assessing look and then met Hernández at the stalker's car. They both put on gloves. Hernández opened the passenger's door while Osso went around to the driver's.

Hernández hesitated and turned to us. "Did either of you touch anything?"

We both shook our heads.

"We need to make sure he doesn't need assistance and then we'll take your statements," she said.

"I've got this," Osso said. "You go ahead and get started. I'll call in the coroner."

"Oh, great," I said.

Hernández paused, pulling off her gloves. "See if you can get Andy to come. I think he's back on nights."

Osso nodded and then hit the trunk button. When it opened, Hernandez, Declan, and I saw a hatchet, a tire iron, and an unzipped duffle bag with rope, zip ties, and duct tape. Whatever else was in there, I couldn't see and didn't want to know about.

Hernández moved to block my view of the trunk. "Why don't you guys go in and we'll come for your statements in a few minutes?"

Osso joined her at the trunk and gave Declan a look before

tilting his head. I read it as well as Declan, who stood and pulled me up with him. They wanted me out of here.

"I really do appreciate you guys trying to protect me, but I already know what he planned to do with me." The sun had finally set, and the scene was getting dark. "I'll put on the outdoor lights. We'll be in the studio when you're ready."

Hernández nodded. Declan grabbed my backpack and we headed in. I knew the man's death had been his own fault, that he'd pulled the trigger, but even though there was one fewer man in the world who wanted to hurt me, I couldn't help but feel like there were too damn many to begin with.

The Benefits of a Sturdy Table

When we went in, I hit the outdoor lights switch and then locked the door.

Declan paused and studied the painting progress. "Looks like you were able to do some work today."

I nodded. "Not much, but at least I finished the big wall."

He stared into the corner, at the short wall connecting the road side of the gallery and the parking lot side. "I don't know how you did it, but that triangular storage room in the corner disappeared."

I smacked his arm. "Right? It's an optical illusion I created through brushstroke angles and paint colors. If it was bright in here, you'd see it." I flicked my fingers and the overhead lights came on.

He shook his head. "I see it because I'm looking for it. If I wasn't, my eyes would have gone right past it. You better watch out. You're going to get people running into that wall."

"I have big, glass-fronted display cases that go there. And it's not a storage room. I'll be using it to give readings. I can't do that out here once I open, and I don't want clients in my studio. Too much of what I see is painful. I don't want that energy in my creative space."

"Is there anything in the room yet?" he asked.

I shook my head. "The gallery is the priority. I haven't scheduled any readings for a little while so I can get the main space ready."

"Let's look. Do you have the furniture you need?" His fingers slid down my arm before clasping my hand.

As we walked across the huge space, I said, "I know what you're doing."

"Checking to see if my girlfriend needs me to make any pieces for her reading room?" He gave me a look that caused mad flutterings.

"Yeah. That's it." I played along, knowing full well he was trying to take my mind off the man who'd intended to hurt me in dark and varied ways.

It was a decent-sized room, somewhere between a small storage room and a large walk-in closet, but it worked fine for what I did. I made sure there were tall windows so clients didn't feel too claustrophobic.

"Nice light," he said, looking up.

I'd had Phil's guys install an antique chandelier. It was a French nineteenth century fixture, with elaborate black iron scrollwork holding five candles. I flicked my fingers and the candles lit. Declan reached over to the light switch on the wall and turned off the canned lights forty feet above, leaving the candles flickering in the now dim room.

Declan pulled me into his arms and kissed me until I forgot where I was and what I was doing. "Oh," he growled, "I like this room." He palmed my butt and then lifted me up so I could wrap my legs around him. Pressing me into the wall, he kissed up and down my neck. "I could install a Murphy bed."

I glanced around, judging distance. "Maybe just a really sturdy table."

"Done." And then his mouth was on mine.

I was pulling his shirt out of his jeans when I remembered we had cops outside. Patting his shoulder, I said, "Wait a minute."

Wolf gold eyes met mine.

"Dead guy. Cops. Statements." I wasn't any happier about it than he was.

His head dropped to my shoulder. "Forgot."

I saw his truck outside in the parking lot. "Let's go get dinner from your rig and I'll spell your tires and windshield against random acts of wolf violence."

Blowing out a breath, he set me back on the floor. "Yeah, okay. But don't forget where we were." He rubbed his hands over his face and then finished untucking his shirt. "I'll get my measuring tape too, so I can see how much room I've got to work with in here."

"How much room do you need?" I ran my hand down his thigh.

"Watch it, woman." He took my hand and led me out. "Don't forget to turn off the lights."

Laughing, I flicked my fingers, snuffing the candles. "You seem to be walking a little funny. You okay?"

"What did I say about watching it?" He swung around, picked me up, and threw me over his shoulder, one large mitt of a hand on my butt. "That's a little too much lip outta you."

"I thought you liked my lip."

He opened the back door and came to a sudden stop. I pushed on his back to lift my upper body and see what was going on.

"You put her down this instant," Bracken ordered.

Declan did and I stepped in front of him. Bracken was about to nail Declan with a spell.

"I'm okay. We were just messing around."

"There are police officers here. One came to my door and wanted to talk with me." He looked both outraged and concerned. "She said someone had tried to hurt you and asked if I saw anything, which, of course, I hadn't. And then this." He gestured at a very tall and muscular Declan.

Stepping forward, I rubbed his shoulder. "Thank you for looking out for me, but I'm okay. The guy who was looking in my windows earlier? He came back with a gun."

Bracken stood rigid, his expression furious.

"I spelled the gun to jam so when he tried to shoot me, it exploded in his face. This one," I said, pointing at Declan, "pulled me out of the way so I didn't get hurt. The cops are out front investigating. We were going to his truck to get dinner. It's Mexican. Are you sure you don't want to eat with us?"

His eyes brightened at *Mexican*. "Oh, I don't want to intrude."

"It's no intrusion. In fact, you can come help me now. There are some local wolves causing Declan trouble, trashing his rig. Let's go get the food and add some protective spells."

Bracken nodded, turning back toward the parking lot. "I know just the one to use."

After my uncle and I each added our own protective spells, we all headed back in for dinner.

"You could probably enter that truck into a demolition derby now," I said.

"Do they still have those?" Bracken asked. "I remember hearing advertisements for them. They were quite irritating, *Sunday, Sunday, Sunday*," he mimicked. "*Come to the monster truck rally.*" Shaking his head, he added, "Humans are odd."

Declan grinned at me and then pointed at the studio door. I took me a minute and then I saw it too. Three little noses were hanging over the edge of the roof.

"How do they keep getting up there? There are no trees that brush up against the gallery."

Bracken paused and looked up. A smile slowly spread across his face. "You have raccoons?"

"I don't have them. They just show up," I said. "They're Otis, Daisy, and Jasper."

Bracken raised his eyebrows. "You named them?"

"In her defense," Declan said, "she names everything."

"That's true," I confirmed.

"And she feeds them," he continued.

Bracken and Declan shared a look.

"Arwyn," Bracken began, "they're wild animals. You can't make them reliant on humans. It's unsafe for them."

"I'm not! It was just Otis at first. He looked really hungry but was too polite to ask, so he just sniffed at the basket where I had a muffin. He sat like a little gentleman by the basket, waiting to see if I'd share. I mean, come on. Look at them. What? I'm supposed to say, *Starve, you adorable little forest creature. I have more than enough food to share, but I'm selfish and won't.* Is that it?"

"Bracken, I don't know if you understand how hard she's fighting the impulse to run inside and get them food right now." Declan scratched his beard, trying to hide his grin.

"Oh, shut up." I ran inside and got three cinnamon oatmeal raisin muffins. I'd been experimenting. Mom had said it wasn't a popular flavor, but those few customers who bought one really enjoyed it.

I defrosted them in my hands, adding a bit of warmth while I was at it. When I came back out, Declan and Bracken were sitting on a bench, looking up and chatting—that was nice. I looked up as well but didn't see the raccoons' noses. Thankfully, it only took a moment before they popped back out again, sniffing the air.

"Okay, you guys." I held up the three muffins, so they knew they'd each get one. "Otis, you're first." I tossed up a muffin and little paws shot out to grab it. "Daisy, you're next." I tossed and more little paws. "Jasper, are you ready?" One last toss and two more paws shot out. "Have a warm meal and then enjoy your adventures tonight. But be careful up there!"

I turned to the men. "Let's eat."

Bracken went in but Declan pulled me into a hug. "How worried are you about them falling off the roof?"

I slumped into him. "Very. They're babies and it's so high up there. Where are their parents? That's what I want to know."

He kissed the top of my head and pulled me into the studio. "Come on. I'm hungry."

When we went in, Bracken was sitting at the worktable, correctly assuming it was also the dining table. "Declan, can you give the food boxes to my uncle? He can warm up the food while I get plates and utensils."

The studio filled with mouthwatering smells as boxes were opened and spells were used to heat the food. I put out the plates, silverware, and napkins. "What would you two like to drink? I have water, milk, soda, beer, and tea."

"I don't suppose you have horchata?" Bracken asked as he continued to spell the boxes, heating up the food.

Declan and I shared another look. "I'm afraid I don't."

"Oh, well. Water will do fine for me. Thank you, dear," Bracken said, finally sitting back down.

When I returned with drinks, our feast began. All our plates were piled high and still there was more food. Of course, Declan loved leftovers. They took the guesswork out of the next day's lunch.

Bracken finished quickly and then went back to his motorhome so he could continue his research, leaving Declan and me alone. He'd just shoved his plate aside, his eyes wolf gold, when we heard a knock on the back door.

Slumping back in his chair, he growled.

I waved Hernández and Osso in.

"Oh my God," she said, "that smells amazing!"

"I'll get two more plates." I hopped up. "What would you guys like to drink?"

"No, no," Hernández said. "We don't want to take your food."

"Speak for yourself," Osso grumbled. "I'm starving."

Hernández, of course, relented. Neither had eaten anything since breakfast.

Once they were done eating, they moved back into detective mode, asking each of us to give our statements.

Osso tapped his notebook in the table. "You gave him a shove—"

"Two," I clarified.

"Two. And your uncle gave him one earlier today. Any idea why he kept ending up back here?"

I shook my head. "Originally, it could have been something as simple as he drove this road to and from work, so even though we redirected him, every time he drove by, the obsession was re-engaged. Today, though, I felt my cousin, the sorcerer's hand in it."

"And this guy was never a client, right?" Hernandez asked. "He never came for a reading?"

I shook my head again. "I'd never seen him before a couple of days ago."

"He was off," Declan said. "The first time we noticed him, I caught his scent and wanted him away from her den. I kept putting myself between them and I couldn't get her away soon enough. He smelled like sickness."

Osso nodded. "I caught that under the blood, sweat, and gunpowder." He pocketed the notebook. "Okay. We're going now. You should be fine," he said to me. "He's the one with the gun. He's the one who pulled the trigger. You can't be held responsible for his gun backfiring." He gave me a look. "At least not in a human court."

"I guess that's something," I said, walking them to the back door.

Once they were gone, the door locked and the shutters drawn, Declan threw me back over his shoulder and took the stairs to my loft two at a time.

THIRTY-THREE

Death by Boat

"Remember where we were?" he growled, referring to our time in the reading room.

"Up against a wall?" I was bracing myself on his butt, trying not to laugh.

Instead of dropping me to the floor or tossing me on the bed, he slid me from his shoulder and down his body, his hands on my butt, holding me a foot off the floor.

Mouth on my neck, he walked us over to my bed and turned, falling backward to keep me on top. Such a gentleman. I straddled him, grinding down just a little. On a groan, he unhooked the straps of my overalls and relieved me of my top.

Rolling us over, he climbed off the bed and then yanked off my overalls, taking my shoes and socks with them. His gaze lazily roamed. "I've been dreaming of you all day." He quickly undressed and then pounced.

At turns laughing and moaning, we couldn't get enough of each other. Eventually exhaustion rather than satiation had us both passing out, still twined together.

I woke alone after the sun had risen, but only just. No messages waiting. No one knocking on my door. Flicking my fingers, I opened the shutters to soft pink light. With any luck, the rest of the world would forget all about me and I could get the walls painted. First, though, I needed something to wash off all the death of the last couple of days.

I put on a pair of swim leggings, a long-sleeve rash guard, and water shoes before jogging down the stairs and out the back door.

"Good morning, guys!" I climbed up on top of the railing and dove into the ocean, instantly feeling stronger and more myself. I swam under the deck, looking for Cecil. I was just about to give up and assume he was away from home when a tentacle shot up from a rock, coiling around my ankle and tugging.

Cecil's color changed as he uncoiled himself, dancing in the water beside me. I put out my arm and he wrapped himself around me, all but one tentacle that he used to point deeper under the deck. I swam where he indicated and found his friend was still here. Ah, young octopus love.

I shall name you Poppy, as she was a beautiful poppy red right now. She undulated in the current, her tentacles recoiling underneath her. In that movement, I saw the eggs she was protecting.

Cecil! I was so excited. We'd soon have baby octopuses floating under my dock. Well, not too soon. As I recalled, they took six months to hatch. Then I remembered another important octopus reproduction fact. *You two are still getting along okay, right?* His tentacle wrapped around my hand and squeezed.

No going crazy or dying on me, all right? You two are the exceptions to the rule. You're both going to live long lives, okay? Dad, are you listening? Cecil and Poppy are special.

They both seemed completely fine, but now I was terrified I'd say *good morning* and he wouldn't be there to slap the water. He uncoiled himself and danced beside me again, as though trying to reassure me I didn't need to worry. *I'm holding you both to that.*

Something knocked into my shoulder and I turned to see Wilbur racing away. I'm a strong, fast swimmer, but I'm not a seal. He disappeared and I was left spinning, trying to find him before he sneaked up on me again.

When the pressure in my head got painful, I surfaced and

took a breath. Dad's DNA meant I could stay under without drowning, but the longer I went without air, the bigger the headache.

Something bumped my hip, the little sneak, and I dove down to give chase. He was teasing me, letting me get tantalizingly close and then racing off. I'd been so distracted, worrying about how long I'd have Cecil in my life, that it took too long to realize I'd swum too far out.

Surfacing, I got swamped by a wave, the wake of a fishing boat. *Damn it.* What the hell was wrong with me? Exhausted, muscles trembling, I looked for the gallery and couldn't see it. Another huge wave dragged me down and spun me around. When I finally surfaced again, I wasn't sure which direction to go, and I felt a flutter of fear in my chest.

I'd barely gone ten strokes when I was nudged again. This time, however, it wasn't Wilbur. It was a dolphin, who circled me once before sidling up beside me. I wrapped my hands around his dorsal fin and let him tow me back to shore, with two more dolphins who seemed to be serving as guards. A last big wave brought me home, the dolphins circling until I'd climbed the rope Declan had installed for me. At the top, giving me a hand over was Emrys, Wilbur in his other form, that of a slight, pale fae man with translucent hair.

"Mistress, are you well?" He waited, unconcerned with his nakedness.

"Yeah. The nice dolphin gave me a ride back. What was that, though? Why were you leading me so far away from the shore?"

He'd already begun shaking his head. "Never would I put your safety in jeopardy, Mistress. That wasn't me. That was Ash, who has always been a good and loyal soldier to your father." He lowered his head. "He is being stripped of his seal skin as we speak. Your father is furious that he would try to harm you."

I dropped onto a bench, my muscles quivering. "Does my father know we have a sorcerer and her demon targeting us again?"

Emrys—which is how I thought of Wilbur in this form—hissed at the word *demon* and then nodded. "He has been informed."

"Does Ash interact with humans around here, or is he primarily in the ocean or in Faerie?" I was getting a sneaking suspicion as to why Ash was suddenly trying to kill me, to make me afraid of my safe place.

"Both. He recently found a mate and has been granted permission to live in this realm."

"Please let my father know that he could have been spelled or even possessed to behave as he did. Though I believe possession leaves the possessed dead. If he's still alive, it's possible my cousin spelled him." I paused, considering. "I wouldn't have thought our magic strong enough to spell the fae, though."

"Your father is listening to your words through me. He asks that you spell me as an experiment." He stood braced and ready.

"Emrys, I'd never hurt you. The vast majority of spells don't cause pain. I understand my father orders it, but are you okay with this? I won't do it otherwise."

Solemnly, he nodded, looking like he was facing a firing squad.

"Father, if you can hear me, this isn't a perfect experiment. Wicches are all different. We have different strengths and gifts. My magic is even more different, as I also possess fae gifts. If Ash's betrayal was orchestrated by Calliope, her magic would be run through with demon power. Does Ash smell of sulfur? I have a half-demon, half-wicche friend who says that if demons are involved, sulfur will be present."

Emrys kept his head bowed. "Your father is having Ash checked, though he still asks that you spell me."

I flicked my fingers, and he waited.

"Look at yourself," I said.

He lifted his hand in wonder. His pale skin was now the speckled gray and brown of his seal skin.

"Have you altered my skin or my own perception of it?"

"Your skin. And you might notice you're no longer standing on the deck."

His focus quickly moved from his arm to the deck he hovered six inches above. "I see. Your father asks—and I second—can you undo what your spell has done?"

I flicked my fingers and he was as he had been.

"I'd be more inclined to believe Calliope and her demon poisoned Ash than he suddenly chose, all on his own, to try to hurt me." I really didn't want some poor selkie being punished for freaking Cal's actions.

"Your father understands your concern and commends your empathy. He assures you he will investigate before Ash is punished, if he is indeed punished."

"Thank you," I said.

Emrys nodded, donned his sealskin, and leapt over the railing, diving into the ocean.

Sopping wet and still shaky, I did a quick drying spell so I didn't track seawater everywhere, and then went in to shower properly. Once I was cleaned, my hair conditioned and beginning to dry, I crawled onto my bed and pulled a blanket over me.

The ocean had always been my happy and safe place. When the nightmares and visions were too much, when the haters got to me, or the obsessives wouldn't leave me alone, I had the water and all the wonderful creatures in it. Now Calliope was trying to take that away from me.

Curled up and shivering, I called Declan.

"Good morning. Hey, it's almost nine. Hopefully that means you slept well," he said.

A let out a breath. Just hearing his deep voice helped me feel not so alone. "I woke up early, but I was feeling pretty good."

"What's the matter? You sound funny."

"I'm okay now. I was just feeling a little shaky and wanted to hear your voice."

"I'm on my way,"

"No, Declan. I'm fine. You have a crew there and work to do. Really, I'm okay."

I heard a tire squeal, a honk, and then road sounds. "Can you unlock the back door? I'm coming around the side now."

Flicking my fingers, I unlocked it a moment before it opened and was relocked. Then I heard heavy steps pounding up the stairs.

"You didn't need to drive over. I didn't mean to scare you." I watched him round the bed and sit down before kicking off his boots and rolling in behind me, his powerful arm pulling me in tight against him.

"I had a nice jog. Now tell me what happened."

I rolled over, put my head on his chest, and told him.

"How far out had he led you?"

"I don't know. I have excellent eyesight. Not as good as yours, but still. I couldn't see the gallery." I let out a sigh. "I wasn't panicking. It was more of a *What the fuck did I just do?* I mean, what was the worst that could happen? My arms were too tired to swim, so maybe I sink and walk back with a headache? I don't know. It was more that Wilbur, someone I loved and trusted, had tried to hurt me. Goddess, it was my childhood all over again."

"And the real Wilbur—"

"Emrys," I corrected.

"Right. Emrys says it was this Ash selkie who was actually leading you into boating lanes."

I flinched.

He hugged me even tighter. "I think that was the endgame. As you said, other than being tired, it was more of a mean prank. Once you introduce humans in boats with large engines and propellers, it rises to attempted murder."

"I watch the fishing boats go in and out of the harbor every day, right where I was treading water. One had passed right before I went up for air and still that hadn't occurred to me."

"You were too busy worrying about Cecil and Wilbur."

That was true.

"So, can you do me a favor and start wearing your dad's earrings?"

I thought about it a moment and then nodded. The earrings had been given to me by my Aunt Sylvia when I graduated from high school. I'd only found out recently at her wake that they'd actually been a gift from my father, one my mother had refused to give me. Sylvia didn't agree with Mom's decision and gave them to me herself.

Unfortunately, she hadn't told me or anyone other than my Uncle John, her husband, where the earrings had come from. Consequently, the cousins—especially Sylvia's daughters Serena and Calliope—hated me even more. Why did I receive a gift far nicer and more expensive than anyone else? It went along with their contention that I had been given preferential treatment since birth.

The earrings were stunning, with a large, lustrous pearl in the middle and triangular fiery blue-green opals surrounding it, like petals on a flower. I'd only ever worn them once, at Sylvia's wake, when Calliope tried to kill Gran. That was also the night Emrys introduced himself and told me that if I ever wanted my father's attention, I need only touch the pearl and he'd be listening.

It was hard to explain, even to myself, why I didn't start wearing them every day after that. I had told Declan I was afraid of being eavesdropped on, which was true, but I really just wasn't ready. After wondering who my father was all my life, suddenly he was a thought away and I hadn't been prepared for that.

It was time, though.

THIRTY-FOUR

Death to Square Dancing

Declan went back to work and I was feeling stronger, better. Having someone I could call who'd quite literally run over to check on me was a strange and amazing gift. Another was the earrings my father had given me. I went into my closet, opened the small box, and felt that same rush of wonder I'd had when I first saw them.

Spelling them first against paint, I put them on and went down to work on the gallery. I had too much work to do to wallow all day.

It was late in the afternoon when I finished the far wall and took a quick break to eat something and move the scaffolding to the wall in common with the studio. This wall would be more complicated because of the little tea shop area and the built-in shelves. I had to take down the weathered-looking gray wooden shelves before I began to paint. Arranging them on the floor in the order I'd taken them from the wall would hopefully make putting this all back together easier.

I went out on the deck to sit on a bench and feel the ocean breeze as I ate a sandwich, one hastily assembled and rather bland. I had to remember to order more groceries. A seagull flew toward me and my food and then abruptly flew in another direction.

"That's right. Keep moving," I mumbled. I hadn't been a fan of seagulls to begin with, but after Calliope and her demon had sent a horde of them to attack me, I'd spelled against them. A side benefit of the spell was no bird poop on my beautiful deck.

I finished, filled up my water bottle, and got back to work. Arms already hurting before hours of painting, I decided to start moving some of the display cases, pedestals, and tables into place. They were the same light gray wood as the cash wrap and tea shop. The countertops in both spots were stained concrete, like the floor, but in a light seafoam.

Spelling the fixtures into place was taxing in a different way, one I could live with, as my muscles were sore. When I was mostly done—I wasn't doing anything on the studio side of the gallery because I was afraid the scaffolding would knock things over—I went into the fire room and started loading up a cart and rolling my glass sculptures out. I'd been mulling over placements for months, so it went quickly.

I knew I'd be tweaking the setup right until the grand opening, but I'd been dying to get started on this part for so long, I couldn't tamp down the giddy. My own gallery. I brought out the octopuses first. As the Sea Wicche, the glass octopus was kind of my signature piece. I'd made a hundred, at least. Depending on intricacy, size, and price, some needed to be displayed in locked cases, while others were arranged on tiered tables.

At the top of the table, on an elevated platform, was a five-foot glass octopus. His head was a deep indigo, his irises gold. The color slid down his body, blue to purple to raspberry to orange to tentacles tipped in yellow. The suckers were pearlized. He was one of my favorite things I'd ever made. I'd have to put *Don't touch* signs everywhere, but I wanted him to be out where people could see him, where he could glow in the light.

Flicking my fingers, I turned on one of the spotlights on the ceiling, training it on my octopus. Perfect.

I filled in the lower shelves with far smaller and more affordable octopuses. I brought out starfish and whales, mermaids and jellyfish, sea anemones and rays. I had a collection of ocean waves, as well as an array of bowls and vases. After training spotlights on those displays, I went back to start hauling out my pottery.

I hadn't realized how late it had become until I heard a gruff and grumbly, "Oh my God." I almost dropped the huge vase I was holding when I spun at the words.

Declan held up his hands, staring at my work through the open windows to the deck. "I had no idea you already had all of this made."

I placed the vase and then went to the back door to unlock it for him. I gave him a kiss and said, "I've been working for years, selling some along the way to support myself, stockpiling the rest for the gallery I knew I'd have some day."

"I'd wondered how you could possibly fill up this entire space and now I'm not sure you have enough room." He glanced at the watery walls. "You don't even have your paintings and photographs up yet." Patting his chest, he said, "It's racing. Your gift…" His gaze continued to travel around the gallery. "This must be how da Vinci's boyfriend felt."

"Oh, stop," I said, glowing on the inside.

"I came to measure that reading room and take you to dinner. Now I just want to study everything you've made." And he did just that, strolling around cases and pedestals, watching the light change the pieces.

While he perused, I went back to the shelves in the fire room and brought out another cart of pottery, including an oversized bowl I'd sculpted to resemble a cresting wave.

"Amazing. It looks heavy, though." Declan was beside me again.

"Not as heavy as the octopus, but, yeah, it's heavy."

"I can't do any of this, but I can lift heavy things. Where do you want it?"

I pointed to the center of a tiered table in the pottery section of the gallery. The warning to be careful was on the tip of my tongue, but it was unnecessary. He held my work with the care one would an infant.

"I'll measure while you finish up," he said, heading to the reading room corner. "Think about what you're hungry for."

I waited for him to hear what he'd said.

"Besides me," he called from inside the room.

Grinning, I pushed the cart to the tiered display and arranged a series of vases in graduating sizes.

"Whoa."

I turned at the deep voice and found Osso and Hernández staring through the open windows. Flicking my fingers, I said, "It's unlocked."

They came in and wandered the gallery much as Declan had, with Osso carrying a black bag.

"I knew you were good," Hernández began. "I've seen the paintings and the tentacles." She gestured out the windows. "But —holy crap—I had no idea."

It was funny. The art world knew my name. My pieces sold for a lot of money. My agent told me that the legend around me was of a recluse who occasionally popped her head up to introduce some new masterpiece into the world. The people who knew me, though, were forever surprised that the odd, curly-haired psychic in overalls was actually a successful artist. I supposed it had to do with perspective, which was something I understood quite well.

"How much is this?" Osso asked, pointing to a glass mermaid with dark skin and long, curly black hair fanned out around her face. "My daughter would love this."

She was way too much for a police officer to afford, unless he had hidden wealth and just worked for fun. "I'll make her a smaller version."

He looked at the mermaid again. "Was that a stupid question?"

"Not at all, but she'll go for at least ten thousand. Maybe more." I hated the idea of putting price tags on my work, but it had to be done. My agent had been publicizing the opening and said there were quite a few collectors flying in for it. Since she was afraid that left to my own devices, I'd undervalue my work, she said she'd visit next week and we'd decide on prices together.

Osso took a step away from the expensive mermaid, eyeing it warily.

"Did your kids like the octopuses I made them?"

"Yeah," he said, watching where he moved, now hyperaware of being surrounded by expensive art. "They love them. Thanks."

"The mermaid's pretty tricky to make and I'm going to be swamped for a while, but I will make one for her."

He held up a hand. "That's okay. Never mind."

"I'll do it. Just give me some time. When's her birthday?" I asked.

"September ninth."

Nodding, I pushed the empty cart back toward the studio. "I'll have her made by then. Let's go sit down and you can tell me why you guys are back."

When I returned from the fire room, Osso and Hernández were on the couch and Declan was sitting on the wobbly stool, pulled up beside my chair. "I'm going to need to buy more furniture, aren't I?"

"Probably a good idea," Hernández said.

I sat down, kicked off my shoes, and pulled up my feet, sitting cross-legged. "So what's up? Am I in trouble for the stalker?"

Osso glared at me. "Why would you be?" he said slowly, like he was talking to a child. "He shot himself. You're the innocent victim."

I nodded solemnly. "I am."

"One might even say helpless," Declan added with a grin.

"Let's not go too far," I protested. "I took a self-defense class."

"You did?" Hernández asked. "But you can…" She wiggled her fingers.

"I do have excellent finger dexterity. That's true," I said, causing Osso and Declan to laugh. "I had a great P.E. teacher who taught self-defense instead of tumbling or square dancing or whatever."

"I had to square dance," Hernández said, outraged.

"Did you have Ms. Smith in seventh grade?"

She shook her head. "Mr. Gillespe."

"There you go. She was a first-year teacher and more progressive than the rest. My cousins had Gillespe and said he was super old-school."

"Yeah," she agreed. "Sexist old creep. If a guy showed up late, he was told to hustle. If a girl was late, she was told to stop wasting time fixing her makeup or to deal with period stuff on her own time, not his."

I'm not sure what look I had on my face, but Hernández nodded in agreement.

"I wanted to punch that guy in the gut so bad," she said. "I hear he finally retired. Anyway, no, we're not here about the stalker."

Osso picked up the black bag on the floor and placed it on the coffee table. "We think we found the dean's murder weapon." He pulled out a plastic evidence pouch holding a glass award.

I felt a jolt of recognition. "That's it. Where did you find it?"

"It had been thrown in the school pool," Hernández explained, "which was actually a great hiding place. You couldn't see it down there. Thankfully, a girl had lost a very expensive ring and was running her hands along the bottom, trying to find it. She found a heavy glass award instead."

"It's already been fingerprinted, right?" I asked.

Both detectives nodded.

I picked up the plastic bag, put it in my lap, and slipped off a glove.

"My father will kill me. You said you could get me an A on that paper. I paid you for that A. Now, not only did I get an F—an F!—but the dean is going to fail me for the whole semester? Harvard is going to rescind their acceptance." The teen paces the small room, his pale face flushed with anger and fear. He wears the uniform of a Cypress Academy

student, though his tie is loose at his neck and his blond hair disheveled from being yanked at.

A man stands in the shadows, arms crossed, leaning against the wall and watching the frantic boy. "I'll take care of it."

"How? How can you take care of it? The report's been submitted. The dean already knows." He pulls at his hair again and then stops. "Plagiarized? I could have plagiarized the paper myself. I paid you three thousand dollars to get me an A so I can make up the assignment and get my diploma. What. The. Fuck?"

"As I've now said multiple times, I'll take care of it."

The teen resumes his pacing. "You can't. People know. The dean is calling my father in the morning. He's already furious he had to contribute to the building fund to get them to let me walk at graduation with my class. I have to pass this class with an A. The only reason Harvard is waiting for this grade, that they haven't rescinded my acceptance yet, is because my family has attended Harvard for generations. My family's name is on the damn pool," the teen whines, causing the man to smirk, not that the teen notices in his agitation. "And I'm sure Father had to make another donation for this too." He wipes at his face. "Now it's all fucked up because that damn teacher had to be such a hardass."

"The best thing you can do is go back to your room and act naturally," the man says. "Relax. Nothing bad has happened. You'll pass the class. You'll get your diploma. You'll attend Harvard in the fall. Leave it to me."

"I already left it to you once and now I'm fucked."

He steps out of the shadows. "Enough. I said I'd take care of it, and I will. You don't see that teacher scurrying around causing problems anymore, do you?"

"Ms. Lopez? She was out sick today," the teen says, confusion clear on his face.

"It's quite a bit more permanent than that."

The teen takes a step back. "What?"

"Nothing you need to concern yourself with. I'll persuade the dean or, if that proves too difficult, I'll have the headmaster overrule him. You come from a good family that has always supported this school. He won't

allow one paper to ruin your future. Or his Ivy League stats. Go now. I have work to do."

The teen walks to the door, the rage he was feeling just moments before is subsumed by fear. What happened to Ms. Lopez? What has Dorian done?

THIRTY-FIVE

And So It Begins...

The image goes dark and then…

The dean tumbles down the stairs, the noise so loud it must wake the students still on campus for the summer session. He readies a story, sure someone will open a door and find him, but nothing happens. For the space of five precious seconds, nothing moves or makes a sound.

Still gripping the bloody block of glass, he quickly retreats down the hall to his room. They gave him the same room he had as a student when he returned to observe. That was what he told the headmaster, in any case. The ridiculous man believed that he was considering a teaching career. Lord. As if he'd ever stoop so low.

He did well at university but failed to embark on a career after graduating. His father set him up on a few interviews: One to clerk for a judge, hoping to spark an interest in the law, another for a wealth management firm, and still a third at his own medical practice. As if he wants to spend his days under his father's scrutiny.

He takes the block of glass to the bathroom sink, cleaning it as well as his own hands. Should he return it to the table? Yes. That seems the most sensible. He dries it off and then carries it in a towel to the door. When he opens it, he finds the new housemaster leaving his own room in running shorts and a t-shirt.

"Good morning. Up early as well, I see." The man is in his early thir-

ties and is fit and happy. How odd in a housemaster. "Are you getting in a workout before school too?"

Dorian looks down at his Oxford shirt, trousers, and loafers before staring at the man haughtily. "No." *He keeps the hand holding the award behind the wall, out of sight.*

There's an awkward silence before the man finally says, "Okay, I'm going to hit the track."

Dorian watches the man, who thankfully jogs to the other end of the corridor and the far staircase, the one closest to the track. He waits a moment and just as he's about to return the award, another door opens and a girl starts knocking at the room next door.

Dorian closes the door and considers his options. He loves the weight of the glass in his hand, the potential power. He can't wait to tell Brandon what he's done. He's right. There's something so satisfying, so savage, about blunt force trauma. Brandon had that experience with the Civics teacher. Now he knows too.

He admits, at least to himself, he prefers using his bare hands. He strangled Pearl, the nosey bitch. It might have taken over a decade to pay her back for ruining his summer, but it was worth it. He wasn't even cheating. He barely glanced at her test. Of course, that didn't stop the dean from calling his parents nor his father from refusing to allow him to stay home alone over the summer while they traveled. "Apparently, we can't trust you." *He'd been looking forward to the freedom all year and then it disappeared because of a stupid girl's groundless claim. If he could, he'd choke her again.*

What his father will never understand is that his current endeavors are far more entertaining than a career. What drudgery an office would be. Of course, seen in a certain light, one could call what he and Brandon did a career. A calling, perhaps. A vocation.

He pulls up the blinds, opens his window, and scans the empty grounds. It's still early, the sky going gray. He throws the block of glass, and it sails out the window, landing in the pool with a small splish. There. That's taken care of at least. Time to wake Brandon with the news.

The image goes dark and then…

The same room but different. Textbooks piled in the desk. His blazer tossed over the chair. Whispers, ideas becoming profound and revelatory by virtue of being uttered in the dark. Brandon isn't sure. Dorian explains. Right and wrong are constructs, a way to keep the populace in line. Children are taught from an early age to do what benefits the majority. But what about those special few who see through the construct, who recognize the hypocrisy? What about the ones who can think for themselves, who make decisions based on what they know to be right, rather than what society dictates?

Brandon is trying to follow but is floundering. "But there are rights and wrongs. Killing is wrong."

"Unless you're killing a killer," Dorian counters, excited to finally have someone to discuss these things with. "The government puts criminals to death. So, it is wrong or right?"

"But that's punishment for doing wrong," Brandon says, scratching at the pimple on his chin, still trying to understand.

"True, but who decides what's right and wrong? Soldiers kill and we give them parades. Police kill unarmed citizens with impunity."

"With…yeah. Impunity," Brandon echoes.

"Without punishment," Dorian clarifies. "In some parts of the country you can shoot someone for ringing your doorbell. You can shoot someone for making you fear for your life, even if they've done nothing threatening. My point is, laws are made by men, and men are biased and fallible. It's like that moron we have as headmaster, or worse yet, the dean. Men who weren't smart enough, important enough, to get good jobs but they're in charge of us? They get to determine what's right and wrong?

Dorian, lying on his bed, staring up into the dark, slams his fist on the bed. Brandon is sitting on the floor, leaning against Dorian's bed, looking over his shoulder at his friend.

"You and I are far more intelligent than those two and yet we have to follow their rules. The same goes for these teachers. Why are we bound by what small-minded, mediocre people say? Why is our future determined by jumping through their hoops? Who are they?"

"Especially Collins," Brandon says.

"Good. Yes." Dorian is pleased that his friend is finally catching up. "Collins is a prime example. Collins made you all do that ridiculous

group assignment. All your grades were pulled down because Ainsley decided to go off on a tangent about museums stealing artifacts from other cultures." He scoffs. "It's an Art History final assessment. She already brought the topic up in class and Collins shut it down. So what does she do? She does it again on a project where you all share a grade. Now that's a wrong."

"Yeah. Collins thought we were all in on it. I needed that A," Brandon complained, not for the first time.

"The whole idea of group work is asinine. They always say that we need to learn how to work together. No, we don't. My father is a surgeon. Yes, there are other people in the operating theater, but he calls the shots. He doesn't stop to ask the surgical residents or the nurses if they agree with what he's doing. He doesn't take a vote. He's in charge and he tells them what to do."

Brandon nods in the dark.

"My mother chairs the Carmel Mental Health Awareness charity. She has to coordinate a dinner dance every year and says it's like herding cats. She has to deal with everyone on the committee wanting a say in the event, even if they're idiots and their ideas are ridiculous. One woman suggested food trucks and a night of roller disco at a local rink."

Brandon grins. "That sounds kind of…stupid. Totally."

"She always says it would go far smoother," Dorian continues, "if she could just make the decisions herself and be done with it."

"Yeah," Brandon agrees. "I hate groupwork."

Dorian pauses, trying to get the discussion back on track. He made an unfortunate detour into group work to help Brandon along and now his friend seems stuck there. "What I was saying before, though, about us not being tied to what society says. You understand that, right?"

Brandon looks confused but says, "Yes."

"Good. Good. I've been thinking we should try an experiment." Dorian's mind is spinning with possibilities.

"What kind?"

"Well, if it's correct that we are better than the average idiots around us, it follows that the rules created to keep those idiots in line don't apply to us. Right?"

"*Uh.*" *Brandon doesn't finish the thought.*

"*So, who has wronged us? Much like society or the headmaster creating rules and laws to punish wrongdoing, we, as superior individuals, should set our own rules and punishments. Right?*"

"*Oh. Yeah.*" *Brandon perks up, his eyes glowing.* "*Yeah, okay.*"

"*Good. Now, who has wronged you?*" *As much as Dorian wants to go first, he knows he needs to let Brandon have this. He can tell his friend isn't entirely convinced. Besides, Dorian has been taking his pound of flesh for years. He believes, though, that having someone to share it with will make it more enjoyable for him.*

Brandon ponders for quite a while before responding, "*Spencer.*"

Dorian nods in the dark. Of course. His friend is obsessed with Spencer McCutchin. Brandon was in the middle of asking Schuyler to the Winter Formal when Spencer, older, richer, and better looking, walked up, laughed at Brandon, and threw an arm around Schuyler, walking her to the dining room for lunch. Yes. That sort of humiliation deserved recompense.

"*What kind of punishment were you thinking?*" *Dorian asks.*

"*Holding him down and shaving his head. Maybe spitting on him. No, acid! We make acid in the Chem lab and then throw it on him.*" *Brandon is positively glowing at the thought.*

"*I like where you're going with this, but remember, we don't want to be caught. He'll see us if we do those things. The police will be called in and there will be a huge investigation. What can we do to Spencer that won't come back on us?*"

"*You mean like laxatives in his food?*" *Brandon asks.*

"*No. That's a prank. What does Spencer love?*"

"*Himself,*" *Brandon sneers.*

"*True. What else?*" *Sometimes it's exhausting needing to lead his friend like this.*

"*His car?*" *Brandon suggests.*

"*Yes. He is quite proud of that, isn't he? So what can we do to his car to punish him?*" *Dorian knows what he'd do but he's interested in what his friend comes up with.*

"*We could slash his tires,*" *Brandon suggests with relish.*

"We could. Of course, that makes Spencer the victim and then the dean, or maybe the police, will look for whoever did it."

"Yeah, that's true. Sugar in the gas tank?" Brandon says.

Dorian waits.

"I wish I knew how to cut brake lines," Brandon says on a huff of laughter.

"Now that's *interesting..."*

Blinking, I glanced around the studio. Declan was still beside me, but Osso and Hernández were out on the deck.

"Detective Hernández got a call, so they went out there to take it. Neither wanted to disturb you," Declan said.

Since neither seemed to be on the phone now, I flicked my fingers, opening the back door. Both detectives looked over and I waved them in. They closed the door after them and resumed their seats.

"What did you see?" Osso asked.

"I know who they are."

THIRTY-SIX

Here, Mark!

Hernández and Osso took out their notebooks.

"Dorian killed Pearl and the dean. Brandon killed Ms. Lopez and Mr. Garza. The thing is, though, they started this as students. Look for a car accident involving someone named Spencer McCutchin. They were talking about cutting his brake lines. He would have been Brandon's first, but Dorian had been at it awhile. I don't know if he was killing yet, but he'd been lashing out at whoever he'd felt wronged him."

The detectives scribbled down names.

"Dorian's dad is a surgeon." I pointed to the corridor painting. "The last door on the right is his bedroom. He's staying there now. It was also his bedroom when he was a student. He told the headmaster that he wanted to observe the teachers, that he was considering going into education, but he was just trying to get close to the people they'd targeted."

"Let's start at the beginning," Osso said. "Why Pearl?"

"Let me check something first." I pulled out my phone and dialed my aunt Hester.

"Hello, Arwyn. Guess where I am?" she said.

"Where?" I was so happy to hear the light in her voice.

"I'm playing with the neighbor's dog. I was helping Mitchell, the neighbor, in the garden all day and when he mentioned he had a date, I volunteered to babysit his daughter Emma and their German Shephard Mark."

"The dog's name is Mark?" I loved that.

"I know." She laughed. "It tickles me every time I call him. Come on. Let's go in." The background sounds changed. "I already put Emma to bed, but I was giving Mark some exercise and throwing the ball for him. So, how are you?"

"I'm okay. Can I ask you a question about Pearl, though?"

"Oh. Of course." Her voice lost its lilt.

"Did she ever attend Cypress Academy?"

"Yes, but only for a semester. It was the beginning of sixth grade. Your uncle said it was an excellent school and wanted her there, even though it was mind-numbingly expensive. She hated it. The students were cruel. She was so smart, though, she was in advanced classes with older students. There was one boy in particular who wouldn't leave her alone. He scared her. It caused a huge fight, but I took her out and got her away from those people." She paused. "Why do you ask?"

I considered whether it was okay to tell her and decided those secrecy rules didn't apply to me, as I wasn't a cop. "I had a vision."

Hernández gestured to stop me, but Osso shook his head at her.

"I believe that boy who harassed her at Cypress Academy is the one who killed her."

"What?" Her voice caught. "But they were children. Why would he do that?" I could hear the tears, but she deserved to know.

"Because he's a sociopath and a narcissist. She caught him cheating off her paper and told the teacher. That was it. But it was enough for him to never let it go."

"I don't understand."

"That's because you're nothing like him. I'm with the detectives now. I hate having to upset you, especially when Mark was making you happy, but I needed to make sure what I saw was correct. I didn't remember ever hearing that Pearl had attended Cypress."

It took her a moment to speak. "I want to know. Even if it upsets me, I want to know. And I'm glad the detectives are there and can find him now. Can you tell me when he's caught?"

"I will," I said.

"I'm not sure if Mark is allowed on furniture, but he just crawled up to comfort me, so I'm letting him stay."

"Can you put Mark on the phone for me?"

Hester released a breath. Her voice was distant when she said, "Go ahead."

"Good boy."

She chuckled. "Whatever you said got his tail wagging."

"I'm sorry to bring darkness into your evening. I—"

She cut me off. "That wasn't you. That was him. You're the one who's going to get justice for my girl. And tears are all right. I have Mark here to keep me company."

"Okay. Remember to come by anytime for a muffin and tea."

"I will." She sniffed.

"Good night."

I blew out a breath as I disconnected. "Pearl attended Cypress for the first semester of sixth grade. You heard what I told her. She turned him in for cheating. He waited over ten years and then killed her for it."

Declan took the bag with the award from my lap and returned it to the coffee table before reaching for my hand.

"Did you get last names?" Hernández asked.

I shook my head. "There's gotta be a list of graduating seniors somewhere. Dorian isn't a common name. And if he's around campus—enough to be arguing with the dean early in the morning—other staff members must have seen him. That new housemaster probably knows his name."

Osso nodded. "We'll check."

"He was going to put the award back on the table after he cleaned it, so no one missed it. People were waking up and moving around the halls, though, so he tossed it out the window of his bedroom that overlooks the pool."

More scribbling. "Anything else?" Osso asked.

"One thing. He was excited about having a friend to share his passion with. He talked about them being superior and rules not applying to them."

Hernández looked up. "Oh. Only us peons have to follow laws, huh?"

Nodding, I explained, "As superior individuals, they set their own rules. They aren't obligated to follow the laws created by mediocre minds."

"Once you identify them, you should probably check their colleges," Declan suggested, "see if there are any unsolved murders."

Osso nodded, standing up. "Yeah, I know."

Hernández picked up the black bag and stood. "We need to get on this. Thank you again."

After they were gone, Declan got up and led me to the couch, both of us collapsing onto it. "You've done what you could. You've given them the killers. Now they need to do their job."

I nodded slowly, bone weary. "I hate having those voices, those thoughts in my head. They make me sick to my stomach."

"Like you said to your aunt, that's because you're not like them." His stomach growled. "Sorry. I could go get us food or maybe order a pizza."

"Yeah, let's do that." I had to do a better job of having more food around for the poor guy. I pulled up a meal delivery service on my phone and ordered two large pizzas.

"Thanks for getting two."

I leaned into him, and he wrapped an arm around me. "Sixth grade. She was eleven years old. And you know a school like that was probably all about their high standards and academic integrity. She's new. Trying to do what they told her was proper in that school. A creepy kid's cheating off her, so she goes to her teacher. That was it. She was on borrowed time after that. He was just planning how to do it and get away with it."

Declan kissed my temple, listening.

"A little over ten years later, he's her first boyfriend. She was painfully shy. He comes in and sweeps her off her feet so he can involve her heart, so his attack is not only terrifying but heartbreaking and humiliating. She'd thought he liked her, but he was just biding his time until it hurt more."

"You found her killer and he'll spend the rest of his life behind bars," Declan said.

"Yeah. It doesn't bring her back, though." Her poor mother would never be the same. "I can't imagine everything you go through as a parent. All the colds and skinned knees, the heartaches and joys, school, friends, hugs, conversations, adolescence, periods, bras, all of it. A life. And he decides he can't handle being reprimanded in middle school, so that life is snuffed out."

His thumb brushed back and forth on my arm. "You identifying him means other innocent people, like Pearl, won't lose their lives because he felt offended or inconvenienced."

Tucking my shoulder under his arm, I rested my head on his chest. "I don't understand it. I don't think I ever will. Most people are just living their lives, trying to do what's right. He considers them limited, mediocre, the weak ones who knuckle under to society's rules. He, though, is special. Superior. He leaves mourning loved ones in his wake, and it doesn't signify."

He was like all those men who had been preying on me all my life. Who I was, what I wanted, those things weren't important. I wasn't important. The only thing that mattered was that their own needs be met. It was like the rest of us were background players in the story of their lives. We pantomimed actions and mouthed nonsense, waiting to be addressed by the lead, waiting for our lives to gain meaning through them.

My phone buzzed and I pulled it out of my pocket. I had a reminder on my screen. The full moon was tomorrow.

"You put it in your calendar?" He sounded surprised and amused.

"I'm dating a werewolf, so it seems like pretty important information. And this particular full moon has me scared." I hugged him tighter. "Please can I come? I'll stay in the truck. You won't even know I'm there."

"No."

It was essentially Declan against a pack of wolves, but I was supposed to sit back and have faith that all would be fine?

"I can hear you worrying, but you don't need to. I've seen them. I understand the dynamic. Will they cheat to win? Absolutely. Because I know that going into it, my strategy changes. There's no expectation of honor or fair play, so I won't hesitate to put them down."

He leaned back so he could meet my gaze. "Logan is a weak Alpha, more concerned with having the position than doing the work. His men are likewise weak."

I scoffed. "They're werewolves."

He nodded. "They are, but they don't train. They're not a cohesive unit, working together. They're a loose group that shares one thing: They shift into wolves once a month. They're like weekend warriors, dressing up in army fatigues to play war before going back to their office jobs on Monday. The pack members run in their fur once a month and then ignore that side of themselves the rest of the time. He hasn't helped the pack integrate man and wolf. If he had, they'd be far harder to fight."

"That all sounds nice, but I haven't forgotten that it's at least twenty to one. Daniel and Kenji are good men, and they were part of the pack. There are probably others," I said, referring to the two who had left the pack, recognizing Declan as the true Alpha.

"They are and the hope is that once Logan is down, I can get them to step up to truly be a pack."

"You've never been a member of a pack before," I pointed out. "How do you know what one should be?"

He kicked off his boots and put his feet up on the coffee table, crossing them at the ankles. "Excellent question. I've hung out with wolves, who by the way don't have a dictatorial Alpha leading them. Wolf packs are more like families. They work cooperatively. What we consider Alpha is usually just the breeding pair, leading the family.

"I've also read books on Biology, History, Psychology, Sociology. Basically, I studied to better understand what I am and my place in the world. What I've found is that it's the human side of us that wants a dictator to lead the pack. For many two-natured beings, the human is almost entirely in control. As I said about the Big Sur pack, they get together once a month to shift; otherwise they shun the wolf. They're not a pack. They're guys with a similar affliction.

"Single-natured wolf packs are together all the time. They live, work, play, hunt together as a unit. Decisions are made based on the safety and health of the pack. They're family, so lots of different personalities and temperaments, but a cohesive working unit.

"Dual-natured wolf packs are rarely that. With the human side comes ego and envy, mindless aggression. It's the werewolf packs that engage in battles to the death to demonstrate dominance and superiority, not natural wolves. Wolves fight for food or territory, but the goal isn't to kill the interloper, just to make the threat go away.

"Human psychology mixed with an apex predator's strength often leads to overt aggression and a need to rank themselves first, second, third in a group of individuals who don't feel the safety and security they should. They're constantly on edge, waiting for an attack, which is why they like the dictator Alpha. If he's telling me what I can and can't do, some of that anxiety settles. Someone's in charge and it's not me. He'll be the one to deal with threats. The problem with that type of arrangement is if you end up with a weak Alpha, like Logan, the pack members feel it and never settle."

He shook his head. "For some of these guys, anger is their

entire personality. The first thing I'm doing as Alpha is instituting mandatory yoga and meditation sessions."

I laughed.

"They need *something*. I know we hide what happens in the supernatural world from the humans, but I'm surprised more violence hasn't bled over and exposed us."

I thought about it. "Maybe it has but there are members of our community in the police. Like Osso hiding what I am and what probably happened when they came to investigate my stalker's death."

"Good point," he said as my phone buzzed.

I pulled it out of my pocket. "There's no way the pizzas are here that fast." I tapped the screen, swiping through to find the link to the security cameras. "It's probably my raccoon buddies."

Declan stood and growled, hearing something I couldn't. "It's not raccoons." He sprinted to the gallery as I pulled up footage of three guys attempting to break my glass tentacle.

I Didn't Know Raccoons Could Knock

"Wait!" I called, running after him. "This is what they want. They're probably here to hurt you, stab you, something so that Logan wins."

He stood by the door, fists clenched, his breathing ragged. This close to the full moon, I couldn't believe he'd listened and stopped.

"This is my home. Allow me." I could see on the video that they were trying to grab the tentacle but then were quickly pulling their hands away. I'd put a protective spell on it so anyone trying to destroy it would receive a sting, much like a jellyfish's. They were shaking out their hands, the red welts already rising.

Raging, they pounded the door, the wall, the railing, and each surface gave them more stings. Watching them on my phone, I held up a hand, a spell at the ready, and shoved them off my porch.

When they were scrambling up from the gravel, I flicked my fingers, adding a layer of protection to the stairs and porch so they couldn't come back up. Twirling my index finger, I spun a spell I hadn't had to use for a while. When I flicked my finger, the men stopped slamming at the invisible wall. Their red, swollen hands flew to their eyes and then shot out before them.

"What did you do?" Declan had settled down and was now looking over my shoulder at the video feed on my phone.

"I blinded them."

The men were yelling at each other while rubbing at their eyes. I gave it another thirty seconds and then lifted the blindness. With one more shove, they took off running to the truck they'd hidden down the road.

"I heard tires squealing. They're gone." After a moment, he added, "I also hear knocking on the back door." When I turned to go answer it, he said, "Don't forget your force field or we'll never get our pizzas."

"Oops." I waved a hand and then jogged back into the studio. I didn't see anyone through the door, but Declan was chuckling behind me.

"Look down."

Otis lifted his little paw and knocked again.

"Just a minute," I called, going to the kitchen to collect three muffins. "It's like getting trick-or-treaters at the door."

Declan sat on the couch. "Maybe I should pick them up little pumpkin buckets."

Defrosting the muffins in my gloved hands, I said, "Could you? I'd love that." I went out on the deck. "Hi, guys. I hope you're all doing well this evening."

Otis and Daisy sat with their paws clasped in front of them. Jasper had his paws up, reaching for the food. Otis made a sound somewhere between a hiss and a chitter. Jasper lowered his paws and mirrored his siblings.

Crouching, I handed the first muffin to Otis, who took it carefully and then moved away. Daisy was also quite polite. Jasper snatched and ran, causing his siblings to chitter and screech. Poor Jasper was getting it from both of them. He eventually came back and placed the muffin in front of me, stealing a quick bite and then going to sit beside Otis and Daisy. I nodded my thanks and then picked it up and held it out to him again. He looked at his siblings first and when neither yelled at him, he scampered over and took it gently from my hand.

Standing, I said, "You three be careful out there. We've had some wolves in the neighborhood." I left them to their dinner and went back in. My phone buzzed again. When I pulled up the video feed this time, it was the delivery guy leaving the pizza boxes on the gallery porch.

"Pizza's here. Be right back." I readied a spell in case the three stooges returned. Thankfully, my porch was wolf free. I bent down to pick up the boxes and heard, "It *is* you."

Righting myself, I watched a tall, dark-haired man walk into the porch light. "You're the sea wicche, aren't you?"

"I am." I smiled nervously, luring him in. The face was a little different, the cheeks more prominent, but he was wearing the false chin again. There was nothing he could do about the dead eyes, though. "Can I help you?" I lowered my walls, listening to his plans for me, including the syringe in his pocket.

"I'm a fan of your work. I purchased one of your paintings last year when I was summering in London. It hangs in my study." He gave me a self-deprecating eyeroll and grin, as though realizing that sounded pretentious as hell.

I nodded, my eyes darting to the door. I hadn't been stalked by predators all my life without learning a few things, like how much they love to prey on those they see as small, weak, and frightened.

"I didn't mean to interrupt your evening," he said, taking another step closer.

Three pairs of eyes shined outside the circle of light, watching. My sweet little raccoon buddies had my back.

I met Dorian's gaze and saw it: an image of myself, at the base of the stairs at Cypress Academy. I'd been lost in a vision before snapping my head up and staring into his eyes. He'd followed Detective Hernández here and then had begun watching me, trying to suss out why an artist was consulting on an accidental death investigation.

He gestured to the boxes in my hands, the ones I tried to look as though I was hiding behind. My reputation as a recluse was working to my advantage. "Am I interrupting a party?" he asked. In other words, was I alone?

"Oh." I ducked my head, letting my hair fall in my face. "No. It's silly. I just—I bought two pizzas so I can have leftovers for the next couple of days." I shrugged. "I should eat healthier, but I'm racing to get everything ready for the opening and I was too tired to cook."

"I'd love nothing more than to take you out to dinner. I know a quiet bistro you'd love." That grin again. "It's close by. A woman as gifted as you shouldn't have to worry about such mundane things."

I heard a low growl on the other side of the door, but Dorian, with his human hearing, did not. Poor Pearl. She'd been too overwhelmed, too flustered, to see behind the mask.

"That's very kind, but I don't want to be a bother," I responded, glancing at the door again.

He leaned in and said with a wink, "Spending time with such a beautiful woman is never a bother."

I ducked my head again, waiting for the lunge with the syringe, but he was having too much fun. Control and power. They were a heady combination, and he was drawing this out longer than he'd intended.

"Here," he said, taking the pizza boxes out of my hands. "Those must be getting heavy." He balanced them on the railing before turning back, a feral grin on his face. "There. That's better. Now I can see you."

I gave him a wide-eyed, deer in the headlight stare and I felt his adrenaline race. Laughing, I dropped the scared schtick and said, "She never saw you coming, did she?"

He was too busy looking me up and down to notice the change. Lost, fantasizing about how he'd kill me once I was overpowered and restrained, it took a moment to meet my gaze.

"Sorry. I didn't get that." He reached out for my curls, and I ducked away from his hand. I was *not* letting him put his hands on me.

"My cousin. She couldn't see past the face putty and makeup to the entitled sociopath from her middle school class."

He stepped back, the grin slipping off his face.

"I know exactly who you are." Fingers twitching at my side, I had spells locked and loaded. "Poor baby. The world has been so cruel to you, hasn't it? A wealthy family, the best of everything. I can see how that kind of privilege would make you vengeful."

His mouth opened and closed. I felt his shock, his disbelief.

"How will a superior individual, such as yourself, deal with prison? I mean, they're the unwashed masses, right? The ones who have to follow laws and be punished when they break them. Not you, though, huh?"

Sneering, I added, "Maybe not too superior after all. Poor little Dorian needs a murder buddy, though. You pull Brandon in so you can plot and plan together, so you can build each other up and pretend you're strong and important. Special. Brandon's a weak-willed follower with sadistic tendencies you helped him uncover. You, though, are a true narcissist and psychopath. It's more than you *deserving* everything you want, isn't it? You believe it's owed you."

His hand went to his pocket. Face red, eyes murderous, he said, "You have no idea who you're dealing with."

"Trust me, I do. And what brings me comfort is knowing when you finally shake off this mortal coil—you'll get shivved in the prison cafeteria because you're insufferable—you're headed to Hell, a place I happen to know is real."

On a wail of fury, he lunged, his thumb on the stopper of the syringe. I flicked my fingers and he froze as three little raccoons leapt and bit him, their sharp claws digging through his clothes.

Grinning, I leaned in. "How does it feel, being on the other side? Do you enjoy being at my mercy? Not being strong enough to overpower me? Not really even understanding what's going on?

You should get used to this feeling. You're going to experience it a lot where you're going."

Sirens sounded in the distance and sweat broke out on Dorian's forehead.

I whispered in his ear, "Pearl may be dead, but she's in a good, loving place now. You, my young serial killer, will know nothing but pain for the rest of your days, and that brings me comfort."

The sirens were getting close, so I moved back to where I'd been standing when I froze him. With a flick of my fingers, the cameras began recording again, and he completed his lunge. I spun out of his reach, turning and punching him in the back of the head. My hand may have hurt like hell, but Dad's DNA helped me do it with enough force to knock him out.

"Okay, you three, hide. The cops are coming. And thank you!" They scampered off the porch and into the night.

When a cop car skidded to a halt, I stepped back from the sprawled figure.

The same cop who'd drawn his gun on me before did it again. I pointed at the unconscious man.

"It would be cool if you'd stop pointing your gun at me," I said. "He's the one with poison in a syringe who just attacked me."

The cop kept his gun on me while he talked into the radio on his shoulder.

Thankfully, Hernández pulled up and slammed out of her car. "What the hell are you doing? You have a gun pointed at the victim, a woman who is a police consultant, while the serial killer hasn't been cuffed and still has a weapon in his hand."

Hernández couldn't see it as she was walking up the steps to me, but the gun moved in her direction before he finally holstered it. She was asking me something, but I was focused on him. Lots of rage in that one. And fear. He hated to take orders from a *racial slur *gender slur.

When he moved back to his car, I turned to a concerned-looking Hernández. "He hates you," I whispered.

She looked down at Dorian. "I'm not fond of him either."

When she started to move away, I grabbed her elbow and pulled her back. "The cop. Don't trust him. In fact, see if you can get him off the force. Someone like him, someone who only respects white men, shouldn't have authority and a gun."

She blinked and then looked over her shoulder.

"He's filled with rage and righteous indignation, believing you and Osso leapfrogged over him, took his detective's badge, because of your ethnicities."

Her expression turned to stone. "Is that so?"

"He's not that different from this one. The world owes him. He doesn't look inward to question himself, only outward to blame everyone else. Because of that badge and gun, though, his petty grievances are worked out on the general public with impunity." The cop looked back in our direction, and I tipped my head so my hair blocked his view of my mouth. "I mean it. You have to get that guy fired. Get someone higher up to check his record. They're going to find more complaints than normal for a cop with his number of years on the job. Lots of little cruelties. That's what he enjoys."

"I'll take care of it," she said. "Tell me what happened here."

I gave my head a quick shake, pushing Josh, the asshole cop out of my head. "Dorian showed up as I was coming out here to get the pizza." I scanned the porch before remembering he'd put them on the railing. "Can I take these in now? Declan needs to eat."

"Do they have anything to do with what happened here?"

I shook my head. "They were just something I was holding." I grabbed the boxes and opened the door, finding a huge wolf. "Give me a minute," I said to the detective. I closed the door quickly and the wolf knocked the boxes out of my hands, crowding me against the door, sniffing me furiously.

I petted the top of his head. "I'm fine. He never laid a finger on me. He's human: no special powers, no unique protections. He never had a chance. Really, I'm fine."

He reared up on his back paws, his front paws on the door above my shoulders, and rested his head in the crook of my neck.

"I know what it must have cost you not to come out and kill him when you realized I wasn't talking to the delivery guy. Thank you. This is much cleaner and ultimately safer for me. There's no body to hide, no crime scene to clean up, no lies that have to be remembered. He's human and the human authorities are dealing with him. Okay?"

He rubbed his head against my jaw and then went back to the floor.

"And don't eat all the pizza," I added, slipping back out to the porch.

Dorian was cuffed and being walked to the police car by Officer Cross, the one who'd helped get me home when I was consulting on the child abduction case.

"Do you know who my father is?" Dorian blustered. "This is outrageous. I'll have your badges, all of you. I'll be bailed out in an hour and then you'll be dealing with a multimillion-dollar lawsuit for wrongful arrest." He kept yelling, but once Cross slammed the door, we didn't have to hear it.

"Did you get the syringe?" I glanced around the porch, not seeing it.

Osso, who'd joined Hernández, nodded. "It's been bagged and is heading to the lab. Do you know what's in it?"

I shook my head. "I don't think he intended to kill me here. I think it was something to put me out so he could kill me at his leisure elsewhere. He wanted to draw it out so it was more pleasurable for him."

"Okay," he said, pulling up the voice recorder on his phone. "Tell us what happened."

I did, leaving out my freezing him and the raccoons. "I have cameras up. I can give you the tape."

He turned off the voice recorder. "Is there audio?" Eyebrows raised, he knew they'd probably hear something that would be hard to explain.

"No."

"Good. We'll take that with us." He put his phone away. "We'll need you to stop by the station tomorr—"

"I'll bring it to her to sign," Hernández said. At Osso's look, she added, "She doesn't drive."

"Right. Of course. We'll bring the statement to you to sign." He took one last look at the porch and then nodded to himself. "We'll get out of your hair. Lock up," he said, going down the stairs. "There's still one more out there."

"Thanks for that," I grumbled. "Like I don't have enough trouble sleeping." When I went back in, Declan was once again himself and sitting on the floor.

"Hey, did you eat?"

"Yeah." He stood and picked up the boxes.

"Did you leave me a couple of slices?"

"I only ate one pizza." He took my hand. "Are you really all right?"

I glanced over. "Are you kidding? I got to scare the crap out of the asshole who killed my cousin. I'm great. And kinda hungry."

Waving a hand, I closed most of the windows, leaving the rows at the top open to continue airing out the paint fumes. I'd spelled the windows a while ago to only let air in and out. I didn't want to worry about randos crawling in at night, but I still felt more comfortable with the windows closed and locked.

We settled back in the studio with pizza and drinks, Declan lowering the screen so we could watch another British mystery.

"I fell asleep last time. Who done it?" I asked.

"The brother-in-law," he said, taking another big bite, the open box on his lap.

"What? I thought for sure it was the governess." I donned thin rubber gloves and then slid two pieces onto my plate.

"You missed some important details while you slept, namely that the brother-in-law was having an affair with the murder victim, who turned out to be pregnant."

"No."

He nodded.

"The bastard. Did you know more pregnant women die by violence from their partners than pregnancy-related issues?"

Declan stopped eating. "That can't be true."

"Yup," I said, shaking my head at the injustice of it all.

He closed the pizza box and placed it on the coffee table. "Bastards," he grumbled.

"Exactly."

He hit play and we watched the opening scene where the dead body was found. When the title sequence started, I turned to him. "Are we talking about tomorrow night?"

He shook his head. "I just want a nice, quiet evening with you, and I'll do what I need to do tomorrow so I can continue having nice, quiet evenings with you." He met my gaze. "Okay?"

Nodding, I took a bite of pizza and settled in to figure out who had killed the poor old lady.

THIRTY-EIGHT

An All-Around Shitty Day

When I woke the following morning, it was still early. I hadn't had a nightmare, exactly. It was more a bad dream about the full moon tonight, about Declan fighting for his life, about me losing someone I'd just found.

We hadn't discussed what might happen tonight, but we'd made love with an intensity that we hadn't had before. Both of us knew it might be our last night together. I had faith in Declan, but I also knew Logan would do anything to win.

After showering and dealing with my hair, I put on work clothes and went downstairs. I had a ton of work to do and all day to do it, but I mostly wanted to crawl back in bed and sleep until the Alpha challenge was over.

Instead, I went down, grabbed a muffin and a cup of tea, and sat on the edge of the deck, the way I used to. "Good morning, Cecil." A tentacle rose from the water and slapped the surface before sinking back down. "Poppy, I know you're busy right now, but good morning. Charlie, Herbert, it's lovely to see you." I didn't see his tennis ball, but I called, "Good morning, Wilbur."

I broke off a bite of muffin. It was dry and tasteless, which I thought had more to do with abject fear than my baking skills.

"And good morning to you, Arwyn."

I turned to find Uncle Bracken sitting on a far bench, near his RV, drinking from a mug.

"Good morning."

"Hmm, it doesn't sound good. Are you all right, dear?"

Standing, I gathered my stuff and went to sit with him. "I can't eat. Would you like this?" I held out the chocolate raspberry muffin.

He took it. "Thank you. I was just sitting here thinking I was feeling a bit peckish, and you arrive with food. Providence." He broke off a piece, popped it in his mouth, and hummed, smiling. "Delicious."

"Is this working out for you?" I asked, gesturing between the water and his motor home.

He nodded. "Very well indeed. The sound of the ocean is quite relaxing. And there's something about being close to family." He patted his chest. "I feel more settled."

"Good."

He took a sip of his tea. "Now tell me what has you so sad this morning."

I turned the mug in my hands, warming them. "Full moon tonight."

"It is," he said, taking another bite.

"Declan is a very powerful wolf, a born wolf. A Quinn. Other wolves can't stand having him in their territory. They want to challenge him. Normally, he just moves on, but it's different now."

"Of course it is. He wants to stay so he can be with you."

I nodded, staring out at the waves. "The Alpha challenge is tonight. In order for Declan to stay, he needs to take over the pack. The fight should just be between him and the local Alpha, but they're all going to attack. It'll be Declan against a pack of wolves."

"Well, that's easy. Let's go and help him."

That made me smile. "I had the same thought, but I've been forbidden to attend."

"That's ridiculous. I'll drive us and we'll park far away. They won't even know we're there. We can level the playing field for him." Bracken took another sip of tea, as though the whole thing had been decided.

"That's what I said and was told no."

Bracken opened his mouth to argue.

"In order for Declan to be accepted as the true Alpha, there can be no question about his strength. If we're there, he'll always be doubted. They'll assume his wicche girlfriend fixed the fight. And these are wolves. They see and hear for miles. They'll know we're there. Even if we could come up with a scheme to shield ourselves, I couldn't. I promised him I wouldn't interfere."

"That was silly of you," he said.

"I know."

"You went and chose an honorable man, eh?"

"Looks like."

He sighed, took another bite, and watched the waves with me.

"Did you just wake up or are you going to bed soon?" I had the feeling he was a night owl.

"Bed soon. I love watching the sunrise before I go to sleep. I find I have fewer bad dreams." He crossed his legs. "Shall I give you good news?"

I turned to him. "Yes, please."

"I've found references to a house laden in black magic."

I sat up straight. This could be it. The house where Calliope was doing her sorcery.

"I've been going through books and journals since we spoke. If I'm right and all the disparate references I've found relate to a house of sorcery, then what we know is that it's been in the family for generations, probably from when Coreys first moved here. The original house burned down perhaps a hundred years ago, and a far grander one was built in its place."

He scratched at his cheek. "It's hidden behind a large wall of stone and sits on the water. It's two stories high, but the upper floors are largely empty. The basement is where the sorcery is conducted. Candlelight and torches."

"Yes," I said. "I've seen her in a basement with sconces on the walls. She's sitting at a large, dark wood table that holds a grimoire."

"That sounds right. I haven't found an address, but it was referred to as The Shades once. The shades is another term for Hell, so I don't know if it's a description of what goes on there or the name of the house. The capital T and S make me hopeful the house was named, as that gives us another avenue to research. I'll keep looking this afternoon."

"Thank you, but you need sleep first."

He stood and stretched. "I do. I've found the breadcrumbs, though." Walking to his RV, he said, "Try not to worry. The valiant are often victorious."

Often, not always. That was what had me worried.

I went in and got to work, painting the wall on the café side of the gallery. It was difficult with the shelving brackets and the café area itself, which helped keep my mind focused on what I was doing, not on what I might soon be losing.

Taking a break at midday, I went to have some leftover pizza and realized I still couldn't eat. My mom called, asking if Bracken was with me. I told her he was parked here and was researching where Calliope might be holed up. She was happy he was settled and very interested in what he'd learned. I told her I'd call her if he found anything we could use and ended the call.

Sitting on the couch, I willed myself not to consider the possibilities, while also envisioning every possible way Declan could be overpowered and killed. These weren't visions, just me terrified and imagining the worst.

When I couldn't stand my own thoughts any longer, I turned on the gallery sound system, turned it up to eleven, and played heavy metal while I painted.

Hours later, brain numb, I turned off the music and climbed down from the scaffold for the last time, studying the wall I'd just completed. I looked at the other two walls and then back at this one. A storm was brewing over here. The ocean was churned up, with tsunami-sized waves forming at the surface.

The last wall to paint, the wall of original cannery windows, would be the most difficult. This was the closest to the light and therefore just under the surface of my watery gallery. The sunlight, the sea-foam, the paint colors here would be lighter, all of which was fine. The annoying part was trying to create that image while painting around five rows of twenty-five windows. I had only the strips of wall between windows as my canvas.

I was starting to move the scaffolding when I noticed the sun setting. My stomach cramped, watching the sky go red and gold. I wasn't ready for night. I wasn't sure how long I stood there, dreading what was coming but unable to stop watching the encroaching darkness.

A knock at the backdoor broke the spell and got me moving again. I headed to the studio, wondering if Otis and his siblings were back, and then I heard the knock again. It was the gallery's back door, not the studio's.

Moonlight shimmered on the water behind Declan. I opened the door and he pulled me into his arms, lifting me off the ground.

"I needed to see you before I headed out," he said, his voice a deep growl in my ear.

"How far away are the pack grounds?" *Please, let me go with you.*

"Hour and a quarter. Maybe hour and a half. It's a ways up into Big Sur."

"Does it start at a specific time? The Goddess and I will be having a talk at that time."

He blew out a breath, chuckling into my hair. "Put in a good word for me."

"What do you think we're going to be talking about? Dummy." I squeezed him tighter, not wanting to let go.

"How are you going to feel if the last thing you say to me is calling me a dummy?"

"I'm going to feel just fine. You have a powerhouse wicche in your pocket and you're leaving her at home." I kissed his neck. "Dummy."

"Probably, though not for that."

His scratchy beard rubbed against my jaw, and I never wanted something to drag out longer. I also needed to get him some beard conditioner. "What time?"

"Midnight, though I have a feeling it'll start as soon as I get there."

I leaned back to see his face. "Midnight? But you have plenty of time. That's hours away."

He shook his head. "I think you got caught up in painting." He studied the walls and then all the pieces I'd already placed. "You really are extraordinary, and I feel so lucky to have known you."

"Know, not known. No one wants your past tenses around here. You're going to go kick all the other wolves' asses and then you're going to come right back here and show me that everything's okay. Okay?"

"Yes, ma'am."

"I mean it. Right back here."

He kissed me then, with a desperation that broke my heart a little more.

When he finally put me back on the floor, he coiled one of my curls around his finger. "See you soon, Ursula." He walked out, the sound of his heavy boots growing faint until they were gone and I was alone.

THIRTY-NINE

The Full Moon

I checked the time on my phone. After ten. Declan was partially right. I had lost track of time, but it wasn't because I was working. I'd instead been watching the light leave the sky as dread built. I put the gallery to rights for the night and then went into my studio to endure what was going to be one of the longest nights of my life.

As I had until recently spent most nights baking when I awoke from nightmares, I fell back on old habits to fill the time. Mind too scattered to concentrate, I went simple and made brownies, what I'd offered him on the day we'd met.

I took the brownies out to cool and was starting on the cinnamon rolls I'd promised him when a thought occurred to me. I ran out onto the deck, yanking off my gloves. Pulling up a fountain of seawater, I ran my hands through it, fortifying my magic and washing off Declan's nulling effects before jogging up the stairs to the loft and lying down on the bed. Breathing deeply, centering my magic with a prayer to the Goddess, I placed a bare, wet hand on his pillow. *Show me Declan.*

I was in the cab of his truck as he turned off a gravel road onto an even narrower one. When the trees opened, he was driving onto the pack grounds I'd seen in a vision. There was a huge meadow ringed with towering pines, rising into the mountains. Two dozen wolves paced in the center, growling and snapping at one another.

Declan parked, turned off the engine, and sat, readying himself. He took a pair of my green gloves out of his shirt pocket and breathed in my scent. Placing them on the passenger seat, he stepped out and began to undress. Howls rent the air as some wolves pawed at the ground, eager for the violence to begin.

He placed his belongings in the truck, shut the door, and walked naked across the meadow. A couple wolves couldn't control themselves and came racing toward him. He continued forward, unconcerned. When one came too close, Declan stopped, his wolf gold eyes boring into the other, whose legs buckled before he turned tail and ran back to the pack.

He was glorious and I, like the rest of the wolves, couldn't take my eyes off him. Something, though, was niggling at me. I wanted to watch Declan, but something was pulling my attention into the woods.

The compulsion was too strong, as though the Goddess Herself was directing me. I scanned the surrounding woods, looking for the threat.

There. A flash of metal in the moonlight. My consciousness went straight there and found Logan standing naked in the trees, looking up at a high branch where another man was perched, arms braced, a rifle in his hands.

"Keep him in your sights. As soon as it starts, take him out. Everyone will be too amped up to notice. I'll get out of the way and they can tear him apart."

"Yes, boss," the man said, Declan even now lined up in his scope.

"And be careful. Don't fucking hit me."

"No, boss."

Logan got down on his hands and knees and began to shift. It was a lengthy and painful process. Declan, a Quinn, was a born wolf. He could shift with a thought. For other, bitten wolves, it took some minutes. As Logan was the Alpha and it was a full moon, he was able to speed the process. Logan shook out his fur and then put a paw into a bowl of liquid. All four paws took a turn in the bowl, and my stomach sank even lower. He'd planned more than a sniper. I didn't know for sure, but I was guessing there was now poison on Logan's claws.

Declan stood outside the white chalk ring, waiting for Logan. The rest of the pack kept their distance, pacing between the far side of the ring and the trees.

"Big Sur Pack." Declan's voice boomed across the meadow. "I have come to challenge your Alpha. I would have lived peacefully in your backyard, but I wasn't given that option. If my only choices are leave or fight, then I fight."

Focusing all my attention on the sniper in the trees, I kept one hand on the pillow, needing to maintain the link, and circled the fingers of my other hand, building a spell strong enough to travel far from me.

"Please, Goddess," I whispered. "Please."

I flicked my fingers to jam the rifle. I didn't feel the snap I normally did when I knew my spell had landed. It hadn't worked. No, no, no. Declan was going to die by gunshot or poison while I watched, unable to do anything.

I was desperately readying another spell when I finally felt the snap. Sobbing out a breath, I tried to calm myself. I'd never set a spell from so far away. The distance must have caused a delay, meaning my magic would be useless in the fight, my spells arriving too late. Declan was going to get what he wanted. I wouldn't be able to help.

As Logan stalked out of the trees, Declan shifted to his wolf and stepped into the ring. The rest of the wolves raced around to close the circle.

I built another spell to neutralize the poison, sending it hurling across the mountains.

Logan shot forward but Declan didn't move. Waiting. A shot went off and then a crash in the woods, causing the ring of wolves to jump and bark, some howling, all agitated and searching for the source of the sound. Logan paused a few feet from Declan, no doubt expecting him to crumple to the ground. Instead, Declan sprang, taking Logan down, his jaws clamped tightly around Logan's neck as he shook him fiercely from side to side.

Logan's claws ripped into Declan, but still he held on, crushing Logan's neck. I felt the spell's snap too late to stop the poison from running through Declan's blood. I wasn't a healer, but I spun another spell, this one to pull the poison from Declan. Panicking, trying to build it as quickly as possible, I feared I'd screw it up and cause more harm than good. Praying, I flicked my fingers.

When Logan whined, two wolves jumped into the ring, causing chaos. They knew only the Alpha and the challenger could enter the ring, but more and more danced on the edge, putting a paw in and then stepping out.

The wolf in them wanted to save their Alpha and kill the intruder, but the men knew a fair fight was law. Declan had to let Logan loose, as he now had three to fight. Logan moved back, limping, the scent of blood heavy on him. The other two protected him, keeping themselves between Declan and Logan. They made moves to attack but didn't want to leave their Alpha unprotected.

Declan lurched to the side, almost losing his paws beneath him. I felt the snap and then saw him shake his fur. Body convulsing, he vomited up something black. The two wolves saw weakness and leapt, driving Declan to the ground and tearing into him.

Declan reared back, shaking them off. He snapped his jaws around the neck of one and heaved him out of the ring. The other closed back in on him. I worried that Logan would join in and overpower Declan, but he must have been too hurt to move.

When the wolf leapt, Declan slashed his razor-sharp claws down his opponent's side before tossing him out of the ring as well. Declan could have gutted him, could have killed the first one, but he was holding back, showing mercy, something the pack didn't seem familiar with.

The bloodshed excited the wolves pacing around the outside of the ring, prompting three more to cross the line and join the fight. Four against one.

The three moved in, circling Declan, trying to keep him from their wounded Alpha. Heads down, snarling, they each dove at him, biting and swiping his shoulder and flank with their claws. Declan howled and the wolves cringed away before shaking off his influence and moving back in.

Declan stilled, seeming to reassess. The wolves outside the ring were losing control, snapping and lunging at each other. The dead sniper had been found and dragged out into the open. A mournful howl went up, followed by others. The presence of a dead body, even one they knew, was sending them over the edge.

A fight broke out at the far side of the ring, with others quickly joining in. Attention moved from the Alpha fight in the ring to the larger brawl outside it. Declan, though, kept his focus on Logan.

Logan's three defenders were distracted by the other fight, their heads swinging back and forth. Declan wasn't moving, so the howls, barks and whines drew them. One shot off to join the other fight; the other two remained but were torn. Declan leapt over the top of them, landing beside Logan, who sprang to his paws and backed away, clearly not as wounded as he'd been feigning.

Instead of fighting his own Alpha challenge, he was letting others do the dirty work, and his wolves saw it, saw the strength in his stance, heard the steadiness of his breathing.

The two who had been circling moved back, leaving the ring. Others, at the periphery of the brawl, moved back to the line, seeming to understand what had happened. No longer were his wolves pawing at the ground, desperate to defend their Alpha. The group had gone quiet, shamed by their Alpha's cowardice.

Declan shifted to human and lunged for Logan, picking him up in his powerful arms, muscles bunching, and crushed Logan's ribs. He fought, snapping at Declan, clawing at him, scraping his claws up Declan's jaw, opening a deep wound, but Declan squeezed tighter.

The snap of bones breaking echoed across the field. All the

combatants had come back to the ring to watch the Quinn crush their Alpha. When Logan finally went limp, Declan grabbed him by his muzzle and, using his razor-sharp claws, ripped through his neck, decapitating him.

Spattered with blood, fur, and dirt, he lifted his head, howling his victory to the moon, and the pack dropped to their bellies. Declan walked around the ring, staring down each and every wolf. The message was clear, even to me. He would take on all comers. No one moved.

"I am the Quinn, the Origin, the rightful Alpha of this pack."

The wolves rose, barking, yipping, and howling for their new Alpha.

"This is not a social club. We are wolves." He pounded his chest and the pack sounded off again. "We will work together. We will train together. We will help one another. Pack is family." More barks and howls. "If you want to stay in this pack, you will return here in three days. We will meet and we will train. I don't care how things used to be done. This is our way now."

He looked over his wolves again. "Tonight, the moon sings to us and we will answer. We will hunt as a pack." He lifted his nose to the wind. "Deer."

Shifting to his wolf, he howled again, and the pack joined him. When it quieted, he tore off across the meadow with the entire pack following him, ready to bring down the first deer of the night.

I left then. It was okay. I felt a harmony in the pack. They recognized him as Alpha and were following him. This was private wolf business, so I left them to it. I went back downstairs to put away the cinnamon roll ingredients so I could instead bake a celebratory cake and wait for my man, Monterey's new Alpha.

FORTY

Where Did You Get One of Those?

There was a knock at my back door. I slid the cake tins in the oven, one vanilla, one raspberry, one lemon, closed the oven door, and then followed the sound of the knock. Opening the blinds, I saw Bracken with a journal in his hand. I let him in.

"Good evening. I know it's late, but I saw your light on. Any word from your man?"

I waved him in and closed the door. "I—actually I'm not sure what I did—astral projection, maybe? Anyway, I was able to be with him and watch the challenge. He won. The pack seems content to have him at the helm, so I'm hopeful and baking a cake. I already made some brownies, if you'd like one."

He blinked, taking all of that in, and then nodded. "Yes, thank you."

"Great. Why don't you have a seat?" I went back to the kitchen. "What would you like to drink?"

He thought a moment. "Milk, if you have it."

"I do." I brought him a plated brownie, a glass of milk, and a napkin before going back for my own, a tea mug, and a fork.

He took a bite and closed his eyes. "The Goddess favored you with many gifts. This is divine."

"Thank you. So, what's in the journal?"

"Oh, yes." He put down his plate, wiped his fingers clean, and then picked up his journal. "I found another reference to The Shades. It's at the water's edge and spelled to be hidden, like your grandmother's house. If a human were to stumble upon it, they'd see a derelict hut that looks like it's one strong gust of wind from collapsing. They'd also be struck with a desperate need to get away from it.

"For those with a magical eye, it appears to be a vacant stone cottage. One has to pass through a ward—from what this says, a very powerful ward—in order to see the real house."

"Any more specific information on location?" I asked.

"Well." He held up a finger and pulled from the back of the journal a ragged piece of paper that looked as though it had been folded and refolded countless times. "This is a hand-drawn map of the area dated 1854. There is what I believe to be the word *Shades* on the tip of this cliff right here."

I moved over to sit beside him and study the map.

"Now, unfortunately, this wasn't drawn by a cartographer, so it bears little resemblance to the actual coastline. If, however, we assume this curve here is the Monterey Bay, then this outcropping would be Pacific Grove and the Del Monte Forest, and that would put The Shades somewhere near the Lone Cypress."

"Isn't that Pebble Beach?"

"Not all of it, no. There are residences as well. And again, if this is private property that's been spelled to look like trees and bushes hiding a derelict shack, it's no doubt been overlooked."

"That's the 17-Mile Drive. Tourists are driving by all the time."

He nodded. "It's a powerful spell." He refolded the map and tucked it back into his journal. "I could be reading it wrong, but I don't think so. What do you say we go for a little drive tomorrow?"

Forgetting, I grabbed his wrist, and he only flinched a little. "Thank you so much for coming, for all the work you've been doing. We never would have gotten this far without you."

"Oh, well." He looked embarrassed but pleased. "I'll get back to my research and let you cook. May I?" He gestured to the plated brownie and milk.

"Absolutely. Take it. I know where to find you."

Chuckling, he stood, pocketing the journal before picking up the glass and plate. "You do, indeed. If I find anything more and your lights are on, I'll tell you."

"Perfect. And I'll bring you some cake tomorrow." I went with him and opened the door, as his hands were full.

"Something to look forward to," he said as he shuffled back home.

I started on the frosting while the cake layers baked. Declan had once said he liked coconut. I hoped that was true because I was making coconut frosting.

While the layers cooled and the frosting was refrigerated, I received a text.

Detective Hernández: Call me when you get up.

As I was up, I called.

She answered on the first ring. "Why are you awake? Is this a bad night?"

"No. It's a full moon night. I'm waiting up for Declan," I said, plopping down on the couch.

"Full m—oh. So that's true about…" She trailed off.

"It is."

"Okay. Something to think about later. I just wanted you to know we have Brandon in custody too."

"What? That was fast."

"We got a warrant to search Dorian's room on the Cypress campus and found blood in the bathroom sink drain. We also found a document on his laptop where they'd been recording each incident of revenge since they were in school. Brandon was easy to find once we knew who Dorian was. Since you said Brandon was the weak link, we interrogated him first. He was trying to play it off like it was all a big misunderstanding, so he didn't call for a lawyer."

"Putz."

"Truly," she said. "Anyway, we were able to hit him with so much information from you that he was crying in no time and rolling over to put all the blame on Dorian. Now, Dorian is no fool. His lawyer's doing all the talking at this point, but we have the dean's blood in his drain—we're pretty sure. We're waiting for the lab to confirm.

"And we have the document that clearly states he killed Pearl because she had turned him in and ruined his summer. We also found the case with the makeup and face putty he'd used to alter his appearance enough that Pearl didn't recognize him. And, of course, we have the photos Brandon had taken of Garza right before he killed him, his fingerprints on the shovel, as well as years of texts between the two, crowing about their successes."

"So, that's it," I said. "They're locked up and can't hurt anyone else?"

"Mostly. As they both come from wealthy families, they'll probably end up with bail, but they'd be idiots to do anything more before trial. We're going to get them, Arwyn. We'll get justice for their victims. Oh, and you were right. There was a kid named Spencer who died in a car accident during his senior year. He also came from a *very* wealthy family, and we now have the ability to give his family the truth about their son's death."

"*And* you'll have an influential guy helping to push for these two to go to jail," I said.

"Oh, did I forget to say Spencer's dad is a judge and his mother is an heiress to like a billion-dollar fortune and that they were both devoted to their son?" She scoffed. "*Do you know who my father is?*" she mimicked. "No, but I know who Spencer's parents are.

"Brandon's pathetic," she continued. "Still a cold-blooded killer, but he just wanted to impress Dorian. He took lives to seem cool to another sociopath. Dorian, though, scares the shit out of me. I look into his eyes and they're dead. I've heard that term before, but I've never experienced it. He's evil."

"Yes," I said, feeling sick to my stomach that Pearl had spent any time with him at all, that anyone had.

"Oh, the other reason I was calling is to see if you wanted to let your aunt know they've been arrested or if you'd prefer it came from us."

"Thank you. I would like to be the one to tell her. I'll visit tomorrow. Thank you for thinking of that."

"Okay, good. Listen, I'm beat so I'm going to hang up now, but not before I thank you—Arthur and I both thank you. We never would have found them this quickly without you. More people would have died. On behalf of the police and those assholes' future victims and their loved ones, thank you."

"You're welcome. Now go to bed," I said.

"That I can do. Goodnight."

I sat with it for a bit, hoping they truly had been stopped and would soon be locked up for life. A chill ran down my spine. We had to find Calliope and her demon. They had to be stopped before their sorcery bled darkness into more pockets of our community.

I checked the time and forced myself to shake off the ugly thoughts. Declan was alive and well and I had a cake to frost. Working quickly, I assembled the cake, adding strawberry slices to the frosting between the layers, which may have been overkill, but it sounded good.

As I finished frosting, a thought occurred to me. Declan should drive Bracken and me tomorrow. Bracken's huge RV on that narrow, twisty road sounded harrowing. Plus, Declan could watch the road while we searched magically.

Knowing Bracken was up and I needed to kill time, I went to go talk to him. I was halfway across the deck when I heard the sound of heavy boots. On a yip of excitement, I spun and ran back as Declan came around the corner. I almost threw myself into his arms, but I felt something off, something dark, and skidded to a stop.

The silhouette of Otis, Daisy, and Jasper's heads popped out from the roofline and hissed.

Grinning, he held out his arms. "I did it! I'm the Alpha."

I moved back a few steps.

He kept his arms open. "Come give me a kiss and congratulate me."

I moved back another step. "Are you okay?"

"Never better." He finally dropped his arms and looked in the studio. "Mmm, have you been baking cookies?"

"I was worried you'd been hurt." Where was the wound on his jaw? The other bites and cuts could be under his clothes, but Logan had opened a gash on his jaw. And Declan would have recognized the scent of my brownies.

"Nope. I won easily." He lifted an arm and flexed his muscles. "Come here, honey."

I dove over the railing and into the ocean. This where my magic was at its strongest and I was going to need it, because that wasn't Declan.

When I surfaced, he was leaning on the railing, watching me. His eyes were off, though. They were full black, no whites around the irises. "Now, why would you do that?"

"Because you're a close personal friend of Calliope's." I flicked my fingers, pushing him back a foot.

On a laugh, he recovered and leaned on the railing again. "You'll have to do better than that. And we're not friends so much as colleagues. She's not terribly friendly, is she?"

That was just my opening salvo. While the demon chuckled and made a show of not being bothered by my magic, I was silently reciting the spell Sam had shown me in her grimoire. I sent it sailing and the demon went rigid, his black eyes going wide. His mouth opened in a silent scream and then he disappeared.

Unsure if that meant he was really gone, I continued to tread water for a few minutes. Cecil wrapped a tentacle around my arm and I rubbed it. "I'm okay now." He let go and I swam to the rope ladder Declan made me.

When I got to the top, I stood dripping for a moment, trying to decide if I should do a drying spell or if I had time to take a shower before Declan returned.

"That was rude." Demon Not Declan walked back around the side of the gallery. "You're going to come with me now or I'm going to destroy every piece of art in that gallery." His dark eyes gleamed with the threat. "Oh, you don't like that, do you?" He glanced over his shoulder in the direction of the back door. "I should do it anyway for causing me pain."

He smiled sharply and I heard glass shatter.

Heart sinking, I leaned against the railing, ready to dive back in. "What does she want?"

"That's easy. To destroy you." His black eyes glittered in the moonlight.

"Why? What did we ever do to her?"

He waved a hand. "Who listens? She's like a gnat, buzzing in my ear." He clasped his hands together. "I have a proposal for you. If you come with me now and work with me, I'll help you become the most famous, most lauded artist in the world."

Shaking my head, I said, "I can do that on my own."

"Oh, careful." He waggled a finger at me. "Pride is one of the deadly sins."

"I don't truck with demons."

He tilted his head, studying me. "More's the pity. We always end up with ones like your cousin knocking on our door." He rolled his eyes. "What you and I could do together, though, would be amazing. Epic." He paused. "In fact, if you wanted me to take away that pesky inability to touch people without seeing and feeling horrors, I could do that. You could live a long, happy, horrorless life with me."

"I don't know. That sounds pretty horrific." My voice was steady, but I was trembling on the inside. My magic clearly wasn't up to battling demons.

"No." He shook his head. "It's not. But together, there's no limit to what you could accomplish."

I put up every mental block I could think of. *Shit, shit shit.*

"Oh, good," Bracken said. "Home safe and sound." He shuffled toward us, head bent, paging through his journal. "I've just found the most interesting passage and I believe it relates to what we were discussing earlier. Right here," he said, turning a page, "but then again, here it might contradict. I want to show you both."

No, no, no. Not poor Bracken.

The demon glanced at me, eyebrows raised, clearly tickled by this latest development.

"You can show us tomorrow," I said. "We'll come see you." *Please, go away!*

"Young love," he said, still staring down at the page. "I promise not to take up too much time. Where is it? Let's see, let's see." He turned another page. "I just had it."

I touched my earring, my lifeline to my father. "I need help."

The demon gave me a pouty face and then returned his amused gaze to Bracken.

Bracken stopped right beside Not Declan. "Ah, here it is." He tilted the page to show us a passage. He looked into the demon's gaze and said, "You see now, don't you?"

The demon's eyes went wide. His skin cracked open, revealing flames, and then he popped out of existence, leaving Bracken holding a journal in one hand and a dagger in the other.

A huge wave swamped the deck and a tall, muscular, very naked man with hair like mine, golden skin, and aqua blue eyes raised his silver sword, stalking toward Bracken.

"Wait!" I shouted. "Not him. That's my uncle. He just killed a demon." I turned to Bracken, who was sliding the dagger back into a leather sheath. "How did you do that?"

He shrugged, tucking the weapon into the pocket of his oversized cardigan. "I have a demon blade, and this seemed like the time to use it. I'm going to get back to work and let you catch up with your father." So saying, he turned and strolled back to his RV.

The man and I looked at each other. I kept my gaze trained above his neck.

"Pants would be good," I said.

He glanced down. The sword disappeared and fabric appeared.

"A toga?" I asked, quite confused.

"They're very comfortable. Pants are constricting. Is this all right?"

I nodded. "It's a good look on you."

He stood a little straighter. "You called for me."

"I did. There was a demon—"

He hissed, expression thunderous. "Foul things."

"True enough." There was an awkward silence and then I asked, "Would you like to sit down?" I gestured to one of the benches.

He was bigger and broader even than Declan, but he sat, leaving room beside him for me. "I like your home," he said. "The tentacles are a nice touch."

"Thanks." This was my father. I was sitting with my father. Shooting the shit with Dad. "Um, thanks for showing up so quickly. And with a sword. That was cool."

"You're welcome, but never thank the fae," he said.

"That's real?" Look at me, learning things from Dad.

"It is for some. Not for me, of course. It's best to be safe, though. If you instead said something like, *It was good of you to come save me, Father*, that would be nice."

Grinning, I said, "It was good of you to come save me, Father."

He nodded benevolently. "Anything for you, my child." Glancing around, he added, "You are an artist, are you not?"

"I am." Twenty-eight years of giddy bubbles were filling my insides. My dad was interested in me. He wanted to see what I did. I started to stand and then dropped back down on the bench. "Can you visit again, maybe on opening night? I mean, if you're busy and you can't come back, I'll give you the tour now, but it's not ready. I'd love for you to see it when I'm done painting and all my pieces are placed. If you can."

He looked out over the ocean. "You're inviting me back?"

"Yes, please. Unless you're too busy." *Please come back.*

Brow furrowed, he met my gaze. "What could be more important than my child?"

Eyes flooding with tears, I shrugged. "Tsunamis. Sharknados?"

He gave me a puzzled look and then said, "The ocean waits for me. Yes, I will return at your gallery opening."

I stood with him. "You will?"

"I'll even wear pants." The twinkle in his eye made the bubbles inside me burst with happiness. His head turned. "Your man has arrived." He tipped my chin up, studying my face before running his hand over my hair. "It's good to finally meet you, daughter." He leaned down, kissed my cheek, and then dove over the railing, disappearing into the ocean.

Declan walked around the corner, a huge gash on his jaw. He looked at me and then at the ocean. "Did I just hear a man call you *daughter*?"

"Yes!" I clapped like a demented toddler, jumping up on the bench so I was tall enough to then jump on Declan.

He caught me, spinning me around and kissing me senseless.

When we finally came up for air, I dropped little kisses all over his face. "You did it! Congratulations, Mr. Alpha!"

He laughed. "That's Sir Alpha."

I put my hand over his eyes, even though I totally knew it was him. "What did I bake tonight?"

"Brownies, which make me very happy, and something else. Vanilla, lemon, berries, sugar…did you make me a cake?"

I gave him one last loud kiss and then smacked his shoulder to let me down. "Yes! We have cake and brownies to celebrate. You're the new Alpha. My dad is coming to my opening. It's been a big night. Oh, and Bracken killed a demon."

He followed me into the studio and then stopped short. "He did what?"

"Come on in. I'll tell you all about it."

Read on for an excerpt of WICCHING
HOUR: The Sea Wicche Chronicles

Chapter One:

It's a Talent That I Always Have Possessed

Opening night of The Sea Wicche gallery and tea bar was finally here. I'd been planning it since I was little and saw the abandoned cannery for the first time. At first, I wanted to live here, but when I got a little older and would sneak down here to break in and run around, leaping over stagnant ponds of dirty water and playing with rusty machinery, I saw it for the potential it had. I started bringing my sketches with me, taping them up on the walls.

And now look at me. The cannery remodeled into a huge, forty-foot-tall gallery with my studio and apartment taking a quarter of the space. The floors were dyed concrete that looked like a deep ocean blue. I'd painted the walls to look like water as well, from deep sea to surf.

If one looked closely enough, high on the wall above the front door, in the deepest part of the ocean, there lurked a sea monster, watching and waiting. The exterior of the gallery told us he wasn't waiting long. I'd built thirty-foot long tentacles coming from the water under the cannery, appearing to be pulling the gallery into the ocean. It gave the local fisherman quite a start when they'd first seen them.

I'd also painted one whole side of the building to look as though the gallery were still an old condemned building that had tentacles breaking through the rotting boards. There'd been a number of articles written about the exterior of my gallery, which probably had something to do with why there were so many people packed in here tonight.

On the one hand, I'd done it. Having my own art gallery was a dream come true. On the other, having all these people touching and judging my pieces was making my stomach churn and causing my head to pound.

I don't do well in crowds. I'm a Cassandra wicche, meaning I can see the future. And the past, come to that. I'm an empath, who keeps covered neck to fingertip and toe, because psychometry is also a gift of mine. I wear gloves always, as I don't want to touch someone and drop into a vision, learning every hidden thing in their lives. Unfortunately, far too many people here tonight seem intent on shaking my hand.

What I hadn't anticipated, though, were the hugs. Yes, my body was covered, but my face wasn't. Hugging meant my highly sensitive skin touching cheeks or hair. I didn't want to drop into a vision, so my boyfriend Declan, the werewolf Alpha of Monterey, and my agent Mary Beth, were flanking me, keeping people at a safe distance.

I'd been working with Mary Beth for some years. She was half fae, like me, but her other half was human. She was one of the most respected agents in the art world. She had an almost encyclopedic knowledge of all art. No matter the medium, the time period, or the location, she knew it. Most saw her as a hard-ass agent who knew all the major players and always got her clients the best deals, but I knew her as my slyly funny friend who was also my biggest champion, refusing to let me undersell myself.

She'd arrived four days ago because she didn't trust me to price my own art. She was clearly right to do that, as I would have gone much lower. As it was, pieces were still flying out the door and I was going to be set for a few years.

"Okay, shorty, I see a couple of live ones," Mary Beth said. "Where did your mom go?" She glanced around and then made a quick movement with her hand. "She was talking to your Aunt Hester. Okay, Mom's on her way." She glared at Declan. "Do not leave her side." She glided off, the masses separating before her.

In my defense, I'm not short. Am I as tall as my six-and-a-half-foot, super hot, bearded boyfriend? No. No, I was not. I'm five-three and a half, which is a totally respectable height. Did I usually round up to five-four? Of course. I was simplifying.

Mary Beth's mom was a beautiful Black woman who was herself an artist. I'd met her once when I went to New York to work with Mary Beth. Her mom was free and funny and open to the world. She was also a gifted sculptor. I was pretty sure Mary Beth's father was a warrior elf, given she was at least six feet tall, with long, white-blonde hair, luminous golden-brown skin, and piercing gray eyes.

She arrowed through the crowd, stopping beside an elderly couple in windbreakers and walking shoes who looked as though they'd wandered in by accident.

"Do you know who they are," Declan asked quietly, his arm protectively around my waist.

I shrugged. "No idea."

My mom stepped in front of a wild-eyed man coming straight at me. Her fingers twitched at her side and he turned sharply, wandering off.

"Thanks," I said.

Because it was opening night, we also had waiters weaving through the gallery, offering wine and appetizers. Mom was sipping the wine, but I couldn't handle alcohol on a queasy stomach.

"I worry, darling," she said. "I know you've always wanted

your own gallery, but this gives people too much access to you. And that security guard you hired isn't watching people to make sure they don't steal. What is he even doing?" My mom was used to being in charge and I'm sure this all felt too chaotic to her.

"You look beautiful," I said. "I told you the blue dress would be perfect tonight." Mom was gorgeous to begin with, with shoulder-length black hair, fair skin, and Corey green eyes. It had taken some doing, but I had talked her out of her very conservative black suit and into a flowing, wraparound silk dress in blues and greens.

"You do look very pretty, Ms. Corey," Declan said.

Staring out at the crowd, she said, "Yes, well, that's nice to hear, but I'd rather discuss your security."

"Oh, that's right," I said, bouncing on the balls of my feet. "I haven't told you. Bracken and I created a ward. If someone tries to steal one of my pieces, tries to hide it and walk out—that part's important—it disappears from their pocket or bag and reappears in its original spot."

Mom's focus snapped to me. "What? How—that's amazing. You need to share it with me so I can share it with the family. Excellent," she said, nodding. "No more pilfered goods in our shops." She thought a moment. "So, is your guard just for show?"

"No," I said. "That's Carter, Detective Osso's younger brother." Like Declan, he was six and a half feet tall, with shoulders even broader than a werewolf's. He was a dark-skinned Black man who, like his brother, wore a perpetual scowl. "He's working on a PhD in Marine Biology. We'll only be open a couple days a week, so it won't cut into his dissertation time too much. The ward should keep my artwork safe. He's here to watch people."

"Oh," Mom said. "Good. But I still don't see how you can possibly make a living only being open two or three days a week."

"And by appointment," I said. We'd already had this discussion a few times. "Collectors prefer private viewings. Anyway," I said, trying to change the subject, "that earpiece Carter's wearing? It's not hooked up to a security system or whatever. He's listening to audiobooks."

Declan laughed. "Nice."

"Are you sure he can handle one of your obsessed stalkers?" Mom asked.

Carter turned to us from his spot across the gallery, eyebrows raised.

Leaning into my Mom, I whispered, "He's a bear shifter. He can handle any of them; probably all of them."

He nodded and went back to surveying the room.

"Mary Beth's walking them to Cecil 2," I whispered.

"Who?" Mom followed my gaze, studying the couple for a moment. "Oh. Your agent is very good, darling. The Winslows look like middle-class tourists, but the wife's from serious old money and the husband used it to make them even more. They're committed philanthropists, so at least they're doing a lot of good with it." Mom elbowed me. "You should feel honored they're here. They live on the East Coast. Connecticut, I believe."

"How do you know all this stuff about them?" I asked.

"I read an article on the charity work they do. I never would have recognized them if your agent hadn't singled them out."

"Aaaand there they go." My hopes sank. Not only did they not buy my five-foot glass rendering of Cecil, they didn't even pick up a starfish paperweight. *Damn.*

Mary Beth moved back to us, the crowd parting and then coming back together behind her. "Sybil, that dress is gorgeous on you," she said as she went behind the cash wrap.

My aunt Elizabeth's kids Frank and Faith were working the cash register, ringing up and wrapping purchases.

Mary Beth went into a drawer and pulled out a roll of *Sold* stickers.

"Did they buy something?" I whispered, hope bubbling up.

She rolled her eyes. "Oh, you sweet summer child. It would be easier to tell you what they didn't buy. Cecil is gone. They've put in an order for one hundred and seventy-five of the large octopuses." At my look of shock, she said, "I explained you'd need time for an order that large. They're planning to give them to the top executives in their companies as holiday gifts. I told them we could deliver by November fifteenth. That works, doesn't it?"

She was referring to the twelve-inch octopuses. There was only one five-foot rendering of Cecil. I considered and then nodded.

"We'll hire a team when it's time to ship. We do *not* want them arriving with broken tentacles. They also bought three of the paintings, seven of the framed photos—your underwater series—and an assortment of this and that. They want to come back tomorrow before opening so they can browse properly. We'll pull out any of the big pieces you still have in the fire room for them to see." She stopped. "No. We'll take them to the fire room so they can see what you do. That's better. They get to feel themselves close with the artist. Ten tomorrow morning. I'll get here first." She looked out over the crowd. "It's going well. Let me get these stickers on.

"And we have another collector who just walked in. He's going to be very annoyed the Winslows got here first." She hurried off, stickers still in hand.

I was reeling, doing math in my head.

Declan picked me up and kissed me soundly. "Congratulations, Ursula. Looks like The Sea Wicche is a success." When he put me down, I had to hold on so my knees didn't buckle.

"I'm so proud of you, Arwyn. And you were obviously right about only needing to be open a couple of days a week." Mom looked as dazed as I was feeling.

I felt it when he walked in. The air changed. Mom made a noise and I followed her gaze to the door. He'd come. He'd promised he'd come, and he did. Dad.

Larger than life, he stood just inside the door, taking it all in. He wore a dark gray suit with a snowy white shirt and a watery blue tie. His hair was cut short, making his aqua blue eyes stand out even more.

I grabbed Mom and Declan's hands, giving patrons a mental push out of the way so we could go to him. Mom resisted, but I pulled harder. She hadn't seen him since before I was born, since she'd done what the family said and broken up with him. To say this meeting was frought was an understatement.

He met us halfway across the room. "Daughter, I like your gallery very much." He may have been speaking to me, but his eyes were on Mom. "Sybil, it's good to see you."

She swallowed and then nodded.

His focus swung to Declan. "And you. Are you strong enough to protect my child?"

Declan said, "I am," just as I said, "I'm strong enough on my own, thanks."

"That's true," Dad said, taking my gloved hand. "You have a lot of me in you." He tucked my hand into the crook of his arm and moved us away from the other two. "Show me what you've created."

———

To pre-order WICCHING HOUR: The Sea Wicche Chronicles, click here

Acknowledgments

It's always so funny to me how things I don't even realize I'm thinking about come out in my writing. I recently lost my parents, my dad two years ago and my mom a few months ago. I had no intent to make this a mothers and daughters book, but the scenes that make me cry every time, are Hester and Pearl's farewell, and Arwyn and Sybil finally clearing the air. Hopefully they resonated with you too.

Thank you to Peter Senftleben, my extraordinary editor. You have the enviable knack of getting to the heart of the story and then helping me to see my own work through a different lens. Thank you to Susan Helene Gottfried, my exceptional proofreader who always knows exactly where the commas go (unlike myself).

Thank you to the remarkable team at NYLA! You've made every step of publishing a little easier with your wit, compassion, and expertise. Thank you to my incomparable agent Sarah Younger, the fabulous Natanya Wheeler, and the incredible Cheryl Pientka for working together to make my dream of writing and publishing a reality.

Dear Reader,

Thank you for reading **Wicche Hunt: The Sea Wicche Chronicles**. If you enjoyed Arwyn and Declan's second adventure together, please consider leaving a review or chatting about it with your book-loving friends. Good word of mouth means everything when you're a writer!

Love,
Seana

Want more books from Seana?

If you'd like to be the first to learn what's new with Sam and Clive (and Arwyn and Declan and Owen and Dave and Stheno…), please sign up for my newsletter *Tales from the Book Nerd*. It's filled with writing news, deleted scenes, giveaways, book recommendations, first looks at covers, short stories, and my favorite cocktail and book pairings.

I hope you enjoyed Arwyn's latest adventure. **Wicching Hour** will be arriving in the spring of 2025. Stay tuned for more…

If you're a Sam Quinn fan, **The Bloody Ruin Asylum & Taproom** will be out October 1, 2024.

What else has Seana written? Well, I'll tell you…

The Slaughtered Lamb Bookstore & Bar
Sam Quinn, Book 1

Welcome to The Slaughtered Lamb Bookstore and Bar. I'm Sam Quinn, the werewolf book nerd in charge. I run my business by one simple rule: Everyone needs a good book and a stiff drink, be they vampire, wicche, demon, or fae. No wolves, though. Ever. I have my reasons.

I serve the supernatural community of San Francisco. We've been having some problems lately. Okay, I'm the one with the problems. The broken body of a female werewolf washed up on my doorstep. What makes sweat pool at the base of my spine, though, is realizing the scars she bears are identical to the ones I conceal. After hiding for years, I've been found.

A protection I've been relying on is gone. While my wolf traits are strengthening steadily, the loss also left my mind vulnerable to attack. Someone is ensnaring me in horrifying visions intended to kill. Clive, the sexy vampire Master of the City, has figured out how to pull me out, designating himself my personal bodyguard. He's grumpy about it, but that kiss is telling a different story. A change is taking place. It has to. The bookish bartender must become the fledgling badass.

I'm a survivor. I'll fight fang and claw to protect myself and the ones I love. And let's face it, they have it coming.

The Dead Don't Drink at Lafitte's
Sam Quinn, Book 2

I'm Sam Quinn, the werewolf book nerd owner of the Slaughtered Lamb Bookstore and Bar. Things have been busy lately. While the near-constant attempts on my life have ceased, I now have a vampire gentleman caller. I've been living with Clive and the rest of his vampires for a few weeks while the Slaughtered Lamb is being rebuilt. It's going about as well as you'd expect.

My mother was a wicche and long dormant abilities are starting to make themselves known. If I'd had a choice, necromancy wouldn't have been my top pick, but it's coming in handy. A ghost warns me someone is coming to kill Clive. When I rush back to the nocturne, I find vamps from New Orleans readying an attack. One of the benefits of vampires looking down on werewolves is no one expects much of me. They don't expect it right up until I take their heads.

Now, Clive and I are setting out for New Orleans to take the fight back to the source. Vampires are masters of the long game. Revenge plots are often decades, if not centuries, in the making. We came expecting one enemy but quickly learn we have darker forces scheming against us. Good thing I'm the secret weapon they never see coming.

The Wicche Glass Tavern
Sam Quinn, Book 3

I'm Sam Quinn, the werewolf book nerd owner of the Slaughtered Lamb Bookstore and Bar. Clive, my vampire gentleman caller, has asked me to marry him. His nocturne is less than celebratory. Unfortunately, for them and the sexy vamp doing her best to seduce him, his cold, dead heart beats only for me.

As much as my love life feels like a minefield, it has to take a backseat to a far more pressing problem. The time has come. I need to deal with my aunt, the woman who's been trying to kill me for as long as I can remember. She's learned a new trick. She's figured out how to weaponize my friends against me. To have any hope of surviving, I have to learn to use my necromantic gifts. I need a teacher. We find one hiding among the fae, which is a completely different problem. I need to determine what I'm capable of in a hurry because my aunt doesn't care how many are hurt or killed as long as she gets what she wants. Sadly for me, what she wants is my name on a headstone.

I'm gathering my friends—werewolves, vampires, wicches,

gorgons, a Fury, a half-demon, an elf, and a couple of dragon shifters—into a kind of Fellowship of the Sam. It's going to be one hell of a battle. Hopefully, San Francisco will still be standing when the dust clears.

The Hob & Hound Pub
Sam Quinn, Book 4

I'm Sam Quinn, the newly married werewolf book nerd owner of the Slaughtered Lamb Bookstore and Bar. Clive and I are on our honeymoon. Paris is lovely, though the mummy in the Louvre inching toward me is a bit off-putting. Although Clive doesn't sense anything, I can't shake the feeling I'm being watched.

Even after we cross the English Channel to begin our search for Aldith—the woman who's been plotting against Clive since the beginning—the prickling unease persists. Clive and I are separated, rather forcefully, and I'm left to find my way alone in a foreign country, evading not only Aldith's large web of hench-vamps, but vicious fae creatures disloyal to their queen. Gloriana says there's a poison in the human realm that's seeping into Faerie, and I may have found the source.

I knew this was going to be a working vacation, but battling vampires on one front and the fae on another is a lot, especially in a country steeped in magic. As a side note, I need to get word to Benvair. I think I've found the dragon she's looking for.

Gloriana is threatening to set her warriors against the human realm, but I may have a way to placate her. Aldith is a different story. There's no reasoning with rabid vengeance. She'll need to be put out of our misery permanently if Clive and I have any hope of a long, happy life together. Heck, I'd settle for a few quiet weeks.

Biergarten of the Damned

Sam Quinn, Book 5

I'm Sam, the werewolf book nerd owner of The Slaughtered Lamb Bookstore & Bar. I've always thought of Dave, my red-skinned, shark-eyed, half-demon cook, as a kind of foul-mouthed uncle, one occasionally given to bouts of uncontrolled anger.

Something's going on, though. He's acting strangely, hiding things. When I asked what was wrong, he blew me off and told me to quit bugging him. That's normal enough. What's not is his missing work. Ever. Other demons are appearing in the bar, looking for him. I'm getting worried, and his banshee girlfriend Maggie isn't answering my calls.

Demons terrify me. I do NOT want to go into any demon bars looking for Dave, but he's my family, sort of. I need to try to help, whether he wants me to or not. When I finally learn the truth, though… I'm not sure I can ever look at him again, let alone have him work for me. Are there limits to forgiveness? I think there might be.

The Viper's Nest Roadhouse & Café
Sam Quinn, Book 6

I'm Sam, the werewolf book nerd owner of The Slaughtered Lamb Bookstore & Bar. Clive, Fergus, and I are moving into our new home, the business is going well, and our folly is taking shape. The problem? Clive's maker Garyn is coming to San Francisco for a visit, and this reunion has been a thousand years in the making. Back then, Garyn was rather put out when Clive accepted the dark kiss and then took off to avenge his sister's murder. She was looking for a new family. He was looking for lethal skills. And so, Garyn has had plenty of time to align her forces. When her allies begin stepping out of the shadows, Clive's foundation will be shaken.

Stheno and her sisters are adding to their rather impressive portfolio of businesses around the world by acquiring The Viper's Nest Roadhouse & Café. Medusa found the place when she was visiting San Francisco. A dive bar filled with hot tattooed bikers? Yes, please!

Clive and I will need neutral territory for our meeting with Garyn, and a biker bar (& café, Stheno insisted) should fit the bill. I'd assumed my necromancy would give us an advantage. I hadn't anticipated, though, just how powerful Garyn and her allies were. When the fangs descend and the heads start rolling, it's going to take every friend we have and a nocturne full of vamps at our backs to even the playing field. Wish us luck. We're going to need it.

The Bloody Ruin Asylum & Taproom
Sam Quinn, Book 7

I'm Sam, the werewolf book nerd owner of The Slaughtered Lamb Bookstore & Bar. My husband, Master vampire Clive, has been asked to go to Budapest to interview for a position in the Guild, a council of thirteen vampires who advise the world's Masters. The competition for the recently vacated spot is fierce. I worry about Clive, as it quickly becomes apparent that the last person to hold the position didn't leave voluntarily.

Ever the supportive wife, I'm tagging along. I researched Budapest and had a long itinerary of things to do. That is, I did. When we arrive, we find out that the Guild headquarters is in the ruins of an abandoned insane asylum. Awesome. If there's one thing I love, it's being hounded by mentally unstable Hungarian ghosts.

Let's just say this isn't the romantic getaway I'd been hoping for. With Clive in top secret meetings and a bunch of creepy Renfields skulking around corners, nowhere is safe. I want to help Clive because I know he really wants the job, but the other Guild members are ancient and scary powerful. Between you and me, I thought Vlad would be taller.

Wish us luck! We're going to need it.

Bewicched: The Sea Wicche Chronicles
Sea Wicche, Book 1

We here at The Sea Wicche cater to your art-collecting, muffin-eating, tea-drinking, and potion-peddling needs. Palmistry and Tarot sessions are available upon request and by appointment. Our store hours vary and rely completely on Arwyn—the owner—getting her butt out of bed.

I'm Arwyn Cassandra Corey, the sea wicche, or the wicche who lives by the sea. It requires a lot more work than I'd anticipated to remodel an abandoned cannery and turn it into an art gallery & tea bar. It's coming along, though, especially with the help of a new werewolf who's joined the construction crew. He does beautiful work. His sexy, growly, bearded presence is very hard to ignore, but I'm trying. I'm not sure how such a laid-back guy got the local Alpha and his pack threatening to hunt him down and tear him apart, but we all have our secrets. And because I don't want to know his—or yours for that matter—I wear these gloves. Clairvoyance makes the simplest things the absolute worst. Trust me. Or don't. Totally up to you.

Did I mention my mother and grandmother are pressuring me to assume my rightful place on the Corey Council? That's a kind of governing triad for our ancient magical family, one that has more than its fair share of black magic practitioners. And yes, before you ask, people have killed to be on the council—one psychotic sorceress aunt stands out—but I have no interest in the power or politics that come with the position. I'd rather stick to my art and, in the words of my favorite sea wicche, help poor unfortunate souls. (Good luck trying to get that song out of your head now)

Wicche Hunt: The Sea Wicche Chronicles
Sea Wicche, Book 2

I'm Arwyn Cassandra Corey, the Sea Wicche of Monterey. Want a psychic reading? Sure. I can do that. In the market for art? I have all your painting, photography, glass blowing, and ceramic needs covered in my newly remodeled art gallery by the sea. Need help solving a grisly cold case? Unfortunately, I can probably help with that too.

After more than a decade of being nagged, guilted, and threatened, I've finally joined the Corey Council and am working with my mother and grandmother to hunt down a twisted sorcerer. We know who she is. Now we need to find and stop her before more are murdered.
The evil the sorcerer and her demon are doing is seeping into the community. Violent crimes have been increasing and as a result Detectives Hernández and Osso have brought me another horrifying case. I'll do what I can, because of course I will. What are a few more nightmares to a woman who barely sleeps?

Declan Quinn, the wicked hot werewolf rebuilding my deck, is preparing for a dominance battle with the local Alpha. A couple of wolves have already left their pack to follow Declan, recognizing him as the true Alpha. Declan needs to watch his back as the full moon approaches. The current Alpha will do whatever it takes to hold on to power, including breaking pack law and enlisting the help of a local vampire.

And if Wilbur, my selkie friend is right, I might just be meeting my dad soon. Perhaps he'll have some advice for this wicche hunt. I'm going to need all the help I can get.

Wicching Hour: The Sea Wicche Chronicles
Sea Wicche, Book 3

I'm Arwyn Cassandra Corey, the Sea Wicche of Monterey. My new art gallery is finally open, my boyfriend is the new Alpha of the Big Sur pack, and my sorcerer cousin is still on the loose. It's been a lot. I'm just sayin'.

Detectives Hernández and Osso are asking for my help again. Bodies have been found torn up in the woods in a manner that has those in the know thinking werewolf. Declan, as Alpha, will need to investigate his pack and help hunt the killer.

We're narrowing in on Calliope and her demon. She can't hide forever, and my uncle might just have the map to where she's been holed up. If it's the last thing I do, I'll make her pay for her treachery.

Did I mention there's a new podcast, hosted by a human, who is coming dangerously close to telling the kind of secrets the supernatural community kills to keep quiet? His latest season is about a certain artistic wicche.

Oh, and I finally met my dad. Like I said, it's been a lot.

Titles by Seana Kelly

The Sam Quinn Series

The Slaughtered Lamb Bookstore & Bar
The Dead Don't Drink at Lafitte's
The Wicche Glass Tavern
All I Want for Christmas is a Dragon (short story)
The Hob & Hound Pub
Biergarten of the Damned
The Banshee & the Blade (short story)
The Viper's Nest Roadhouse & Café
The Nocturne's Gatekeeper (short story)
The Bloody Ruin Asylum & Taproom

The Sea Wicche Series

Bewicched: The Sea Wicche Chronicles
Wicche Hunt: The Sea Wicche Chronicles
Wicching Hour: The Sea Wicche Chronicles

About Seana Kelly

Seana Kelly lives in the San Francisco Bay Area with her husband, two daughters, two dogs, and one fish. When not dodging her family, hiding in the garage to write, she's working as a high school teacher-librarian. She's an avid reader and re-reader who misses her favorite characters when it's been too long between visits.

She's a *USA Today* Bestselling Author and is represented by the delightful and effervescent Sarah E. Younger of the Nancy Yost Literary Agency.

You can follow Seana on Twitter for tweets about books and dogs or on Instagram for beautiful pictures of books and dogs (kidding). I also love collecting photos of characters and settings for the books I write. As I'm a huge reader of young adult and adult books, expect lots of recommendations as well.

𝕏 x.com/SeanaKellyRW

instagram.com/seanakellyrw

facebook.com/Seana-Kelly-1553527948245885

bookbub.com/authors/seana-kelly

pinterest.com/seanakelly326

www.ingramcontent.com/pod-product-compliance
Lightning Source LLC
Chambersburg PA
CBHW061055100726
47911CB00012B/229